UNLOCKING THE MILLIONAIRE'S HEART

BELLA BUCANNON

FROM BEST FRIEND TO DADDY

JULES BENNETT

MIX

FSC

FSC C007454

This book is produced from independently certified FSC™
paper to ensure responsible forest management.

For more information visit: www.harpercollins.co.uk/green

Printed and bound in Spain
by CPI, Barcelona

MILLS & BOON

First Published in Great Britain 2018
by Mills & Boon, an imprint of HarperCollinsPublishers,
1 London Bridge Street, London, SE1 9GF

Unlocking the Millionaire's Heart © 2018 Harriet Nichola Jarvis
From Best Friend to Daddy © 2018 Jules Bennett

ISBN: 978-0-263-26486-9

38-0418

Bella Bucannon lives in a quiet northern suburb of Adelaide with her soulmate husband, who loves and supports her in any endeavour. She enjoys walking, dining out and travelling. Bus tours or cruising with days at sea to relax, plot and write are top of her list. Apart from category romance she also writes very short stories and poems for a local writing group. Bella believes joining RWA and SARA early in her writing journey was a major factor in her achievements.

National bestselling author **Jules Bennett** has penned over forty contemporary romance novels. She lives in the Midwest with her high-school-sweetheart husband and their two kids. Jules can often be found on Twitter chatting with readers, and you can also connect with her via her website, www.julesbennett.com.

Thank you to family, friends and fellow writers, whose encouragement and support were invaluable during the highs and lows of this particular writing journey.

To my husband, always willing to brainstorm when I'm stuck for a word or idea, always reassuring.

To Kim for special insight.

To Victoria and Laurie for their advice and guidance.

CHAPTER ONE

NATE THORNTON SHOOK the rain from his hair with vigour before entering the towering central office block in Sydney's city centre. He'd had to reschedule planned video meetings to make the train trip from Katoomba at Brian Hamilton's insistence, and he'd been further frustrated by his evasive remarks.

'It has to be Thursday the ninth. I think I've found a resolution for your hero and heroine interaction problem. And there's a publisher who's interested in seeing a revised copy of your book.'

Late-night research had shown Brian Hamilton to be one of the best literary agents in Australia. After initial contact he had asked for, and read, Nate's synopsis and first three chapters, then requested the full manuscript. His brutal honesty on its marketability had convinced Nate he was the contract negotiator he wanted.

Attempts to rewrite the scenes he'd specified, however, had proved that particular aspect wasn't his forte. And when he'd been tempted to suggest cutting them out, the feeling in his gut had told him it wasn't that simple, and to ask if the agent could find a better solution.

It wasn't the possibility of income that drove Nate to his computer. Astute investment of an inheritance and a significant part of his earnings while working abroad meant he was financially secure for years. Or, as his brother claimed, 'filthy rich'—a phrase he detested. Although he envied Sam the satisfaction he'd achieved as a pilot in the air force, currently stationed at Edinburgh, north of Adelaide.

His compulsion to write had been driven by the need to put the hardships and traumas he'd witnessed as an international reporter where they belonged—in his past. Those harrowing images of man's inhumanity to man were still in his head, though for the most part he managed to keep them buried.

There was nothing he could do regarding the way he now viewed life and interacted with new acquaintances. The walls he'd built for his own emotional protection were solid and permanent.

Frowning at the number of floors all six lifts had to descend before reaching him, he punched the 'up' button and tapped his fingers on his thigh. Okay, so he wasn't so hot on the touchy-feely sentimental stuff. Hell, the rest of his hundred thousand words were damn good, and his target readers weren't romantic females.

No disrespect intended.

The street doors sliding open drew his attention. The woman who came in brushing raindrops from her hair held it. He had a quick impression of black tights, then a flash of blue patterned fabric under a beige raincoat as she unbuttoned and shook it.

His mind registered long brown hair, a straight nose and red lips above a cute chin—*great descriptive characterisation for an author, Thornton*—then, as their eyes met, he felt a distinct jolt in his stomach.

Dark blue eyes framed by thick lashes stared, then blinked. Her smooth brow furrowed, and she swung away abruptly to study the board on the wall. He huffed in wry amusement at having been dismissed as un-noteworthy— not his usual first reaction from women.

The lift pinged and he moved aside to allow an exiting couple room. Another quick appraisal of the stationary figure of the woman, and he stepped inside.

* * *

Brian's personal assistant had notified Brian of Nate's arrival, and in less than the time it took her to hang his damp jacket on a stand in the corner the agent was greeting him with enthusiasm.

'Punctual as always.' He peered over Nate's shoulder, as if expecting someone else. 'Come on in. Coffee?'

'Yes—if it's going to be rough and take that long.'

Brian laughed. 'It all depends on how determined you are to have a successful publication.'

He followed Nate into the well-appointed corner office, waved at the four comfy leather armchairs round a long low table and went to the coffee machine on a built-in cabinet.

'Strong and black, right?'

'Please.'

Nate sat and studied the view of nearby commercial buildings: hundreds of glass pane eyes, letting in sunlight while hiding the secrets of the people behind them. He'd need to be a heap of floors higher to get even a smidgeon of a harbour view.

'How was the journey down? Ah, excuse me, Nate.' Brian walked over to answer the ring from his desk phone, said 'Thank you, Ella,' then hung up and went to the door.

'I won't be a moment, then we can get started. Your coffee should be ready.'

Spooning sugar into the mug, Nate added extra, figuring he was going to need it. He heard Brian's muted voice, and a quiet female answer. Distracted by the sounds, he drank too soon, letting out a low curse when the hot brew burnt his tongue. This day wasn't getting any better.

'Come in—there's someone I'd like you to meet.'

A second later he was experiencing the same reaction as he had a few moments ago on the ground floor. The woman who'd caused it stood in the doorway, her stunning eyes wide with surprise. And some other, darker emotion.

The absence of her raincoat—presumably hanging up with his jacket—revealed a slender form in a hip-length, blue-patterned, long-sleeved garment with no fastening at the front. The black tights drew his gaze to shapely legs and flat black laced shoes.

This close, he appreciated the smoothness of her lightly tanned skin, the blue of her irises and the perfect shape of her full lips. Not so acceptable was her hesitation and the glance behind her. An action that allowed him to make out the nuances of colour in her hair—shades of his teak table at home.

One look at his agent's satisfied expression and his brain slammed into full alert. This young woman seemed more likely to be a problem for his libido than a resolution for his fictional characters' relationship. What the hell did Brian have in mind?

With Brian urging her in, Jemma Harrison had no choice but to enter the room, pressing the tips of her left-hand fingers into her palm. The man from the lobby seemed no more pleased to see her than she felt about him. Down there, with the length of the foyer between them, his self-assured stance and the arrogant lift of his head had proclaimed his type. One she recognised, classified and avoided.

She'd dismissed the blip in her pulse as their eyes met, swinging away before her mind could process any of his features. Now, against her will, it memorised deep-set storm-grey eyes with dark lashes, thick, sun streaked brown hair and a stubborn jaw. Attractive in an outdoor, man-of-action way. The tan summer sweater he wore emphasised impressive pecs and broad shoulders. He'd teamed it with black chinos and sneakers, and she knew her socialite sister, Vanessa, would rate him as 'cool.'

'Jemma, meet Nate Thornton. Nate, Jemma Harrison.' Brian grinned, as if he'd pulled off an impossible coup.

Jemma stepped forward as Nate placed his mug on the bench and did the same. His cool eyes gave no indication of his thoughts, and his barely there smile vanished more quickly than it had formed.

For no fathomable reason her body tensed as he shook her hand, his grip gentle yet showing underlying strength. A man you'd want on your side in any battle. A man whose touch initiated tremors across her skin and heat in the pit of her stomach. A man she hoped lived a long way from her home town.

'Hello, Jemma. From your expression, I assume Brian didn't tell you I'd be here, so we're both in the dark.'

Against her will, she responded to the sound of his voice—firm and confident, deep and strong, with a hint of abrasion. The kind of voice that would stir sensations when whispering romantic phrases in a woman's ear.

Oh, heck, now she was thinking like one of her starry-eyed heroines, and feeling bereft as he let go and moved away.

'Brian invited me to come in any time I was in Sydney. He didn't mention anyone else being here today.'

'I'll explain once you have a drink,' Brian said. 'Coffee, tea or cold?'

'Flat white coffee with sugar, please.'

She settled into one of the chairs. Nate retrieved his mug and dropped into the one alongside. She was aware of his scrutiny as she scanned the office she'd been too nervous to admire during her first appointment here. It was furnished to give the impression of success with moderation—very apt for the occupant himself.

Average in appearance, and normally mild-mannered, Brian let his passion surface when speaking of books, of guiding authors on their journey to publication and the joy of sharing their triumphs. In assessment he was never condescending, highlighting the positives before giving honest evaluation of the low points, and offering suggestions for improvement.

Why had he invited Nate Thornton to join them? She'd bet he had no idea of the romance genre, and wouldn't appreciate any relevant cover if she held it up in front of his face.

Brian placed a mug in front of her, sat down with his and smiled—first at her, then towards Nate.

'We have here an agent's dilemma: two writers with great potential for literary success, both with flaws that prohibit that achievement.'

Jemma turned her head to meet Nate's appraising gaze and raised eyebrows and frowned. Why wasn't he as surprised as she was at this announcement?

Brian regained her attention and continued.

'Discussions and revision attempts haven't been successful for either of you. But, as they say in the game, I had a lightbulb moment after Jemma told me she was coming to Sydney.'

He took a drink before going on, and Jemma's stomach curled in anticipation—or was it trepidation? She wasn't sure she wanted to hear any solution which meant involvement with this stranger by her side.

'Nate has a talent for action storytelling—very marketable in any media. Regrettably, the interaction between his hero and heroine is bland and unimaginative.'

That was hard to believe. Any man as handsome as he would have no trouble finding willing women to date and seduce. She'd seen the macho flare in his eyes when they'd been introduced, and her body's response had been instinctive.

'Jemma's characters and *their* interaction make for riveting reading. But the storyline between the extremely satisfying emotional scenes has little impact and won't keep pages turning. So, as a trial, I'm proposing we combine your strengths in Nate's manuscript.'

Nate's protest drowned out the startled objections coming from the woman on his right. It took supreme effort not to surge to his feet and pace the room—a lifelong habit when agitated or problem solving.

'Oh, come on, Brian. You know the hours and the effort—physical and mental—that I've put into that book. I can understand bringing someone else in…could even accept an experienced author…'

He struggled for words. Huh, so much for being a great writer.

'You expect me to permit an unproven amateur to mess with my manuscript? Her hearts and flowers characters will *never* fit.'

'Isn't your "amateur status" the reason you're here too, Mr Thornton? I doubt you've ever held a romance novel, let alone read the blurb on the back.'

The quiet, pleasant voice from minutes ago now had bite. He swung round to refute her comment, so riled up its intriguing quality barely registered.

'Wrong, Jemma. Every single word of one—from the title on the front cover to the ending of that enlightening two-paragraph description—to win a bet. Can't say I was impressed.'

Her chin lifted, her dark blue eyes widened in mock indignation and her lips, which his errant brain was assessing as decidedly kissable, curled at the corners. Her short chuckle had his breath catching in his throat, and his pulse booting up faster than his top-of-the-range computer.

'Let me guess. It was selected by a woman—the one who claimed you wouldn't make it through the first chapter, let alone to the happy ending.'

Shoot! His stomach clenched as if he'd been sucker-punched. Baited and played by his sister, Alice, he'd read every page of that badly written, highly sexed paperback to prove a point.

Brian cut in, so his plans for sibling payback had to be shelved for the future.

'Relax, Nate. Your hero and heroine's action stories are absorbing and believable. It's their relationship that won't be credible to the reader. I'm convinced Jemma can rectify that.'

'You're asking me to give her access? Let her delete and make changes to suit her reading preferences?'

No way. Not now. Not ever.

'No.'

'No!'

Their denials meshed.

Brian was the one who negated his outburst.

'No one's suggesting such a drastic measure. To start with I'd like the two of you to have lunch. Get to know each other a little. If you can reach a truce, we could start with a trial collaboration on two or three chapters.'

Lunch? Food and table talk with a woman who'd shown an adverse reaction to him on sight?

He sucked in air, blew it out and shrugged his shoulders. What did he have to lose? A book contract, for starters.

He matched the challenge in Jemma's eyes, nodded and forced a smile.

'Would you care to have lunch with me, Jemma?'

'It will be my pleasure, Nate.'

Her polite acceptance and return smile alleviated his mood a tad, though the option he'd been given still rankled. He disliked coercion—especially if it meant having a meal with an attractive woman who was somehow breaching the barriers he'd built for mental survival. Another reason for not entering into a working relationship with her.

He avoided entanglements. One heart-ripping experience had been enough, and was not to be chanced again. It was only his fact-finding skill that had prevented his being conned out of a fortune as well. Any woman he met now had to prove herself worthy of his trust before it was given.

Brian had been straight and honest with him from the start. And Jemma had shown spirit, so she might be good company. He'd enjoy a good meal, and then...

Well, for starters he'd be spending a lot of time reading writing manuals until he'd mastered the art of accurately describing a relationship.

It was warming up as Jemma exited the building with Nate. The rain had cleared, leaving the pavements wet and steamy and the air clammy. With a soft touch to her elbow he steered her to the right and they walked in silence, each lost in their own thoughts.

She was mulling over the recent conversation between the two of them and Brian, and assumed he was doing the same. Agreeing to Brian's proposition would mean being in frequent contact—albeit via electronic media—with a man whose innate self-assurance reminded her of her treacherous ex-boyfriend and her over-polite and social-climbing brother-in-law.

But unlike those two Nate also had an aura of macho strength and detachment. The latter was a plus for her—especially with her unexpected response when facing him eye to eye and having her hand clasped in his. Throughout the meeting she'd become increasingly aware of his musky aroma with its hint of vanilla and citrus. Alluring and different from anything she'd ever smelt, it had had her imagining a cosy setting in front of a wood fire.

Other pedestrians flowed around them, eager to reach their destinations. Nate came to a sudden stop, caught her arm and drew her across to a shop window. Dropping his hand, he regarded her for a moment with sombre eyes, his body language telling her he'd rather be anywhere else, *with* anyone else.

'Any particular restaurant you fancy?' Reluctance resonated in his voice.

'I haven't a clue.' She arched her head to stare beyond him. An impish impulse to razz him for his hostile attitude overrode her normal discretion and she grinned. 'How about that one?'

He followed her gaze to the isolated round glass floor on the communications tower soaring above the nearby buildings. His eyebrows arched, the corner of his mouth quirked, and something akin to amusement flashed like lightning in his storm-grey eyes.

'The Sydney Tower? Probably booked out weeks ahead, but we can try.'

'I was joking—it's obviously a tourist draw. If we'd been a few steps to the right I wouldn't even have seen it. You decide.'

'You're not familiar with Sydney, are you?'

His voice was gentler, as if her living a distance away was acceptable.

'Basic facts from television and limited visits over many years—more since some of my friends moved here.'

'Darling Harbour's not too far, and there's a variety of restaurants there. We'll take a cab.'

'Sounds good.' She'd have been content to walk—she loved the hustle and bustle of the crowds, the rich accents of different languages and the variety of personal and food aromas wafting through the air. Tantalising mixtures only found in busy cities.

She followed him to the kerb, trying to memorise every detail while he watched for a ride. Once they were on their way her fingers itched to write it all down in the notepad tucked in the side pocket of her shoulder bag—an essential any time she left home.

As a writer, he might understand. As a man who'd been coerced into having lunch with her, who knew *how* he'd react?

Erring on the side of caution, she clasped her hands together and fixed the images in her mind.

CHAPTER TWO

THE FORMAL ESTABLISHMENT Nate steered her towards was a pleasant surprise. She'd been expecting something similar to the casual restaurants she'd passed on her way to Brian's office from the station. White and red linen, crystal glassware and elegant decor gave it a classy atmosphere, and made it look similar to her parents' current venture in Adelaide. The difference was in the plush red cushioning on the seats and the backs of the mahogany chairs.

They received a warm welcome, and at Nate's request were led to a corner table by the window. The view of moored yachts and the cityscape behind them was postcard-picturesque, and would be more so at night with the boats and buildings lit up. She made a mental note to return to the area after dark with Cloe, the friend she was staying with in North Ryde.

Occasionally taking a sip of the chilled water in her glass, she perused the menu options carefully. Having grown up experiencing different flavours and cuisines, she loved comparing the many ways different chefs varied tastes.

'What would you like to drink, Jemma?'

Looking up, she encountered a seemingly genuine smile from Nate. Pity it didn't reach his eyes. But at least he was giving her a choice—something her ex had rarely granted. She placed her menu down, food decision made, and flicked back the hair from her right cheek.

'White wine, please. I'm having fish for both entrée and main courses.'

'Any special kind?'

That impulsive urge to rattle his staid demeanour rose again: *so* not her usual behaviour.

'I guess I should pick a local label—though our South Australian ones are superior.' She raised her chin and curled her lips, daring him to dispute her statement.

She achieved her aim and then some.

His eyes narrowed, drawing his thick dark brows obliquely down, and his mouth quirked as he spoke in a mild tone. 'We'll save that war until later. For that quip, *I'll* select.'

His flippant remark left her breathless, lips parted and with tingles scooting up and down her spine. She drained her water glass, incapable of forming a retort. He was smart—a fast thinker. A man not to be toyed with.

Her mind inexplicably recalled the adage *Make love not war*, and a hot flush spread up from her neck. Lucky for her, a young waiter arrived for their orders, and she ducked her head to read from the menu.

I'll start with the smoked salmon with capers,' she told him, 'and have the barramundi with a fresh garden salad for my main.'

Nate chose oysters with chilli, coconut and lime as an entrée, followed by grilled salmon and steamed vegetables.

The wine he ordered was unknown to Jemma, and the hours she'd spent stacking refrigerators and racks had given her an extensive knowledge of labels. She'd also filled and emptied many a dishwasher, so figured she'd earned any offer to dine out for years to come.

'You obviously enjoy seafood.'

Nate's upper body leant forward over his crossed arms on the table, his intent to follow their agent's suggestion of becoming acquainted evident in his posture. Pity there was little affability in his tone, and a suspicion there was more to his manner than giving her access to his writing began to form.

'Barramundi is my mother's specialty. I like to compare other offerings with hers.'

'She's a good cook, huh?'

Jemma laughed. 'Don't ever call her that if she has a knife in her hand—which, by the way, will always be sharp. Both she and Dad are qualified chefs, and live for their profession.'

A speculative gleam appeared in his smoky eyes, holding her spellbound, feeling as if he were seeking her innermost thoughts. His features remained impassive, his voice with its intriguing hint of roughness calm. The only sign of emotion was the steady tapping of two left-hand fingers on his right elbow, an action he seemed unaware of.

'I'm guessing that didn't leave much time for child-rearing.'

'I didn't mean—'

The waiter appeared with their wine, sending the next words back into her throat. She'd have to set him straight—hadn't meant to give that impression. Yet as Nate sampled the small amount of wine poured into his glass she couldn't deny the facts. There *had* been little time for any of the usual parent/child activities, though they'd encouraged and financed Vanessa's modelling courses. They'd gained publicity, of course, when she'd won an international contract.

On Nate's approval, her glass was filled. As she savoured the crisp, dry flavour he raised his glass to her without speaking, drank, then set it down.

'This *is* good. I approve of your choice, Nate.' She took another sip and let it linger on her tongue, waiting for him to continue the conversation about family. He didn't.

I presume you don't write full-time? Do you have another career?'

'I paint pictures of Australian flora and fauna, mostly on small tiles, and work part-time in the gift shop where they're displayed. I also sell them at local markets.'

'Let me guess—koalas and wombats top the list?'

Hearing the hint of condescension in his voice, she clenched her teeth and felt her spine stiffen. She tightened her grip on the stem of her glass and held back the retort his words deserved.

'They're up there. Mother animals with babies are my bestsellers, along with bright native flowers.'

'And where's home?'

Firing questions seemed to be his idea of becoming acquainted. She obliged, giving him only the information she wished to reveal.

'The Adelaide Hills.'

'South Australian bushfire territory? I was there in 2015. The risks don't worry you?'

Nate saw the flicker of pain in her eyes and the slight convulsion in her throat—heard the hitch in her voice when, after gazing out of the window for a moment, she answered.

'That year was my first summer as a resident there. A close friend lost property, some sheep and their pets—a cat and two dogs. Meg and her family were devastated, yet they stayed, rebuilt and adopted from the animal shelter. They taught me how to minimise risks, and although the worry is there every year, it's balanced by living with fresh air in a friendly, small-town atmosphere. Big cities are for holidays and shopping sprees. How about you?'

Sprung. He'd kept his questions basic, complying with the intent of Brian's words if not the spirit. He hadn't expected to hear a familiar story—one he'd heard a few times since he'd moved to the mountains. Given her parents' profession, he'd pictured her living in Adelaide or one of its suburbs.

Bracing himself for her reaction, he answered.

'The Blue Mountains.'

He was treated to a sharp intake of breath between

parted lips, a delightful indignant expression and flashing eyes. Against his will, his gut tightened in response.

'That's the New South Wales equivalent. *You* have flare-
ups every year.'

Stalled by the arrival of their entrées, Nate waited until
they were alone before replying, surprising himself with an
admission he didn't normally disclose to strangers.

'I know. I help fight them.'

She tilted her head as she scrutinised him, as if mem-
orising every feature and nuance. He'd already achieved
that in the office. He might not have her reputed eloquent
descriptive powers, but her face was indelibly imprinted
on his mind. Again, not intentionally.

'You're a volunteer firefighter?'

Her apparent admiration was gratifying, if not truly
merited. He shrugged it off. Living in the country meant
embracing its culture and values.

'You live in the area—you should do your bit. The training keeps me fit, along with exercising at home.'

He scooped up an oyster and let it slide down his throat,
savouring the spice and tang as he watched Jemma arrange
salmon and capers on a cracker, and take a delicate bite.
Her glossed lips fascinated him, conjuring up thoughts better left unsaid, and his sudden surge of desire was totally
unexpected.

He knew the myth that oysters were an aphrodisiac, so
maybe they'd been the wrong choice.

Risky selection or not, he ate another before asking,
'How much writing have you done?'

It came out more curt than he'd intended—caused by his
inability to curb her effect on his mind and body. If he was
attracted to a woman his rules were not negotiable. *Keep
it simple, keep it unemotional and don't get too involved.*
Strictly adhering to those rules since his short disastrous
affair—never discussed with anyone, not even family—

ensured mutually satisfying relationships with women of similar views.

Jemma wrote romance. She'd be a sentimental believer in happy-ever-after who deserved flowers—hell, she even *painted* them—and love tokens. She'd want commitment, and would no doubt one day be a devoted wife and mother.

He might fantasise about her, might desire her, but the pitfalls of sexual entanglement had taught him to maintain control. Whatever feelings she aroused now, they would pass once they'd parted company.

She sipped her wine and made a lingering survey of the room, before facing him with enigmatic features. Not one to open up willingly to someone she didn't know. He waited patiently. As things stood now, his literary career wouldn't be taking off any time soon.

'Poems and short stories since childhood—most of the earlier ones consigned to the recycling bin. A computer file of thirty thousand-word partial manuscripts with varying degrees of potential, plus this finished one.'

'Which Brian deems in need of drastic revision?'

'Ditto, Mr Thornton. Is this your first effort, or are there others waiting for your help too?'

She gave a sudden stunning smile that tripped his pulse, shaking his composure.

She rattled it even more when she added, with unerring accuracy, 'No, you'd see any project through to the bitter end before starting another.' Leaving him speechless.

He scooped out the last oyster, trying to fathom why a woman so dissimilar from those who usually attracted him was pressing his buttons with such ease. Down to earth rather than sophisticated, she had that indefinable something he couldn't identify.

Shelving it to the back of his mind, he pushed the tray of empty shells aside. 'Point conceded. And the name's Nate. Unless you're trying to maintain a barrier between us?'

The soft flush of colour over her cheeks proved he was right. His own rush of guilt proved that his conscience knew his curtness was partly to blame.

He drained his wine glass, set it down, and thanked the waitress who cleared away the dishes. A new topic seemed appropriate.

'How well do you know Brian?'

Jemma blinked as he switched topic again. This was almost like speed-dating—which she'd never tried, but she knew women who'd described it. Except she and Nate weren't changing partners, and she definitely wasn't in the market for one.

'Mostly by email, but I trust him. He read my novel, then when I came to Sydney in December we met in his office. Not my happiest encounter ever, as he gave me an honest, concise appraisal of my writing proficiency. Unlike you, my inept storyline passages way outnumber the good scenes. You?'

'Similar scenario. You're not bothered that agreeing to his proposal means putting your novel on hold while you work on someone else's?'

'No, I'm dumbfounded by the offer, terrified of the implications if I fail, and thrilled that he believes I'm worthy of being part of something he seems keen to see published. If you're as good as he's implied, adapting those scenes yet keeping them true to your characters and story will be beneficial for my career too.'

'Hmm.'

He appeared to be considering her declaration as their mains were served, pepper offered and accepted by Nate, and their wine glasses refilled. She waited for him to continue, but instead he began to eat.

The fish was delicious, and her *mmm* of pleasure slipped

out. Glancing up, she found Nate watching her with a sombre expression.

'How does this chef's barramundi compare to your mother's?'

'As good as—though I'd never tell her. It's different, and I can't pick why. I prefer the natural taste of food, so I don't use many herbs and spices and I can't always identify their flavour. How's your salmon?'

She hoped her answer would satisfy him, and save her from having to admit that her limited cooking knowledge came from her aunt and recipe books, because her parents claimed they didn't have time to teach her.

'Up to the usual excellent standard. I've never had a meal here that wasn't.'

They ate in silence for a few minutes, with Jemma wishing she had her sister's gift to attract and charm people of any age. Apart from when she was with close friends Jemma hid behind a façade of friendly courtesy. Though she had her moments when she couldn't hold back—like when someone irked her as *he* had a few times. Or when her curiosity was aroused. Like now.

'How do you make a living while you're waiting for the book sale royalties to come flooding in?'

Nate's head jerked up, his face a picture of astonishment. Instead of the comeback she'd assumed he'd give, he chuckled, and the deep sound wrapped around her, making her yearn for a time when trust had come easy.

'I'll let you know when they do and we'll celebrate.'

The memory of a similar pledge slammed through her, taking her breath away and freezing her blood.

I'm expecting good news. When it comes we'll have a special celebration.

Two days later she'd found out that the man she'd believed loved her and intended to propose was sleeping with a female colleague to gain promotion. He'd even gone to meet her after taking Jemma home that night.

'Jemma, are you all right?'

She shook her head, dragged in air and looked into concerned grey eyes.

'You're white as a ghost.'

'The ghost of a bad memory. Best forgotten.' She managed a smile and he relaxed into his seat, keeping watch on her pale face. 'Truly, I'm fine.'

'I'm not so sure, but…'

He let out a very masculine grunt and she was totally back in the now, reaching for her wine, sipping it as he gave her a serious answer.

'I was a reporter. Now I'm an investment advisor.'

'A good one?'

'Good enough to pay the bills.'

Jemma pondered on his succinct job description. She could visualise him investigating a story, chasing information to find the truth, but the switch to an office job didn't gel.

'Why the career move?'

She watched his chest expand under the tan sweater, hold then contract. He seemed to be deliberately assessing how much to disclose. Preparing to keep secrets and lie like her ex?

'Things happen and you make choices. My gap year—travelling in Europe with a friend after we graduated from uni—became a rite of passage lasting seven years that made me who I am now.'

She empathised, and was convinced his matter-of-fact tone belied his true feelings. Her parents selling their house—her home—to invest in a restaurant, and her ex's betrayal were the two events that had forced her to re-evaluate her future, and they had a continuing effect on her viewpoint and life choices.

'Four years ago, my father had a health scare, prompting him to semi-retire and move with my mother to the south coast. It was my motivation for coming home for good—a decision I've never regretted in the slightest.'

She heard honest affection in his voice and envied that relationship. She couldn't imagine her parents or sister giving up their careers for anyone—hoped she'd be more compassionate.

Sensing he'd divulged more than he'd intended when he'd agreed to lunch with her, she didn't reply and finished eating her meal.

Nate had no idea why he'd revealed private aspects of his life he usually kept to himself. Or why he found it almost impossible to take his eyes off her enchanting, expressive face. His attraction to a woman had never been so immediate, so compelling. So in conflict with his normal emotionless liaisons.

A growing need for open space was compelling. He had to get away from her—away from her subtle floral perfume that had been tantalising him since he'd stepped near enough to greet her. Native rather than commercially grown city flowers, it was delicate and haunting.

He didn't fight his urgent compulsion to pace and consider all the implications, including any legal ramifications, of collaboration. He needed to think and plan away from the distractions of other people, away from Jemma and his reactions to her, physical and mental.

Noting her plate was empty, he placed his cutlery neatly on his.

'Do you want dessert or coffee here? Or we could take some time apart to consider our options and meet up later.'

This time her scrutiny was short. yet no less intense.

With an understanding smile he'd rather not have seen, she nodded. 'That's a good idea.'

Muscles he hadn't realised were tight suddenly loosened.

'I'll need your phone number.'

Unease flickered in her eyes before she reached for her shoulder bag on the floor. Had it anything to do with her adverse opinion of him at first sight?

He held his mobile towards her, allowing her to input first.

Their empty plates removed, and anything else politely declined, she leant her elbows on the table and cupped her chin on her linked fingers as they waited for the bill.

'Do you commute from the mountains every day?' she asked.

'Electronic media means I can do a fair amount from home. I come in when necessary, or for socialising.'

He hadn't yet bowed to the pressure to commit to full-time employment with the family firm, wary of the daily sameness stretching into his future.

'Like today?'

'Like today.'

And he'd be staying until his flight overseas on Sunday morning.

He settled the account on the way out, irrationally torn between needing to be alone and reluctance to let her go. After saying goodbye, she headed for the railway station without glancing back. He watched for a moment, then strode towards the Harbour Bridge.

CHAPTER THREE

JEMMA TOOK NO notice of the world around her as the train sped to Central Station, and as she deliberated on which way to go when she alighted. Her brain buzzed at the compliments Brian had given her, coupled with the sensations from Nate's few touches and her own responses to his looks and his voice.

Could she handle being in frequent contact with him? Even by email? How would she deal with someone who was averse to allowing her to read anything he'd written?

Consider our options.

Like heck. He oozed the authority of a man who knew exactly what he wanted and rarely settled for less. He'd given no indication of his point of view on their two-way deal, focussing only on his novel.

Brian's appraisal of her work had been honest and unemotional, letting her know the downsides while still giving her hope of a satisfactory solution. Already aware of her weakness when she'd submitted to him, she was open to any suggestion for improvement.

Could Nate remain impartial to the romance genre when he read her work? How did he feel about helping to transform her inept storytelling? He'd been very forthright about his aversion to allowing her access to his manuscript. Her emotions wavered from exhilaration that she might achieve publication to apprehension that Nate's expectations might be hard to satisfy.

She walked out of the station and turned towards Circular Quay. Window shopping in Pitt Street would pass the time and occupy her mind. If he didn't call... She banished that thought. He'd phone—even if it was only to dash any foolish hopes she might have allowed to take seed.

A new dress and two fun presents for her friends later, she was watching the ferries dock and depart as she devoured a fruit and nut bar. She wandered over to where groups of excited people were dragging suitcases towards a huge cruise ship. A holiday to inspire a romance novel? Maybe one day she'd take one.

A brochure she'd picked up on the way showed it wasn't far from here to the historic Rocks area. If she hadn't heard from Nate by the time she'd explored the old buildings she'd catch the next train to North Ryde.

Did he like Jemma? Way too much. Nate had kept his emotions under tight restraint since he'd narrowly escaped being duped into a sham marriage, but he'd had trouble curbing them around her. She'd had doubts concerning *him* on sight, which had him wondering who he reminded her of.

Did he trust her? Not yet. Experience in dealing with the darker side of life had taught him that trust had to be earned rather than given freely.

Did he want her? His body's response to any thought of her gave him an instant reply. But that didn't mean he'd follow through.

Mental arguments for and against dual authorship had got him nowhere, and he was still uncommitted as he reached the waterside. Swinging left, he took the steps leading up to the bridge walkway. After skirting a group of photo-snapping tourists, he took a deep breath of salty air and began to run.

He maintained a steady pace until he reached the apartment block at North Sydney. His grandfather had bequeathed a twenty-third-storey unit jointly to him, Sam and Alice, and all three of them had lived there, alone or together, at various times. It was always available for family and friends when they came to the city.

A long, refreshing shower cooled his body, but didn't clear his mind. Dressed in fresh clothes, and with a stubby of cold beer in his hand, he stood on the balcony, staring at the buildings around him. Not far away by foot was the office block housing the family brokerage firm, which had offered him a lucrative job for life.

Far away up in the mountains was the home he'd designed, with an architect's help, to suit the lifestyle he planned to live. Mostly solitary, with occasional guests, pleasing only himself. Closing his eyes, he pictured the view as he woke in the morning, ate his meals and chilled out in the evenings. And in that instant his decision was made.

Somewhere in the thriving metropolis across the bay was the woman Brian believed could help him realise literary success. All he had to do was have faith and stay in command of his libido.

But before he committed to a trial partnership he needed to reinforce the life oath he'd made years ago, during the lowest point of his life. He took the dog-eared leather notebook he always travelled with, flipped it open to a coded page, and read the vow he'd made never to get involved out loud.

Then he phoned Jemma Harrison.

It took three rings for her to answer, and he heard traffic and the rattle of a train in the background.

'Hi, Jemma, where are you?'

'Taking photos from the Harbour Bridge.'

He surprised himself with a spontaneous burst of laughter.

'What's so funny?' There was a spike in her voice, though she didn't sound offended.

'I ran over it on the way here. Which end are you nearest?'

'Um… I guess I'm about a third of the way along from the quay.'

'Keep coming north. Don't rush. I'll meet you at the steps going down to the road. We can sit in the park nearby. Would you like me to bring you a hot or cold drink?'

'No, thanks. I have a bottle of water.'

'Okay, see you soon.'

He grimaced at the screen after disconnecting, and then went to put on socks and sneakers. Having his pulse hiking and his mouth drying, even his palms itching, was something he might have to become accustomed to if they were going to be in regular communication.

Anticipation of seeing her had him moving faster than normal. It was not the way he wanted to feel.

Nate saw Jemma approaching as he reached the top of the steps so he waited, admiring the natural sway of her hips as she came towards him. The extra bag in her hand and the bulge in the one over her shoulder, proved she'd been shopping. Her smile as they met had him steeling his arms at his sides to prevent greeting her with a hug, and the sunglasses hiding the expression in her beautiful blue eyes was a disappointment.

'Hi—would you like me to carry the bag?'

'Thanks, I'm fine.' She waved her arm in a wide sweep. 'I'd love to sit and view all this on a stormy day—or preferably night.'

'You like thunder and lightning?'

She laughed, causing an unfamiliar and yet not unpleasant effect over his skin. Causing him to take a quick breath. Causing him to fortify the reason he was meeting her. To get his book published.

'From a safe vantage point—oh, yes.'

'They can give you a spectacular display in the

mountains—especially when watched from a heated room with a beer or glass of wine at your side.'

Berating himself for conjuring up an image of them sharing wine and nature's dramatic show, he guided her down to the ground and across to the lawn area at the edge of the water. Partial images of the Opera House and the southern side of the bay were visible through the semi-circle of palm trees. A small oasis of green surrounded by acres of concrete and buildings was behind them, and the expanse of deep water in front.

Jemma placed her bags on the ground, sat and curled her legs to the side. He joined her, leaning on his elbows, legs stretched out in front of him. For a moment or two there seemed no need for conversation. The serenity of the small area compensated for the traffic noise from the bridge.

Having resolved his mental conflict, and acutely aware of her beside him, he accepted that she'd now be a presence in his life. How prominent depended on how often they had to meet in person.

Few women he knew would wait so quietly, so patiently, for a man who'd told her he needed to consider his options, expected her to hike across the bridge, and then didn't initiate conversation. Another difference from the women he dated.

Her profile was as appealing as her full face. Delicate smooth skin invited a caress, thick brown lashes enhanced the dark blue of her eyes, and her slender neck with its curtain of...

Where the heck had all that come from? And where the hell had it been when he'd tried to write such descriptions on the computer?

'Jemma?'

His raspy tone came from the absence of moisture in his throat, exacerbated by the expectancy in her eyes as she faced him. He coughed, swallowed and retried.

'Do you have full virus protection on your computer?'

Her chin lifted and her eyes narrowed in umbrage. 'The best—and regularly updated.'

'Would you be willing to send me some examples of those scenes Brian claims will improve my novel to a marketable level? I'm aware it means one-sided trust, but—'

Her laughter—natural, musical and matched by the sparkle in her eyes—cut him short.

'My text is less than fifty thousand words, a fair proportion of which need cutting or rewriting. Most of your...' She tilted her head and her eyebrows rose in query.

'One hundred and ten thousand.'

'Not only pass muster but have earned Brian's praise. You have the right to be protective. How about I email three chapters?'

He puffed out what little air was left in his lungs. This could either be the start of a new career or the most turbulent phase of his life. Even seeing her face-to-face online would test his tenacity.

Jemma tried to hide the elation coursing through her. If he approved of her style of writing there was a chance he'd send her a partial to test her competence in blending with his. A *limited* partial, if she was any judge of men—a talent she could hardly claim, having had no inkling of her ex's infidelity.

Nate Thornton, with his solemn expression and deep-set thoughtful eyes, was hard to read. He rarely smiled, but when he did he stirred feelings she'd sworn she'd never allow to rule her again. And his touch had her hankering for pleasures she'd renounced, tainted by betrayal. An electronic, detached co-author partnership would be the ideal answer.

'You'll need my email address.' He pushed himself into a sitting position, and took out his mobile. She gave him her ever-present notebook and a pen, and had no trouble reading the neat script, wishing hers was as legible when she jotted something down so fast. He recorded hers in his phone—a much newer model than she owned. Something she might have to research and rectify in the coming weeks.

'I've got a USB back-up with me, so I'll send them tomorrow.' She grinned at him; no use being precious about her failings. 'Try to skim over the boring bits. Brian left me with no illusions on the quality of the storyline, but I hope to amend that failing by taking relevant courses.'

He returned the smile. 'Maybe I *should* read them. They're the reason he recommended you work with me instead of offering your novel to a publisher. I'll do a print-out for my flight to Europe on Sunday morning—preferable to reading off a screen for me. I'll get in touch on my return in a week or so.'

'However long it takes.'

She couldn't seem to break eye contact since he'd smiled at her, and wondered whether she ought to take the initiative and leave. Go home and start preparing dinner for her friends or watch some bad afternoon television. Even better, lose herself in the character charts and life histories of the hero and heroine of her next novel. One for which she intended to have Brian begging her to sign a solo contract.

Nate's sudden rise to his feet broke her reverie and dulled her mood. Now the main issue had been settled he'd be anxious to go, and she understood—she truly did. Accepting his helping hand, she rose, taking her shoulder bag with her. He bent to pick up the other one, and maintained his hold.

'How are you getting back?'

'Walking over the bridge, of course. Who knows when I'll have another chance?'

As he'd met her from this direction, she assumed he'd be staying in this area.

'Suits me, Jemma. I'll shout you coffee on the southern side.'

She had no right to feel elated, or for her heart to beat faster, but both happened as he spoke. And the air in her lungs seemed to have dissipated, making her sound breathy.

'Your offer is accepted with gratitude, Nate.'

Since when had she spoken with such formality?

I don't even allow my characters that uptown privilege. Maybe I will in a future book of mine, and their love interest will have a rougher background for conflict.

Her fingers itched to jot down notes on upbringing, and childhood environment. Instead she set the idea into her head as they returned to the walkway.

On her journey across it she'd become used to the noise of the traffic speeding past, separated from her by a steel and mesh safety fence. On the water side there were shoulder-and-head-high gaps in the corresponding mesh to allow for clear photography.

She stopped a short way along to take photos from this end, turning from Nate as she aimed her mobile upward, marvelling at the size and power of the metal beams and the majestic arches above their heads.

'It's so incredible—so powerful and strong.'

'Walking up there is an entirely different experience. Keep it in mind for another visit.'

Swinging round, she bumped into his body as he stepped forward, pointing his finger to the top of the bridge. Her pulse surged as he caught her by the waist for support, and it didn't ease off when he let go.

'Not for me,' she stated with emphasis.

His eyebrows rose and he grinned—a genuine magnetic smile, stirring butterflies in her stomach. Heat flooded her veins and her heart pounded. Such potency…she was glad he normally withheld it from her.

'You're toned and fit. What's the problem? Fear of heights?'

He'd checked out her body? Fair was fair...she'd checked out his.

'No, I just have no inclination to try anything I consider extreme.'

Or to become involved with the self-assured, super-confident men those activities attract.

'Ah.' He straightened his back and crossed his arms in mock umbrage. The quirk at the corner of his mouth and the gleam in his eyes belied his stance. A new personality was emerging—one that was engaging and amiable, much harder to keep at a distance. With luck it was only transient.

'And that encompasses skydiving, mountain climbing and abseiling, huh?'

His words sounded deeper too, making the abrasion more appealing.

'I'm not *anti* them. I can almost understand the compulsion to try them. But not the repeated temptation for disaster. Everyday life is challenging enough.'

'Don't you ever feel the need for an adrenaline rush?'

'Mine come from seeing a koala with her new baby, or a rainbow appearing over the hills in a rainstorm.'

His soft chuckle evoked an alien feeling in her stomach, warm and exciting.

'Oh, darling, you are *so* missing out on life.'

Her mood altered in an instant and she moved away towards the city. He walked by her side, seemingly oblivious to the word that had rendered her speechless and torn at her heart. It marked him as a man who used endearments as a matter of course, making them meaningless; it had been a habit of her ex.

Glancing at him, she caught his lips curling as if she'd amused him and the penny dropped. He'd listed the extreme sports he'd participated in, was prepared to risk his life for the so-called 'rush' she'd heard people rave about. Nothing they'd said had ever convinced her to try any, and she doubted reading about them—they had to be part of the action in his novel—would change her mind.

Was he even now classifying her as boring, doomed to fail in her attempt to revise some of the passages in his high-adventure book?

She stopped and swivelled to face him, square-on. 'You've done all those activities?'

Nate couldn't deny the accusation. He shrugged his shoulders and nodded. 'Multiple times—plus a few others over the years, here and abroad.'

If they stayed in touch for a lifetime Nate figured he'd never get used to the way she breathed slow and even, her lips slightly parted and her eyes wide and focussed as they studied his face. It made him feel virile, yet vulnerable at the same time—a totally alien sensation.

Better she didn't know that some of those activities had been to gain access to high-risk areas, following leads for stories. Others *had* been for the adrenaline rush—to prove he was capable of feeling after the sights he'd been exposed to had completely numbed all his emotions.

Racking his brain for something to divert her attention, he saw it over her shoulder. 'Where does sailing qualify?' he asked, gesturing towards the water.

She twisted to follow his gaze. A few yachts had emerged from under the bridge and were tacking from side to side, skilfully avoiding impact.

Moving to the mesh protection, she craned her neck to watch. 'Mixed. My sister and brother-in-law in Melbourne own a yacht, and I've sailed with them. I love the wind in my hair, the smell of salt water and the sense of the ocean below us as we skim across the waves. *Wearing life jackets*. Ocean-racing in rough weather—like the Sydney to Hobart some years—is *out*.'

He'd bet any advance he might get on his book that she

had no idea how captivating she looked: features animated, eyes sparkling and hands gesturing. Or how the inflections in her voice proved that she wasn't immune to the thrill—no matter how much she said so.

CHAPTER FOUR

NATE DIDN'T DO YEARNING, or hankering for unattainable dreams. So why did the image of him standing on a boat, his arms on either side of her, guiding her hands on the wheel as they sailed along the coast, imprint itself into his mind?

There had been no conscious thought to move nearer. Had he shifted? Or had it been she who'd taken a step? He'd swear there'd been an arm's length between them a moment ago.

The uneven breaths he took filled his nostrils with her subtle aroma. Time froze. Sounds blurred. And Jemma's face filled his vision. The strong-minded man he believed he was might have fought the urge to kiss her. Here, in this moment, there was no option and he bent his head.

With a shudder she jerked away, remorse replacing the desire in her eyes. Guilt and wanting warred for prominence inside him. Neither won nor lost, and his mind was blank of any words to appease her.

Her gulp of air was followed by a short huff—an unsuccessful attempt at a laugh. 'I don't go there very often. They have full social lives, and I have my work and commitments.'

It was an addition to her last statement, spoken as if those few special moments hadn't happened.

She glanced towards the city, took a step that way, and his regret was heightened at seeing her effort to regain composure.

He fell into step beside her, leaving extra space between them and taking up the conversation where she'd finished.

'In the Adelaide Hills? Apart from the firefighting trip, the only time I've been to South Australia was in my teens, when my family holidayed on the South Coast. Great beaches and surfing. My brother Sam, who's with the air force at Edinburgh, reckons it's a cool place to be stationed.'

'I like it. *Oh!*'

She gasped and he turned his head in time to see a speedboat and a yacht come close to colliding.

'Does that qualify as extreme?' he asked as the vessels swung away from each other.

'Only the attitude of whoever's steering the motorboat.'

'If the yacht's skipper reports him he's in trouble. If not, I hope he's had a sobering scare.'

She didn't reply, and he let the conversation lapse, thinking about their near-kiss and cursing himself for his moment of weakness. It might have screwed up any possible co-writing deal, and that was what this was about.

He presumed Jemma was a stay-at-home girl—painting and writing syrupy love stories, never taking any chances outside her comfort zone. But, no, not quite. It took guts and willpower to send a manuscript to a stranger for assessment and possible negative feedback.

Submitting had been *his* intention from the moment the characters and plot had first formed in his head. How long had Jemma dithered before pressing 'send'? And why this strong attraction when there were gulfs of difference between them?

Jemma opted for a café with outdoor seating near the quay. She ordered a banana and caramel ice cream sundae and a glass of water—well-earned by all the walking she'd done today. Nate opted for sultana cake and coffee.

Having him hold the seat she chose, and adjust the umbrella to shade her, was flattering and she thanked him.

'My pleasure.'

He sat on her left, shuffled along until their knees bumped, then pulled back. The contact sent a tremor up her leg, spreading to her spine. It didn't seem to affect him at all.

He'd told her he'd run over the bridge after lunch, which explained his damp hair when they'd met, and his change of clothes. It also signified that he was staying somewhere on the North Shore. With friends? A girlfriend? She didn't want or need to know, but would be amazed if there wasn't one. He didn't wear a wedding ring, although... *Not going there*—it implied personal interest.

'You run regularly? Apart from the bushfire training?' An acceptable question as *he'd* initiated the topic.

'I like to run or swim every day—sometimes both. There are some great hiking tracks near my home.'

His phone rang. He turned his head and held it to his left ear. She averted her gaze to allow him privacy, concentrating on the passing pedestrians.

'Hi, Dave.' He listened for a while. 'No, we're good. Tess will be there Saturday night, so we'll arrange it then.' A shorter pause, then he said goodbye and tapped her arm.

One side of his lips quirked as he peered over her shoulder 'This looks positively *evil*, Jemma.

Leaning away to allow her dessert to be placed on the table, Jemma felt her eyes widen at its size. And Nate apparently found her dilemma amusing.

She flashed him a fake warning glare and then, with a honeyed tone, thanked the waitress and asked, 'Could we please have an extra spoon for sharing?'

'Of course. I'll bring one out.' She set Nate's plate in front of him and walked away.

'Don't worry about your figure, Nate, you can always run over the bridge again.'

Her laughter slipped back into her throat as their eyes locked and the amusement in his slowly morphed into something deeper. Something perplexed and conflicted. Or was she transferring her own feelings?

He blinked, and she found herself facing the sombre features he'd shown at their initial introduction, as if he'd reverted to his distrust of her. How could he switch so fast? And *why*?

Nate's jaw tightened and his stomach clenched as Jemma's mirth abated and her eyes softened and glowed, mesmerising him. He'd allowed his guard to slip, had forgotten how easily a woman could deceive with her inviting glances and enticing lips.

He'd paid a life-changing price once, and wouldn't ever risk the pain and humiliation again. This relationship must be kept casual and friendly—nothing more. Proximity had to be the reason for the desire Jemma aroused, and that would end when she returned home.

'Water, a long black and another dessert spoon. Enjoy.'

The waitress broke the spell and was gone in the time it took him to refocus. Jemma bent over as she picked up a spoon, her long hair falling forward to hide her face. She didn't brush it away.

They needed to set ground rules and fix boundaries for their own protection. Nate reached across the table and covered the hand dipping to scoop up ice-cream. Ignoring its trembling, he held on until she raised her head, her expression wary.

'Trust me, Jemma, I don't want you to have any regrets for the decisions either of us make.'

Her lips parted and her eyelids fell, concealing her emotions, and her chest rose as she breathed in, drawing his attention, threatening his resolve. Her fingers fisted under his, and he became aware of his thumb caressing her knuckle.

Then, with a sudden loosening of her fingers, a deep intake of air and a challenging message in her dark blue eyes, she replied in a clear, steady tone, 'I won't commit unless I understand exactly what's required of me, and I'm sure I can deliver to your satisfaction.'

Sensation akin to a lightning bolt shot through him at her ambiguous statement. Innocent or deliberate, it created mental images that would keep him awake tonight. Or give him memorable dreams.

He released her hand, tore open two sugar sachets and stirred sugar into his coffee, his mind searching for a topic to discuss that would avoid personal revelation.

'How do you rate a visit to Sydney against Melbourne?'

Her hand froze centimetres from her parted lips and her eyes grew bigger, highlighting their colour. Hell, she was alluring—even when caught unawares. And she was smart, cottoning on to his diversionary tactic in an instant.

'That depends on the season and the reason for going there.'

A discussion followed, with inputs about Adelaide from Jemma, centred on the city's central attractions and the entertainment value of international musical celebrities.

Nate ate the remainder of her sundae without mentioning that he wasn't fond of such sweet offerings. Nor did he protest when she checked her watch and said she needed to leave. He insisted on escorting her to the station, told her he'd be in touch, and shook her hand for slightly longer and with slightly more pressure than convention dictated.

As he climbed the steps up to the bridge he remembered her gentle goad. Setting a steady-paced jog, he recalled their meetings, her reactions to the things he'd said and done and his own to her.

A seagull flew past, soaring upward, and he followed its flight to the top curved girders. If the chance arose in the future, maybe he'd persuade her to take that climb.

Jemma had the electric jug boiling and an open packet of biscuits waiting on the kitchen table for Cloe's homecoming after work. She'd missed the closeness she shared with her best friend since her wedding and move to Sydney. Somewhere in her future there *had* to be a man who'd love her as faithfully as Mike loved Cloe.

The one secret she'd kept from her was the love stories that she'd expanded into full novels. Brian's review had proved her judgement to be right. But if she was ever offered a contract Cloe would be the first to know.

'So how did you spend your day?' Cloe arched her back to relieve the kinks of the day and sipped her tea.

'Window shopping, exploring The Rocks area and walking over the bridge. Plus two meetings that are confidential at the moment. Oh, and I *did* have lunch with someone who'll be involved if the project goes ahead.'

She tried for nonchalance, not mentioning Nate, but heard the new inflection in her tone and felt her cheeks flush.

Cloe jerked upright, scanned her face with narrowed eyes, then clapped her hands. 'You *like* him.' A delighted grin split her face. 'You're blushing, Jemma! You like him *a lot*. Come on—give.'

'Nothing to tell. He was at the morning meeting and we had lunch together. He lives here, and as far as I know may have a wife or girlfriend. I live in South Australia, and am *not* interested in a relationship.'

She told herself it was the truth, attributing her reaction to him as natural in the presence of a ruggedly attractive man. So why hadn't it happened when her friends had set her up for dates in the three years since her break-up?

The back door opened, distracting Cloe. Jemma had often witnessed Mike's loving kisses for his wife, so why the blip of her heartbeat and the sharp wrench in her abdomen this time?

That night, after an evening of reminiscing and lively conversation, she snuggled into her pillow, mulling over the past. Her initial reaction to finding out that the man she'd contemplated marriage with was cheating on her had been gut-wrenching anguish. She'd hidden away and cried, cursing them both to the walls of her bedroom, and had deleted every image of him—even shredding printed copies.

A few weeks later a koala with a baby clinging to her back had trundled across in front of her on a photo-taking walk in the hills. She'd stopped, her hand over her mouth in awe, silently watching their progress into the scrubland. Being that close to an active mother and her joey had been awesome. Inspiring.

She'd laughed out loud, realising that life went on and that it was only her pride and self-esteem that had suffered damage. Her heart might have cracked a little, but it wasn't broken and it would heal with time.

That was the moment she'd decided to move from the city.

Later she'd become aware that her ability to trust had been the thing most affected.

Deep inside she still harboured a dream that there was someone out there who would love her as Mike loved Cloe, and would show it proudly and openly. She'd know him the moment he gazed into her eyes, held her in his arms and kissed her.

Nate Thornton intrigued her, and she'd felt a physical reaction to his smile and touch that was normal for any mature female. It could be a sign that she was ready to move on—though not to trust on sight.

She woke in the morning with a smile on her lips, ready for a day of shopping with Cloe and their friends, plus a lunchtime meet-up which would last all afternoon.

Sunday afternoon at the airport, Cloe hugged her and whispered in her ear. 'Let me know if your meetings lead to anything. Of any kind. Your happiness is my greatest wish.'

* * *

Some time in the early hours of Friday morning Nate jerked upright in bed, throwing the sheet away from his sweat-soaked body. Heart pounding, he swung his feet to the floor and bent over, dragging great gulps of air into his lungs.

The details of the nightmare—his first for over a year—were already fading apart from occasional vague shadowy images, but the aftermath stayed. He strode to the wardrobe, dragged on a pair of shorts and went out onto the balcony, to look at the welcoming view of the city lights.

Why now? Long ago he'd accepted that images of the horrific sights he'd seen in war zones and wherever terrorists preyed on the innocent would have a lasting effect on him. Others reported the sickening acts—he'd chosen to write about the indomitable spirit of the victims and their families, keeping a tight control on his own feelings.

He'd got past the initial bad memories and traumatic dreams when he'd written the novel, repeating the mantra, *These are only words on a page*. Nothing had changed, except...

He gripped the railing as a shiver ran down his spine—always a danger sign.

Jemma. Caught unawares when he'd first seen her, he'd let her slip past his guard, triggering emotions he'd tamped down, refused to acknowledge unless for family.

Fetching a cold bottle of beer from the fridge, and a chair from the dining room, he straddled the latter, leant on the back and drank slowly. He'd joined a tight-knit trauma support group overseas, kidding himself that it was to *give* help rather than receive. Only when Phil and Dave had cornered him in a bar late one night, had he admitted he needed counselling. It was the hardest decision he'd ever made. And the smartest.

As the sun rose he retrieved his mobile from his bedroom

and paced the balcony as he accessed a number, not wanting to wait until the group meeting Saturday night.

'Hi, Phil. No, Tess is fine. It's me. Are you free to talk? Yeah, another nightmare…out of the blue.'

The following evening he walked into the back room of a city hotel, thankful for a restful night and willing to admit to the episode in front of the group.

He hadn't mentioned Jemma to Phil and nor would he tonight, having persuaded himself that the attraction wouldn't go any further. He was flying out tomorrow, with an undetermined return date, and he was certain he'd be able to greet her with impartiality the next time they were in contact.

At six in the morning Nate stashed his carry-on case in the overhead locker, settled into his seat and tucked the document wallet containing twenty-nine printed pages, a clipboard and assorted pens and highlighters by his side.

Before retiring late on Friday he'd followed his nightly habit and checked his emails. True to her word, Jemma had emailed her initial three chapters earlier in the evening. He'd resisted the impulse to ring her, and had sent a standard 'received and thank you' reply.

He'd noted the title, printed the pages and slipped them into a clear plastic sleeve. His intention was to read it all in one session on the plane, have a break, then take it scene by scene. Trial and error had proved that worked best for him when editing his own work.

His usual patience through the pre-take-off safety talk eluded him, and he put it down to the anticipation of finding out if she was as good as he hoped. Once airborne, he ordered a beer, clipped the pages to the board and began to read.

Within a few paragraphs he was reaching for his drink. The confrontation between her male and female characters blew him away. Their believable actions and dialogue were portrayed with a minimum of words. He could pinpoint people he'd met like them, yet wouldn't have nailed it as she had. His characters' interactions paled in comparison.

Jemma was good. Until her hero and heroine parted. Then it was as if someone else had taken over the keyboard.

He suspected that Jemma had been hurt in the past, and had deep-buried misgivings regarding men. But she was also intelligent, and ready to stand up for her beliefs if they were challenged. A stimulating paradox from whom he was having trouble distancing himself.

He flipped the pages, his emotions and his temperament riding a rollercoaster with the changing expertise of the author. In spite of the articulate wording, the basic story was, as Brian had implied, mundane and boring.

His respect for his agent grew for the tactful way he'd handled both him *and* Jemma, along with a surge of sympathy for him at being placed in this position of needing to spell out a truth Nate had struggled to accept.

He replaced the printout in the wallet, finished his beer and lay back with his headphones on. At times like these his choice of music was classical jazz.

By the time he landed in Athens he'd read the printout twice and made notes in the margins with a red pen.

And he was still puzzling over the enigma of Jemma Harrison.

CHAPTER FIVE

ON THE TUESDAY evening after she'd come home to Hahn-dorf, Jemma had been surprised to receive her limited script back from Nate, with comments in the margin. And she'd been thrilled by his second email, asking her to have a go at his attached first two chapters.

Have a go! As if it were a sideshow stall at a fair.

As she'd requested when she sent hers, he'd included back stories for his main characters.

From the opening paragraph she'd been drawn in and captivated; by page seven she'd begun to understand Brian's proposition. By the end of chapter two she'd known it was too good not to be published—even if Nate did it himself. It was a genre she'd never have chosen, yet if she'd had the whole book she'd have continued reading, glossing over the stilted, uninspiring interaction between the hero and heroine.

She'd acknowledged receipt and spent all her free time from then until Saturday morning revising the four rele-vant scenes, two of them quite short. She double-and-triple-checked, determined not to leave a single mistake. Unsure of the normal procedure, she'd highlighted anywhere she'd made changes in one version, then deleted and amended in red text in another, allowing him to compare.

Dead on noon, with fingers crossed, eyes shut and her lips mouthing a silent prayer, she pressed 'send.'

Late on Wednesday morning of the following week, as she walked into town, she counted her blessings: the beauti-ful natural setting of her home, fresh air to breathe and the one she loved most tucked into a cotton shoulder bag clutched to her chest.

There was a cruise ship in Port Adelaide, which she knew meant buses full of tourists who'd keep her too busy to fret over the absence of any response from Nate. And she was right. By mid-afternoon she'd hardly had time to take sips from her water bottle, let alone make tea or coffee, since she'd taken over at noon from Meg, who owned the business.

'My mother's going to adore these miniatures,' an American woman gushed as Jemma wrapped three of them in bubble wrap with care. 'It's so hard to find anything small, light and tasteful to take home.'

'Your grandchildren will love the cuddly Australian animals too,' Jemma replied, placing them into a carry-bag.

'Lucky I saw the kangaroos in the window, else I'd have gone straight past. My husband likes to be back at the coach early—keeps me on my toes when we're travelling. Thank you, dear, have a nice day.'

'And you enjoy the rest of your cruise.'

Grateful for an empty shop at last, she hunkered down to drink from the bottle under the counter, relishing the cool water as the doorbell rang with the customer's exit. The murmur of a voice didn't register as she looked at her watch, which showed it was more than an hour until Meg returned. But by now the last of the cruise buses would be heading back to the port, so there'd be fewer shoppers around.

The hairs on the back of her neck lifted as if caught by a light breeze or someone's warm breath. A quiver ran down her back. Not daring to hope, she came upright with slow ease and glanced across the shop.

Her throat dried, her fingers curled into her palms and everything around her faded into mist as her blue eyes met perturbed storm-grey in enigmatic features. It was as if he was unsure of why he was there. Then light flared in his eyes and he gave her the smile she'd spent all the time since she'd been home telling herself she didn't miss at all.

His unique aroma filled the space between them, stirring her senses. Up close, he looked tired, and she noticed that the fine lines at the corner of his eyes were deeper, more pronounced.

'Hello, Jemma.'

Two everyday words in an unforgettable voice with a rusty edge. Absolutely no reason for her suddenly to feel hot all over. No reason for her stomach to clench and her pulse to race.

Feigning control, she met his gaze with what she hoped was a calm, unruffled demeanour. 'Hello, Nate. You're a long way from home.'

The bell rang and they both turned their heads to watch the door open, hear a male voice say, 'Let's have a drink first,' and then see it close.

Jemma saw Nate frown as he scanned the shop and peered at the open doorway behind her.

'Are you on your own? What time do you finish?' He frowned again, as if aware of how terse he sounded. 'Sorry, I'd like to talk to you. Should have let you know I was coming, but...'

He shrugged, as if that were explanation enough. She ought to be annoyed at his arrogance—wasn't that a major factor against all those she deemed were that type of man?—but instead energising anticipation bubbled through her. The reason for his presence *had* to be to discuss Brian's solution. Why come all this way if he wasn't seriously considering it?

'Would you like coffee? I'm dying for a hot drink.'

She sounded like a flustered teenager. Exactly how she felt.

At his nod and 'Mmm,' of acceptance, she went through the doorway and into the small kitchen, not expecting him to follow. The compact space seemed to diminish when he came in, watching as she filled the electric jug, set out two mugs and measured coffee into both.

'Two sugars, right?'

The sound of the bell impeded his reply and she handed him the spoon.

'I take one and milk, and mine's the mug with a possum on it. There's biscuits in the square tin.'

Leaving the room meant squeezing past him and another intake of musk, citrus and *him*. Another aspect of the man she'd missed—which was crazy, considering the limited time they'd spent together. Fixing a smile on her lips, she smoothed her hair and stepped past the counter to greet the new customers.

In the time it took for the water to boil and for Nate to make the coffee the bell rang twice, and he figured he'd made a mistake coming during shopping hours. He hadn't warned her, hoping to gauge her true reaction to him, but had seen a delightful range of astonishment, pleasure and annoyance, leaving him unenlightened.

He hadn't factored in the lack of privacy. He'd be lucky to find a quick moment to arrange a quieter place for their essential conversation on co-operation. Success was now a feasible goal, and his plan for co-writing depended on her availability and commitment. One read-through of her suggested amendments and he was fully on board. With reservations.

She'd done a brilliant job, bringing fiery passion to the bland interaction between his leading characters. And she'd nailed the way the male he'd visualised would respond to a female whose presence had upset his life's equilibrium. His heroine was now feisty and flawed—a worthy match for his hard-bitten, battle-worn hero.

Mug in hand, he went to take a surreptitious peek at

her. She was showing a couple with a young girl a display of colourful teddy bears. Staying out of sight, sipping the hot drink, he admired her genuine pleasure at serving all three. Two women were browsing the shelves… Another was peering in the window.

Why was she having to cope alone? Was it always this busy? If so, it might affect his proposal. And why the hell did she have to be as alluring in jeans and a loose green top as she'd been in the outfit she'd worn in Sydney?

His fingers gripping his mug were white-knuckle taut. Forcing them to relax, he returned to the kitchen. Hanging around was distracting for him, probably the same for her, and would achieve nothing.

Between customers he brought her a fresh coffee, the first one having gone cold.

'Thank you. This is much more satisfying than quick sips from a bottle of water under the counter. It's been full on this afternoon.' She cradled the mug in her fingers and savoured the invigorating flavour.

'Are you always on your own? When do you get a break?'

Her eyes flashed and she stepped away. He shouldn't have asked so abruptly.

'I can manage. Meg had to go home for personal reasons just after I came in at twelve. She'll be back around four.'

'I'm concerned—okay?'

He pressed one finger to her mouth, preventing the words she'd taken a breath to say from being voiced. Had to fight not to caress a path to her cheek.

'Will you have dinner with me so that we can discuss how good your rewrites are?'

His breath caught in his throat and his pulse tripped, then surged as her face lit up and her eyes shone, as dazzling as the stars he gazed at from his balcony in the mountains.

Idiot! That was the greeting she'd deserved—not the uncivil questions he'd fired at her. His hand fell to his sides.

'You're happy with them?' Her voice was husky and animated, making him feel like Father Christmas.

'Yes—so we need to have a serious discussion on how we proceed.'

She blinked, and appeared to consider the implications of his words.

'There's quite a few good places to eat and I'll be free at five-fifteen.'

'We'll need privacy.'

Again there was that assessing scrutiny he was beginning to anticipate. Then she smiled, as if pleased at his words.

The shop bell rang again.

'I could get to hate that sound.' There was a low growl in his voice, fuelled by frustration.

She heard it, and a light blush flowed over her cheeks, easing his tension. He wasn't alone.

In an effort to hide her expression, she dipped her head to finish her coffee. 'I have a customer. Would you rinse the mugs and leave them to drain, please, Nate?'

For another smile he believed he'd clean the whole kitchen—floors, walls and all. On his way out, he called, 'See you later, Jemma,' and held the door for the teenagers entering.

His replies were a quick wave from her and giggles from the girls.

Jemma relaxed as he strode past the window and gave her full attention to her current customer and those who'd followed until the shop had emptied. She'd been on edge since he'd waltzed in—well, strolled in as if he was expected, barking out questions. In hindsight, remembering his demeanour, he'd obviously been disconcerted at finding her serving alone.

The conflict between anger at his assumption that he could act as if they'd arranged this meeting and her emotional and physical response to his presence was unsettling. He muddled her brain—*not* conducive to giving good service.

She brewed herself a chamomile tea, and drank it while automatically tidying the shelves—a no-brainer task allowing her to imagine future scenarios for his battle-scarred ex-soldier and the girl who'd lost everything because of the military.

Meg arrived and was pleased with the sales, giving Jemma due praise.

'The extra tourists helped. Always eager to buy Australian souvenirs.'

'I'll finish closing up if you want to go home and put your feet up.'

'I'm fine—a friend's coming to meet me at a quarter past five.'

'Going to dinner? That'll be a treat.'

Her words gave Jemma reason to think. She preferred to keep her personal life private, except for the facts she chose to reveal to a few close friends. Yet enough local people knew her to make her being seen dining out with Nate open to gossip. A takeaway at home would be better.

As she unpacked and displayed new stock she found herself glancing through the window every few minutes. By five she was ready to leave, and the instant he appeared she collected her two bags and said goodbye to Meg. Resolving to be calm and businesslike, she joined him outside.

She wished he wasn't so ruggedly attractive—like those guys on television who starred in exotic nature series, travelling the wildernesses of the world in their four-wheel drives.

Quivers skittled up and down her spine as he perused her from head to feet and back…as far as the cotton bag clutched to her chest. A bubble of laughter rose in her throat at his puzzled frown.

Nate jerked as if he'd been sideswiped. A moment ago, he'd been admiring how fresh Jemma looked after a busy day in the shop—now he couldn't take his eyes from the wriggling bulge in the colourful fabric she was hugging.

'It's moving.'

He glanced up as her lips parted in a burst of delightful laughter and then she opened the unfastened top. A small tortoiseshell head popped out, tawny eyes blinking at the bright world.

'Hey, it's cute.' He liked animals, and rued the fact that his travelling prevented him keeping any at the moment.

'Isn't *she*?'

'She comes to work with you?'

He stroked the kitten with his forefinger and she leant into it, then licked him. Lifting her out, he cradled her to his chest, and Jemma's eyes showed approval of his gentleness.

'It depends on my hours and how she seems. I've had her less than a week—it's a learning curve for the two of us.'

'I grew up with an assortment of cats and dogs, along with various other pets my brother and I found or brought home. Until I built my own home I couldn't imagine one without any animals. I assume she's not coming to dinner with us?'

She dropped her gaze to his hands, still wrapped around her pet, seemingly unsure of how to answer.

'Jemma?' His fingers itched to cup her chin and see why she'd hidden her expression from him. Instead he tickled the kitten's ear, and waited.

'I thought…' It was mumbled and faint.

She let out a slow breath, breathed in, and then her eyes, cool and determined, met his.

'I thought we'd go to my home to talk…then order take-away.' Firm and assured now.

It was new and strange, this feeling of being honoured by her offer of trust—a gift he was convinced few men were granted. Having guessed she was vulnerable, he resolved not to break it and kept his tone casual.

'Okay by me. Whatever you choose.'

'It's a fifteen-minute walk along the track—unless you'd rather take the road. I assume you have a car?'

'I'd prefer to go through the local bushland. My hire car's parked behind the hotel I've booked into for the night. May I carry…? What's the little fur ball's name?'

'Milly.'

She took off the bag and slipped it over his neck, leaning towards him. Allowing him to breathe in her floral aroma. Forcing him to fight the urge to find out with his lips if her skin was as soft as it appeared.

As they set off he could feel movement through the bag's material as Milly purred in her sleep, snuggled against his chest. It was a comforting feeling he remembered from nights of having pets sleep on his bed in the innocent times of youth.

Some time in the future he'd persuade her to tell him why she'd chosen the name.

He kept the bag open, allowing him to see Milly, and occasionally stroked her head, causing a deepening of her contented sounds. This was one of the comforts missing from his life that he intended to rectify soon. His dilemma was cat, dog or both.

At the end of the shopping area Jemma led him down a side street and onto a track that wound through native scrub and trees—some recognisable from his mountain home surroundings.

'This is where I find my painting inspiration. All the seasons of nature are right here on my doorstep. I keep extensive files of photographs in my computer because nothing stays the same in bushland.'

Her face lit up as she indicated plants she'd painted, adding the fact that she ensured every tile ended up unique. Her passion for her art moved him, and when he queried the canvas paintings he'd seen on the shop wall she admitted they were hers too, and gaining interest.

As they approached a bend she caught his arm to slow him down and touched her finger to her lips. When she stopped and pointed upwards he followed her finger's direction and felt his throat clog. A koala sat in the crook of a gum tree within climbing reach, a joey clinging to her chest. He couldn't remember when he'd last seen one in the wild.

She didn't stir and appeared to be dozing, completely oblivious to their presence.

After a moment or two they continued on, and Nate waited until they were some distance away before speaking, though he was certain his voice wouldn't have disturbed the sleeping pair.

'That was a rare sighting for me. We don't have koalas in the Blue Mountains—wrong type of gum trees.'

'They're plentiful here, but often hard to spot. She's been in that tree for a week, and I haven't seen her awake once.'

They hadn't gone much further when Jemma pushed between two shrubs, and he followed her onto a narrower, rougher, more overgrown dirt path.

'My hidden entrance. I keep it that way to prevent hikers assuming it's another trail and coming to my back door asking for directions.'

That he understood—though it was rare that anyone ventured near his fenced-off property, which was on a clifftop away from the main road.

The track brought them into a cleared area behind a

stone cottage with a corrugated iron roof, its long garden surrounded by a vine-covered, weather-worn wooden fence. It was classic Australiana, by his estimation over a hundred years old, and the house nearest to town in a row of three.

CHAPTER SIX

JEMMA OPENED THE gate and led the way along a crazy paving path between a vegetable garden and patch of lawn on one side, and fruit trees and a flowerbed on the other. Wide steps ended on a veranda that stretched across the back, furnished with an old-fashioned three-seater swinging seat, a small outdoor table and two chairs, and a number of potted plants.

They entered a compact kitchen fitted with modern appliances, with a dining area through an archway on the right. Jemma placed her bag on the mottled stone benchtop and stepped in front of him to take the kitten.

Nate willed himself not to move a muscle. He was in her home on trial. A wrong action or word could have him banished with no chance of appeal. He leant against the bench, admiring the harmonious blend of old and new decor. Admiring Jemma's supple movements as she crouched down, gently placing Milly onto a blue-cushioned bed in the corner behind the back door.

'Is the house yours or rented?'

He could imagine her scouring magazines for furniture and colours to suit, fired with enthusiasm. Picturing her in an ultra-modern house—like his?—wasn't difficult either.

'I bought it, along with some of the seller's furniture, three years ago this coming June. The only difference is the colour. I painted the walls in the bedrooms, study and lounge.'

'You?'

'Not a big job with such small rooms. Do you want coffee, tea or water?'

He grinned. 'You need to ask?'

This was polite small-talk—a prelude to the serious conversation ahead. Her earlier fractured invitation, and the way her lips didn't quite make a return smile now, had him guessing she was nervous. Because he was a relative stranger or because he was a man?

He watched in silence as she clicked on the electric jug and took two mugs from the hooks on an antique hatched dresser. This was her domain, and the less he intruded the quicker she'd accept his presence.

When the drinks were ready he offered to carry them. She thanked him and walked into the hall that stretched to the front door. The compactness of her sitting room was eased by the light sandy-coloured paint, and the space around the furniture. Two suitably-sized paintings—a stormy sea and one landscape—had been hung on the walls.

He appreciated the furnishings: a traditional patterned sofa and armchair, a wooden coffee table and a classic sideboard with mirror, all smaller than regular size. A television sat on a mobile trolley in one of the nooks either side of the stone fireplace. The other held a packed floor-to-ceiling bookcase. And, although modern, the imitation log heater suited the setting.

Polite as always, Jemma thought, as he waited until she'd taken her coffee and settled into the armchair, sliding back, keeping her body erect, and crossing her ankles to one side.

From this position he appeared to dominate the room the way he had the kitchen in the gift shop. Her heartbeat skidded to a stutter as his eyes held hers captive. She refused to be the one to initiate the discussion. He'd requested it—he should air his views first.

Breaking eye contact, he flicked a glance at the window behind her, huffed out a solid breath and sat on the two-seater. He took a drink, placed his cup on the table, and then, keeping his body equally upright, clasped his hands between his knees.

'You have trust issues with men.' It was a simple statement of fact rather than an accusation. 'One in particular or more. Either way, every man you meet has to field the blame.'

'That's…'

'True, Jemma.'

She stared at her collection of stones in a bowl on the table, accepting that he was right. She believed it was justified to protect her heart. He had no right to disparage what for her was a necessity.

She tamped down her irritation and, feigning a neutral expression, replied, 'I have good reason.'

His oblique nod showed that he understood—to a point.

'I don't doubt it. However, the best way for this collaboration to succeed will be for us to work closely together. And that requires your trusting me to treat you as an equal colleague. If—'

Her spine stiffened and her fingers scrunched the bottom hem of her cotton top as she cut in.

'Trust is a two-way street. Your initial greeting was superficial, at best, and you weren't exactly receptive to my having access to your novel.'

His eyes narrowed for a second or two, and then he stunned her by chuckling at her outburst. The realisation that she'd missed a sound she'd only heard a few times shook her. Unusual and gravelly, it was imprinted in her memory. *For ever.*

He leant back, his elbow on the sofa-arm, wiped his hand across his mouth and made no attempt to hide his amusement. 'We must be making progress, Jemma Harrison. You forgot to call me Mr Thornton.'

She really, *really* wanted to glare at him for sending her up, but her facial features and her body refused to co-operate. Her lips were mimicking his smile, her pulse was giving the impression she was running a relay, and a warm glow was firing up in her abdomen.

'I'll put a reminder in my calendar.'

Any bite she might have meant to give was negated by the suggestive breathy sound that came from her dry throat. A swallow of coffee didn't ease it at all—but then, the cause was right there, watching her with fascination.

'And I'll try not to warrant it.' He extended his hand over the table. 'Truce?'

She reached out to meet his gesture, and had to wriggle to the edge of the chair. 'Truce.' They both had much to gain by co-operation.

Wishing she didn't like the feel of his skin against hers so much, she sank back and curled her legs up onto the chair.

'So, will you be sending me the next chapters? Do we need some sort of written agreement? I have a back stock of paintings and can begin work any time from now.' She couldn't wait to read future instalments of *Trials of a Broken Man*.

'I'd rather not send them but, yes, that suits me—with provisos. I suggest we ring Brian tomorrow and find out the legal ramifications. Will you be free in the morning?'

She nodded, puzzled by his first answer and unable to speak.

'How obligated are you to your hours in the gift shop?'

'It's pretty flexible. There are two young mothers who don't want to be tied to regular shifts but are happy to go in for odd days or an occasional week.'

He nodded again, as if pleased with her answer, and then fell silent, his inscrutable gaze making her squirm and gulp the remainder of her drink. She almost choked when he spoke again, churning the words out without pause.

'We'll talk to Meg as well. The sooner we finish the

amendments the better. Emailing partials back and forth and waiting for each other to check them will take too long. Would you be prepared to come to Katoomba and stay with me until they're finished?'

'Stay with you?'

Idiot! Of all the phrases he used, that was the point you zero in on?

Her cheeks burned but she didn't dare look away, needing to see his reaction. She inhaled and exhaled in slow deliberation, her mind processing all he'd said. An elementary fact, an obvious problem and a logical solution. Practical and impassive. *So* him.

Every cell in Nate's body clamoured to go to her, take her in his arms and reassure her.

Yeah, a great way to prove you'll act like a gentleman and keep the relationship platonic.

He hadn't meant to shock her—to him it had been the best answer to a logistical problem. One which meant breaking his rule not to have any unrelated women staying in his home. Any liaisons were conducted in Sydney, in his apartment or at their homes.

This was the exception to break the rule. They'd need time with no distractions—somewhere they could take breaks, walk or run at will. Somewhere they could work, eat and sleep at odd hours as needed. That was the way he'd lived while typing most of those hundred-thousand-plus words. *And* all the ones he'd deleted or cut and saved.

Now he hoped to persuade Jemma—who probably only typed in her spare moments—to accept his way until they'd finished.

'It could take weeks.'

He started—had been so lost in thought he hadn't noticed she'd recovered from his startling proposition.

'There's no way of knowing. *You're* the one who emailed

to say that my characters' emotional relationship will affect every aspect of their lives. Being able to discuss any possible revisions and do them on the spot will speed up the process.'

'I get that. It's just the idea of leaving with no idea of a return date. That's asking a lot of my neighbours, who keep a watch on the house if I'm away. And I can't foist Milly on anyone for that long.'

'Bring her.'

Hell! That had shot out, bypassing any thought process. *Not* what he'd been thinking when he'd made his earlier decision, though having to buy bowls and a pet bed would strengthen his resolve to get a dog or cat of his own...

It suddenly struck him that expecting her to drop everything and come to his out-of-town house had been arrogant.

'I apologise, Jemma. I'm wound up and I want to get things rolling. Plus, I've lived solo for so long I've got used to making autocratic decisions. How about we allow a fortnight, to give us an idea of the timeframe we need? Then we can take a short break, or continue back here with me staying in the hotel.'

She didn't answer—just swung her feet to the floor, held out her hand for his now empty cup and, holding both, stared at the floor for a moment.

Then she sat down again. 'We're strangers. I've never lived with anyone but my parents.'

His heartbeat soared with an adrenaline rush he refused to attribute to her second statement, blaming it on her consideration of his offer.

'We both want success, so we'll agree on boundaries and work through any issues that come up. Compromising should get us through.'

Being surrounded by the house he'd designed as a refuge to keep him from ever again falling prey to romantic fallacies would be a constant reminder to him to stay objective and focus on the end result.

'Starting when?'

'Your decision. Whenever you can come.'

He heard a plaintive mew from behind him, and she looked past him to the doorway.

'Milly's hungry. I'll see my neighbours in the morning and phone Meg to arrange fill-ins. The takeaway menus are in the kitchen drawer.'

He waited until she'd gone before giving a short, triumphant fist-pump. This was no night for tinfoil cartons. They had a deal to celebrate—albeit a verbal one.

As he joined her in the kitchen, a phone number already punched into his mobile, Jemma closed a drawer of the dresser, turned and held out a handful of pamphlets.

'There's one from every takeaway in town. Pick what you fancy'

He might be in trouble if he did—and, anyway, for this evening he had an alternative plan.

'How long will it take you to get ready to go somewhere special for dinner?'

His muscles tightened, and his gut clenched at her enchanting reaction: cheeks colouring, lips parting in an O and beautiful eyes blinking. The sound she made was a delightful mixture of huff and laughter. He'd have to surprise her more often. *Or not.*

'To celebrate our agreement on collaboration. It's a milestone for both of us. Forty minutes, okay? That'll give me time to walk back for my car.'

At her audible intake of air and quick nod he pressed the already accessed number for the restaurant. A short conversation later he had a reservation for eight o'clock, with some leeway for the unfamiliar route.

'Where are we going?' She'd found her voice, and was eager for information. 'Casual dress?'

'Windy Point. My brother Sam's recommendation, and luckily they have a table. I've been staying with him for the last two days.'

If he'd thought he couldn't surprise her even more he'd been mistaken. Her eyes clouded for a millisecond, shuttered and then sparkled on reopening. 'It's back on my wish list. We were booked in a few years ago and had to cancel. The view is meant to be stunning—especially at night.'

'I'm glad you approve.' Her happiness lifted his spirits higher and gave the promise of an unforgettable evening. 'You did say it's quicker to town by road?'

'Yes—I'll let you out the front door.'

She squeezed against the wall of the narrow hallway, her perfume filling his nostrils as she passed, tempting him to press a light kiss on her lips.

Fingers held tight to his thighs, he crossed the threshold and told her he'd see her soon. With purpose in his stride, he pondered her *back on my wish list*. Why had it been crossed off? And who was the *we* she'd referred to?

Jemma leant against the closed door, shaking from head to foot, fighting to unscramble the sensations churning inside her.

She'd agreed to revise essential scenes in his manuscript. *In his home in New South Wales.* She would be taking time off from her part-time job, and wouldn't have time to paint while she was there. She was excited, overawed and nervous. And scared by how easily Nate had undermined her vows to stay detached.

She'd also agreed to go to a restaurant that not so long ago would have evoked dark emotions. The evening she and her ex were supposed to have had dinner there he'd rung to postpone, claiming an impromptu office meeting. They'd never rebooked, and a few weeks later she'd learned of his infidelity.

On the way to her bedroom she mused on the diverse changes in her life since that time. As she showered she vowed to embrace these latest ones and relish every moment, even while keeping her heart guarded and Nate at a distance.

Wrapped in a towel, she studied the selection of dresses in her wardrobe and chose two, holding them up in front of her to view in the mirror. They'd be eating in a popular venue with floor-to-ceiling glass windows, overlooking the city and the ocean, the sun setting on the horizon. Her aim was to be dressed appropriately and to appear stress-free while being escorted by Nate.

A quick calculation told her she had time to research the restaurant, and the images online helped her decide on a simply styled electric blue dress, with thin shoulder straps and a below-the-knee hem. Cloe's Christmas present to her—a similar-coloured, long-sleeved lacy knitted jacket—would be perfect when the temperature cooled. Comfy, medium-heeled shoes and silver jewellery completed the ensemble.

Well aware that she'd never challenge Vanessa's impeccable fashion sense, Jemma still found herself grinning as she nodded at her nice-but-nothing-special image in the mirror. Her sister would never write a book, let alone a good one—no riveting and satisfying emotional scenes worthy of being published.

Jemma's basic storyline *was* a problem, but she'd already decided not to hold Nate to his revision of a full story for her characters. It was too far out of his comfort zone. But she'd study his prose as she worked on it, talk to him and ask his advice. When his book was finished she'd enrol in writing courses and hopefully resolve her particular ineptitude.

Her phone, keys, tissues and emergency money fitted into her black clutch bag, and she left it on the hall stand while she checked on Milly. Finding her curled up asleep in her bed in the dining area, she shut the door to the hall so she wouldn't come out and hide while she was alone.

Waiting had never been a problem for her. She let her mind wander to plots and scenes, and never noticed time passing. Tonight was different. Her mind refused to co-operate, and would only dwell on her encounters with Nate.

She was grateful when the glare of his headlights in her driveway announced his arrival.

She went outside—and almost lost her footing stepping off the front porch as Nate came around the front of a silver sedan and stopped, taking his time to look her over.

Wow, he *really* scrubbed up well for a date. Not that this *was* one—it was a meal between two literary associates. All she had to do was ignore the pheromones bombarding her senses and stay calm and unaffected. Easy, right? *Like heck.*

Freshly shaved, and wearing a dark suit and a navy tie over a pale grey shirt, he'd draw *every* woman's attention. Her fingers itched to dishevel his neat, thick hair, which would make him even more desirable, and even more dangerous to her never-to-be-hurt-again plans for the future.

She dug one set of fingers into her palm and firmed the other on her bag.

'Hi, Jemma, you look…good.'

For an irrational moment she'd have given anything to know the word he'd caught back. But, sliding into the vehicle while he held the door open, giving her the full effect of newly applied cologne, she resolved not to care. If he wouldn't say it out loud, it wasn't worth hearing.

Buckled in, with the motor running, he turned to face her. 'Do you have any problem taking the winding route? The GPS offers that. Or do you want to go right down to the suburbs and up another way?'

'I'm lucky—never suffered from motion sickness.'

'Good.' He selected the setting and backed into the road.

CHAPTER SEVEN

A DISTURBING BATTLE raged in Nate's head. Taking Jemma—whose appearance deserved a much more flattering word than the one he'd stumbled over—to dinner being purely business against the growing desire to be closer to her. To hold and kiss her.

On the way to pick her up he'd reinforced every reason he had for staying unattached and alone. His failure to distinguish the lies behind the sweet talking of a scheming woman, which had taught him to be cautious. The suffering he'd seen which had left him sceptical of the façades most people projected. He never took anyone at face value.

He'd believed he was in control until she'd stood there, sweet and delectable, her blue dress and matching jacket making the colour of her eyes appear darker and more alluring. He'd stopped dead, his throat had dried up, and his pulse had rocketed. And he'd barely managed an inane remark not even worthy of a randy teenager.

Glancing at her composed profile, he saw her chin lift a little, as if she'd sensed his action. *Was* she projecting a façade, like him? If he could see her eyes he might know. Unlike many of the sophisticated women he knew, she hadn't learned the art of deception. For the sake of the man who'd one day win her heart, he hoped she never would.

'You're very quiet, Jemma. Having doubts?'

'Over agreeing to come to Katoomba or to dinner? The answer's no to both, Nate. You're driving a hired car on a curving hilly road and the sun is beginning to set. You need quiet to concentrate.'

He recalled places where there'd been the added dangers

of military conflict and gave a wry smile. 'Thank you for
your consideration, but I prefer conversation over silence.
How come you had to cancel your previous booking at Windy
Point?'

Her barely audible intake of breath, and the hitch in her
tone, told him more than her verbal answer.

'My date's sudden meeting—compulsory attendance.'

'Hmm. So we get to share the pleasure of a first visit
here?'

She surprised him by laughing—a melodic sound he
wished didn't stir him so easily.

'You've travelled around the world. You must have eaten
in exotic and famous places I've only heard of or seen in
magazines.'

'True. But I've also eaten meat and vegetables I wasn't
game to ask the name of or to refuse. Consider every offer
you're given, Jemma. Even bizarre memories are better
than nights of wondering *what if?*'

'I've accepted yours.' She was resolute and firm.

'And I swear you'll never regret it. Make sure you pack
warm tops; the evenings can be quite cool.'

'Like here?'

'Yeah, I guess it's pretty similar.'

'Except your winters are more severe and your snowfall
higher. Do you ski?

Jemma's question threw him for a moment. He hadn't
skied since returning home—didn't want to revive memories of covert trips in wintertime Europe.

'Not for a long time. I've been otherwise occupied. Do
you?'

'I've taken a few weekend trips with friends. Never got
higher than the beginners' slopes but I had lots of fun.'

He pictured her in a fitted ski outfit, hair flying, cheeks
flushed and radiant, eyes sparking with joy. Hands tight on
the steering wheel, he sought for a diversion.

'I'm serious about bringing Milly. Write me a list of everything she'll need—or, better yet, email or text. Then I'll have it on my phone. I'll be shopping before you come.'

'She's not fussy…likes wet or dry food. Do you have a rug or old towel she can sleep on?'

'Not on your bed? That wouldn't worry me—our pets always did. Mum tried to dissuade them—and us. Eventually she accepted the inevitable.'

'I'd prefer she has a familiar setting—like a corner somewhere. I'll bring a couple of her toys.'

For the rest of the trip he told stories of the pets in his past, and Jemma loved listening to the escapades he, Sam and Alice had got up to, growing up in the suburbs.

She had a few dim memories of playing with Vanessa, but had rarely experienced sibling moments like her friends. Midway through her teens she'd realised the six-year gap between them wasn't the reason. Her sister had always been focussed on a modelling career and had had no time for games or any distraction such as a younger sister.

They arrived in the restaurant's car park earlier than expected, and Jemma felt pampered when Nate walked around to hold her door as she alighted.

'Can we go and watch the sunset?'

As a teenager, she'd often come here with friends—some of them dates, hoping for a kiss. Or more. She was glad her ex hadn't been one of them and her memories of this place were sweet.

'Fine by me. Looks like our timing is perfect.'

They walked down the path to a lookout, then further to a lower one at the edge of the hill, where the vista was partially blocked by trees. In the gaps there was a clear view, with the city sprawled from left to right from the lower tree line to the ocean's edge. Just below them cars negotiated the bend in the road, some with headlights already on.

Jemma sucked in a breath and blew out a long, *'Ohhh...'*
How could she have forgotten how incredibly beautiful it was?

The sun hung like a glimmering yellow-and-gold UFO,
appearing to be balanced on a wisp of dark grey cloud
above the horizon. Its mirror image skimmed across the
translucent blue sea towards them. Above and below, and
spreading across their vision, the spectacular colours
morphed into oranges and reds. Fascinating. Soul-warming.

As the lower curve of the sun dipped behind the cloud
Jemma pulled out her mobile and snapped a few shots. She
gasped with joy and clicked three or four times in succes-
sion as the dark shape of a plane, climbing after its take-
off from the airport, flew across the split sun.

Glancing at Nate's face, seeing him moved by the experience too, made her feel light-headed.

'Different, isn't it?' Even though there was noise from
the traffic below, she found herself whispering.

'Incomparable is a better word. A panorama of city and
suburbs, with true blue gumtrees almost within reach, and
the ocean and the sunset in the background. Indescribable.'

'Not for an aspiring author, surely?'

His brow furrowed, then cleared as he twigged that she
was ribbing him. 'Is that a challenge, Jemma?'

'Not tonight.' She looked away from his too-knowing
eyes. 'As the sun sinks lower those colours intensify, then
fade, leaving the sea pitch-dark unless there's a boat passing. Shall we go in?'

Neither her dim memories of glimpses through the window nor the photos on her computer did justice to the dining area, with its curved glass windows ensuring a clear
panoramic view for every table on each of the three levels.
Jemma noted very few were unoccupied as they were led
to a setting for two on the highest.

She had less than a minute to admire the crisp white of
the linen, the soft glow of candles on each table and the

comfortable upholstered chairs, before the roof began to open up, letting natural light in.

'Oh, someone told me that you dine under the stars, but I'd forgotten. It doesn't happen all year round, so our timing's perfect.'

'Sam mentioned a unique attraction and wouldn't clarify. Now I understand why.'

He stared upward for a moment, then scanned across the view and back. Jemma had already memorised it, and sensed he was doing the same.

'I remember thinking that at night-time, with all the different coloured streetlights and building lights, it looked like a true fairyland.'

A waitress brought them a carafe of water and asked if they would like to order drinks. She looked towards Nate, to ask if he wanted to share a bottle of wine, and felt her pulse hitch at the warmth of his direct gaze. It sped up at his words.

'Seeing as I'll have a special cargo on that winding drive home, I'll have one glass of wine and then stick to water.' His voice lowered to a conspiratorial tone as he added, 'We're in your territory, so you may choose a red to complement my Scotch fillet.'

She'd happily comply if only she could find her voice after his compliments—the first more amazing than the second. Her reply sounded foreign, breathy and a little exotic, as she asked for two glasses of her favourite Shiraz, having already decided she would have the lamb dish from the online menu.

They chose Turkish bread to start, and Jemma declared she'd skip an entrée in favour of dessert if she wasn't too full.

Leaning forward, and keeping his voice low, Nate said, 'I've researched the selection and I'm betting you won't be able to resist.'

Outwardly she pretended to bristle, but inside she quivered at the intimacy of his soft yet edgy tone, her reaction heightened by the knowledge that he was probably right.

He requested medium rare for his fillet, and she shivered. He noticed, waiting until they were alone before asking, 'Not the way you like it?'

'It's a matter of taste. I prefer overcooked to under every time.'

'But don't let your parents know, huh?'

She joined in his laughter.

'They guessed when, aged around eight, I took some slices of roast beef back to the kitchen and grilled them.'

Their wine arrived, and he repeated the salute he'd given in Darling Harbour. This time she echoed his movement, and he nodded in response. After savouring the flavour, she set her glass down and traced her finger around the base. He'd seen her home, how she lived, but had only mentioned the location of his.

'Is your home old or new?'

'As modern as yours is colonial. It has everything I want and need and nothing I don't.'

'You designed it?' Of course he had—from the bricks to the door handles.

His shrug drew her gaze to the perfect fit of his tailor-made jacket, and she had a sudden vision of his toned, sculpted torso, glistening in the sun as he stood poised on a diving board.

The clatter of cutlery from an adjoining table broke her reverie in time for her to catch his next words.

'With professional help. The location was paramount, and there was no problem with demolishing the seventies-style building in need of major repairs. My architect drafted the original plans from a rough sketch of mine and included everything I deemed essential. I now have the home I visualised.'

She'd bet her favourite paintbrush there'd been nothing 'rough' about his sketch. Every line would have been straight, and all the extras neatly depicted.

'I'm looking forward to seeing it.' She knew she'd learn more about his true character in a short stroll through his home than he'd revealed so far. 'Is it cat-proof?'

He smiled. 'Should be. Guess we'll have to keep an eye on her and find out. I'll add "research flight regulations" to tomorrow's list. How old are you?'

His out-of-the-blue question took a few seconds to register. Did it make a difference?

'Twenty-eight. Is that relevant to our agreement?'

'No—journalistic interest.'

He gave that almost-smile she was beginning to find endearing.

'I turned thirty-two the day before Brian told me how awful my one-on-one scenes were.'

She tried not to chuckle…didn't quite succeed. 'Happy birthday, huh? How does the view compare now?'

Apart from the discernible trees near the building, they were surrounded by a band of black. Its furthermost reaches were sprinkled with lights, their number and variety of colour and size increasing until they ended in a ragged edge of darkness to infinity, broken only by the rising moon and its reflection. Above them stars were beginning to emerge in the ebony sky.

Nate didn't say a word, and his enigmatic features hid whatever he was thinking.

Jemma sipped her drink, torn between intrigue over his reporting years abroad and the necessity not to become familiar with his history and personality. Agreeing to live with him for two weeks made the latter hard to maintain. But not impossible.

'I have to admit, Jemma, this is unique. Who'd have

thought Adelaide could compete with the sunset spectacles of the world?'

'Every true Adelaidean,' she declared with pride, and was rewarded with genuine laughter.

'Remind me to show you some photos while we're in Katoomba!'

Nate had expected his unease regarding having Jemma in his home for two weeks to grow stronger as his body responded to her enthusiasm for the sunset and the venue. Instead curiosity about the woman he'd aligned his literary aspirations with overrode any misgivings—though only at surface level. There was a line in the sand he'd sworn never to cross. If that danger surfaced he'd walk away—even if it meant breaking their deal.

Her skin glowed and her eyes sparkled at even the smallest event—like the timing of that plane moving through the sunset. She was bright and intelligent…an enchanting dinner companion. There had been no awkward silences as they ate their main courses, approving of the flavours and the choices they'd made. The discussion had progressed to sunsets around the world, and places she'd seen in movies and would love to visit in the future.

As he'd predicted, she was now poring over the dessert menu, seesawing between two items before selecting sorbet with fresh fruit and herbal tea. He ordered the same, with coffee.

'Doesn't drinking coffee this late keep you awake?' Jemma asked him.

'I guess I've grown immune to the effects over the years. There are places I've been where you couldn't rely on the quality of the water, or what the coffee grinds or tea leaves might actually consist of. Boiling hot coffee became the safest bet, and I caught the habit.'

Her eyes had widened as he spoke, and he pressed one

hand against his thigh and the other into the arm of his chair to prevent either from reaching for hers across the table. To prevent himself wrapping her fingers in his and caressing across her soft skin with his thumb.

Their desserts were served, their flavoursome tang enhanced by the complimentary handmade chocolates accompanying their hot drinks. An ideal ending for a memorable evening.

His only regret was the way it was going to end: saying goodnight at her front door with space between them. At this moment the idea of shaking hands and walking away didn't appeal at all.

Late the following Tuesday afternoon Jemma sank into her plane seat, worrying about Milly all alone in another part of the aircraft. Their visit to the vet for the required certificate for flying—luckily she was over the minimum age—had gone smoothly. The delay had been because this flight was the first available to have an allocation for pets.

Nate had arranged for a specialist firm to handle Milly's transportation in a regulation carrier from Hahndorf to Adelaide airport, and to collect and deliver her to them in the Sydney terminal. He'd also emailed chapters three to six of his book to her computer between phone calls on Thursday, while she'd prepared a ham and salad lunch. The final few pages needing her revision were in her satchel, to be worked on during the flight, along with a book and magazine.

On Saturday he'd asked her to send him her full romance, telling her he needed to read it all to assess the storyline. Their contract was for him to advise and help her, but she hadn't expected him to want it so soon. He'd flown out later that day, promising to be there to collect them when they landed, and she'd instantly both missed him and felt slight relief when he drove away.

Two full days of seeing his efficiency at work had left

her wondering what she'd agreed to. And whether she could stand up to his strong will if they had a conflict of opinion. She hadn't had a skerrick of unease for her physical safety—not for a second since they'd met. It was the underlying allure, the subtle dismantling of the rigid barriers she'd erected to protect her heart, that caused concern.

Well aware of her limited knowledge of legal matters, she'd let him and Brian do most of the talking during their call to the enthusiastic agent. As promised, he'd already sent the relevant information to them both.

Meg and her neighbours had accepted her excuse for going away: 'It's a personal matter.' And friends who'd wanted details, believing it was because of a man, had been stalled. They were right, but in a very different way from what they hoped for her future happiness.

Nate was an enigma. Polite and charming, with a definite soft spot for animals, and yet there were times when his eyes were veiled, hiding secrets she'd rather stayed that way.

Keep things professional, get his manuscript viable for publication, and on the way, learn, learn, learn.

The doors were sealed and the plane began to taxi along the runway. Instead of opening her satchel she closed her eyes and let her mind wander to an isolated farm and a tormented hero. She knew little of Outback Australia, but that was where the heroine in her next novel was going.

CHAPTER EIGHT

STRICT RESOLUTIONS TO stay impervious to Nate's charm dissolved into mush the second Jemma spotted him, standing apart from the waiting crowd. Wearing dark jeans, a black polo top and black sneakers, he depicted exactly the struggling man of her air-flight thoughts. Except with deliberate determination she'd given *him* green eyes, jet-black crew-cut hair and features as different from Nate's as possible. In addition, her hero's clothes and country boots were well worn from hours of hard physical labour.

'Hi, Jemma. Good flight?'

He reached to take her overnight bag, his fingers brushing lightly against hers. Tingles radiated from his touch. Mush got mushier.

It wasn't fair that he appeared immune as they walked towards baggage retrieval, his voice its normal tone. 'Milly's being collected and we'll pick her up by the luggage carousel. Do you have the bag you carry her in?'

'Yes, but…'

'I have a regular cat carrier in my vehicle. You look tense.'

Nate's chest tightened with a pang of guilt as he spoke. *Probably due to me.* He'd cajoled her into agreement, had told her nothing of his apartment, little of his home, and had avoided mentioning the intricacies of sharing. In fact he hadn't even mentioned they'd be staying in Sydney tonight.

'I'll be fine. The full reality of our co-writing agreement began to really sink in as I packed yesterday. I don't think it's going to be as simple as you made it sound, Nate.'

'My fault, Jemma. The prospect of finally having a

finished product made me push too fast and hard. Are you having regrets?'

'A few—all minor. Not enough to make me back out. It'll be a win for me too, remember?'

'From now on I promise to answer any questions you have with as much detail as you want.'

As long as they were literary, legal or general. Nothing personal. And he'd have to fudge any questions pertaining to how he'd gained the gritty basics of his story.

'Thank you.'

Suitcases and bags were already jostling around the turns of the conveyer belt, and passengers, two and three deep, nudged others in attempts to spot and retrieve theirs. Not being in a hurry, Nate and Jemma stayed away, leaving room for the impatient ones to succeed and leave.

'How many suitcases do you have?' Nate asked, glancing around for an available trolley.

'One. Bright blue, with purple and yellow ribbons tied on the handle.' She held her handbag, and the bag for Milly. The other two were on the ground between them.

'One? That's all? Plus this carry-on and the satchel? I'll admit your handbag's big, but for a two-week trip…'

Her shoulders relaxed, and she laughed. 'You *do* have a washing machine in your remote humpy, don't you, Nate? Unless you're planning for us to go dining and dancing every night, I have all I'll need.'

'There's all the amenities a lady requires,' he kidded, ignoring her jibe, glad to see her relax. 'And if we make good progress by the end of the week I'll drive you into town for a hamburger.'

Her smile widened. 'A true Aussie incentive.'

She twisted to allow a couple to pass, and glanced across the terminal.

'Looks like Milly's here.'

A man in a labelled uniform was walking towards them

holding a pet carrier. Milly's plaintive mews became audible as he grew nearer. Nate signed the form and retrieved the kitten, which tried to climb up his arm.

'Steady, little one—watch the skin.' He slipped her into the material bag now hanging over Jemma's shoulder, and moved over to join the few remaining people by the carousel. Within minutes they were exiting the lift on the fifth floor of the car park.

Nate stopped at the rear of his SUV, pulled his keys from the pocket of his jeans and activated the locks. He stowed Jemma's suitcase, turned, and then frowned at the sight of her perplexed expression.

'What?'

'It's an Outback monster for travelling and camping in the bush.'

'And that's a problem because...?'

It was perfect for him—it could go anywhere and carry any load required.

She made that huff-laugh mixture sound he liked as he tucked the other two pieces of luggage in safely.

'I assumed you'd have one of those sleek modern cars they advertise on television. I have no idea why. I guess it's the aura you emanate.'

He straightened up, throwing his head back and laughing out loud, causing the couple passing by to stare, and Milly to wriggle against Jemma's chest.

'I emanate an *aura*? Before I allow you anywhere near my friends or family I'll need a solemn vow you'll never repeat that remark to *anyone*, Jemma Harrison.'

He guided her to the front passenger seat, unable to contain his mirth. 'Mind you, I do like the way saying it has made you blush. Let me take Milly while you hop in. I've secured her carrier behind the driver's seat so she'll be able to see you.'

Cradling the kitten to his chest, he walked round and

put her into the brand-new carrier. She vocally made her dislike of being caged for a second time quite clear.

'Opinionated little devil, isn't she?' he said, backing out with care. 'Not surprising after today's new experiences.'

There was little talk as he drove through the heavy traffic. When it became apparent they were heading north across the Harbour Bridge he heard her sharp intake of breath.

'Did I mention we'll be staying here tonight and heading off in the morning? We'll get a better run through the traffic and it'll give Milly a break.'

'No, you didn't. But I agree. I'd like my first view of the mountains to be in daylight. I might even take a few photos.'

'For painting or writing? Have you started a new book, or are you still labouring on the current one?'

'I've typed up a rough synopsis and filled in character charts for my new hero and heroine. But they've been sidelined until yours is finished.'

'Do you want to discuss it?'

'No.' Sharp and abrupt. 'Sorry. One fictitious romance at a time for me.'

Convinced she'd suffered a painful break-up in the past, he bit back a quip about them being preferable to real life.

The scenes she'd revised had shown genuine anticipation of hope for a shared future between the man and woman. If she taught him how, he'd be able to go solo again. Perversely, instead of being motivational, he found the prospect disheartening.

With that disturbing thought running through his head he exited the highway.

'Not far to go. I've got a tossed salad in the fridge and steak ready to grill for dinner. I'd like to leave early tomorrow, and stop for breakfast when we're clear of the city.'

'Sounds good.' Jemma's answer was automatic, her mind focussed on the buildings they were passing. Each one was tall—multi-storeys tall—the iconic apartment blocks of all the pictures of the northern side of the harbour.

How far was 'not far'? How long until they reached more moderate dwellings? *Were* there any near the water in this area? If this was where he usually stayed… She raised her head, trying to count floor after floor heading skywards as he turned off the road and stopped to activate the gate leading into an underground car park.

'We're staying *here*?'

He flicked a glance at her. His chest rose and fell, and she knew without the slightest doubt that he was in a how-much-to-reveal? mindset. That capacity to blank all emotion from his features must have been an invaluable asset for a reporter. Add his knack of knowing when to hold back on giving information himself, and it was no mystery how he'd become a success.

She dismissed the girlfriend angle, and the chance of it being a friend's place, because he'd have mentioned either of those. It had to be family owned or his. Which meant…

He negotiated the downward curves to the second level as she mulled this over, and parked in an assigned spot.

'You're rich.'

It came out as a negative personal trait.

Switching off the engine, he unbuckled his safety belt and faced her.

'Yes, compared to some—minor league compared to others. Wealth is relative, Jemma.'

The blunt edge to his tone should have warned her not to stoke the fire, but completely out of character she continued.

'An apartment in this area puts the owner in the big league—especially if it's a second home, just for when you're in town.'

Add to that however many shares he owned, plus income from advising others on buying and selling… It explained his assured demeanour, and how he could take his time writing a lengthy stand-alone novel.

His guttural growl and narrowed eyes shook her from her reverie.

'What the hell difference does it make, Jemma? Does it mean you want to break our agreement?'

No! The word resonated in her head and contrition set in. Why had she raised the subject? She wanted to be the one to take his bad scenes apart, twist and tweak them and add magic to enchant the readers. More than she could ever remember wanting anything else in her life.

His economic status had nothing to do with their professional relationship. She had no idea why she was reacting this way—unless it was as a diversion from her responses to his smile, his voice. To the mere presence of him in her life. He'd awoken feelings she'd deliberately blocked since her betrayal, and she was in danger of having them torn apart again if she didn't regain control.

'No—and I apologise. Please forgive me.' She unfurled fingers pressed subconsciously into her palms and instinctively reached out to touch his arm, pulling back before making contact.

He moved quicker, clasping her hand in his with firm yet gentle pressure.

'I only take credit for what I've earned, and I concede that I'm doing okay. My siblings and I moved in here after my grandparents relocated to their house on the coast, which now belongs to my parents. The three of us inherited it seven years ago, after our grandfather died. He was the one with the foresight to invest in the building project and buy a unit off the plan.'

He released his hold and clicked her seat belt open.

'Let's go up. I think Milly's ready for a run-around.'

His tone decreed the subject closed.

They exited the lift into a small foyer. Nate turned left,

unlocked the door and allowed her to enter first. She walked in with confidence, believing that movies, television shows and her sister's mansion had prepared her for a luxurious sight.

But TV screens showed mere backdrops, and Vanessa's home was at ground level. This was high in the sky and had an almost touchable illusion. Jemma halted a few paces into a spacious kitchen with a marble-topped island, taking a slow panoramic scan of the open-plan design encompassing dining and living areas too, with a view of city lights at sundown. It ran the whole width of the apartment, with floor-to-ceiling windows on two sides.

It took a moment for her to refocus and acknowledge the quality of the dining and multi-piece entertaining settings. The light colour of the beech wood furniture complemented the bright blue shadings of the modular lounge, the two large deep-pile rugs and the open curtains. The scattering of mismatched bright multi-coloured cushions was the only aspect that didn't appear home-stylist-selected.

For her, it was too neat and clean—like a show home waiting to impress a buyer and lure them into a purchase contract. Or as if there was no permanent resident.

She looked at Nate, who was watching her with an amused expression. 'It's very impressive, Nate.'

'It's just an apartment, Jemma. One that isn't lived in much at the moment, but is regularly serviced by a cleaning firm. Let me release Milly, then I'll show you to the guest room.'

He placed the pet carrier on the sparkling clean mottled tiles and released the catch. Milly came out in a rush, stopped to look around, then began to explore her new surroundings with interest. Jemma empathised with her curiosity, and wished she felt as unperturbed.

Earned or inherited, Nate had fortune beyond anything she'd ever realise, and he accepted it as normal, his due right. Her ex had aspired to material possessions, and been willing to take a shortcut up the corporate ladder. Could she differentiate between the two?

'It's like a magazine picture, Nate. Like the luxury hotels I've researched. Like my sister Vanessa's new home in Melbourne, exclusive-decorator-furnished and ultra-modern, but…'

Her voice trailed away. She had to admit it would be a perfect setting for Vanessa, just as Nate fitted easily here.

'It's not your style? We did a full upgrade after we inherited—designed it to make a base for us when we are in Sydney, and a family place for visiting relatives and friends. Feel free to take photos or make notes for literary descriptive purposes.' He gestured towards the lounge area. 'This way.'

Carrying her big handbag, only used for travelling and shopping expeditions, and her laptop satchel, she followed him to a door in the wall that backed most of the open area. Opening it, he went in far enough to place her case and overnight bag on the floor, then stepped away.

If Jemma had been asked what she'd expected, the monster of a bed against the wall wouldn't have made the list, however long. She'd be lost in it alone.

Turning to ask if there was a smaller alternative, she was beaten by Nate's ready answer. 'They're *all* that big— and very comfortable. No chance of falling out when you roll over.'

The words were barely out when his expression changed. His lips firmed into a tight line, his throat convulsed and his eyes darkened. He seemed to have trouble speaking, and sounded huskier than he had a moment ago.

'En suite's through there. I'll be in the family room.'

He strode out, closing the door behind him, leaving her bewildered by the change. Trying to fathom its cause, she laid her suitcase flat and took out her toiletries bag.

There'd been nothing in his demeanour or tone as he'd described the bed's merits and glanced from her to it.

And then she was back on the words 'when you roll over.'

Had he imagined a similar scene to the one in her head as she'd stared at that great expanse of supportive mattress and the cosy light green quilt? *Not going to happen.* Bad move for them both. His novel was number one priority.

After freshening up in the immaculate, clean en suite, she listened for a moment at the open door, shy at the prospect of facing him, and afraid that her face would reveal her imagined scenario.

An intriguing jingling sound and the low hum of his laughter drew her out. Apart from those in front of the dining area the curtains had all been closed, making the large space seem homelier.

Nate was sitting cross-legged on one of the carpets, dangling a ball on a string, up and down, and chuckling as Milly tried to swat it. Both were apparently absorbed in the game. There was no trace of the emotion he'd displayed in the bedroom, though she noticed his shoulders flexed before he turned his head in her direction.

Scooping the kitten up and tickling her ears, Nate rose to his feet. Being physically occupied with a simple task, he'd tried to clear his head of visions of Jemma in that room and bolster his need to treat her as a working colleague. The amendments had to take precedence, and he needed to focus on her writing skills—her most important attribute as far as he should be concerned.

After his previous responses to her he'd steeled himself, and once again reinforced his defences on the drive to the airport. Outwardly he believed he'd succeeded, but inside his heightening reactions had him determining to… to *what*? Stay away from a house guest with whom he was supposed to be collaborating? Go for long runs, leaving her alone?

He'd known Jemma was near. The back of his neck had tingled, he'd breathed in through his nostrils, seeking an elusive aroma, and his pulse had quickened. He'd twisted his head and seen her watching him, body stiff, eyes wary.

Her newly brushed hair flowed neatly down her back, and he so wanted to muss it up a little, or have a few strands lie across her shoulders, so he could lift them into place, or run them through his fingers. Her short-sleeved loose top with its yellow leaf pattern and her tan trousers were ideal for travelling. But the image imprinted in his head was of the blue dress she'd worn for their dinner date.

Not a date. A celebration of a business deal.

'Hi, take a seat while I start dinner. The TV remote's in the drawer of the coffee table.' He bent to put Milly on the floor. 'You stay out from under my feet, okay?'

The expected background noise didn't come as he activated the grill and took the bottle of white wine he'd opened last night and the steaks from the fridge. Leaving the meat on the benchtop, he turned towards the dining table, already set for two, including two glasses in an ice bucket at one end.

Jemma was standing by the uncovered window, staring at the twinkling view. He ought to pour their drinks. Instead he walked up behind her, and knew she'd sensed him by the hitch in her shoulders.

'Would you like to go outside?'

Spinning round, she nodded. 'Yes, please.'

'It'll be windy. You might need to wear something warmer.'

She sped off to her room, and he went to put the steaks on a slow grill, then unlocked the glass door leading out onto the balcony. As Jemma returned, pulling on a navy zip-up jacket, his firm intentions began to crumble. Her face was flushed and her eyes as bright as the city lights.

Images of numerous kisses, stolen with the excuse of protecting or keeping a girl warm, flooded his mind. The memories of fighting to control rampant teenage hormones had dimmed, and couldn't compare to the burning desire of a mature man coursing through his body.

He steeled his resolve, and made sure Milly was nowhere near before pushing the door open enough to allow them to slip through, shutting it behind him.

CHAPTER NINE

A LIGHT BREEZE caught her hair as she moved over to the glass and metal railing, lifting the ends to make them float behind her, tempting him to fulfil that secret wish. He followed, leaning on his arms by her side, the railing cold on his skin. She didn't seem to notice, her fingers gripping it as she peered over and swivelled her head to take in the full view.

'It's even better out here. I checked through the window of my room just now—it has a balcony, but no way onto it.'

'There's a sliding door on three sides, and the kitchen wall is the divider between the two apartments on this level.'

She walked towards the corner and he followed, knowing the wind might pick up there, ready to steady her if it did. She was occupied with the view and continued round, noting the rooms they passed after the lounge.

'This one's mine, and the corner one has windows on two sides *and* a door. Lucky devil.'

Nate tamped down the temptation to admit it was his room, and show her. She'd already invaded his nights; how much hotter would his dreams be if he had an image of her inside his bedroom?

She stopped at that corner, her features animated as she picked out buildings and landmarks. Her enthusiasm was contagious, making him feel as if he was seeing it all from a new and different perspective.

Unable to resist, he placed his hands on the railing either side of her, telling himself it was to protect her from the wind. Leaning in, he breathed in the fresh lemon scent of her hair as it blew across his face, and had to tighten his grip to prevent himself from running his fingers through the silken strands, all the way to the ends near her waist.

For Jemma, seeing the iconic view from pictures and movies was like living a dream. So incredible from this height, and such a vast array of lights in every conceivable colour, blinking and pulsing as if alive. A spectacle for her...a common scene for Nate.

She'd paused here to breathe in the aroma of the harbour. Instead her lungs were filled with Nate's special blend of vanilla, citrus and musk. Three scents that would haunt her for ever.

She glanced at his hands, firm and strong, one on each side of her, enclosing; protective. Heat flared in her core at the thought of those long, tanned fingers tangling in her hair, caressing her cheek and stroking her body until she melted against his. Crazy. Impossible. Taboo.

For a second she thought the low guttural sound of need she'd heard came from her. But it was Nate, his mouth close to her ear, his hot breath fanning her lobe. He surrounded her, yet there was no physical contact. Foolish to desire any.

Her heart beating as if she'd climbed the twenty-seven flights of stairs, she swung round, her breath catching in her throat at the fire in his storm-grey eyes as his head jerked back. They both froze. If an earthquake had struck she wouldn't have moved, wouldn't have been able to break the spell.

Nate leant in again, his intent obvious, and a flashback triggered in her brain, causing her to echo his recent movement away. He stopped, eyes narrowing and brow furrowing. His chest rose, and his breath was audible as it fell.

Stepping back, he allowed her room to leave the railing. 'We'd better go in. I need to check on the steaks.'

* * *

Jemma watched a quiz show while he served up dinner, taking little notice of the screen in front of her. Why would a man of Nate's status, with two homes and the means to support himself while he wrote a long novel—he'd mentioned how time-consuming his research and revisions had been—want to kiss *her*? She wasn't sophisticated, didn't do social chitchat, and hadn't the flair to host dinners or parties like Vanessa. She could never even begin to compete with her sister, had never wanted to.

All she had to offer was her talent to imagine and describe believable relationships between a man and a woman.

Her fingers balled into fists in her lap, and she bit her lip to prevent any sound escaping. Was that why he'd come so close? Had appeared to be going to kiss her? Did he intend to use charm to keep her sweet and willing to help him? Her ex had had no qualms on that score, and there was no doubting Nate had plenty to spare.

She knew nothing of his personal life. Maybe there was someone—a woman who didn't live with him—or perhaps they had a casual mutually satisfying relationship.

'Dinner's ready, Jemma.'

It took a moment for his words to penetrate as she suddenly realised he'd never asked *her* about any ties either. She clicked off the television, stood and walked over to the dining table. The overhead lights in the whole open-plan area went on and off automatically, leaving the dining area with a surprising sense of privacy as they faced each other. She refused to think intimacy.

'Are you okay having white wine? I opened the bottle for pasta last night, but we can take it with us if you'd prefer red with the steaks.'

'Purists would be shocked. But I don't mind.' She thanked him as he filled both glasses, waited until he'd taken his seat, then lifted her drink towards him in a gesture that was becoming a habit.

'Thank you for cooking dinner.'

He dipped his head, returned the salute, and after drinking began to eat.

Jemma's steak was tender, cooked exactly to her taste. The salad was crisp and the dressing tangy without being overpowering. She'd be happy to do all the cleaning and let him cook every meal if he kept up this standard.

'You enjoyed being outside? Great setting for a romance scene, huh?'

Looking up, she met a guarded expression. His tone didn't quite match the casual words. But if he wanted to ignore the episode outside she'd play along, and ensure she never found herself in the same situation again.

'One that's been used so many times, in so many locations around the world. The trick is in finding a new angle. How about for your rough and tumble scenes?'

His eyes softened and she sensed his shoulders relax, caught a hint of a smile.

'That was one of my grandmother's favourite sayings when Sam, our friends and I came into her kitchen, grubby from playing and wrestling. I've got a couple of fights on balconies, even guys falling off. If you feel any of those is a better place for any of the interactive scenes, go ahead and relocate them.'

She stared at him, and the hand holding her fork in front of her parted lips stilled. Less than three weeks ago he'd vehemently opposed her having any access to his manuscript, and since then they'd spent limited time together, spread over four days, before her flight this afternoon. Now he was saying he'd allow her to change a location?

Her hand dropped, the food left uneaten. He seemed oblivious to the enormity of his statement, and then his lips curled.

'I'm impressed with those scenes in your novel—and I do still have right of veto.'

He was teasing her, yet there'd been a serious undertone in his voice. Pushing it to the back of her mind for dwelling on later, she took a drink of the fruity wine as he changed the subject.

'I stocked up with enough fresh fruit and vegetables for a few days this morning. Any time you want anything I'll drive you into town, or you can take the SUV. I'm—'

'Whoa. Are you referring to that monster down below, or do you have another vehicle in the mountains? I've never driven anything that big, and I wouldn't feel comfortable trying it on unfamiliar country roads.'

Mouth agape, he blinked and his brow furrowed. Her stomach tensed and she wished she'd said nothing, just ensured the situation never arose. She assumed the women he associated with were competent in *all* fields of life, and she had many failings.

'I'm sorry, Jemma. I'm so used to it I didn't consider its size. Alice won't use it either—claims it's hard to park. I'll take you anywhere, any time, and if I'm not there you can call a cab from town.'

Grateful for his understanding, Jemma thanked him, and they finished their meal talking about the tourist attractions of Katoomba.

Nate insisted on cleaning up, grateful that there'd been no repercussions from his inexplicable behaviour earlier. Berating himself as he'd mixed the salad and turned the steaks, he hadn't been able to explain why he'd come so near to wrecking everything for a moment's pleasure in a moment's madness, caused by her scent and the soft sigh he'd swear he'd heard as he'd craved her lips under his.

The pain in her startled eyes as she'd pulled back had cleared his head and fired up his guilt. Her issues with men ran deep, and he had no intention of exacerbating them. He had enough personal issues of his own. And with her now on her guard, keeping control should be easier.

He went looking for her to suggest coffee, and found her in the hall between the bedrooms and the laundry. She was staring, transfixed, at the massive built-in bookcase that reached to the ceiling, every shelf filled with books of various sizes and piles of magazines.

There was no sense of order or filing system, no attempt to line up by height or writer's name. This was generations of his family, taking books out and putting them back, re-reading them and returning them to any available space.

He stood behind her and watched for a moment, empathising with her joy. As if mesmerised, she scanned the books, running her fingers over remembered titles and authors and sighing with happiness.

'We're all avid readers, and there's a lot of old favourites on those shelves. Wouldn't part with them for the world.'

She pivoted, and laughed, oblivious to the rapture evident on her face.

'Oh, I envy you. Children's books to science fiction, with every genre in between. For years I relied on libraries, and hated having to return those books I loved.'

'You now have quite a collection yourself.' He grinned. 'One of the first things I noticed in your lounge room. I've put the jug on if you want a hot drink.'

'What time do you want to leave in the morning?'

'Is six too early? I've learned it's the best time for getting clear of the city and avoiding multiple traffic hold-ups. No guarantees, but… And, like I said, I know the best places to stop for breakfast.'

'Six is fine. It's been a long day, so I'll put Milly in the laundry and go to bed. We'll have to shut her in, otherwise she might wander and hide.'

'Leave her to me. She can keep me company for a while.'

'Okay.' She crouched down to stroke the kitten, who'd

trotted over to join them, then stood up. 'I'm very grateful for the opportunity you're giving me, Nate.'

'Works both ways, Jemma. You have a good night's sleep and we'll talk on the way, once we hit the highway. Goodnight.'

Jemma didn't move—couldn't as Nate's grey eyes locked with hers, holding her entranced. His arms lay rigid at his sides, fingers curled, and she was acutely aware of his Adam's apple bobbing, and the steady movement of his chest in the rhythm of his breathing.

She licked dry lips, her heart pounded and she could swear the air shimmered between them.

Suddenly from nowhere the sharp pain of her ex's infidelity cut deep inside, breaking the spell.

She dropped her gaze, scrunched her eyes shut for a second to regain control and faced him again. 'Goodnight, Nate.' Only the slight tremor in her voice betrayed her.

'Goodnight, Jemma.'

He moved aside and she walked past him to her room.

Alone in the shower, she tried to compare the two men and failed. It seemed that over the years images of her ex had blurred, leaving behind only the deep-rooted anguish of betrayal, making her treat any handsome man with charm and aspirations of becoming wealthy as if they were in the same mould. It was because of his and her brother-in-law's social climbing endeavours that she avoided mixing with anyone she deemed prosperous or elite.

Nate fell into both of those categories, though she couldn't imagine him cheating for money. But his literary aspirations were different, strong, maybe even obsessional; he had a drive to prove he could achieve his goal. What would he do and who would he manipulate to have a copy of his published novel in his hand?

Some time later she vaguely heard music—soothing,

classical. Groggy with sleep, she turned over, snuggling deeper under the quilt.

Woken by her alarm in the morning, she was dressed and packing her suitcase when she heard a clatter through the adjacent wall. From the big corner bedroom. Where Nate must have slept.

Nate had hoped for a six o'clock getaway, would have settled for six-thirty, and was pleasantly surprised to be exiting the car park at ten to six—an hour or so before sunrise. Jemma looked relaxed and rested, which shouldn't have irked him but did, seeing as it was she who'd kept *him* awake for most of the night.

It had been one of those rare occasions when low music and the night sky view through open drapes had failed to lull him to sleep. Trying to equate the demure woman in the room through the wall behind his head and the sensual scenes she'd written had rattled his brain. Had they been penned from imagination or experience?

She used her pain as a shield, which was something he understood and emulated, along with his compelling desire to purge his own dark memories in his story. It never quite worked—merely pushed them a little further into the deep recesses of his mind.

Love scenes were different. Passionate and personal. He'd done with feelings and emotions, which explained his stilted written relationships. But was describing their sexual encounters cathartic for women?

In frustration, he'd turned the overhead light on and accessed her full manuscript, the relevant scenes highlighted in his tablet. He'd scrolled to each one, concentrating on the interaction, physical and verbal, and the varied ways she'd depicted loving gestures and emotions. Not his business, but his gut had tightened as he'd speculated on how she'd gained so much knowledge.

Waking from a restless sleep, he hadn't been able to remember his dreams, yet knew they'd been hot and steamy. Dressed, bed made and suitcase ready, he'd reached for his watch on the bedside cabinet—and knocked his clock radio onto the tiled floor.

Now, even with a meal break, they'd be at his property by mid-morning. Unless Jemma wanted to, there'd be no need to stop in the town.

'Do you mind if I listen to the news, Jemma?'

'No worries. Is keeping up to date with the news important for your writing? I assume you've started a second novel?'

'It's more for the effect current events might have on the share market. But, yes, I'm in the planning stage with different settings.' He gave her a quick smile and turned the radio on. 'I'll contact you for help when I get to a schmaltzy scene.'

'*Schmaltzy?* That, Mr Thornton, sells millions of books every year—print and digital.'

The chuckle he tried to hold back came out as a splutter. 'I surrender, Jemma. For now. One day we'll debate the pros and cons over a good bottle of wine.'

'And chocolates?'

The news began and Nate adjusted the volume. Jemma took a book from her handbag on the floor, wriggled a little until she was comfortable and began to read. Discussion followed the news, and as the traffic was building up Nate tuned to a more relaxing music station and gave his full concentration to the road.

Being in control of a reliable vehicle on good roads was a unique feeling—power with responsibility. Rattling along potholed dirt tracks in uninhabited areas overseas, wrestling with a clapped-out wreck and with no certainty of reaching your destination safely, was empowering—with the added pungency of danger.

Jemma was the perfect companion in peak traffic, occasionally looking up at the road or checking on Milly, otherwise absorbed in her reading. Nothing in her gentle demeanour even hinted at those torrid scenes he couldn't get out of his head. Even the milder ones raised his suspicions over where and how she'd researched them. And with whom.

CHAPTER TEN

THEY ATE IN a highway fast food outlet and shared a daily newspaper. Before setting off again he gave Milly a few minutes' freedom in a safe area behind the building.

The traffic was light now, and he was familiar with the road, and still those questions were drumming in his head. Having a fervent dislike of banal small talk, he broached the subject full-on—a habit from his reporting days.

'That him/her stuff you write, Jemma—how do you do it? Where does it come from?'

He sensed her eyes on him, figured he was getting the usual penetrating scrutiny, and surprisingly didn't mind at all.

'Define *"it,"* Nate.' Her voice was flat, with a hint of umbrage.

'You know darn well, Jemma. That intensity and interaction with sensual undertones. That emotion and the different ways you write it. The actual physical encounters. If there's a how-to-write book on *that* I'd like a copy.'

'I'll give you a list. If that's how you describe making love you'll need it. Reading well-written scenes you want to emulate is also a great teacher.'

'Plus practical learning?'

Her gasp coincided with his oath of regret, and he immediately tried to make amends.

'I'm sorry, Jemma, that was crass and uncalled-for. It sure didn't work for me.'

A quick glance at her pale face deepened his self-contrition. And his next remark would probably fuel the fire.

'I can't offer any excuse because there isn't one. I read

what you've written and I can't believe the variety of ways you describe the same actions and feelings. Can't help wondering how.'

He'd screwed up—virtually accused her of sleeping around—and wouldn't blame her if she told him to fix his inadequate scenes himself. What the hell had possessed him? Stupid question. She intrigued and bothered him.

The women he dated—which was hardly the correct description for mutual sexual satisfaction sometimes preceded by dinner or a function—were experienced. Jemma was a far cry from their determined-to-stay-independent and career-absorbed personalities. There was no explanation for his reactions towards her. He needed her brain, her description expertise, nothing more.

Yeah, that's why you can't stop thinking of her enticing blue eyes and her soft lips ripe for kissing. Why you take deep breaths to inhale her perfume. And why you pushed for this personal collaboration when your head argued for electronic contact only.

'Are you claiming actual participation in every aspect of your hero's covert operations, Nate?'

The biting tone of her challenge slammed him back to the present situation. The breath he hadn't realised he was holding whooshed from his lungs, and for a second his head spun.

Sucking more air in, he framed an answer he hoped would satisfy her without revealing the complete truth. 'I've met military personnel in a number of places, and worked with some to gain access to remote areas, normally inaccessible. Friendships with them and a few corporate employees working for international companies have been beneficial to my job. A lot can be learned from conversation over food or drinks if you're prepared to listen and be discreet.'

He hesitated, stared at the number plate of the camper van in front, and then inexplicably shared more.

'I've never betrayed nor had reason to regret any of those relationships. And being involved with a social group who meet in Sydney every month has aided my return to normal day-to-day life. The support they give is unconditional—never questioned and never denied.'

Jemma heard the words he spoke and filled in those he'd held back. Nate Thornton would refute any suggestion by others of being affected by his experiences, and yet she sensed he'd turned to these members for help at some time.

'If you're part of it, it's not just for ex-military?'

His eyes met hers for a brief moment, cool and confronting with an underlying warning.

No questions. I've said enough.

'Your business. Just keep in mind that any alterations I make in your characters' relationship will impact elsewhere.'

'As in...?'

'As in the friendlier they get, the more intimate details they'll learn, and the more likely it will be that they'll think of each other when apart...even at inappropriate times.'

Like I think of you, though you've never held me; we've never kissed.

'My amendments will influence how they react to each other in future scenes, Nate. They can't become involved without some changes in their behaviour.'

'Hmm...'

She gave him a moment to absorb what appeared to be a new concept for him, though he'd already accepted the few revisions she'd made outside her specified scenes. To continue, she needed to know about the couple's individual futures.

'It would be helpful if I could read the entire manuscript and get some idea of how often they'll be together and what happens to them. They had long breaks away from each other in the last four chapters I saw, but the action was so riveting it didn't matter.'

'In your story they seldom had a page apart.'

'Different genre. Different reader expectations.'

'You added music to mine too—something I hadn't considered. Even nailed the heavy rock band my hero listens to. The man I based his character on was a diehard fan.'

'Which means *you* nailed the character. Who, by the way, wouldn't appeal to *every* woman.'

'That was the furthest thought from my mind when I was writing.'

The atmosphere in the vehicle had changed—or maybe it was Jemma herself. Without being conscious of any deliberate action she'd accepted her irrational attraction to Nate, *and* the understandable apprehension of staying with a man she barely knew. On all but one level she trusted him. She no longer deemed him arrogant, but to her he was still the self-assured, I-can-handle-any-situation macho male she'd pegged in that foyer.

At her request, he switched radio channels to one playing contemporary hits. They discussed the merits, or lack of, in the music and performers, and agreed to disagree when their tastes didn't mesh.

The warmth of the sun through the windows and the steady purr of the engine combined with her early rising made her drowsy. She turned her face towards the window and slept.

Some time later she became aware of an almost familiar song as she drifted towards consciousness. Eyes shut, she tried to identify it and realised it was Nate, singing along with the radio. His voice wasn't bad at all, especially with the abrasive edge favoured by many hard rock fans.

The music finished and she didn't move, not wanting to embarrass him. As if *anything* could shake the man's composure. Opening her eyes, she saw tall trees flashing past, backed by blue sky, not the peaks and stunted tree-growth she'd pictured from television images of the Blue Mountains. They were different, though, and not as lush as those in Hahndorf.

Reminding herself they were at a much higher altitude, she stirred, straightened up and caught Nate's quick smile towards her.

'We're about fifteen minutes from Katoomba. We'll bypass it—unless you want to stop for a drink or anything?'

She checked her watch. It was twenty to nine. He'd mentioned living out of the town, but not how far.

'No, I'm all right. Shouldn't I be able to see the mountains now?'

He laughed. 'Not when you're driving along the top of them. Don't worry—you'll get plenty of photo opportunities in the next two weeks. I've got tourist brochures at home from when Dad and Mum stayed with me.'

'Will there be time for sightseeing?'

This time his glance included an eyebrow quirk.

'You agreed to come thinking I'd work you without any breaks, Jemma?'

His smile told her he was teasing, and she responded the same way.

'You said you wanted my input as soon as possible, Nate.'

'Ah, but even *I* take time out for pleasure.'

The phrase, *What kind?* formed on her lips, but thankfully didn't get spoken—although she was sure he'd give plausible answers. He ran to keep fit, and trained with the firefighting service. He had family and friends to socialise with. But he had given no indication of there being a regular woman in his life.

She'd been first to the dining area with her luggage this morning—not quite first, as Milly had been eating a small portion of dry food in her corner. Kneeling to stroke her, she'd heard the sound of Nate's suitcase wheels on the tiled floor, turned, and felt suddenly bereft of air and logical thought. Why was it no other man in jeans and a muscle-sculpting T-shirt had that power?

She'd love to ask if he'd had any requests to pose for those firefighter calendars like the one she'd bought for a friend's Christmas present last year. If Nate had been featured she'd have that month on her wall permanently.

'Jemma? You've gone very quiet. It's a bit late to change your mind.'

'I'm not. I was wondering how far from town you live. You said it was too far to go by foot.'

'Ten-point-seven kilometres along the road—plus four hundred metres from the turn-off to my house. I *have* walked it on occasion. My normal routine is to leave the SUV in town with a friend if I catch the train to the city.'

'Are there other homes nearby?'

'No—that's part of the attraction for me. If you're worried about safety it's textbook fire-and-storm-protected, and I clear any surrounding bush-growth every spring or when needed.'

She went quiet, noting the small number of turn-offs before he slowed down and drove into his which was un-marked and barely discernible, consisting of solid-packed dirt and weaving around a large tree for a few metres in, then veering off again.

'You don't have a mailbox?'

'Anything I can't get on email goes to a post office box in Katoomba. I cleared it last week.'

'And the house isn't visible from the road? Is all this land yours?' There were more trees than she'd expected, given his statement regarding safety and clearing land.

'Yes. Privacy is important to me. Anyone I invite here knows where it is.'

A final bend and they were in an open area with a view of a mountaintop across a valley. For Jemma, it was like seeing a picture from a classic architectural magazine for real. She couldn't conceive of a more perfect home in such a setting. Everything she'd imagined it might be flew out of her head.

Nate was justifiably proud of the house he'd helped design, with every eco-friendly device and technology available. Built on rising ground as a split level, with a solar-panelled sloping roof, the house's colours blended with its natural surroundings, and was fronted with a wide area of neutral-coloured pebbles. Beyond there was a variety of naturally growing, widely spaced low scrub bushes. The nearest trees wouldn't reach the building if felled by fire or man.

He drove around to the right, activated a remote control and stole a glance at Jemma as what appeared to be part of the side wall slid upwards into the ground-floor ceiling. Her wide-eyed response was all he'd hoped for, as it had been when family members and friends had first visited.

His parents had loved the comfort of cooling and heating, the views and the peaceful evenings. His brother-in-law and Sam had wanted to try every piece of gadgetry and know how they worked. Alice had been enthusiastic about everything, and had made playful fun of him for living there alone.

Reversing down the ramp, he experienced the same heightened anticipation as he had the first time he'd completed the manoeuvre. As if Jemma's opinion was significant.

If the smile on her face as she gazed around the illuminated garage and workshop was any indication, he'd earned her approval.

She was out of the vehicle and scanning his tool shadow board and built-in workbench and shelves before he had a chance to get around and open her door.

'Wow, are there any tools you *don't* have, Nate?'

'I bought these while we were building. Haven't had many yet, but I like to do my own repairs except when a licence is needed.' He pointed to the far corner. 'Laundry's over there—use it any time you need.'

Turning back to the vehicle, he went to the rear and began unloading their luggage, carrying it to a small lift near a set of stairs. She collected her handbag from the front seat, then unbuckled the cat carrier and took it over. Two more trips and everything was inside, ready to go up.

Nate caught her arm as she was about to enter and led her round the side. Between the lift and the ramp was a large back-up generator and an electricity switchboard. He gave her a quick rundown on the switches.

'Blackouts are rare, and the generator should cut in if one occurs. If I don't happen to be here, and it doesn't, you can do it manually. There's a torch and spare batteries in the bottom of your bedside cabinet, and in a kitchen drawer.'

'You've really covered everything, haven't you? Even putting in your own lift.'

He looked down into enchanting blue eyes, deep and alluring as the Mediterranean Sea, and the desire to dive into the tantalising depths was overwhelming. Only dredging up the memory of another pair of bewitching eyes kept him from dipping his head those few centimetres and claiming her lips with his.

A flash of wariness flickered in her eyes, but was gone as quickly as it came. Heeding its warning, he moved away.

'Useful when there are three storeys, and it cuts out arguing with Dad about him carrying suitcases up flights of stairs.'

Jemma went in first, standing sideways on to Nate in the small space left by the luggage, her eyes fixed on his chest as he closed the door and pressed the top button. The air she drew in was scented with his cologne, and it would take little effort for her to rise onto her toes and press her lips to his manly jaw.

Contrary emotions. A moment ago, she'd been afraid *he* was about to kiss *her*.

'We'll drop off the luggage, then go down to ground level,' he told her as they halted, stepping out to allow her to exit with her handbag, satchel and carry-on.

The wide corridor stretched the width of the house down to a picture window with shutters.

'You're in the first on the left, and the light switch is on the left by the door. I leave all the drapes closed and the blinds down when I'm away.'

Nate followed her with the two suitcases, set hers down near the bed and left with his. A good move for her, because she was incapable of speech, in awe of the suite she'd be occupying during her stay.

With her love of nature, this was her dream room. The soft green décor with traces of pale yellow, including a leaf motif on the enormous bedspread, pillow and an armchair, was soothing. She loved the way it was teamed with the light brown of the bedside cabinets, the desk table and chair in one corner, and the small round coffee table alongside the armchair by the window.

A double door which slid into the wall revealed a large walk-in wardrobe, with a dressing table and full-length mirror. She assumed every bedroom would be similarly furnished, with different designs. His? Or had he hired an interior decorator? She couldn't picture him flicking though swatches of fabric.

She'd begun to slide the single door open, catching a glimpse of a continuation of the colour scheme in the en suite bathroom, and heard him coming back. Whatever he'd been about to say was lost as she gave him a knowing smile, well aware that her eyes would be gleaming with mischief.

'That must have been quite a bulk deal you got on those beds, Nate.'

He chuckled, clearly appreciating her sense of humour. 'Nearly four years apart, but from the same dealer. You *did* find yours comfortable last night?'

'Very—I slept peacefully until my alarm. Seriously, Nate, I think this room's worthy of a five-star hotel.'

Nate was tempted to make a quip about twenty-four-hour room service but refrained, deeming it might be misconstrued.

'Thank you. Now, let's get Milly to the ground floor and free her before she starts objecting.'

Downstairs, he opened the shutters and green drapes, flooding the open area with light. Before releasing the kitten he latched the gates he'd installed across the stairs, up and down, preferring to keep her on one floor until she settled.

From the moment he'd driven onto his property his senses had been attuned to Jemma, trying to gauge her reaction to everything he'd designed, chosen, sourced and put in place. Although he'd valued his family's opinion, it hadn't impacted on him. It disturbed him that hers might. So far every reaction had been positive, lifting his spirits.

The similarities between here and the Sydney unit were deliberate, with ceiling-to-floor glass along one long wall, facing a panoramic view of the mountains across the gully. Here the colours were various shades of green, and the furniture teak. This was a subdued version, conducive to relaxation, quiet evenings and a peaceful atmosphere for writing.

Partial glass on the side wall and front ensured plenty of natural light and a true living-in-the-country atmosphere. And behind the kitchen was a surprise he hoped she'd share with him.

CHAPTER ELEVEN

HE WATCHED HER walk the length of the open-plan area, her eyes focussed on the true-life mural through the glass, swivel for a slow scan of the décor inside, then turn to him with a bemused expression. Unable to gauge her reaction from where he stood, he moved closer.

'Sydney was awesome, Nate, and this is spectacular. What's your next project? A castle or a palace? Is it *all* your personal taste?'

'It took time, but everything here is exactly what I want, right down to the salt and pepper shakers, and it will suit me until I grow old.'

As he spoke he recalled selecting it all with a fierce determination that no one else would have any input, that his home would have only his stamp in every room.

Jemma was the first woman not related to him he'd invited here and he wanted her to approve, to feel relaxed and at home. *No!* He fisted his hands at this thought. Relaxed and comfortable for *writing*—not as if it were her home. She was a transient visitor, and on completion of the assignment she'd leave.

He switched topics. 'Where I write depends on my mood: in here, or outside—even in winter on occasion.' He flicked his hand towards a desk and chair in the far corner. 'Or over there, or in my study. You go wherever you feel comfiest.'

'Thank you. May I see the study?'

He led her to two doors in the lounge area, opposite the long veranda.

The first room was set up like an executive's office, with

top-notch furniture and equipment, and was showroom-neat and tidy. The bookshelf held a few photographs, and books that were all reference books.

Noting her frown at the latter, Nate quickly ushered her out and into the next room, standing to the side to watch her expression. He wasn't disappointed. She gasped, her lips parted and her eyes widened in ecstatic surprise.

Jemma coveted this room more than any other she'd seen in either home. Two full walls and the space under the window held replicas of the bookshelves in Sydney, even the random higgledy-piggledy stacking of reading material. In the centre was a comfy old armchair, with its footrest out and a coffee table alongside. She closed her eyes, envying his having both rooms, wishing that maybe one day...

'You approve, Jemma?'

Her heart blipped and her eyes flew open. She'd been so wrong at their first meeting. Forget romantic phrases—his soft tone against her ear would stir sensations even if he were reciting a dull repair manual. She swallowed, and managed to nod in agreement.

'I'll take that as a yes. Come with me. I think you'll like this too.'

He reached for her hand; she pulled away at the first touch—too late to stop the tingles shooting across her skin. He didn't appear affected.

She followed as he strode towards the front corner of the house by the kitchen, to a door with no handle in the side wall. He placed his right-hand fingers into a metal insert at his head height, she heard a click, and then it slid to his left, disappearing into the wall.

The humidity hit her and she knew what she was going to see apart from the weights and bench press in her immediate view. Past a screened change area and shower there was a lap pool, clear and inviting, extending nearly the width of the house. A lat pulldown machine stood in the furthest corner.

Her mind boggled, trying to take it all in: the actual building with its solar panels, the double-glazed floor-to-ceiling windows on almost every wall, and the underground area—what the heck would digging *that* out have cost? Add in the fixtures, fittings and furniture...

Her brain couldn't, *wouldn't* process the figure, had gone numb trying.

Her eyes met Nate's gaze. It was hopefully expectant—as if her opinion mattered, as if he really wanted her endorsement. But that was crazy thinking, and she countered it by voicing the silly thought that had flashed into her head.

'What? No spa?'

Instead of being insulted, he burst out laughing and raised his eyebrows.

Idiot, of course there was. Probably in *his* bathroom. No, probably in all of them. His approach upstairs had prevented her from looking right into hers.

As if he read her mind, he answered. 'How could I possibly enjoy my own spa if my guests had to settle for less? Apart from the colour scheme, and some difference in size, the bedroom suites are all the same. Did you pack bathing suits?'

She refocussed at his question. 'Yes, I checked out the nearby aquatic centre online, hoping to use it for exercise and an alternative to walking. This is amazing, Nate. You really are self-contained here, aren't you?'

She heard the envy in her own voice. He hadn't been joking when he'd said his home had everything he wanted. How she'd love to design her own home from scratch. How she'd love to have enough money even to consider it.

'As long as you're here, consider the pool yours as well. Do you want to unpack now, or go for a walk?'

'I'd love some fresh air and exercise, please.'

'Walk it is.'

* * *

Nate took two small water bottles from the fridge and they left via the front door, walked across a porch area and down two steps to the pebbles. The width of the path varied, constantly forcing the gap between them to widen and narrow. Each time they were close Nate flattened the fingers of his left hand to his thigh, fighting the desire to touch her and have her even closer to his side. Once or twice, when they were further apart, he became aware that his fingers were tapping, a sign of agitation he fought to control.

His solitary walks in the mountains would never be the same. They would now be imbued with the spirit of Jemma—her tranquillity as they strolled, her affinity with nature and the scent of her floral perfume.

He'd have to modify his lifestyle while she was here. He couldn't expect her to fit in with his erratic hours— sometimes he was up through the night and cat-napping in the day. It only happened here. Even if he was alone in the Sydney apartment he lived by regular business hours.

'Do you have a work schedule, or do you go with the creative flow?'

Grateful for the sudden question requiring him to refocus, he answered readily. 'I can write any time, anywhere. If you like, I'll rustle up some food while you unpack, then you can choose where you'd like to set up. We can sort out breaks as we go.'

'Sounds good to me.'

Jemma was enjoying the feel of the pebbles under her sneakers, loving the crunch of fallen leaves and undergrowth along the track even more. The filtered sun through the trees warmed her back, and the T-shirt and cotton pants she wore were perfect for the different activities of the day.

A slight breeze cooled her skin, and their footsteps were

the only sound apart from the occasional rustle of nature. It seemed they had the world all to themselves—or at any rate, this tiny part of it. She memorised the sights, sounds and smells, the latter a mingling of musk, vanilla and citrus. And the essence of Nate.

Their discussion on the return trip included aspects of living in the same house, morning rising and meal times, plus music and television show preferences. She admitted that her exercise consisted of walking to and from town as often as possible, spasmodic yoga classes and summer trips to the beach with friends. She kept quiet about her love of dancing whenever she was inspired by music...most often at home and alone.

Although she'd been at ease during the walk, Jemma's trepidation resurfaced as she mounted the stairs to her room, her fingers clenching and opening. Nate had a knack of disconcerting her with words, looks and limited touches. And an equal talent for bringing her back to equilibrium with the same.

Shutting her door was an unwarranted gesture. She was convinced he'd never enter uninvited. It was for her own benefit—a physical obstacle she needed because her emotions were rapidly dismantling her internal barricades.

The quick peek she'd given the bathroom confirmed its luxury, and now she pushed the door into its recess. It was as if he'd perused the same décor magazines and top hotel rooms she had in her research. She'd described it in her book and he'd built it. She'd fantasised about soaking in bubbles while he actually relaxed in them. Tonight, she'd be joining him.

No, no, *no*. Not together. Heat shot through her—head to toe, skin to core—as she tried to distance her imagination from her innocent thought process. Too late. And splashing cold water over her cheeks did little to diminish the colour or the burning.

Vowing to stick to showers, she left, shutting the door behind her, knowing that sooner rather than later she'd renege.

She knelt by her suitcase and began to unpack her everyday clothes in this room which deserved the kind of designer clothes her sister's closet held. Suitcase empty, she stowed it away and crossed to the window, overlooking the track they'd taken. Pushing the curtains further apart, she was thrilled to find a door leading onto a balcony. The beauty of the ancient peaks against a brilliant blue sky spurred her to capture this moment of nature's tranquillity, to have it as a permanent memento.

A few minutes later she had photographs taken from there, and others of the gully view from the corner of the house in her camera.

Shamed by her stubbornness in resisting her friends' pressure for so long, she stood for a moment, reinforcing to herself who she was and the reason Nate had invited her to his home.

You are here because you have an invaluable talent. Because Brian and Nate believe in your ability to enhance this novel. Because Nate trusts you. Because you are worthy of his trust.

He was also attracted to her, and she was vulnerable.

Only if you allow yourself to be.

She vowed to focus on the reason she was there, to complete her task as soon as possible, then return to Hahndorf, where she belonged, with no regrets.

Nate put the two covered plates of ham and salad in the fridge, wondering how long it took a woman to unpack one suitcase and a carry-on. He opened a bottle of beer and drank, leaning against the island. His fingers tapped on his thigh and he grunted, trying to understand why her approval of his home was so important.

Every moment spent with her tested his resolve to stay platonic, as he'd promised himself. She amused him, provoked him and stirred desires he'd sworn never to fall prey to again. When she'd decided where she wanted to work he'd pick another area, out of sight of her, where her evocative perfume didn't reach.

Huh, as if *that* would diminish how aware he was of her. Like right now, as the hairs on his nape stiffened, sensing she was near.

He squared his shoulders and sucked in his stomach. Twenty-five chapters to go—each with a minimum of one confrontational scene between his prime characters. In all, too many discussions with Jemma about feelings, emotions and sex.

He turned his head and smiled as she approached, looking cool and refreshed, while *he* was in definite need of a cold shower.

The rest of the day was spent as he hoped a fair portion of their time would be.

Jemma chose to work at the lounge room desk, with the full manuscript on her laptop and a printed copy she could make notes on. He took his computer, containing all the chapters she'd revised, his canvas folding recliner and a soft drink to his favourite spot on the ground-floor veranda.

They compromised on non-vocal music from classic movies in the background, and to limit distraction he pulled the middle blinds, blocking their view of each other.

That didn't stop him from being aware of the regular breaks she took to stretch or move around. But it was no fault of hers that he was as aware of her as he was of the words in front of him.

She went to the kitchen once, and twice brought a page

to him for clarification. Mid-afternoon they stopped for coffee and biscuits, and he called a halt at five, telling her he'd fix a chicken stir fry for dinner and she could cook tomorrow.

When Jemma yawned and said goodnight Nate stayed in the lounge, giving her time to fall asleep before he retired.

The tactic didn't work. He stared open-eyed at his ceiling, picturing her along the corridor, silken hair spread over her pillow, soft skin glowing in the moonlight through the window, her delectable lips curled as she dreamt of one of her heroes.

Hell, who needed sleep anyway?

Somewhere between two and three in the morning he gave up trying, and flung himself out of his crumpled bed. After showering and dressing in T-shirt and shorts he grabbed a sandwich and coffee, and stretched out on the long sofa. Milly, woken by the lights, came looking for attention, and he scooped her up onto his stomach.

'You're almost as distracting as your mistress, Scamp.' The name from his past came more easily than Milly. He tickled her ear, and she swatted his hand. 'The pair of you are getting under my skin, and that's not good.'

She curled up and closed her eyes, making him chuckle, and the movement of his stomach caused her to lift her head and blink at him. He stroked her and she settled.

Dragging his mind from an image of Jemma being in Milly's place, he tried and failed to mentally plot the opening scene of book number two as he ate and drank. Images of his encounters with her dominated, messing with his mind.

With an exasperated curse, he pushed upright and gently set the kitten down. If he couldn't sleep, he'd at least be productive.

He fetched his laptop and settled down with it on his lap, his feet on a padded footstool. After booting up, he created a new folder and file, blocked from his mind the figure asleep upstairs and typed.

SHADOWS OF A HAUNTED MAN
CHAPTER ONE

The only sound greeting Jemma when she descended the stairs at twenty past seven in the morning was the ball being patted across the tiles by Milly. She'd meant to ask Nate about a morning swim last night, but had been tired from the long day.

He wasn't in the pool. He must either be in his room or… He was running, according to the note attached to the coffee machine.

She brushed off irrational disappointment. Expecting to be included in an exercise she rarely participated in was selfish—as would be asking him to slow down to accommodate her leisurely pace.

She made coffee and toast, wandering as she ate, studying the photos attached to the few walls. It was easy to identify his family—his brother was so much like Nate, apart from a carefree look and shorter, trimmed hair. Had Nate's eyes been that clear and untroubled before he'd gone abroad? Or had being naturally sombre steered him towards the more thought-provoking stories he'd chased?

A movement outside caught her attention. Nate was moving fast and sure towards the house on a track opposite the one they'd walked yesterday. She drank in the power of his fluid motion, his feet pounding and arms pumping, eyes fixed straight ahead.

The desire to have that intensity focussed on *her*, that energy overriding her fears and that power sweeping her away to delights unknown swamped her, inciting tremors down her spine.

A second later, icy chills overrode all that.

There were stones and bits of broken branches on that uneven trail. How far did he run? What if he tripped and got injured? Couldn't make it back to the house? Did he take his mobile with him?

And why was she panicking about something that shouldn't concern her and might never happen?

His head jerked up as if he'd become aware of her presence, his eyes seeking her out through the window.

Please let him be too far away to see what I'm feeling.

Her prayer was answered with a light wave of his hand and, she thought, a smile. So if she couldn't see his mouth, then he couldn't see her expression. She began to deep-breathe, figuring she had roughly three minutes before he was in this room. Counting to ten with each inhale and exhale, she went to fetch her coffee.

His chest heaved with audible puffing as he came through the door, perspiration glistening on his skin and soaking the white tank top and black shorts, which left oodles of bare, tanned and toned muscle for her eyes to feast on. His eyes shone with exhilaration.

Clinging tightly to her hot mug, she prayed the internal waves of desire he created simply by standing in front of her, hands on hips, didn't show externally. His quick smile and back-arch reassured her that he hadn't noticed.

Both pieces of his clothing and his black and green running shoes looked worn and comfortable, but she didn't have to see their tags to know they'd be an international brand.

'I thought about waking you—wasn't sure what sort of reception I'd get after yesterday's early start.' He headed for the kitchen tap.

'A moan and the sight of me disappearing further under the blankets, if your appearance now means you've been gone for a while.'

He swallowed a glass of water in one gulp and leant on

the edge of the sink, grinning at her. How could a sweaty and dishevelled man look so gorgeous? He tugged at her heart strings and booted up her pulse to danger speed.

CHAPER TWELVE

JEMMA NEEDED A DIVERSION—something to distract him.

'Do you want coffee?'

Mundane but, with luck, effective. He shook his head.

'I was wide awake before dawn and left just as the sun rose. It's a great time to be out there. If you leave your drapes open the sun will substitute for an alarm. I'll take a shower and eat, then we'll get to it.' He walked towards her, arms outstretched, lips curved in a devilish grin. 'Wanna hug?'

Jemma's brain was trying to process 'get to it,' and her body was fighting the heat its connotations had fired up. He was within the required arm's length for the action before she reacted. She jumped back, and blushed even hotter at his roar of laughter as he gave her chin a gentle flick on his way past.

She mustn't... She wouldn't... She did. She twisted and watched him take the stairs two at a time, looking as hot and heady from the rear as he did face to face.

By the time he returned she was reading his script on the veranda, a glass of water and a bowl of mixed nuts by her side. It was the coolest place she could find, short of going into the basement.

'Hey, time for a break. D'you fancy a swim?'

Jemma started, blinked and dragged her mind from the ruins of the battered European town in his novel to the peaceful mountain scene in reality. Her laptop told her it was nearly two-thirty, and Nate was standing in the veranda doorway, watching her.

She'd chosen to remain outside after she'd returned from her solitary short walk after lunch. Declining his offer to accompany her, she'd claimed that solitude was preferable for forming mental images of the current scene. The crisp mountain air had been invigorating, and she'd begun to understand why people settled in the area, even with its cold, snowy winters.

'Sounds great.'

Clear water to refresh her mind and body after the stimulating scene she'd been working on, intensifying the characters' relationship, forcing the hero to admit to himself he might have feelings for the heroine.

Standing in front of the wardrobe mirror, she scrutinised her figure in the blue one-piece swimsuit, bought in the January sales. Cloe had often told her she'd look great in a bikini, but she couldn't shake her own negative comparison with Vanessa.

She swivelled in a circle and decided she didn't look too bad. The alternative was not to use the pool at all. Shoulders squared, she splayed her fingers at her image and left the room.

Keyed up with anticipation, and needing to expend nervous energy, Nate powered up and down the length of the pool, checking for Jemma at every end.

Her appearance was worth every second of the wait, and he was grateful for the distance of the pool between them, and for the fact that only his head and shoulders were above water as his body immediately reacted to the perfection of hers.

A shade lighter than her eyes, the blue swimsuit moulded her breasts and shaped her alluring curves, drawing his attention to enticing thighs and shapely legs. He trod water, fighting for breath, his heart jolting as she balanced on the pool's edge and raised her arms. *Lord, what he wouldn't do for a camera right now.*

Her smooth dive shook what little equilibrium he had left, and with each stroke bringing her nearer he wavered between catching her in his arms and striking out past her to the other end. In the end he kicked to the metal ladder, grabbed it and waited, fascinated by the coiled knot of her hair dipping into the water at each turn of her head.

She executed a faultless turn, then twisted to swim back and hold onto the edge, breathing evenly, her shining eyes and radiant smile directed at him.

'I am now officially envious of you. This would be a perfect way to start any day—or, like now, to ease muscles stiff from sitting and typing.'

He had another way in mind, but refrained from voicing it, not wanting to diminish the moment.

He dog-paddled over to her. 'A tiled hole full of water impresses you more than everything else?'

'I *have* almost everything else—in a more economical price range, of course. You have top-range. I'm enjoying every moment, and I aspire to the comforts, but this is extra-special. One lap and I feel refreshed and alive.'

That's how I feel watching you swim, looking at you now.

'You've had lessons? That was a spot-on turn.'

'In my early teens, with a friend. She made the team and I got toned and fit.'

'I noticed.' He couldn't hold back his grin as his eyes followed the rise of her blush from her cleavage to her forehead.

She retaliated to his teasing, taking him by surprise. Placing her hands on his shoulders and pushing herself upwards, she thrust him under the water before sprinting away. He came up sputtering and followed, passing her halfway along. An easy flip-turn and he surfaced in front of her, forcing her to stop or crash into him.

She saw him and backed away. Pity… He might have had an opportunity to hold her.

'You wanna play, Jemma?'

'No.' She feigned innocence. 'I want to keep fit. How many laps have you done so far?'

'Wasn't counting. How do you get all that hair into that small knot?'

'Practice. You're in my way, Nate.'

'My apologies, ma'am.'

He dipped his head and moved aside, liking the fact that she was more at ease with him than she'd ever been. If this was what it took, he was prepared to swim any time of the day.

Jemma slowed her pace, her movements automatic, her body acutely conscious of Nate whenever he swam past, her mind recalling the strength of his muscles under her palms. And the invitation in his eyes as he'd asked if she wanted to play. She couldn't believe she'd dared to dunk him.

She lost count of her laps and stopped at the far end for a moment, taking deep breaths. He flicked her a grin as he turned, the force of his leg-thrust sending him a fair way underwater before he surfaced. She counted three power-ful arm swings, then took off again.

As they passed his fingers brushed against her and she faltered, almost going under. Trying to ignore the tingles dancing over her skin, she turned at the end, wondering if it had been accidental or if he'd repeat the action.

Instead he caught her by the arm, pulling her to a halt, reactivating the sensation. His other arm slid around her waist, supporting her, holding her captive. She couldn't speak, couldn't find her breath, and he wasn't immune. His chest was heaving for the first time since she'd entered the pool. Desire darkened his grey eyes and a yearning to wrap her arms around his neck flared inside her.

With a sudden shake of his head he refocussed, his raspy tone betraying how much he'd been affected.

'I'm heading out at the end of this lap. Take as much time as you like.'

A gentle caress of her cheek and he swam away, leaving her to scramble for the poolside and hang on. She watched his progress to the ladder, and if she hadn't still had that hand grip as he stepped up she'd have sunk as mind and body went to mush.

From shoulders to calves he was sculpted like an athlete, his taut, trim and tanned image broken only by leaf-green swimming briefs. He was temptation plus, glistening with water sheen, drops flying around him like diamonds as he shook his head.

Her mouth gaped and then dried up. She couldn't breathe, and if her heart beat any faster she thought it might implode. As he began to turn towards her, hand raised to wave, she pushed off, ducking her face into the pool, not wanting him to see her gawking at him.

Three laps later she climbed out, wrapped herself in a towel from the nearby shelf and went to her room. She neither heard nor saw Nate on the way.

Showered and dressed, she went onto her balcony for a few quiet moments to prepare herself for another editing session. There was a light breeze through the treetops, and the distant hum of traffic on the road and an occasional bird call were the only sounds. *Heaven.* She leant her head against the pillar and blanked the rest of the world out.

'Next week at the earliest.'

Nate's voice floated up from the veranda, startling her into the present.

There was silence for a moment, then, 'Nothing that I wouldn't leave to come if you need me, Tess. You know that.'

Jemma backed slowly away from the rail into her room and shut the door, wishing she hadn't overheard.

Nothing he wouldn't leave? What about his declaration of 'the sooner we finish the amendments the better'?

It wasn't until she was in bed, mulling over the events of the day, that she recalled him mentioning a Tess once before, during his phone call at Circular Quay. From his tone, she had to be a friend... Not her business.

She fell asleep, waking early from muddled dreams of hot encounters in foreign places and tender caresses in cool oases.

On being awoken by the sun she went straight to the pool, and Nate joined her after his run. After that, apart from breaks—one of which Jemma spent walking—they worked solidly through the day.

Watching some recorded news after dinner, Jemma realised he always fast-forwarded through any items involving terrorist action or the military.

Did they trigger bad memories? How many of the scenes he'd written had he witnessed? He showed no sign of traumatic stress, but then he'd hardly share personal information like that with her.

Saturday was a repeat of Friday up until mid-afternoon, when Nate came out onto the veranda, where she was working, wearing grey trousers and a green polo shirt. Fashion-magazine-elegant. His mobile lay loose in his hand.

'We have an invite from my friend Grant for dinner tonight. He and his wife, Susie, own a hotel in town. If you want to go in now, we can have a stroll around first. There's a couple of great bookshops you might like.'

She knew—had seen the websites when she'd researched Katoomba and hoped for a chance to visit them. Without hesitation she logged off, stood up and began to collect her belongings.

'Leave that to me. You go freshen up and change. It's

casual and friendly.' He gave her a smile no red-blooded woman could ignore. 'I'll give you fifteen minutes.'

His grey eyes twinkled, and if he'd been trying for severity in his voice he'd failed. The words sounded cajoling, seductive, as if he were suggesting more than a meal with friends.

A sense of excitement accompanied her up the stairs.

Nate, after admiring the view, took her computer and other paraphernalia inside and closed the drapes. He put food and water out for the kitten, and talked to her as if she understood.

'Am I losing the plot, Scamp?' She rubbed against his leg and he picked her up. 'Three weeks ago I was prepared to work from dawn to dusk to get these rewrites done. And I expected, or hoped, that she'd put in good hours too.'

Now he found himself thinking that they were going too fast. At this rate they'd finish within his two-week stipulation, and he'd have no excuse to go to Hahndorf. They'd have a contract tie and, assuming Brian did a deal for them, there'd be publisher's revisions to do. But she might not be involved with them, and it wouldn't be the same as working together.

He determined to spend some extra time on the storyline he was writing for her romance, and then...

He hadn't heard a sound, and yet he knew she was there. He spun round, clutching Milly to his chest, and recognised the blue patterned top from their first meeting, now teamed with blue trousers and black low-heeled shoes.

Her beauty caught his breath in his throat, and quickened his pulse as she turned from closing the stair gate to face him, dark blue eyes sparkling and red lips begging to be kissed.

Wishful thinking, Thornton. Cool down and get a grip.
'I've got two minutes to spare. Shall I go back up?'

The gentle taunt in her tone was rousing, causing his stomach to tighten.

'No.' It came out blunt and harsh, and she halted halfway across the space between them, eyes blinking in disbelief.

'Sorry. Let's settle Scamp and we'll head off.'

'Scamp?'

Eyes flashing, she took Milly from him, cradling the kitten to her body, sending his body into overdrive, and slapped her hand on his chest.

'Her name's *Milly*, Nate Thornton. Don't you *dare* teach her to answer to any other name or...'

'Or you'll revert to calling me Mr Thornton? Can't be having that, can we, Milly?' He tickled her ears and she purred. 'See—she likes my touch.'

He'd looked up at Jemma, and their eyes met as he spoke. If his had widened and darkened to the same awareness as hers they could be in trouble. Were they on the same wavelength? Imagining his hands caressing her body with gentle strokes?

Hell, now he was thinking the way *she* wrote. The sharp tug in his gut told him they'd better get out of here—now.

'Ready to go?' And he was sounding as raspy as she claimed his hero would when interacting with his heroine.

Unless he felt they were warranted, he didn't *do* explanations. With Jemma, he couldn't justify walking away unless she understood. By the end of their stint here she'd probably know his inner self better than Sam or his best mates. But not the deep stuff—not the dark side that kept him from bonding with women, the hard, frozen core preventing him truly trusting again.

He gave a self-justifying grunt as they approached the SUV and he activated the locks. She had personal issues not for sharing too.

Pausing for a moment with one hand on the driver's door,

he swiped the other across his mouth, then gave a wry grin.
He was sliding on ice and had no inclination to jump off.

'Alice got a grey kitten for her sixth birthday and named
her Rosebud…'

They were on the road to Katoomba and it was the first
time either had spoken since her blunt 'okay' to his curt
question.

The straightening of her body and her head-turn in his
peripheral vision told him he had her interest.

'I mean, fair go—what did she expect from Sam and I?
No way were we going to call *that* out when we went looking for her in the garden.'

He heard a stifled sound, suspiciously like a giggle, and
glanced sideways to see one hand trying to smother her
laugh and a sparkle in her eyes.

'So you dubbed her Scamp? I trust Alice got revenge.'

'Oh, yeah—with interest—a year or so later. He was an
Alsatian Labrador cross, big and butch and a great guard
dog. While we were out after school and on the weekends,
she taught him to answer to Snookums.'

Her unrestrained laughter delighted him, and he took
mock umbrage.

'Hey, do you have *any* idea how mortifying it is to have
your mates see the dog you've built up as a fearsome protector race off in answer to such a sooky name?'

By the time he'd described how they'd bribed Alice, persuaded their friends not to tell, and reinstated Wolfhound
as the only name the dog should respond to they were in
town and entering the car park behind his mate's hotel.

He parked, glanced at the names on the two texts that
had come through on the journey in, then put his phone into
his pocket. He saw Grant was busy behind the bar, so he
signalled that they'd be back and led Jemma onto the street.

* * *

Jemma usually loved browsing alone through bookshops, reading the blurbs on new or used novels of assorted genres, and also in second-hand emporiums, inspecting items for collector friends' birthdays or her own home. So why the hollow sensation in her stomach when Nate stopped at the corner, telling her he had to answer his messages?

'One's a client who wouldn't text unless he has genuine concerns, so I'm not sure how long it'll take. I'll catch up with you. Enjoy yourself—and remember we can pick up anything heavy or too big to carry later.'

He took advantage of a gap in the traffic and crossed the road.

She had no right or reason to complain—he'd told her where the bookshops were and given her freedom to wander at will. It was her own fault that she'd let herself look forward to his opinion on anything she might like.

With a sudden change of mind, she walked down a side street, intent on a different shopping trip.

An hour or so later, cheered up by her purchases, she was near the same corner, on the other side of the main street, debating whether to call Nate or stop for a drink alone. Her decision was made at the sight of him through a café window, still talking on his mobile.

His expression pulled her up short, and then had her racing past, praying he didn't look up and see her. That tender expression on his face had torn at her heart, reviving memories of her ex's ability for deception.

She circuited the block, disappointed at herself, and at the speed she'd judged him without justification. He was close to his parents and his siblings—it could be any one of those. Most likely his mother or sister. He owed *her* no emotional loyalty, and she had no right to expect any.

The café was not far ahead now, and she moved to the

kerb, ready to cross over and check from the other side. Her ringtone sounded as she looked to the left and she spotted him, phone to his ear, facing away from her.

She walked towards him, steeling herself to be cool and calm.

CHAPTER THIRTEEN

NATE SWIVELLED AS she came up behind him, his lips beginning to curl into a smile, then falling open as his gaze flitted from the bags in her hands to her face, and back. Twice.

'Someone having an irresistible "going out of business" sale? No sensible offer refused?'

There was genuine laughter in his tone, and her misgivings slid back to the deep, deep place they'd held for the last few years. She smiled, pleased there was no tension between them.

'I've written a novel—even if it's not publishable at the moment—and I have a contract to help revise yours to that status. I deserve to splurge on new clothes. So I did.'

He tucked his hands in the back pockets of his trousers, swaying on his heels, and his storm-grey eyes shone as if backlit by the sun. His quick appraisal of her from face to feet created in her a total body heatwave, and his wide smile sent her heartbeat into triple-time.

'Do I get a fashion parade when we get home?'

He arched his eyebrows like an old movie villain and laughter bubbled up inside her—followed by a sobering image of her sister on a catwalk. She'd never compete with her—wouldn't try—but the pain from this acknowledgment was less than usual.

'No, I'm not a model.'

'But you're beautiful, and every inch a woman. Let's put these bags in the car and have dinner. Maybe if I ply you with expensive wine you'll change your mind.'

Maybe it was his sincere compliment, or maybe she was happy with her new clothes. Or maybe it was purely the brush of his skin against hers as he took the bags from her that sent ripples of electricity across her skin.

One or all of them had her wishing with fervour that he'd take her hand and keep it in his as they strolled to his vehicle.

Jemma dozed on the way home, mentally tired from the day's revisions, her impulsive purchasing spree and staying up late talking to Grant and his wife, Susie. They and Nate shared the kind of close bond she had with Cloe and Mike, but they'd ensured she was included in the conversation.

Her sleepy thoughts churned through the comments Nate had made about his family, the group he belonged to in Sydney and his friends in the Blue Mountains. Did he keep them in isolated pockets of his life? Would they intermingle when he became a successful author? That he would had never been in doubt as far as she was concerned.

She would be an interlude for him. They'd finish the book, he'd help her with her basic storytelling and then learn to write his own personal scenes. She'd resume her solitary life in the Adelaide Hills.

She sighed, only realising it had been out loud when he spoke.

'Tired, Jemma?'

'Mmm. *Nice* tired.'

'Thank you for coming with me tonight.'

She was sinking into a haze of wanting something beyond her reach, so her weary brain must be imagining the emotion in his voice.

She woke at the gentle shaking of her shoulder, the husky sound of her name and hot breath tickling her earlobe. His features were as enticing blurred as they were when sharp and clear. And close enough to share a…

Her head jerked up, she blinked and her vision cleared— by which time he'd moved away.

Unbuckling her seat belt, she slid out and focussed.

'It's been quite a day. Thank you, Nate. I had a great time in town, and I like your friends.'

'The feeling was mutual. I've got your spoils from the trip.'

He held up both hands, clasping the labelled bags she decided she'd unpack in the morning.

'You go straight to bed. I'll see to Milly and meet you in the pool in the morning.'

Nate never bothered with lights on his way to bed, liking the peaceful aura of familiarity in the dark. Tonight, he paused outside Jemma's door, picturing her asleep. Did she curl into a ball, cuddle up to a pillow, or lie on her back? Whichever, her long silken hair would be splayed around her head, as he'd imagined before, and his fingers itched to thread their way through its strands.

She's a romantic lady. A true-love-for-ever lady. Be smart, Thornton, don't get involved.

But that didn't stop him having fantasies of her wearing whatever was in those five bags he'd carried in from the back of his SUV as he tossed and turned.

Whether it was yesterday's outing, dinner with Nate's friends or that morning's vigorous swim, something had energised Jemma. She set herself up on the veranda and lost herself in the intricacies of Nate's story. Breaks were taken at scene or chapter endings, and she found it easy to pick up the action on her return. It was enthralling.

She'd read the full manuscript again, and had reservations on his viewpoint over three of the relationship scenes. She debated whether to list and discuss them now, or deal with them as they were reached. Opting for the latter, she reasoned it would be clearer if the amendments had been done up to each point to be discussed.

Nate had settled inside, occasionally strolling round the house talking on the phone. On a quick trip to town he'd picked up newspapers, magazines and hamburger lunches. Neither of them had lingered over the meal, eager to get back to their individual pursuits.

The bubble burst mid-afternoon. She stared across the gully and huffed out a breath, her stomach churning. This encounter really didn't read true, and Nate wasn't going to like being told he'd got it so wrong. He'd accepted her critiquing and adaptations up to this point, though not without intense discussion. But this was major—a disagreement over his characterisation.

She reread his description of the moment his hero hitched a ride heading back to the capital. Going over it twice, even out loud, didn't alter her judgement. She'd promised him honesty, so that was what she'd have to deliver.

With a tight grip on the highlighted original, plus her revisions, she went inside, finding him sprawled in the lounge reading the financial news. A warm glow flared in his eyes and regret raked through her, anticipating their hardening at this criticism.

'Ready for a break…? Jemma, what's wrong?' He sat up, swinging his feet to the floor.

Her fingers tightened on the papers, and she struggled to swallow past her dry throat.

'This scene…their scene in her flat…'

His eyes darkened and narrowed, and the rest came out in a rush.

'It's *wrong*. He wouldn't cave in like that. Not him.'

Nate rose to his feet, fingers splayed at his sides, his chest puffed out. 'What the hell are you talking about?'

'He grabs her arm as they argue, she slams her hand on his shoulder and he *backs away*. Wouldn't happen, Nate. Not—'

He cut in, exasperation making the rough edge in his

voice hoarser. 'It happened before, in an earlier encounter, and you left it in. What's the difference?'

'*Them.*'

What kind of relationships did Nate have if he couldn't understand that continuing involvement meant more freedom of temperament—especially in tense or emotional situations?

'*Think* about it, Nate. He tried the he-man heavy tactics at their second meeting and she slapped him away. He backed off, as any decent man would. Right?'

Nate nodded with obvious reluctance, muscles tense.

'They've met quite a few times since, and had disagreements, but they can't stay away from each other. He's wound up after a traumatic night patrol, can't get her out of his mind, and he hitches a ride to her—not sure what to expect, but hoping she'll be eager to see him. She's not. Imagine how frustrated he'd be, knowing he only has limited time before reporting back.'

She could see Nate absorbing what she'd said, and instinctively moved closer.

'He'd take hold of her arm, probably more roughly than he intended, needing her to understand.'

Nate wrapped his fingers round her upper left arm, as if caught up in her narrative, drawing her body to his and causing her fingers to tighten on the printed sheets of paper. She struck his left shoulder, and in an instant play-acting ceased.

She was hauled against him and kissed with an ardency that scattered every coherent thought in her head. The papers fell from her hand as he released her arm, wrapping his arms around her and crushing their bodies together. Her fingers gripped his shoulders, then slid across his neck and into his thick, surprisingly soft hair.

Heat flowed through her veins as his heart pounded against her chest, and hers beat with a similar erratic rhythm. She answered the pressure of his lips with a passion that shook her to her core. Frightening. Exhilarating.

There was no day, no night—only this instance in time. And his low masculine growl mingling with her soft mews.

With a harsh gasp he broke the kiss and rested his cheek on her hair. Fighting for breath, she let her head fall to his shoulder, unable to speak, afraid that any words would diminish the moment.

'Jemma...' Her name had never sounded so special, so ethereal. So unique.

She looked up into dazed storm-grey eyes that mirrored her own bewilderment. The trembling of his fingers on her cheek and his rapid breathing were comforting—tangible indications that he was emotionally shaken too.

He kissed her forehead and eased away, holding her arms with a tenderness that allayed any feeling of loss. He swallowed, blew out air and then breathed in again, making a part-laugh, part-groan sound.

'Hell, that was... Jemma, I...I guess I just proved you were right.' He looked away, then into her eyes again, and gave her a wry smile. 'Let's go for a walk.'

She'd barely regained her composure and he'd shaken it again. Those last words were not what she'd expected to hear, yet they were entirely understandable.

A walk. Fresh air and open space. Room to think and process this—for her—emotionally traumatic happening. Room to recover from her tumultuous reaction to his touch and his kiss. Beyond that, she didn't dare anticipate.

'Yes. Let's.'

At first Nate fought the desire to lessen the gap between them as they walked, to take her hand and intertwine their fingers. He caved in before they reached the track through the trees, and the tight knot in his gut eased when she didn't resist.

His body hummed from the exhilaration of having her in his arms and that incredible kiss, like none he'd ever known. He'd been a hair's breadth from losing control, from sweeping her up and…

Don't go there.

For that blissful moment they'd been in tune—as one. He'd never believed it possible, deeming it a fantasy of fiction. Somehow he had to regain normality—though he feared he couldn't backtrack over the line he'd crossed. He had no idea how to explain his actions, and knew there was no way he could promise not to kiss her again. Hell, given the slightest encouragement he'd kiss her right now, and was well aware from her ardent response that she'd willingly kiss him back.

Or was she regretting her uninhibited reaction?

They had to set guidelines. He had to ensure she understood there'd be no rosy future, no wedding bells or settling down. For ten years he'd chosen women who accepted his terms and didn't ask for explanations. Jemma was different—she deserved the truth. Because it was he who'd broken the rules.

There was no pressure to begin a conversation, no urgency to bare his soul. He let himself live in the moment, surrounded by the sounds and smells of the bush and with Jemma's soothing presence by his side. She'd been as affected as he by their shared kiss, yet she now appeared calm. The tranquillity of this mountain area was once again weaving its magic.

He stopped by a group of gum trees, part of one split by lightning, leaning at an angle, its bare branches wedged solid in another. It had been like that for nearly two years, and he often leant against it while he took a break while running.

The undergrowth crunched beneath their feet as he led her over, let go of her hand and leant his back and elbows against the rough wood, its bark stripped away by the elements. Jemma stood on the down-sloping side, taking in the view, giving him the lead without pressure.

Staring straight ahead, he kept his voice level and radio-broadcaster-neutral.

'I'm assuming the reason for your move to Hahndorf was the result of a break-up? You'd have been twenty-five?'

She made no movement he could sense, and no sound, so he continued.

'When I'd just turned twenty-one, and had been requested to send in more reports for publishing, I thought I knew it all and could handle anything life threw at me. In truth I was *so* bloody green. I was an easy target for a woman whose only real interest was my family's money. I had a…a life-changing experience a few days after meeting her, and when she found me blind drunk in the bar of my hotel she was supportive and comforting. I was needy, immature and stupid.'

'Human—like us all.'

Looking sideways, he saw no condemnation in her eyes, only sympathy and understanding. Thankfully she didn't press for the details he'd buried with his shame. He turned towards her, fisting his fingers to prevent himself reaching out for contact. If she couldn't accept his proposition there'd be no touching, no kissing. No making love.

'I have my grandfather to thank for teaching me to always verify what I'm told, though I almost left it too late. Being fooled by her forced me to evaluate my future, who I really was. I stayed overseas, hopefully became wiser, and my perception of people and life altered. I know it's rarely black or white, more a murky shade of grey. I have family, who I love deeply, and friends I'd give my life for. Beyond them are colleagues and acquaintances I treat with courtesy but hold at a certain distance. I live a solitary life, and I intend to keep it that way.'

'For as long as you live?'

'Yes.'

Though he wasn't keen on her choice of wedding ceremony words, it meant she understood his resolve.

'And now? Are you involved with anyone?'

'If I was I wouldn't have kissed you, no matter how strong the temptation.'

Jemma heard the growl in his voice and sensed his resentment of her implication. Either the damage from that deception ran deeper than her own ex's betrayal, or there had been other disloyalties in his life.

Now was not the time to tell him or show him how mindblowingly incredible his kiss had been. How it had felt as if they'd been alone in the universe and how she ached for more. Whatever the future held, that memory would be enhancing and uplifting.

She moved in front of him, placed her hands on his chest and looked him straight in the eyes. He didn't blink, and held eye contact warily.

There'd be no shared expectations of a happy home with children playing in the garden. There'd be no cheating, lying or broken hearts. Her only remorse would come if she declined what he was offering and never experienced the full pleasure of the passion he'd shown in that kiss.

'I want you to make love to me, Nate Thornton. No promises of for ever, no lies, no regrets.'

She went up on tiptoe, pressed her lips to his, and with a deep guttural groan he swept her into his arms. His hands caressed from her shoulders to her hips. Her hands wrapped around his neck, holding him to her, her sigh catching in her throat.

Her pulse shot into overdrive as he pressed her body tight to his. She trembled when he kissed a trail across her neck to her lips. He teased them with the tip of his tongue and they parted, allowing him entry to caress and savour until her head spun and there was nothing in her world but him.

Time had no meaning until the need for air broke them apart. He cradled her head to his chest, brushing his lips over her forehead, his rasping breath stirring her hair. Though there was no gap between them she wriggled to get closer and he groaned again, this time even more roughly.

'Jemma, darling, there's a limit for every man, and I've just about reached mine.' He cradled her face in his hands and gave her a quick tender kiss. 'Let's go home.'

CHAPTER FOURTEEN

JEMMA STIRRED, HER muscles languid and unwilling to move, and snuggled into the warm muscular body alongside hers, her head pillowed on a mat of thick, wiry chest hair. The slightest shift might shatter her dream, and this euphoria could be nothing else.

Gentle lips caressed her forehead and soothing fingers roamed her back. This was reality—and more spine-tingling, toe-curling and floating-to-the-moon wonderful than any dream *ever*. Cosseted and treasured, she wanted to stay right there, forget the past and let the future take care of itself.

'Jemma...'

She burrowed deeper against him, tightening her hold around his waist, loving the sensual touch of his skin against hers, loving the heady combination of musk, citrus, vanilla and *him* teasing her every breath.

His throaty chuckle reverberated through her, startling her into opening her eyes. Pushing up onto one arm, he stroked her cheek, gazing down at her with such a tender expression it melted her heart.

'For a supposedly good author, I'm stuck for words.' He kissed her with soft reverence. 'I've never...' He stopped and looked away, as if uncomfortable with the words forming in his head.

She understood. How could she not when her mind was blank too—and she'd *never* had problems describing passionate encounters?

'Nate, I understand.'

He grinned, and brushed his thumb across her mouth 'I guess we have to write a new love scene, huh?'

'Mmm...' Falling asleep in his arms was her preferred option, but... 'So, working instead of TV tonight?'

'We should.' He bent and blew gently in her ear, laughing as she quivered. 'Would he do that?'

'Not him.' She ran her fingernails over his chest, loving the way he sucked in air at her touch.

'How about this?' He nibbled her neck and she wriggled.

'You should know. You created him.'

'Hey, I penned a fighter, not a lover.' He pulled her tighter against him and she didn't resist. '*You're* the one who claims he'd want intimacy after sex. I visualised him getting up and leaving once the deed was done.'

He twirled strands of her hair around his fingers and dropped a kiss on the tip of her nose.

'But now I figure he'd stay longer. For this.'

He covered her mouth with his, soft at first, then hotter and harder.

She caressed a path up his chest and around his neck, anchoring his head. He parted her lips, allowing him to deepen the kiss as he pressed her into the large, firm mattress.

They'd be in complete agreement over his hero's next action.

Nate had never had trouble with after-sex talk, the non-emotional aspect of his encounters ensuring there were no expectations of romantic platitudes like those in the book Alice had given him and in Jemma's novel.

Today he'd found himself fighting not to say them, biting them back as quickly as they arose. Telling her how special making love to her had been, that she was different from the others, didn't seem right when he couldn't promise a lifetime commitment.

She'd said no promises, no regrets. Alone in the kitchen, he was already regretting letting her go to shower in her own en suite, instead of with him, and that he hadn't planted rose bushes in the garden so he could pick her a bouquet.

He made coffee, wishing it were champagne, and set out biscuits, wishing they were her favourite handmade chocolates—whatever brand they were. He'd have to find out, even if it meant telling her more about himself.

She hadn't mentioned his scars, but she must have seen them even though they'd faded over the years. The jagged pale lines ran over his left hip onto his stomach, and probably wouldn't have been noticeable in the pool. But naked on the bed...

He sucked in air as she came down the stairs, looking so fresh and beautiful she scrambled his vocabulary, leaving him with an inadequate, 'Hi.'

Her face lit up and he was across the kitchen, taking her into his arms even before her, 'Hi, yourself!' left her lips.

He covered them with a long, satisfying kiss he never wanted to end. It was Jemma who eased herself from his embrace and tapped him on the chest—right over his racing heart.

'We're supposed to be *revising* a scene, Nate Thornton, not acting it out.'

The dazzling smile she gave him and the teasing note in her voice blew his mind. For a moment he imagined a lifetime of friendly teasing and laughter and rosy cheeks. Then he tamped it down. Lifetimes were for others—not him. However satisfying it was now, their relationship wouldn't—*couldn't*—last.

He gestured at the neat pile of papers on the dining table. 'I read them as I picked them up. Couldn't fault a word. Or an action.'

He emphasised the final word, recalling her responses to his caresses, and her immediate blush proved she was too. He trailed a fingertip path down her cheek to her chin, cupped it, and pressed a light kiss on her lips.

'Hold that thought until tonight, Jemma.'

They slipped into a flexible routine based around a wake-up swim and walking, and taking quiet breaks between writing sessions. Jemma declined to join Nate in his gym workouts, letting him work off steam alone, and stayed home when he went to fire training.

Only two incidents marred the following four days for her...

On Monday her mobile bleeped as she was cooking her special scrambled eggs for lunch. Probably Cloe sending a promised recipe, she thought, smiling to herself. They chatted every few days, though Jemma hadn't yet revealed where she was, or why.

She called out to Nate, dished up the food, and then sat at the table opening the email. Just to check. Her smile faded and she lost her appetite as her stomach sank.

Vanessa. Her sister had sent her customary reminder for what was, as far as Jemma was concerned, an over-the-top annual charity event she'd conveniently semi forgotten. Her day-to-day life was good, and she'd learned to handle the now dwindling number of bouts of social inadequacy. But being at that particular glamorous function always rekindled her Cinderella complex.

'Bad news?' Nate's genuine concern was comforting.

'Only for me. An evening in a huge room of A-class notables I have nothing in common with and have problems talking to, battling a throbbing headache even if I take tablets before.'

'Don't go.'

'My sister and her husband are on the organising committee. As far as they and my parents are concerned my attendance is compulsory.'

Without shame, he leant over and read the businesslike message. He frowned. 'For a sister, she's not very personal.'

'We're not close.'

'From this I wouldn't be able to tell you were related.'

She bristled at his criticism, even if she did agree. Different personalities and a six-year gap had been insurmountable for them.

'Have your lunch before it gets cold.'

He ate in silence, brooding for a few minutes before persisting with the subject. 'Why the reminder?'

'I decided not to attend three years ago, and pretended I'd forgotten when my mother asked if I'd booked my flights.' She scrunched her nose. 'Hence the reminder missive.'

His husky chuckle brightened her up.

'You always attend solo?' he asked.

She ignored his inference that she couldn't get a date.

'That year only—and Vanessa partnered me with a widowed bank manager in his forties. Nice enough guy, but... I have a bachelor friend who's been willing to act as escort since. I'll ring him and confirm the date.'

She lifted a forkful of eggs to her mouth and chewed, contemplating the inevitability of her fate.

Becoming aware of a difference in the atmosphere, she looked up to meet dark storm-grey eyes studying her with an intensity that made her body pulsate.

'You've already asked him?'

'He knows the date, so...'

His eyebrows arched and her throat dried. Why was he...? He couldn't be suggesting... By then the manuscript would be with Brian or a publisher for assessment, and she'd be painting and tending shop in Hahndorf.

'I am corporate-dinner-trained, and can produce references if required.'

He was joking, yet his voice held an edge reminiscent of their original encounter. She was speechless.

* * *

Nate was acting on instinct, reacting to the cold clamp in his gut when she'd casually mentioned this friend. A male friend. Her tone had negated any romantic connection, so he had no reason to be jealous. That he'd even *think* the word rocked him, making his statement come out more roughly than intended.

He tried to atone. 'Jemma Harrison, would you please allow me the honour of escorting you to your sister's charity do in Melbourne?'

His heart flipped at the sight of her flustered face; cheeks rosy, eyes glistening and her pink tongue licking lips that strove to form words. The tight clench of his stomach proved how susceptible he was to that natural action.

'You might be already booked that weekend.' Breathy. Unsure.

'I'll make sure I'm free.'

Seeing her sudden dazzling smile was like watching the sun rise over the mountains or appear from behind the clouds as the rain stopped. The world was clearer, brighter. A better place to live.

As long as he lived in the moment and didn't plan ahead.

The second incident occurred as they arrived home from a walk on Thursday afternoon. Nate had answered his phone and the female voice at the other end sounded distraught, though Jemma couldn't make out the words.

'Hang on, Tess.' He shrugged and gave Jemma a wry grin. 'I have to take this. Wanna make coffee?'

He brushed his lips over hers and went out onto the veranda.

Tess again. None of her business if his friend needed help. Except he didn't mention it when he came in, just thanked her for the coffee and resumed revising. She brushed her qualms aside, but the seed of doubt had been sown. How often did the woman call when she wasn't there, and why bother Nate with her problems?

A wisp of hair soft as Milly's fur tickled Jemma's face, slowly rousing her from sleep. She sighed, flicked her hand, encountering only air, and buried her face deeper into the pillow. It happened again, this time accompanied by a musky aroma.

She blinked, saw a shadowy figure and opened her eyes. Nate was hunkered down by the bed, his fingers waving strands of her hair over her cheek. It was the most delicious way to wake up—the perfect face to see when she did. And even better when he pressed his lips to hers, reigniting the fires that still smouldered from the night before.

'Good morning, sweetheart. It's Friday morning, and you need to get up. Breakfast in fifteen minutes. Casual dress code today.'

Propping herself up onto one elbow, she double-blinked as the force of his energy swept away any waking lethargy.

'You're lively this morning. I know what day it is, and I thought we—'

He was dressed in a lightweight navy top and chinos, rather than the T-shirt and shorts he favoured at home.

'You're going out?'

'We are.' He slid his hand round her neck, and caressed her cheek with his thumb. 'Do you trust me, Jemma?'

The wariness in his eyes tempered his excitement, and the firm line of his mouth conjured up an image of a small boy not sure if his Mother's Day present would be well received, fervently hoping it would.

'What have you done, Nate Thornton?'

'What? No Mr?'

He smiled and kissed her softly, then harder as her arms wound around his neck. He finally pulled away, breathing rapidly, sat on the edge of the bed and took her hands in his.

'Temptress! I made a vow the day we met. Now I'm hoping to honour it. Shower and pack for two nights in Sydney. I've got the support meeting tomorrow night, so you might like to stay over with Cloe then and I'll pick you up Sunday morning.'

He stood up and strode to the door, looking back and winking before disappearing. She stared at the ceiling, wondering what he had planned. They had six full chapters and a few pages to go, and would have had no problems finishing by Monday—Tuesday at the latest. Probably wouldn't if they spent two days away.

Was he deliberately delaying her departure?

A quiver of delight vibrated along her spine at the thought. She had no illusions of a long-term romance—he'd been adamant on that score. There was, however, the possibility of a continuing professional relationship if she was needed. By email, as urgency wouldn't apply.

Springing from the bed, she gathered up her clothes and shoes and raced naked to her room. Warm weather was predicted, so she wore blue trousers and a new floral top. Remembering the sparkle in his eyes, she packed a new dress, guessing there'd be a restaurant meal included in his plans.

Nate tapped his fingers on the steering wheel, out of tune with the music, as they sped along the highway. Should he have told her before they left? If he told her now and his surprise upset her he wouldn't be able to pull over and reason with her.

'Is everything okay? You look worried and you're tapping.'

He flicked her a smile, liking the way she was concerned about him. He wasn't so sure about her growing insight into his character and what motivated him. Or why he was so determined to be with her in Melbourne and escort her to that function, three weeks in the future. When she would be back in Hahndorf.

'We'll talk in the unit.'

She didn't push the subject and he relaxed. He'd be disappointed if she refused, but it wouldn't be the end of the world.

They arrived at the unit about eleven, having stopped on the way to pick up sandwiches. Nate left Jemma to release Milly and make coffee while he took their suitcases to his room. On returning, he took two recliners and a low table onto the balcony, and set them up so they had a view of the city centre and the bridge.

Delaying his moment of revelation, he voiced the question he'd pondered since being told the name.

'Why Milly?'

Lord, she was gorgeous when she was surprised. Her wide-eyed reaction brought back memories of Alice on Christmas mornings, when his world had been safe and full of fun and laughter. He waited, his chest tightening with pride as he sensed the second she decided to trust him with a personal anecdote from her past.

'Milly was a favourite cartoon character from my early childhood. She was adventurous and feisty—everything I wanted to be at that age and never was. Best of all, she was funny-looking, with a button nose and frizzy hair. I've never forgotten the way she never let that impact on her zest for life, even if I'm not very good at emulating her.'

He dumped his mug on the table, moved across to sit beside her, did the same to her mug and gripped the sides of her seat with his hands, leaning over her.

'You've lost me. There's an implication there that you're neither pretty, courageous nor spirited.'

She shrank away from him and he gave a huff of disbelief, took her hands in his.

'You are *beautiful*, Jemma Harrison. Exquisite and smart. You wrote a book, had the courage to send it to an agent and didn't give up when he gave you honest criticism. You put your own work aside and chanced coming here to help me achieve the goal you wanted for yourself.'

His heart blipped and his pulse raced as her fingers trembled in his, her chin lifted and her lips curled into a shy smile.

'Your book was so much closer to deserving publication.'

'You've shown sheer guts and generosity of spirit, darling. Now, can we harness that spirit for something special? I've booked us in for a walk over the top of the bridge.'

She gasped, and he bent his head to kiss her, smothering any protest. The softness of her lips, her unique Jemma aroma and the caressing touch of her fingers sliding around his neck shot every thought bar one from his head.

CHAPTER FIFTEEN

JEMMA COULDN'T SEEM to focus when he rested his forehead on hers, allowing her space to drag in short puffs of air. How could one man have the power to muddle her thinking and reduce her body to malleable clay?

The bridge? A climb? Reason rushed back and she pushed at his chest, forcing him to lean away, one hand settling by her thigh, the other arm lying across his.

'You think I'm too scared to do it? We're up high *now* and I don't have a problem.'

'Not with fear. Heck, I think you'd tackle a tiger if the need arose. You're a delightful mixture of self-assurance and insecurity, Jemma. You're confident of your ability to paint, to write about intense personal relationships and maintain long friendships. And yet...'

He flicked a hand towards her mobile on the dining table.

'All those photos on your phone—are any of you?'

'They're inspiration for my miniatures, and I'm the one taking them.'

No way can I compete with Vanessa, and nor do I want to be compared with her.

Yet she'd agreed to his escorting her to the Melbourne function.

'You don't like being in front of the camera. The bridge walk, a tandem skydive—they take photos as mementoes, and other participants take shots too. Come with me, Jemma. You don't have to pose, and we won't buy any copies of the photos if you don't want to. Please.'

She looked into the man's eyes seeing a boy's pleading

expectancy, and was overcome by a surge of regret for all the activities she'd denied herself because she'd judged herself inferior to her sister.

'I'm not agreeing with you, but I'll come to prove you wrong.'

With a triumphant, *'Yes!'* he kissed her again.

'You'll love it—and there's an extra surprise tonight.'

'I'm not abseiling down a building in the dark.'

His roar of laughter warmed her from head to toe. Their time together might be short, but she'd have a lifetime's store of precious memories.

Jemma's enthusiasm for the climb grew with each mandatory action—filling out forms, locking away all personal items and wriggling into blue overalls. She listened carefully to the safety talk, conscious of Nate watching her for any sign of nerves.

Every rung of the ladder and each long, flat step taking her higher was empowering. She wanted to surge ahead, race to the top and spread her arms in triumph. Whenever they stopped, she memorised the view, storing it for future moments of self-doubt.

Nate followed her, seemingly enjoying her reaction more than his own experience. Having already been up there, he pointed out the ferry route through The Heads to Manly, the location of the zoo and of his apartment. And he sneaked in a few kisses when she smiled at him.

He put his arm around her for the group photo on the way up, and at the very top joined in her triumphant gestures and laughter. His proud smile thrilled her as her pose leaning back against the sky was snapped for immortality. Together at the edge, he wrapped his arms around her for a single photo, then kissed her with a tenderness that had her melting against him.

The thumbs-up from their camera-clicking guide told

her it hadn't been a sudden whim. She didn't care. She was on top of the world, living out a fantasy she'd given scant thought to—if any. Even if she never did anything else extreme in her life, she'd proved she could and would.

That evening, she stood in front of the full-length mirror, her euphoria from the day's achievement undiminished. She looked good. No, dammit, she *glowed*, and she was stylish enough to compete with the women on the social pages of weekly magazines. Maybe…

Conceding that Nate had been one hundred per cent responsible for her buying this new dress, and for her taking extra time and care with her make-up, she twirled for effect. Staring at her unfamiliar reflection, she relished her new self-confidence—short-lived though it might be once he no longer needed her.

Not unless she let it.

Brushing the negativity away, she picked up her new evening bag from the bed and gave a final spin for luck, loving the way the box pleats flared.

Where *was* she? Nate paced the open-plan area, leant on the back of the modular couch for a moment, then made another circuit.

He glanced at his watch. No problem with time yet, and he *had* told her to dress up for dinner.

Where *was* she?

Her elation hadn't diminished one iota since her jubilant moment on top of the bridge. And on the way home she'd studied the photographs he'd purchased as if reliving her success.

She'd looked so incredibly beautiful, so full of joy, that he'd bought two copies of every one they were in, intending to frame some. And that was part of his dilemma. He didn't want to let her go, leaving him behind with only images of her on his walls.

She'd insisted on working, and they had finished another chapter before showering and changing. Was she eager to return to her solitary life in the Adelaide Hills? It didn't seem that way to him when they made love. Her responses were as passionate as any man could ever desire. And more. She—

She was here.

He pivoted. His chest tightened, his heart lodged in his throat, and a voice drummed in his head. *Keep her. Keep her.*

She was radiant—a glorious vision in red leaving him lost for words. She'd turn heads, and he wasn't sure he was happy with the concept that most of them would be male. How could she not realise how sexy she was in that dress, with the bodice hugging her delectable body and those pleats drawing his eyes to her lovely legs?

His own legs were none too steady as he stepped forward and took her hands in his, not sure whose fingers were trembling.

'You are *gorgeous*, Jemma.'

Her smile and the shimmer in her dark blue eyes made him regret his limited vocabulary in such a situation. He racked his brain for one of the phrases she'd attributed to his hero, felt like he was battling fog, and drew her against him instead.

It was a gentle kiss. Until her soft lips stirred his desire and he wrapped her into a tight embrace.

The sound of his ringtone broke them apart, earning a guttural objection from him. Their taxi had arrived downstairs.

He deliberately left a gap between them in the back seat, and pressed his fingers to his thighs to avoid pulling her to his side. He needed the space to regain control.

As they drove onto the bridge Jemma placed her hand on his arm, pointing upwards. 'I was up there, Nate, right on the top arch. Because of *you*.'

Her eyes sparkled and warmth spread from her touch. Would she now be receptive to other challenges?

'About those other extreme activities, Jemma…?'

She laughed, reminding him of a bubbling mountain stream, making him wish they were on the way home, not heading out for the evening.

'Uh-uh. I'm going to write my own list.'

'Do I get an invite to join you?'

'Do you want one?'

Her eyes, dark and teasing, were issuing a challenge no man could resist. He cradled her cheek in his hand and covered her sweet red lips with his, forcing himself to keep the kiss light and short. Later there'd be the ride home…to his big, welcoming bed.

Jemma thought she'd burst with happiness as Nate helped her from the cab. She craned her neck to stare at the high-in-the-sky restaurant she'd pointed to…was it only four weeks ago? It had been a life-changing month.

'You remembered, Nate!'

'Everything you've ever said to me, Jemma.'

Hand in hand, they walked inside to the allocated lift that sped them skywards in seconds, and she couldn't hold back her, 'Wow!' of joyful surprise.

Nate had booked window seats which were facing inland when they arrived. The circular room was packed, and the hum of happy patrons filled the air. The revolution was slow and hardly noticeable unless they watched the view changing outside. The city light show seemed to go on for ever, broken only by intermittent dark patches of undeveloped land.

Jemma was entranced, and didn't want to miss a single moment. 'It's fascinating. Utterly different to Windy Point.'

'Better?' Nate teased.

'I'd never try to compare them—or your views in Katoomba. And *you* must have seen some unforgettable sights abroad?'

She had a brief glimpse of something dark in his eyes as he swung his head towards the window. It had gone when he turned back to greet the drinks waitress.

Once she'd left they had a quick scan of the menu, then he sent her to the impressive array of serve-yourself food. She did a full circuit before making her selection.

'That's all you're having?' His eyebrows arched at the small portions on the plate she'd brought to the table.

'This time. There's so many nationalities—too many choices for one visit. Oh, what's that weird structure coming into view?'

They ate, talked and laughed. Nate's knowledge of buildings and landmarks was surprising, considering the years he'd spent overseas. And there were so many intriguing designs and shapes that Jemma would have happily drawn out the meal even longer, and vowed to come back with Mike and Cloe on a special occasion.

In the taxi on the return trip Nate drew Jemma close and cradled her head on his shoulder. She sighed, and nestled deeper into his side.

'Today was magic, Nate. A mere thank-you seems inadequate.'

He cupped her chin with gentle fingers, his eyes scanning her beguiling face and his body aching with anticipation of the night ahead. He couldn't repress his rough growl of contentment as his lips settled over hers.

Later, with Jemma asleep by his side, he lay awake staring at the night sky, dark memories clouding his mind, activated by her innocent remark. Some sights were better left forgotten. There'd been no reason for them to surface—

though his recent calls from Dave and Tess and thoughts of tomorrow's meeting, might have activated them.

Sunday afternoon's trip home was delayed by Mike and Cloe insisting Nate stay for coffee, rather than just taking off with Jemma. Knowing how fond they were of her, he didn't mind, but he was eager to return to Katoomba, to spend what time they had left together away from noise and other people.

He'd missed holding her last night, needing the comfort she gave him. He'd opened up more with the support group than he ever had before during the evening—another small step forward. However, he was still light years from believing that one day the damage he carried would lessen.

His spirits lifted with every kilometre they drove towards his home. Accepting that she'd be leaving within days, he determined to make every minute count. Morning swims, talks on a variety of subjects as they walked and watching television curled together on his roomy couch would be enjoyable preludes to having her warm and loving in his bed at night.

The downside would come with the progress they made on the manuscript. Every chapter, every page, every word he accepted as printable would bring her departure closer. And the Melbourne trip seemed too far away, like having to count the days down to Christmas as a child.

The following Sunday afternoon, he went out to the veranda where she was working, knowing that being out here alone would never feel the same as it had two weeks ago. He hunkered down by her recliner and kissed her, savouring the moment, exhilarating in the passion she returned. He had trouble controlling his breathing when he raised his head.

'How will I ever get any writing done without you?'

Her blue eyes clouded, intensifying his own regret that she'd be leaving soon.

'Easier, I guess, without distraction.' Brave words spoken with a tremble.

'The most engaging, welcome distraction a man could wish for.' He kissed her again, lifted her computer from her lap and placed it on the deck. 'I have something for you.'

He handed her a blue folder, labelled on the front with her name. Inside was a wad of printed pages, with her book title as the heading.

'I've expanded and hopefully improved your narrative. You can edit as you feed it in—I'll email a copy to you now I've given this to you.'

Her reaction was as illuminating as a sunburst on an autumn day, blue eyes shining, skin glowing and a beaming smile that sent his pulse soaring.

'How…? When did you manage…? I… Thank you, Nate.' She ran her fingers over the cover as if it were long-sought-after treasure.

Her delightful fluster made the time spent skim-reading the paperback romances he'd taken from Alice's collection in the Sydney apartment worth every tooth-grinding minute. Now, contrary to his own wishes, he had to bring them both down to earth.

'Have you phoned Meg?'

Her smile faded and he couldn't resist kissing her again—quick and light.

'I feel the same, Jemma. Does she need you?'

'She said she can manage, but…'

'We said two weeks only. As things are you'll be finished on Tuesday, and the only flight with pet allocation before the weekend is Wednesday morning. I don't w—'

She pressed her fingers to his lips.

'I know. You'd better book it before someone else takes the spot.'

He nodded, stood up, then hunkered down again.

This kiss was firmer, longer. Hungrier.

Jemma had always loved airports, with their sense of adventure, of jetting off to new and exciting places. Not today. Every muscle was taut with the effort not to break down, her eyes kept misting, threatening to flood with tears, and her heart hurt.

She refused to look at the clock—didn't want to know how little time she had with Nate, who had his arms around her. He'd hardly been out of her sight today, hardly said a word on the drive from Katoomba—but then neither had she. Even Milly had been quiet, as if sensing their mood.

'Jemma?' His voice had never sounded so husky, as if choking in his throat.

She looked up, and her heart squeezed at the sad expression in his storm-grey eyes.

'Hell, it's gonna be a long two weeks.'

An eternity. During heart-wrenching talks they'd agreed he'd come to Hahndorf on the Wednesday before the function, and that they'd fly to Melbourne on the Friday. In the meantime, he'd do a final read-through, send his novel to Brian and visit his parents on the New South Wales coast for a few days.

She'd serve in the shop, paint and begin merging his new text into hers.

There would still be too many empty hours.

The airline staff moved to the check-in point and the passengers began to line up.

Nate kissed her as if his life depended on holding her close, and didn't pull away even when her flight was called.

She was the very last person to board.

CHAPTER SIXTEEN

NATE HAD NEVER been so frustrated in his life. Dressed and ready to go to the charity event, he paced the floor of the suite Jemma had booked at the venue complex months ago. His query as to why she wasn't staying with her sister had received a succinct, 'My parents do. I don't.'

A week ago, he'd put her increasing edginess over the phone down to nerves due to the upcoming function. Now he was convinced of the fact. He'd gone to Hahndorf hoping to coax her into telling him what she feared. Instead she'd refused to discuss it, blaming her headaches on too much painting and typing.

Baloney—she *loved* creating her miniatures, had never had even a slight headache in the time they'd been together. But without knowing the exact problem he could only keep reassuring her that everything would be okay.

Brian's email on Thursday, telling them he was in negotiations with a publisher, had perked her up, and they'd celebrated at a local restaurant. In the morning her tension had resurfaced.

He checked his watch, brushed a non-existent hair from his cuff and tried not to picture her staying here, or at any other hotel, with her 'bachelor friend.'

Impatient to see her, he strode to the bedroom, pulling up short in the doorway.

His eyes focussed on the motionless figure by the window—the entrancing woman who'd somehow become part of his life. She'd teased and cajoled him into reframing so many scenes in his book, forcing him to re-evaluate the bad experiences he'd depicted. Making him a better author.

Stunning, so entrancingly feminine, she'd twined strands of her hair into a knot at the back of her head, but thankfully left the rest to flow down her spine, over the shimmer of silver blended with shades of blue and green moulding her slender form. The full-length gown had thin shoulder straps, and thankfully the only jewellery he could see was a watch on her left wrist.

His chest swelled with pride at being her chosen escort, his pulse raced at the prospect of holding her as they danced and his heart... His heart never wanted to let her go. His head still doubted his capacity to forget, forgive and fully trust.

'Jemma.'

He spoke softly, as steadily as his choked throat would allow, and held his breath as she turned toward him.

His world spun out of orbit, and not one of the thousands of words in his vocabulary came anywhere near to describing the emotion in that split second when their eyes met. That ticking of time when nothing was hidden and their souls were bared.

She blinked and it had gone, replaced by the insecurity that she denied was there. He walked across and caressed her cheek as lightly as he would a baby's.

'Enchanting. You leave me speechless, Jemma. I'll be the envy of every man in the room.'

She dropped her head to break eye contact, and spoke in a whisper. 'Not true, but thank you for the compliment.'

He growled in exasperation, tilted her chin up and stared into her dark blue eyes. They were wary and unsure. He knew nothing he said would change her mind-set at this moment. Instead he took the necklace and bracelet of interlaced gold strands from his pocket and held them up.

'I figured these would suit any colour you wore. A gift for all you've given me.'

* * *

Jemma tried to say thank you through her strangled throat. If only she could open up and explain how it felt to live in someone's shadow without sounding needy. She couldn't, and in a few moments, he'd be able to compare for himself when she introduced him to Vanessa.

'They're lovely. Thank you, Nate.'

Breathy and overwhelmed, she trembled at the touch of his fingers as he fitted the necklace and caressed her arms. His soft kiss on her bare shoulder increased her longing to close the door and stay here. Alone with him.

'Ready?'

She'd never be ready to walk into a roomful of elite society couples—especially tonight on Nate's arm. His height, sculpted build and striking features, along with the comfortable ease with which he wore his black suit and bow tie, were going to draw the eyes of any available woman. And many who weren't.

The reception area was ablaze with lights, reflecting the colours and sparking jewellery of the people queuing up to be greeted on their way in to the dining room. Jemma wished she could guide Nate to *any* line bar the one where her sister and brother-in-law held court. But better to get the introductions over now, when there was no time to stop and chat.

'This way. I have to say hello to Vanessa and Anthony.'

He looked ahead, stared for what seemed like an eon, then faced her with a stunned expression.

'You and she are *sisters*?'

Even though she'd believed herself ready for any comparison, she felt her world shatter. Over the years she'd become accustomed to similar remarks, but coming from him it cut deep. It took every ounce of fortitude she had not to flee the building, and to feign a smile and nod before taking a step nearer to the pain of introduction.

Jemma could never tell if Vanessa's greetings were genuine or part of her social persona. She smiled, returned her sister's hug and air-kiss, then clenched her stomach as she turned towards Nate.

'My friend Nate Thornton. Nate—my sister, Vanessa, and her husband, Anthony Bradshaw.'

She saw Vanessa's green eyes widen, and couldn't bear to see Nate's smile focussed on her, so moved quickly to greet Anthony. He was nice enough in his own way, but she believed both of them cared more about their social standing than the people they associated with in order to get there.

As the men shook hands the announcement for everyone to take their places at the dinner tables was made. Theirs was to the side and one row back, and the other eight guests were already seated. After an exchange of names Nate held her chair as she sat, brushing his fingertips down her arm before taking his place.

She smiled, joined in the conversation and ate the food placed in front of her, all the while wishing she'd never agreed to him coming, wishing she wasn't here. And vowing never, *ever* to come again.

Throughout the meal and the inevitable speeches Nate found reasons to touch her arm, nudge her knee with his or murmur compliments in her ear. An ideal date—if he hadn't also kept glancing with a puzzled frown towards Vanessa at the main table. That she understood. It was his tender attention to *her* that was puzzling. Unless he was maintaining a façade.

Tables emptied as the band began to play, and she half hoped, half dreaded his asking her to dance. He didn't— just took her hand and drew her to her feet, his eyes saying he'd brook no refusal.

Ignoring convention, he held their clasped hands on his chest over his heart, and brushed her forehead with his lips. Overwhelmed by his innate strength and power, she breathed in musky vanilla and Nate and let the world fade away until there was only them and the music.

If anything, Nate's exasperation had grown during the evening. He felt her tension dissipate as they danced, and berated himself for never making the time to dance before, but then relaxed and savoured the sheer joy of the way they fitted together and moved in harmony. He'd never been so in tune with anyone, and his avowed defences for protecting his heart were crumbling, leaving him exposed and vulnerable. And unable to regret it.

She took him to meet her parents and he liked them—though it was obvious within a few minutes that their world revolved around cooking and their restaurant.

Jemma had told him she always left as early as possible, so he was quite willing to go when she asked. The shadows round her eyes revealed her fatigue to him, though she'd sparkled for everyone else.

She left space between them on the way to their suite, and neither spoke, but as soon as he closed the door she turned to him, her features guarded.

'I'm very tired, Nate, and I'd like to sleep alone tonight.'

He reeled back as if he'd been punched in the stomach.

'Why? That's no reason to shun me, Jemma. You know I'd never ask for anything you're not willing to give.'

Her eyes flashed with anger, and if his own temper hadn't been rising he'd have found it stimulating. She'd never shown this spirited side—not even when he'd baited her in Brian's office.

'No, you were brutally honest, and I was never in doubt over the terms of our relationship. Your page-turning text and my emotional scenes complement each other. We've each gained what we wanted, and I don't regret a moment.'

'That's a damn lousy explanation, Jemma.'

He moved towards her and she backed away, breathing

hard and fast. He stopped, hands clenching and splaying at his sides. What the hell had he done? What the hell had changed?

'It's all I can give. You wanted no commitment, no ties. That's what you've got.'

She spun round and, before he could react, was in the bedroom with the door shut.

Pride stopped him from trying the handle and calling her name. Glaring at that barricade and raking his fingers through his hair didn't give him any explanation. Neither did taking a cold shower and going over every action of the day.

Nothing eased the pain of her rejection, and there was no one he could call to talk it out. He could only pray he'd be able to fix it in the morning.

Jemma changed and packed by the light on the bedside table, chiding herself for allowing herself to be so vulnerable and praising her strength in standing firm. Better the pain of a break-up now than the agonising anticipation of its coming.

He'd warned her, and she'd accepted the risk. No promises of for ever. No lies. No regrets. The defences she'd built to protect her heart had been successful until now because she'd never truly loved her ex, nor more than *liked* the other men she'd dated. But Nate had slipped past her barriers and she'd foolishly dared to dream of storybook endings.

Even if what he felt was only masculine admiration for her sister's beauty, she didn't want to live with the comparison. She was what she was, and would no longer settle for being an also-ran. He'd move on, and he still had this Tess to talk to. Whatever that relationship entailed. She didn't know because he'd never explained their connection.

She would… Hell, she had no idea *what* she'd do.

In the early hours of the morning she crept from the

suite, booked out and took a taxi to the airport. By late morning she was home, picking up Milly from her neighbour and ignoring her message bank.

She imagined Nate's brow furrowing, and his storm-grey eyes darkening. Knew he'd be pacing as he waited for her to answer. Knew it wasn't right to leave him dangling.

She sent a text.

Believe me, Nate. It's better this way. We can communicate through Brian on any writing issues.

Cradling Milly for support, she lay on her couch and bit into the soft flesh at the base of her thumb to prevent herself crying.

It didn't work. She sobbed until there were no more tears to shed. Then, after taking a deep lung-filling breath, she pushed herself to her feet, huffed it out and went to splash her face with cold water.

Life didn't stop just because you'd been a fool.

Two afternoons later she wasn't so sure. Unsuccessful attempts to paint or write had left her restless, and long meandering walks no longer soothed her soul. She missed Nate—his gentle touches, his sombre expression that morphed into a heart-stopping smile in an instant. His ardent loving that took them to a world only they could share.

Oh, how she ached to see that smile focussed on her just once more. No, not once—a hundred thousand times more. When she woke in the morning, over the breakfast table, in the evening watching the sunset and in all the special moments in between. And most of all as he cradled her to sleep at night, watching her with tender storm-grey eyes.

It seemed like a lifetime since she'd last heard his unique husky voice—except in her head as she relived their conversations and the sexy teasing words he'd whispered in her ear as they lay in bed.

She'd begun to trust his word, and had sometimes thought, *Maybe this time...* It was the unspoken—those moments of silent contemplation and the times when his eyes had shuttered over a world he kept hidden—that had held her back. And the female voice of Tess and her sister's lovely face clouded her mind when she tried to think.

Her paintbrushes were dry, her keyboard silent and her inspiration absent and unattainable. Without closure she couldn't continue the revisions in her novel, couldn't move forward.

Catching up her phone, she walked outside and sat on the swing, scrolled through her contacts and pressed his name, then stared at the number she'd unknowingly memorised.

He hadn't called since she'd sent her text. Would he talk to her now? He'd wanted to talk on Saturday night, but she'd felt too raw and insecure, too unsure of his motives.

Oh, Nate, why did you hide what you went through from me? Why ask for my trust yet not give me yours? Why can't I tell if you love me?

She sucked in a deep breath, remembering her declaration about recognising love when she saw it. Had she subconsciously been so determined to avoid being hurt again that she hadn't recognised the pain in his eyes? Was he trapped in his past too?

A crazy idea, worthy of her most feisty heroine, shot into her head. Before she lost her nerve she went inside and booted up her computer, crossing her fingers for one piece of luck.

Hours later she slipped into bed, calmer and more optimistic than she'd ever been.

A lifetime of being non-confrontational, of quietly conforming while Vanessa bathed in the limelight and of accepting her ex's excuses and lies without question was over.

Tomorrow—against all the odds—she'd fight for a happy future. If it wasn't to be with Nate, at least she'd know she was strong enough to make it alone.

Nate was up before dawn, prowling from room to room, gut churning, fingers tapping on his thigh, for once oblivious to the scenic views. The plans he'd drawn and amended, the research into furniture and colours incorporating ideas from his global travels and the time and effort he'd put in all withered into insignificance.

His house, *his* home, had been built to suit a perceived lifestyle that no longer applied. Every room reminded him of Jemma. Every intake of air recalled her unique aroma, though it was no longer there. Every sound had him looking round in expectation of her presence. She was in his head...and in his heart.

He wanted her with him, here or anywhere in the world, every day for the rest of their lives. Running until his muscles burned hadn't helped tire him. Lying awake, yearning to feel her soft steady breathing against his chest, had left him antsy and short-tempered.

He'd been an idiot—so focussed on never being fooled again he hadn't seen the sweetest prize of all waiting in front of him. How could he have so totally misread the most important relationship of his life?

He stopped short at the sight of Milly's bed in the lounge area. Hell, he even missed that little fur ball. He'd bet she missed him too—she'd always loved him scratching behind her ears, or tickling her as she rolled onto her back. And Jemma? Did *she* miss his caresses, his kisses? Their making love?

It couldn't end like this.

Letting loose with a fervent curse, he stormed into his bedroom, accessing flight times on his mobile as he went. No suave persuasion or coercion this time. Like the hero he'd created, he'd fight for the woman he loved. Or at the least learn the reasons why.

As he packed he pictured her eyes. Big, blue and sparkling with exhilaration as she'd stood on the top of the Harbour Bridge. Soft and misty after they'd made love. And that was the image he clung to as he drove towards Sydney, towards the plane that would take him to her.

With time to spare at the airport he sat in the departure lounge and hooked one ankle over the other knee, forming a place to balance the clipboard and the sheet of paper he'd brought with him. With Jemma's image as inspiration he wrote from his heart, holding nothing back.

Reality hit home as he watched a woman trembling with anticipation as she scanned the passengers arriving in the lounge opposite, and then heard her cry of joy as she raced into a passionate embrace. Jemma hadn't been happy at his unannounced initial arrival in Hahndorf, and he had less reason to expect a welcome now.

Would she even be there?

His body taut as a drum, he walked while he accessed her number, holding his breath and willing her to answer. He almost buckled at the knees when she did. Tuning out the somehow familiar noise in the background, he heard only the sound he longed for.

'Nate?'

'Jemma, please. I need to see you. Are you at home?'

She didn't reply. His heart sank, but then picked up a little. At least she'd answered after seeing his ID.

'Jemma, please.'

A soft sound like a sigh came over the line, tripping his heart, then a hesitant voice. 'I'm on the Katoomba train.'

CHAPTER SEVENTEEN

'WHAT?'

The familiar noise. The train.

Nate's mind boggled at the irony of their timing.

'You're coming to me? Hell, Jemma. Of all the crazy…
No, not you, darling. *I'm* the one who's been a fool.'

'I've been trying to decide when to call you, or whether
to take a taxi and simply turn up.'

Just as he had. He was stunned by her actions after she'd
broken all contact with him. Adrenaline spiked, followed
by a cold chill of the knowledge that he might have lost her
for ever. It was soon replaced by the primitive male urge
to fight for his mate against any odds.

'Oh, Jemma, my angel. If I'd known I'd be waiting at the
station now. As it is we have a slight problem.'

'You're not at home?'

She sounded disappointed and his hopes soared.

'That's what we get for not communicating, sweetheart.
I'm waiting for my flight to Adelaide.'

'Oh.'

Picturing her sweet soft lips forming an O, and her lovely
blue eyes widening in surprise, he ached to comfort her.

Jemma stared at the mountain scenery rushing by, seeing
only Nate's magical smile, shaking with the intensity of
the elation flooding her. The last skerrick of doubt that she
loved him had dissipated. But whether they'd stay together
depended on an honest, nothing-held-back discussion.

He was on his way to Hahndorf, expecting to surprise her
as he had before. And a man who called her either 'darling,'

'my angel' or 'sweetheart,' in almost every sentence, even while agitated and under pressure, *had* to care. Could she dare to believe he loved her?

She let her head fall back onto the seat. Her heart was racing, she was smiling and her head was spinning in the nicest possible way.

'How far out are you, Jemma?'

'About an hour.'

'Okay, I'm heading for the check-in counter to ask them to unload my luggage. I'll call you in a few minutes. Don't go anywhere.'

'Hardly an option on a moving train. Except to Katoomba.'

'Except to there. Wait for me, darling.' He hung up.

Jemma ended the call with trembling fingers. So much for being calm and cool when they met. She'd become emotional even at the sound of his deep voice with that sexy hint of abrasion. Add his unique Nate aroma and enigmatic aura and she'd crumble at his feet.

'Well, Milly, still think this is a good idea?' She tickled the kitten's ears through the wires of the pet carrier she'd brought as extra baggage, and was rewarded with a contented purr. 'Of course, you do. He's putty in your paws. Maybe if *I* curled up on his lap and licked his fingers, huh?'

Delightful tingles shimmered up and down her spine as she remembered the last time they'd made love in Melbourne, before the gala function. Nate had made her feel she was beautiful, special, the only woman in his world. Then he'd seen Vanessa, and hadn't been able to hide his surprise that they were related or keep from looking at her, and Jemma's lifelong insecurities had crushed her euphoria.

'Good or bad, we're gonna sort this out,' she told the cat. 'Then you and I will either stay, or take another plane ride home.'

She was ready to answer his call before the first ring-tone finished.

'That was quick, darling. They're getting my case off the plane and I'll be on the road as soon as I've picked up the SUV from the apartment. Grant or one of his staff will meet you and take you to the hotel to wait for me. I'm a damn fool, Jemma. If I'd rung last night or this morning we'd be together now.'

'I'm guilty too.'

His light laugh tingled in her ear, heightening her pulse even more. 'We'll share the blame.'

In the pause that followed she heard a guttural sound, as if his throat had blocked.

'I've missed you, Jemma. I want to hold you, talk to you face to face, and convince you I've never lied to you and I never will.'

She couldn't hold back. That was why she was on this journey.

'Evasion *is* a form of lying, Nate, and you kept things from me.'

'Not long ago I'd have disputed that, Jemma. Now—'

He went silent as a male voice called out his surname. A moment later he was back.

'I've got my case and I'm on my way. I… No, that'll wait. I'll see you soon.'

'Soon' was over two hours away. She really hadn't thought this through, had she? Had *he*? If they were both riding on instinct—well, surely that was a truer gauge than the emotional baggage she'd let rule her life for years?

Nate went straight to his SUV on arriving at the apartment building, feeling rejuvenated and alert. This was the most important journey he'd ever take. Jemma was waiting for him, and all he had to do was release the past and embrace a life he'd denied wanting for too long.

Leaving his bags in the vehicle, he raced through the back door to the hotel's reception desk and prayed the couple there, booking in, were impatient to get to their room. It was hard to curb his impatience as they asked numerous questions.

'Nate, you made good time.'

He spun round to accept Grant's extended hand. 'I was lucky with the traffic. Thanks for looking after Jemma.'

'My pleasure. Jemma's in one of the rooms, resting, and the kitten's in my office.'

Nate froze. 'She brought Milly with her?' His elation peaked even higher than when she'd told him she was on the train. She'd come intending to stay a while.

'Friendly little thing. Can't have pets in the rooms, so...' He glanced over Nate's shoulder. 'Amend my previous statement.'

Nate swung round. His peripheral vision blurred, surrounding noise became muffled and his world narrowed to the elevator foyer. Jemma, adorable and enchanting, stood there, regarding him with the same tentative expression she'd worn the first time he'd seen her. And she was wearing the same blue patterned top and black tights.

His hopes clicked a notch higher.

Heart pounding, he moved with purposeful strides towards her, eyes locked with hers, mind racing to find the right words of greeting. She stepped into his open arms and he hugged her to his chest, then lifted his hand to caress her cheek.

'You brought Milly.'

Before he had time to berate himself for the inane greeting she sucked the air out of his lungs with a radiant smile that sent his head spinning. He kissed her as she deserved, with tenderness and reverence. Both of which threatened to morph into red-hot passion when her lips moved under his.

He pulled away, fighting for control, and saw the same battle in her eyes. Heard the same fight for breath and loved her even more.

* * *

The strong, rapid beat of Nate's heart pulsed under Jemma's palms, and the heat from his body matched her own, telling her she was where she belonged. Brilliant storm-grey eyes held hers captive, begging to steal her soul, and she willingly surrendered.

A deep chuckle from behind Nate sent him spinning, with her clasped in his embrace. Grant stood a few feet away, a broad grin on his face.

'You haven't forgotten you have a room upstairs?'

Heat flooded her cheeks, and a quick glance sideways showed Nate was blushing too. A scan of the area proved they were the only three around, and Nate recovered more quickly than she, or maybe covered it better.

'I guess we have.' He gazed down at her with something akin to awe in his eyes. 'Do you want to stay here for dinner?'

Her answer was forming before he'd finished asking.

'Take me home.'

'You only ever had to ask, darling. Let's get your luggage.'

He linked his fingers with hers and addressed his friend.

'We'll pick up Milly when we come down, Grant.'

'I'll be at the desk or in my office.' He was still smiling in the nicest I'm-happy-for-you way.

They rode the lift in silence, as if knowing a word or a glance might trigger the heat rush that simmered close to the surface. Her backpack and suitcase were ready inside the door, and her handbag lay on the barely disturbed bed where she'd lain, unsuccessfully trying to rest.

Nate's eyes flared as he studied the dent in the pillow, then he looked out of the window to the car park below.

'I was watching the cars come and go, and saw you arrive,' Jemma said.

'Ah, that explains your timely appearance downstairs,'

he said, grimacing at the bed as he reached for her luggage. 'And if we don't get out of here…'

His expression filled in the unsaid words. And they echoed in her heart.

They found Grant in his office, teasing Milly with a scrunched-up piece of paper. He put her into her carrier and took it to their vehicle.

'Thanks for your help and hospitality, Grant.' Jemma held out her hand but he ignored it, drawing her into a hug.

'Any time, Jemma. You two are always welcome.'

She wasn't sure what he said to Nate as the two men shook hands, but both were smiling as Grant stepped away and waved them off.

'He's a good friend.'

He nodded, giving her a quick smile. 'Yeah, one of the best.'

Now they were enclosed in a small space, his aura heightening all her senses, the need to sort out their issues was rapidly being overwhelmed by the desire to touch him and reassure herself this wasn't a dream.

She sat on her hands to prevent herself giving in to the impulse, allowing him to focus on his driving. Anything she asked might lead to a prolonged answer and, as he'd said on the phone, face to face was better.

When he pulled up to turn onto the track leading to his home she glanced across and met contemplative grey eyes. How often, especially in the early days of their relationship, had she seen that unfathomable scrutiny? Then he gave his special smile, and in the instant before he faced the windscreen again she saw such an open look of adoration that she doubted her own sight.

Her head spun, heat engulfed her from head to feet and coherent thought vanished. She sat in a daze until he pulled up beside the house, leapt out and strode round to open her door.

'Jemma?'

Refocussing, she swung her legs out of the car. A second later she was lifted into the air, crushed against his muscled chest and kissed with a thoroughness that melted her bones. A much better use of his lips than forming words. She wrapped her arms around his neck and kissed him back with heartfelt longing.

'Welcome home, darling.' His eyes sparked and he jiggled her body against his. 'This time you'll stay until we resolve our problems—perceived or real.'

He nuzzled her neck, sending her hormones crazy.

She wriggled, and he growled against her skin, evoking a whimper of pleasure. Closely followed by a protest from Milly on the back seat.

'I think she recognises your home and wants out.'

Nate set her on her feet with slow reluctance.

'An impatient chaperone might be what we need. You bring your handbag and Milly. I'll get the rest.

Jemma released Milly from the carrier, and watched her totter straight for her two bowls. She had no problems adjusting to another move as long as she was fed and cared for.

For Jemma, life wasn't that basic. She'd lived with her ingrained insecurities for so long she accepted them as a natural part of her being. Now it was time to voice them out loud and deal with them.

By the time Nate had completed his second trip Jemma had pulled back the drapes, unlocked the glass door, and had coffee ready for him and a glass of iced water for herself.

Nate felt as if he was walking on mountain scree, not sure if the ground would slide away beneath his feet. He'd spent the drive home forcing himself to face the road for safety. Her feet had been in his peripheral vision, and her perfume had filled his lungs every time he breathed, and his own contentment had proved Jemma *was* there beside him.

Lifting her into his arms had been the natural act of a man taking care of his woman, and nothing else came near the feeling of rapture when she'd returned his kiss. But he hadn't dared pre-empt the future, and had left her luggage in the bedroom she'd had before.

Seeing her in his kitchen, and Milly crouched over her bowl, his world began to come together. To move forward he now had to make changes, open up to the people he cared for and no longer compartmentalise aspects of his life.

Anything that involved Jemma becoming a permanent fixture had priority. Since bringing her here every morning had begun with exhilarating expectation, and he didn't want—couldn't bear—to go back to being the loner he'd been.

As if sensing his presence, she turned, and her lovely face revealed her apprehension—along with her determination to see this through. He walked across to her, profoundly grateful for her bravery, enclosed her hands in his and relished the fulfilment the simple act gave him.

'I've missed you, Jemma, more than words can ever express.' He drew her into his arms, needing her warmth. 'It's not my first wish, but we do have to talk. Clear the air. And then...'

His pulse stuttered, then hammered under his skin as she studied his face. Oh, how he'd missed the way she seemed to read his soul. And yet, like a fool, he'd held back from sharing his true self, and the events that had made him who he was.

Never again.

'On the veranda.'

Her reply was low and husky. Unsure, yet resolute. He whooshed out the breath he'd been holding.

'I'll grab a couple of chairs—you bring the drinks.'

This was no time for recliners, so he took two of the dining chairs out to the corner protected by an extension of the inside wall, leaving the smallest space he deemed appropriate between them.

Was there a right place to start? Would Jemma consider professional or personal omissions worse?

He raised his mug to drink, trying to decide.

'What do you feel for my sister?'

He spluttered as hot liquid scalded his tongue, and stared at her for a moment before comprehending that the trepidation in her eyes was real. Her knuckles were white from her tight grip on her glass.

'What the hell kind of question is *that*?'

He dropped his mug onto the decking with a clunk, oblivious to the splattering, and leant forward. His gut tightened when her body backed away, then eased as she raised her chin in defiance. His admiration grew as tenacity replaced anxiety in her endearing features.

'I'm not stupid or blind. I saw the way you looked at her, and I understood exactly what you meant by your remark.'

'That's more than *I* do right now. All I said—'

'You *asked* as if it were unbelievable that we were related. Then you kept looking at her. I've always known I can't compete with her looks, but I thought I finally had my envy under control. I guess I'm not immune where you're concerned.'

'Oh, Jemma.'

He sank back, fisting his fingers, not daring to touch her—not while she harboured that crazy notion in her head. But her unintentional confession spurred him on.

'Of *course* I compared the two of you. Vanessa is the perfect example of a genetically attractive woman, pampered with every beauty product and procedure on the market, and showered with expensive clothes and jewels.'

Her body stiffened, her throat convulsed and her eyes

squeezed shut—then opened slowly as if by compulsion. Every movement strengthened his growing belief that she cared for him…cared enough to be jealous of her stereotypical sister.

'Take a photo of her and pin it on a board with a dozen or so other women and you'd be hard pressed to separate them. Yes, I *was* amazed that you're sisters. She'll hate growing older, fight it all the way, and it will show. *You*, my darling, are innately beautiful, and with your love of life and gentle spirit you will be as naturally lovely when you are ninety as you are now. And I'd like to be there to say, I told you so.'

She might not quite believe him now, but he intended to devote his life to convincing her. In Hahndorf, here or anywhere she wanted to be.

'You know there were other women in my life before we met. But there was never one I invited to my home— never one whose presence I wanted to feel or remember there—until you.'

Jemma scrutinised his face. Love, warm and encompassing, had turned storm-grey eyes into molten silver and all traces of reticence were gone—confirmation that she wasn't competing with Vanessa or any other woman. The depth of his unconcealed emotion shook her, had her gasping for breath.

'You're cold.' The words were rasped out. Protective. Caring.

'No. I've hidden behind an imaginary veil for too long. Maybe if there'd been fewer years between Vanessa and I we'd have been closer, more understanding of each other. But by the time I started school she'd already set her sights on a modelling career and was actively pursuing ways to achieve it. There's never been a middle ground for us.'

With a masculine grunt he dragged his chair across the

gap, took her drink and set it down with his, then wrapped his hands around hers.

'It's not too late to find one. Now, will you *please* tell me about the idiot who broke your heart so we can both wipe him from our minds?'

CHAPTER EIGHTEEN

JEMMA COULDN'T HELP laughing at his description of the self-centred man she'd believed she might marry. But she became serious as she remembered how near it had come to being fact.

'We dated for six months. He was handsome, charming and attentive, and said he loved me. He worked in an insurance office, was determined to climb the corporate ladder to high status and an impressive salary. Working extra hours impressed his superiors, and the extra pay was supposed to go towards the upmarket house he wanted.'

As she spoke Nate's expression grew darker, triggering a flush of happiness in her at his obvious jealousy. Though tempted to prolong it, she couldn't. She loved him too much to let him suffer.

'Or so he said. In fact, a lot of his late nights and special meetings were with a senior female colleague who'd promised to help fast-track promotion for him. I found out not long after he cancelled our dinner at Windy Point to be with her. Any feeling I had for him evaporated, and my trust was shattered.'

'Not just an idiot—one with bad taste too. But I commend his faults because they kept you free for me.'

'When I first met you, I saw the same type of good-looking, polite and—to me—arrogant man. The type I deliberately avoided. I allowed you and Brian to coerce me into that writing deal for the chance to be published. When I agreed to come here I had no reason to doubt my ability to resist your charm. In fact I never had a chance.'

He raised his hand to caress her cheek and she almost

melted into his palm. The memory of those phone calls held her firm.

'Tell me about Tess. She has a very distinctive voice.'

She hadn't meant to blurt it out, but now it couldn't be recalled. She bit her lip as his eyes widened and his brows arched. A twinge of guilt spiralled in her stomach at her act of shifting the confession obligation back to him, and then waned as she recalled that they'd both promised frank and open admissions.

Only when every skerrick of doubt for both of them had been voiced and banished for ever could they face a life-time together.

'Tess…'

He seemed to be mulling over the words to explain, his Adam's apple bobbing, his eyes open and clear.

His chest rose and fell, twice. 'You can't have missed seeing the scars on my hip, yet you didn't mention them. I don't know how I would have responded if you had.'

He seemed to focus on the window behind her, but she knew he was in another time and place, reliving some horror.

His voice deepened with anguish as he continued. 'I was travelling with an army unit into disputed territory when we drove over a landmine and were then targeted by insurgents on a hill. The vehicle flipped, trapping me and two of the men. One of them was killed instantly. I…I watched the other die. I'd seen death before, but never that close. Never heard the awful sounds. Tess protected me as she and the others returned fire. She was shot twice before relief came and we were airlifted out. It's a debt of honour I can never repay.'

The last few sentences were rushed, as if he wanted them out and finished. Jemma covered his hand on her face with hers, wanting, needing to comfort him.

'She's a member of your support group?' She spoke in a hushed voice, with awe and respect for the woman she'd been jealous of for no reason. Jealousy that had blinded her to the obvious connection.

'They invited me to be a member before I came home. Any member can call any other, at any time, and he or she will be there, no questions asked. I still have bad dreams of incidents I can't forget, and still feel the helplessness of knowing there's nothing you can do to stop the carnage.'

'Except let the world know the truth.'

Nate huffed and tightened his fingers round hers on his knee, grateful for her understanding.

'Tess buried everything and tried to handle it alone. It's only in the last couple of years she's admitted to needing help. I'll never not take her call, nor refuse to go to her if talking on the phone isn't enough.'

'I'll never ask you to. She has my lifelong gratitude too.'

She squeezed his fingers, as if encouraging him to trust her. He gave a wry smile, lifted their joined hands and pressed his lips to her skin.

Staring across the valley, seeing visions he was glad she couldn't, he continued. 'I believed that keeping family and work, my overseas experiences and the group, and my writing as three separate aspects of my life would make them easier to manage. My obstinacy almost cost me the most precious jewel a man could have.'

He pulled her to her feet, then settled her onto his lap, cradling her tight, no longer ashamed to admit he needed the close contact. In the days, maybe weeks to come, he'd tell her more. Not now, and probably never everything of what he'd experienced. Instead he'd talk about the courage and fortitude of the other victims, and the compassion of those willing to risk their lives to help.

He cradled her head on his shoulder. One more admission and then he could move on to the good stuff, persuading Jemma to be his for ever.

'My last confession concerns the woman I told you about. Luckily for me I followed my grandfather's advice to never take anyone at face value, to always check. She already had a husband, and was counting on a pay-out to keep quiet about a bigamous marriage. Closing down emotion and treating women as colleagues only was my way of ensuring I didn't get duped again.'

Aware of her body stiffening and pulling away, he looked down, and his chest tightened at the sight of her now not-so-tender astonished expression.

'You *researched* me.'

It was stated with true indignation, and he longed to kiss her until her piqued expression became one of desire.

Delaying the inevitable for a moment, he answered honestly. 'I typed in your name, then deleted it. I didn't know why at the time. I just decided I wanted anything I learned about you to come from you or from being with you. It was one of my better decisions.'

Encouraged by the softening in her enticing blue eyes, he kissed her with the reverence she deserved, holding back the passion surging through his body. This was a time for making sure they were in tune and all suspicions allayed.

She couldn't be thinking the same, because she pressed closer, the tip of her tongue teasing his lips.

He pulled away, laughing down at her. 'Temptress. No more questions or fears, my darling.'

'No.'

Her eyes outshone the brightest stars he'd ever seen in the clear skies over the mountains, and it took all his willpower to resist kissing her again.

He stood and pulled her to her feet, and led her inside. 'Did you bring something special to wear?'

Jemma frowned, tilting her head as she stared at Nate, bewildered by his attitude. Why wasn't he carrying her to bed?

She wanted to be taking clothes *off*, not putting others on. And it was way too early to be going out to dinner.

'I have the dresses I wore to Windy Point and in Melbourne.'

'Go put on the silvery one and meet me here.'

He walked her over to the stairs and picked up a folded sheet of paper from the third step. Placing it into her hand, he brushed his lips over hers.

'This is for you. Take all the time you want. I'll be waiting.'

Her legs shook and her heart fluttered as she obeyed, her fingers holding the single sheet as if it were her lifeline. The door to the room she'd originally occupied was open, and her case was by the bed.

Should she read what he'd written now? She looked down at the outfit she wore, chosen because of their first meeting, then thought of the desire that had flared in his eyes on seeing her in the silver gown, and laid his letter on the bed.

After the quickest shower she'd ever had, she sprayed herself with perfume, brushed her hair to lie smooth down her back and slipped the dress over her head.

Curling into the comfy chair by the window, she began to read.

Nate waited in the lounge, wearing a royal blue shirt and black trousers, wishing he had a flower shop full of roses to give to Jemma. Instead he'd offered his heart, and a lifetime of love.

He'd closed his eyes for a brief moment, picturing her beautiful smile and sparkling eyes, and then had let his love flow from his heart through his hand onto the paper. Every expression came with a wish that she felt the same…every phrase held his desire to cherish her for ever.

He glanced at the ceiling, trying to imagine where she

was and how she was feeling. Did she understand that he'd wanted her to change in order to make this special moment even more memorable?

With a wry smile, he realised that he wasn't pacing as he normally did when waiting. He had no right to be this calm and confident, and yet his heart was as certain of her love as he was of tonight's sunset.

A gentle swish of movement and she came into view, taking his breath away and sending his pulse skyward. Shimmers of colour framed a goddess, here within his reach. An engaging mixture of gentle femininity, loveliness and charm. An angel with an endearing sense of fun.

He waited for her to come to him, then took her hand and led her onto the veranda. The sun was beginning to sink towards the mountains across the valley—an ideal picturesque backdrop. Turning to face her, he drew her close, basking in the surge of macho power initiated by having her in his arms.

Eyes sparkling, she gave him the most stunning smile he'd ever seen. As he bent to cover her sweet lips with his she stopped him with a fingertip touch.

'Thank you for the most beautiful and romantic prose I've ever read, Nate. You make me feel precious and loved, as if there's only you and I in our own paradise, and I'll treasure every word for as long as I live. I love you—now and for ever.'

If a heart could burst from a chest with happiness, his would do it now. He tightened his hold, fitting her body to his, rejoicing as she wriggled with pleasure.

'I love you, Jemma. My precious, adorable angel. My own.'

He loved her.

Jemma had known the moment their eyes had met in the hotel lobby. Had sensed it before, but been too timid to accept it. Hearing him express his feelings in his unique abrasive voice released her from the bonds that had imprisoned her for so long.

She stretched up on her toes to kiss him, and he answered with a passion that made her quiver with ecstasy. He caressed in gentle strokes across her back and she responded, running her fingers up his neck, tangling them into his hair.

He trailed a path of kisses across her neck, nibbled her neck as she sighed with contentment, then kissed his way back, stopping with his lips a breath away from hers.

'I love you with all my heart, Jemma Harrison, and more than life. Will you marry me, help me to write romantic scenes, and to create babies as cute and courageous as their beautiful brave mother?'

'Yes, Nate Thornton. I'll marry you, have your babies *and* create novels with you. You are my love, my life, my hero.'

He kissed her for as long as their breath allowed, then swung her into his arms and carried her to his monster of a bed.

Later they celebrated with champagne, their arms around each other as they watched the sunset and planned their future. Here in the mountains, in Sydney and Hahndorf— anywhere life took them. With Milly, their babies and any other pets who joined them. A family together.

* * * * *

FROM BEST
FRIEND TO
DADDY

JULES BENNETT

Chapter One

"It's just one glass."

Kate McCoy stared at the champagne flute the best man held. He'd flirted with her all night during the wedding rehearsal dinner—and by her estimate in smelling his overwhelming breath, he'd had more than enough for both of them. Thankfully he was just Noah's cousin and visiting from out of town. As in, he'd be leaving after the nuptials tomorrow afternoon.

One of Kate's three best friends, Lucy, was marrying her very own cowboy, and Kate couldn't be happier. She could, however, do without Noah's cousin all up in her face.

"She doesn't drink."

That low, growly tone belonged to Gray Gallagher, her only male best friend and the man who always came to her rescue whether she needed him to or not. She could've handled herself, but she wasn't about to turn away backup since Bryan with a Y wasn't taking her subtle hints.

Kate glanced over her shoulder and smiled, but Gray's eyes weren't on her. That dark, narrowed gaze was focused downward at the best man. Which wasn't difficult. Gray easily had five inches and an exorbitant amount of muscle tone on Best Man Bryan.

"Oh, well." Bryan awkwardly held two flutes in his hand, tossing one back with a shrug. "Perhaps I could get you a soda or some water."

"We were just leaving," Gray growled.

He slid his arm around her waist and escorted her from the dining area of the country club. Apparently they were indeed leaving because he kept heading toward the exit.

"I need to at least get my purse before you manhandle me out the door," she said, swiping her clutch off the table closest to the door, where she'd been chatting with some guests. "And for your information, I was going to have a glass."

Gray stopped short in the hallway and turned to her. "You wanted to have a drink with that lame guy? You've never drank in your life."

Kate shrugged. "It's my thirtieth birthday."

"I'm aware of that." Eyes as dark as midnight narrowed. "You're not drinking with him."

Should she clue Gray in on her reasoning for wanting to have her first drink on her birthday and at her friend's wedding?

True, Kate hadn't so much as tried a drop of alcohol since her parents had been tragically killed in an accident. Her father had been thirty-five, her mother only thirty-two.

Now that Kate had hit the big 3-0, she'd started reevaluating everything about her carefully detailed life.

"C'mon." Gray slid his hand around her arm and escorted her out the door into the humid Tennessee heat. "If you're going to have a drink, it's not going to be with someone who can't handle champagne at a damn formal dinner."

Kate couldn't help but laugh. "That wasn't nice."

"Wasn't meant to be. I don't like how he looked at you."

What was up with this grouchy attitude tonight? Well, not just tonight. Gray seemed to be out of sorts for months now and with each passing day, he seemed to be getting worse and worse.

Gray headed toward his truck. He'd picked her up earlier and presented her with a box of chocolate-covered strawberries for her birthday. He knew those were her weakness and it was a tradition he'd started years ago when he'd first come back from the army only days before her birthday. Gray had told her he'd actually ordered her something this year, but it hadn't arrived yet.

"I'm picking you up for the wedding tomorrow, too."

Kate McCoy calculated everything, from matching her underwear to her outfit to the precise inches of curling ribbon she needed when wrapping packages. She had every detail in her life down to perfection and even owned a company that specialized in organizing the lives of others—everything from closets to finances. The Savvy Scheduler was still fairly new, but it was growing thanks to her social media accounts that drove interested viewers to her blog and ultimately resulted in many new clients.

Kate had anal-retentive down to a science. So she didn't like when her plans got changed.

"I'm driving myself in the morning."

Gray knew she calculated everything in her life well in advance. Hell, her planner had a planner. Everything in her personal life and business was not only on paper but also in e-format.

He was perfectly aware of how meticulous she was with every detail. They'd met in grade school on the playground when she made fun of his new haircut. Considering he'd hated it as well, they had a good laugh and bonded when other children would've fought over the mocking. They knew each other better than most married couples, which was why she couldn't pinpoint why he'd been surlier than usual tonight.

From scowling when he'd picked her up and muttered something about her dress, to the rude way he'd just escorted her out without saying goodbye to their friends, Gray's manners were seriously lacking.

"Plans change," he said with a shrug as he released his hold and walked ahead. "Relax."

Relax? The man had been uptight all night, glaring at any male guest who talked to her, but she was supposed to relax? What was up with him?

The wind picked up, threatening to blow her short skirt higher than was within her comfort zone and expose said matching panties. Kate fisted the bottom of her flare dress in one hand as she marched across the parking lot after Gray—which wasn't easy, considering she'd gone with three-inch stilettos for the special occasion.

Stubborn man. He always wanted to bicker, and tonight was apparently no exception. But his unexplained behavior was starting to wear on her nerves.

Honestly, though, she didn't have time to analyze Gray's snarly attitude. It was late and she was tired and sweaty from this damn heat. Coupled with the unforgiving humidity wave hitting Stonerock, she was becoming rather grouchy herself. What happened to spring?

"I *planned* on getting to the church early to make sure everything was ready for when Lucy got there in the morning." Why was she yelling at his retreating back? "Would you stop and listen to me?"

Gray didn't stop until he got to the passenger door

of his black truck. When he turned to face her, he released an exasperated sigh. He hadn't shaved for a few days, had that whole messy head of dark hair going on, and his tattoos peeked from beneath each sleeve that he'd cuffed up over his forearms. If she went for the dark, mysterious type, Gray would fit the bill perfectly. Well, also if he weren't her best friend.

Kate could easily see why women flocked to Gallagher's to flirt and throw themselves at the third-generation bar owner. He was a sexy man, had the whole "I don't give a damn" attitude, but she knew something those women didn't. Gray was loyal to a fault and didn't do flings. He may have looked like the quintessential bad boy, but he was all heart and a true Southern gentleman.

"Noah asked if I would bring you," he told her. "He said Lucy was worried about parking for the guests and he was trying to make things as simple as possible by having the wedding party carpool. I'll pick you up whatever time you want. Is this seriously something we have to argue about?"

One dark brow quirked and she thought for a scant second that maybe this was something they didn't have to argue about. Not that she was ready to concede the upper hand. First the angry attitude, now a lame argument?

"I'll pick you up," she stated, swiping away a hair that had landed right on her lip gloss. "I want my own vehicle there."

"Fine. Hop in." He motioned toward the truck. "I have to swing by the bar and get champagne out of the back stock since more was consumed tonight than originally planned. I'll give you a drink of whatever you want. But your first one will be with me."

"It's late, Gray. You don't have to do that. My list isn't going anywhere."

"List?" He shook his head, muttering something under his breath she couldn't quite make out. "Get in the truck. I should've known you'd have a damn list about taking a sip of alcohol."

Kate blew out a sigh. "I'm not sure, though. Maybe I should just mark it off and move on to the next item."

Gray reached out and tucked a strand behind her ear. "First of all, one drink of champagne or wine is a far cry from the ten empty vodka bottles found in the car of the person who hit your parents. Second, I'd never let you get in over your head. Third, what the hell is this list you keep referring to?"

The breeze kicked up, thankfully sending some relief over her bare shoulders, but making it impossible to let go of her dress. She'd left her hair down, which was a huge mistake. With that thick mass sticking to her neck and back, she'd give anything for a rubber band about now.

"It's silly."

"I live for silly."

Even without the dry humor, she knew Gray was as far removed from silly as any human being.

"Since I was turning thirty, I decided to make a list of things I want to do. Kind of a way to give my-self a life makeover." She shrugged, because saying this out loud sounded even more ridiculous. "Trying a drink is on there."

"What else made the list?"

His eyes raked over her. Sometimes he did that. Like she was fragile. Just because life had knocked her down at times didn't mean she couldn't handle herself.

"Nothing for you to worry about."

She started to edge around him and reach for her handle when he stepped in her path. "Tell me."

Her eyes met his and she could tell by the hard stare that he wasn't backing down.

"I don't know what's up with you lately. You've been a bit of a Neanderthal." Might as well point out the proverbial elephant in the room. "You're pushy and hovering and…well, demanding. Just because some guy flirts with me doesn't mean I'm going to repeat old mistakes. And if I want a drink, I can do that for myself, too. I know you want to protect me, but you can't always do that, Gray. I'm a big girl and—"

In a quick move he spun her around and had her caged between the truck door and his hard chest. Mercy, he was ripped…and strong.

"Wh-what are you—"

"Putting that mouth to better use."

The words had barely processed before he covered

her lips with his. There was nothing gentle, nothing sweet or calm about Gray. He was a storm, sweeping her up before she even knew what hit her.

Wait. She shouldn't be kissing her best friend. Should she?

He touched her nowhere else and she still clutched her dress in one hand. On a low growl, he shifted and changed the angle of the kiss before diving back in for more. The way he towered over her, covering her body from lips to hips, made her feel protected and ravaged all at the same time.

Heat flooded through her in a way that had nothing to do with the weather.

Just as fiercely as he started, Gray pulled back. Cursing under his breath, he raked a hand through his already messy hair. Clearly he was waging some war with himself. Well, he could just get in line, because she had no idea what to do about what had just happened.

"Gray—"

"Get in the truck, Kate."

His raspy voice slid over her, making her shiver despite the heat.

What the hell did that mean? What did any of the past few minutes mean? Kate couldn't wrap her mind around his actions, his words. One minute she was trying to get to the bottom of his behavior and the next…well, she was being kissed by her best friend, and not just any kiss. No, he'd all but devoured her, almost as if he were trying to ruin her for another man.

Gray reached around her for the door handle, giving her no choice but to move. She settled inside and stared ahead, completely dazed. With his taste still on her lips and countless questions swirling through her mind, Kate didn't dare say another word out loud as she buckled her seat belt.

What on earth had triggered such an intense response? And then to just leave like that? She'd already told him that they couldn't be more than friends, but damn it, that kiss sparked something inside her she'd never experienced before.

Why did he have to go and do that to her? Why did he have to make her question her stance on their relationship and leave her aching for more?

More wasn't an option.

Chapter Two

The ride from the country club to Gallagher's had been too damn quiet. Tension had settled between them like an unwanted third party. Never before had things been this tense between them. They bantered, they bickered…that's just who they were.

But now, thanks to his inability to control himself, the dynamics had shifted completely.

Gray wasn't even going to question what had gotten into him. He knew full well that years of pent-up frustration from being relegated to the friend category, seeing her flirt and dance with other men at his bar and then being engaged and heartbroken, and finally that damn dress and heels tonight had all caused him to snap. There was only so much a man could take…especially from a woman like Kate.

And then the list. He wanted to know what the hell was on it and why she thought she needed to re-vamp herself. Not a thing was wrong with her. Who was she proving herself to?

Losing his cool and kissing her may not have been his finest moment, but every man had a breaking point and Kate McCoy had been his for far too long.

Damn, she'd tasted good and she'd felt even better all pressed against him. He wasn't sorry he'd kissed her, wasn't regretting in the slightest that he'd finally taken what he'd wanted. She'd leaned into him and obviously had wanted it just as much.

No, what angered him was the shocked look on her face and the fact he'd just pulled them both across a line they could never come back from. He was her friend, her self-appointed protector. She didn't have many constants in her life and she counted on him, damn it. She *trusted* him.

Now Kate stood at the bar, her eyes never meeting his. No doubt she was replaying that kiss just as he'd been over the past ten minutes.

Gray didn't say anything as he went to the back and pulled out a bottle of champagne that none of his customers would ever be interested in, but it was perfect for Kate. Once he got her home and came back, though, he was going to need something much stronger. Thankfully he could just crawl upstairs to his apartment after throwing one back.

Gray returned to the bar to find Kate exactly how he'd left her. He reached for a glass and carried that and the bottle around to the front side of the bar.

"I assume you still want that drink."

Finally, her blue eyes darted to his. "If anything in my life warranted a drink, this night would be it."

He poured her a small amount and slid the glass over to her. Kate stared at the peach-toned liquid for only a moment before picking it up and smelling the contents.

All of that long, dark hair curtained her face as she leaned down. With those creamy shoulders exposed, he was having a difficult time not reaching out to touch her.

Had he severed that right? Had he ruined everything innocent about their friendship when he'd put his lips on hers?

Damn it. He didn't like the idea of another man coming into her life. It had damn near killed him when she'd gotten engaged while he'd been in the army. Then, when the jerk had broken her heart, it had taken all of Gray's willpower not to pummel the guy.

Tonight he'd nearly lost it when Noah's best man had gotten flirty. Gray saw how Bryan looked at her, like she was going to be easy to take home. That wasn't his Kate. She didn't go home with random strangers.

Kate slammed her empty glass on the bar. "More."

He added a bit more to her glass and was a little

surprised when she tipped it back and swallowed it in one drink. Then belched like a champ.

"Wow. That's bubbly."

Gray couldn't help but smile. "It is. Had enough?"

"I can still taste your lips, so probably not."

His gut tightened as arousal spiraled through him. "Don't say things like that."

She lifted a slender shoulder. "Why not? It's the truth."

Gray took her glass away and set it aside with the bottle. The last thing she needed was to start buzzing, get all talkative and then regret spilling her secrets come morning. Though part of him—the part that had kissed her—would love to keep pouring and get her true feelings to come out into the open.

The low lighting behind the bottles lining the mirror along the bar wall sent a warm glow throughout the space. The main dining section and dance floor were still dark and Gray had never been more aware of a woman or his desire.

Over the years he'd purposely never allowed himself to be in a compromising situation with Kate, yet here he was only moments after plastering her against the side of his truck and claiming her lips.

"You can't be attracted to me," she murmured. "You *can't*, Gray."

If her words had any heat to them, if he thought for a second she didn't feel anything toward him, he'd ignore his need. But the only emotion he heard in her tone was fear and she'd kissed him right back earlier, so...

"You know I'm attracted to you." He closed the space between them. "I've never made it a secret."

"I'm the only woman who comes in your bar and hasn't thrown herself at you. I'm a conquest."

Anger settled heavily inside him. "Never call yourself that."

"Then what's the reasoning?" she tossed back. "Why me? After all these years, you're telling me... what? I need you to talk to me instead of being so damn irritated. Why now?"

"Maybe I'm tired of seeing other guys flirt with you. Maybe I'm sick of you dating losers since your breakup because you know your heart won't get involved."

She'd been burned and her defense mechanism to set her standards low was slowly driving him out of his ever-loving mind. Couldn't she see that she deserved more? She should actually be expecting more.

"Why did you kiss me back?" he asked, shifting the direction back to her.

Gray adjusted his body to cage her in against the bar with one hand on either side of her hips. He didn't want her to dodge him or look away or find an excuse not to hash this out right here, right now.

Maybe it was the late hour, maybe it was the near-darkness surrounding them. Or perhaps it was just time that his war with himself came to an end one way or another.

Kate's eyes widened, then darted to his mouth. That innocent act had arousal pumping through him. His frustrating friend could stir up quite the gamut of emotions. One of the reasons he had always been so fascinated by her. Nobody could get to him the way she could. And nobody could match him in conversation the way Kate could.

She flattened her palms on his chest. "Gray, I can't lose you as a friend."

"I never said I was going anywhere." He leaned in just a bit closer, close enough to see those navy flecks in her bright blue eyes. Close enough for her to realize he wasn't messing around anymore. "Tell me you don't want me kissing you again."

Because as much as he worried he was pushing her, he kept returning to the fact that she'd kissed him back.

Kate's mouth opened, then closed. That was all the green light he needed.

Gray didn't waste time gripping her hips and capturing her mouth. Those fingertips against his chest curled in, biting into his skin through the fabric. She let out a soft moan as her body melted against his. He wanted to hoist her up onto this bar and see exactly what she wore beneath this damn dress that had driven him crazy all night. He wanted those legs wrapped around him, her body arched against his.

Kate tore her mouth away. "We can't… Why does this feel so good? It can't go anywhere."

Like hell it couldn't. She was just as turned on as

he was if the way she'd rubbed herself against him proved anything.

Gray slid his hands over the curve of her hips, to the dip in her waist, and back down. "Tell me to stop and I will."

He leaned in, trailing his lips over her collarbone, breathing in that jasmine scent that belonged only on her.

"Tell me, Kate," he whispered, smiling when she trembled beneath his touch. "I have to hear the words."

He was torturing himself. If she told him to stop right now he would. But damn it, being pulled away after having a sample would be hell.

Slowly her hands slid up around his neck, and her fingers threaded through his hair. "Gray," she murmured.

Music to his ears. He'd always wondered how his name would sound sliding through her lips on a whispered sigh. Now he knew…and he wanted more.

Gray hovered with his mouth right over hers, his hands circling her waist. "You want me."

She nodded.

"Say it."

"I want you," she murmured. "But I need you as a friend. Please. Tell me we won't lose that."

He didn't want to lose anything. He wanted to build on what they had. They couldn't ignore this pull between them, so taking this risk to see where things went was the only option.

When he said nothing, she eased back as much as she could with the bar at her back. "Gray, this night is all we can have. We'll still be friends come morning."

One night? Did she think she'd be done with him that soon?

"And nobody can know," she added. "I don't want Lucy or Tara to know."

Her girl posse. He understood the need for privacy, but at the same time, he didn't want to be her dirty little secret and he sure as hell wanted more than one night.

He was a guy. Wasn't he supposed to be thrilled at the idea of a one-night stand with no strings? He should've had her dress off by now.

But this was Kate and she was special. Always had been.

"I wondered."

Her words stopped every single thought. "What?"

Bright blue eyes came up to his. "About this. I wondered before."

"Kate," he growled.

"I mean it, Gray. Just this night and it stays here, between us."

There was so much he wanted to say, so much he wanted to fight for because Kate was worth fighting for. He'd worry about the semantics tomorrow. He'd come too far and had a willing woman in his arms right now. There was only one thing to do.

Gray lifted her up onto the bar and kissed her.

Chapter Three

Kate didn't want to think about why this could potentially be a disastrous idea. How could she form a coherent thought when her best friend had his mouth and hands all over her? She'd never felt this good in her life and her clothes were still on.

Was it the champagne? Surely not. She'd only had two small glasses.

No, it couldn't be the alcohol. Gray was more potent than any drink he could give her. Why was she just discovering this fact?

Kate's head spun as she continued to clutch his shirt. She didn't want to analyze this moment or her emotions. She only wanted to feel.

Part of her wanted to rip off his clothes, but she'd

never been that brazen a woman. The few lovers she'd had were all calm, tame...and she'd never tingled like this for any of them.

She'd never ached with desire for her best friend, either, but here they were. A new wave of emotions swept her up, giving her no choice but to go along for the ride and enjoy every glorious moment.

Gray's firm hands rested on her knees as he spread them wide and stepped into the open space. He continued kissing her as his fingertips slid beneath her short skirt. Every single nerve ending inside her sizzled. When was the last time she'd sizzled?

Oh, right. Never. How did he know exactly what to do and how was she just realizing that her bestie had skills?

Kate tipped her head back as Gray's lips traveled over her chin and down the column of her throat. She circled his waist with her legs, toeing off her heels. The double thumps of her shoes hitting the hardwood floor sliced through the moment. Gray eased back and pinned her with his dark gaze. She'd never seen that look on his face before—pure hunger, passion, desire. All directed toward her.

Kate looked in his eyes and the need that stared back had her figuring maybe this wasn't a bad idea at all. No one had ever looked at her with such a need before. Something churned within her, not just arousal, but some emotion she wasn't ready to identify that coupled right along beside it, making her feel more alive and needed than ever.

Keeping his eyes locked on hers, Gray flipped her skirt up and jerked her by the waist toward the edge of the bar. Kate was completely captivated by the man before her. This passionate, sexual side of Gray had her reaching for the buckle on his belt, more than ready to hurry this process along. He quickly shoved her hands aside and reached for his wallet.

The second he procured a foil packet everything clicked in her mind. This was real. All of this was actually happening. She was about to have sex with her best friend…and she'd never been more thrilled, more excited in her life.

Shouldn't she be freaking out? Where had all of this come from? Clearly the desire had built up over time.

But she didn't. Kate waited, anticipation coiling through her. She'd address those questions later. Right now, she had a need, an ache, and judging by Gray's urgency, he did, too.

He tossed the packet next to her hip on the bar and unfastened his pants. Then, in a move that both shocked and aroused her, he reached beneath her dress, gripped the strip of satin that lay against her hip, and gave a jerk until the rip resounded through the quiet bar. So much for that pair of panties. They were a worthy sacrifice to the cause.

Kate didn't even get to enjoy the view before Gray sheathed himself and stepped toward her. With his hands firmly circling her waist, he nudged her forward once again, until he slowly joined their bodies.

Oh...my...

On a groan, Kate took a moment to allow her body time to adjust, but Gray clearly was in a hurry. He framed her face with his strong hands, tipped her head and covered her mouth as his hips jerked forward once again.

There was not much she could do but lock her ankles behind his back and match the perfect rhythm he set with their bodies.

"Kate," he muttered against her mouth.

She didn't want words. She had no clue what he was about to say, but she didn't want anything breaking into this moment. Words couldn't even begin to cover the tumultuous emotions flowing between them and she just wanted to feel. For right now, she wanted this man and nothing else.

Fisting his hair in her hands, Kate slammed his mouth back down onto hers. His hips pumped harder and in the next second, Kate's entire body trembled. She arched against Gray, pulling from the kiss. Her head dropped back, eyes shut as the euphoria spiraled through her.

She felt him lifting her before he settled her onto the bar. He whispered something just as his fingertips dug into her waist and he rose to tower above her. For a moment she marveled at his strength, but he started shifting again, moving faster and giving her no choice but to clutch his muscular arms.

Gray's body stilled as he rested his forearms on either side of her head, aligning their torsos. His mouth came down onto her shoulder. The sudden nip of his teeth against her flesh stunned her, arousing her even as she came down from her high. He kissed her there and trailed his lips across her heated skin.

Kate held onto Gray's shoulders even when their bodies completely stopped trembling. She had no idea what to say at this point. They lay on top of his bar half-dressed and had never so much as kissed more than in a friendly manner before, yet they'd just had explosive sex.

That was one hell of a birthday present.

Okay, maybe those shouldn't be the first words out of her mouth. But really, what was the protocol for a situation like this? She prided herself on always being prepared, but nothing could prepare her for what just took place. On a bar top, no less.

Gray came up onto his hands and looked down at her. Fear curled low in her belly. Was he waiting on her to say something and cut through the tension? Did they joke about this or did they fix their clothes like nothing happened?

Considering she analyzed everything from every angle, they would have to talk about this at some point. Maybe not right now when her emotions were too raw and she was still reeling from the fact that Gray had pursued her and torn off her underwear. Just the memory had chills popping up over her skin.

Exactly how long had he wanted her like this? There had been quite a bit of pent-up sexual need inside her bestie. Not that she was complaining. Definitely not complaining. Just…confused, and there were so many questions whirling inside her head, she had no clue where to start.

The muscle in Gray's jaw clenched and the way he continued to study her had Kate fidgeting. The top of her dress had slid down, so she adjusted to cover herself. She lifted onto her elbows and glanced around, anything but having to look right into those dark eyes to see…

She didn't know what she'd see, but she knew awkward tension had already started settling in.

Gray eased down off the bar and took a step back. Kate started to climb down, but he reached up, lifted her carefully into his arms, and placed her on the floor. The cool wood beneath her feet had her shivering, as did the sweet gesture of how he'd just handled her.

Of course, she could be shivering because her underwear was in shreds on the floor and her best friend was walking away. So much for him being sweet.

Apparently he wasn't one for chatter after sex, either. The silence only left her alone with thoughts she wasn't quite ready to tackle.

Kate's pale pink heels lay on their sides and she padded over to retrieve them. She clutched them against her chest like they could ward off the unknown, because she truly had no clue what was going to happen next.

Hell, it wasn't only the next few minutes she was

concerned with. What about long-term? Did this change everything between them? She hadn't been lying when she said she couldn't lose him. Gray was her everything. Absolutely everything.

The only constant in her life other than Tara and Lucy, but Gray was different. He was…well, he was special.

Right now, though, Kate could use some space to think and here on his turf, where her tattered panties lay mocking her, was not the place to clear her head and regroup.

Of all the times not to have her car. Damn it. This was why she always planned things, always had a plan B. But neither plan A nor B had been to leave the rehearsal dinner and have a quickie on the bar top at Gallagher's.

She was at the mercy of Gray whenever he came back and chose to take her home. Maybe then they'd talk and she'd get a feel for what was going on in that head of his.

Kate was stunned at the way her body still tingled. Gray had awakened something inside her, something she hadn't even known existed. But she'd made him promise just one night and that's exactly what she was going to hold on to.

She couldn't afford to lose him as a friend simply because she'd just experienced the best sex of her life. Gray was the one constant male in her life. He had been in that role since they were in junior high, and he'd come to rescue her from some bullying jerk who was new at the school. Not that she'd needed rescuing, but she'd appreciated it at the time, and he'd been her self-appointed white knight since.

So who was going to save her from him? Because now that she'd had him, Kate knew he'd ruined her for other men.

Gray Gallagher had infiltrated her, body and soul, and she'd better just live with the tantalizing memories, because they were definitely one and done.

She couldn't emotionally afford to have it any other way.

Gray took a minute longer than necessary in his private bathroom attached to the back office. The second he'd come back to reality and looked down into Kate's eyes, he'd seen her withdrawing. He'd instantly wanted her to reconsider that one-night rule. But he hadn't even gotten her completely undressed. He'd ripped her panties off, and they'd had a quickie on his bar.

Yeah, real smooth. Perfect way to show her she was special and he wanted to do it all over again. He'd be lucky if she didn't haul off and smack him when he walked back in there. Hadn't he always told her she deserved better? That she deserved to be treated like she was the most valuable woman in a man's life?

Gray slammed his hand against the wall and cursed himself for being such a jerk to the one woman he cared most about. Now he was going to have to go out and face her, make some excuse as to his behavior, and then drive her home in what he was sure would be uncomfortable silence.

What a fantastic way to end an already crappy day. He'd already been in a bitch of a mood when he'd seen that best man flirting with her. He shouldn't be jealous, but damn it, he couldn't help how he felt.

He'd faced death when he'd lost his mother at the tender age of five. He'd faced the enemy when he'd been overseas in the army. He faced his father, who was disappointed because Gray hadn't settled down and started a family. But Gray was not looking forward to facing his best friend, because if he saw even the slightest hint of regret or disappointment in her eyes, he would absolutely be destroyed.

Knowing he couldn't stay hidden forever, he made sure his clothes were adjusted before he headed out. The second he rounded the corner from the back hallway, he stilled.

Kate stood frozen just where he'd left her. She clutched her shoes, worried her bottom lip with her teeth, and stared at the spot where he'd taken her like some horny teen with no experience.

But it was the pale pink bite mark on her shoulder that had him cringing and cursing himself all over again.

Damn it. What the hell was wrong with him? His Kate was a lady. She was classy. She was so far above him and he'd treated her like a one-night stand.

Oh, wait. That's exactly what this was, per her

last-minute request. It wasn't like he gave her ample time to get used to the idea of the two of them together.

Still, Kate deserved better and he damn well was going to show her. Screw the one-night rule. If anyone should be proving to her exactly how she should be treated, it was him.

"I'll take you home."

Kate jumped and turned to face him, her eyes wide. His voice came out gruffer than he'd intended.

With a simple nod, she headed toward the back door. Gray didn't move from his position and ultimately blocked the opening to the hallway. He waited until she stopped right before him. He shouldn't touch her, shouldn't push this topic, but damn if he couldn't help himself. There had to be something he could do to redeem his actions.

Reaching out, he traced one fingertip over the faint mark on her shoulder.

"We good?"

Wow. He'd had several minutes to think of something tender, kind, and apologetic to say, and that's the best he could come up with?

Yes, he saw confusion looking back at him, but there was more. Kate wasn't upset, not at all. She had questions, of that he was sure, but she wasn't angry. Thankfully he hadn't botched this night up too much.

Kate attempted a smile. "We're good," she murmured as her eyes darted away.

She may not be angry, but she was no doubt wondering what they should do next. Kate planned everything and this whole experience had definitely not been planned.

Enter the awkward tension he swore wouldn't be there. He promised her they wouldn't change. He promised they'd be friends just like before.

Yet she couldn't even look him in the eyes.

"Kate."

Her focus darted back to him, but he didn't see regret. Kate's pretty blue eyes were full of desire… Damn if that didn't just confuse the hell out of him. She might be wanting to ask him about what just happened, but she also wasn't sorry.

Gray didn't know what else to say at this moment. The dynamics had changed, the intimacy too fresh. Maybe once they had some time apart and saw each other at the wedding tomorrow they'd laugh and joke and go back to the Gray and Kate they'd been hours ago.

Or maybe they'd find the nearest closet and rip each other's clothes off. Things could go either way at this point.

Gray moved out of her way so she could pass. Her hair hung down her back in dark waves, her dress was slightly askew, and she still clutched her shoes. He'd turned a moment of intimacy with his best friend into forcing her to do a walk of shame from his bar.

He was no better than the prick who'd cheated on her and broke her heart. But Gray would make this up to her. He had to.

Kate adjusted her one-shoulder bridesmaid's dress for the fifth time in as many minutes. Thankfully Lucy hadn't chosen strapless dresses. Kate needed this chiffon strap to cover Gray's mark. She didn't know what she would've done had he chosen the other shoulder.

Part of her loved the mark. She'd be lying if she said otherwise. She'd never had a man lose such control, and the fact he hadn't even been able to get them out of their clothes was thrilling. Sex should be thrilling, or so she'd heard before, and she'd always wondered if that was a myth. Now she knew.

Analyzing this over and over wasn't going to change the future. Gray wasn't going to happen again. On that they'd agreed, so now she had to figure out how to not compare any other man to her best friend. But at least the standards were set and she wasn't going to settle for someone who didn't at least give her a little spark.

Kate had definitely had a happy birthday. At least she had until he'd come from the bathroom and couldn't get her out of the bar fast enough. Did he regret what they'd done? Or worse. Was she a disappointment?

"Hey, you okay?" Tara whispered.

"Fine."

Kate smiled for the camera and hoped they were nearly done with all the photos. What did it matter if Gray found her lacking in the skill department? They weren't doing anything again anyway.

He'd barely said a word when she'd picked him up this morning and she hadn't seen him at the wedding. But the church had been packed, so that wasn't a surprise. She'd see him at the reception for sure. He was in charge of all the drinks and had brought a few of his employees to serve as waiters.

She felt a bit odd not sharing her epic, mind-blowing, toe-curling experience with Lucy and Tara. If this had been any other man she'd had wild sex with late at night in a closed bar, she would've texted them immediately after, but this was Gray. He was different and what they shared was…well, it was something she still couldn't describe.

"I think we got them," the photographer announced. "We'll do more at the reception."

Kate resisted the urge to groan. This was Lucy and Noah's day. She shouldn't be so grouchy, but smiling and posing and pretending to be in a good mood was not working for her. All she could think of was Gray: what they'd done, what she had missed from him that led up to that moment, how he'd react seeing her again.

Kate lifted the long skirt of her dress and stepped off the stage. A hand slid over her elbow.

"Wait a second," Tara said.

Turning her attention to her friend, Kate dropped her dress and clutched the bouquet. "What's up?"

"That's what I want to know."

Tara's questioning gaze held Kate in place. "I'm just going to hop on the shuttle to take me to the reception so I can get some food. I'm starving."

Rolling her eyes, Tara stepped closer. "You've been acting weird all day. What happened from last night to this morning?"

What happened? Oh, just a quickie on the bar top at Gallagher's, third stool from the left. Well, Gray had shoved the stool out of the way when he'd climbed up to her, but still. She'd never be able to look at that space again without bursting into internal flames. Her panties would probably melt right off.

"I just had a late night." Kate opted to go with some form of the truth. "Gray and I left the rehearsal and headed back to the bar so he could pull more champagne and wine from the back stock. I just didn't get much sleep before we had to be up and ready."

Tara's bright blue eyes studied Kate a moment longer than she was comfortable with. Gathering her skirt in her hand once again, Kate forced a smile.

"C'mon," she said, nodding toward the front of the church. "Let's go get on the shuttle so they can take us over to the food and dancing. I'm ready to get rid of these heels."

Tara nodded. "Will you get some pictures of me dancing with Marley?"

Marley, Tara's five-year-old daughter. She shared custody with her ex, Sam Bailey. Sam had brought Marley to the wedding since this was his weekend to have her. Tara had been surprised that Sam had taken Marley to get her hair done and her nails painted.

Kate knew Sam had some issues several months ago, but she saw the man was trying. Okay, using the word "issues" was really sugarcoating things. But addiction was such a delicate topic and Kate still wasn't sure how to approach it with Tara.

But Kate saw Sam fighting to get his family back. The man had gone to rehab, he'd gotten a new job, he'd gone to counseling. There was a determination in him now that Kate hadn't seen before. Tara wasn't ready to see it and Kate worried irreparable damage had been done and their marriage was over for good.

None of that was Kate's business and she had her own issues to worry about right now. Like seeing Gray at the reception. She didn't like the silence that had settled between them this morning. That wasn't like them. They were always bantering or arguing or joking about something. It was their thing. They lived to annoy the hell out of each other and for some strange reason, it worked for them.

Damn it. She knew sleeping with him would change things, but she'd been unable to prevent herself from giving in. One second they were friends, and the next he'd kissed her against his truck and made her want things she never realized she was missing.

Chapter Four

Gray checked on the status of the bottles, confident they'd be just fine with the extras he'd brought. He asked around with his staff to see if they were doing okay or if anyone needed a break. None of them took him up on his offer.

He had such amazing, loyal employees at his bar who would work any venue when he asked. Honestly, they could run the whole place themselves and probably didn't even need him around.

Damn it. He was out of things to do other than watch Bryan try to hit on Kate again. Didn't the guy take the not-so-subtle hint from the rehearsal dinner?

Gray had been jealous last night, but seeing him make a play again tonight had him feeling all sorts of rage. Which was absurd. Kate was a grown woman and they were just friends. They'd slept together and now he was letting that incident cloud his judgment.

Actually, he didn't care. Kate was better than Bryan and Gray didn't like the way the guy kept looking at her.

Gray walked around the perimeter of the country club dining area and glared at Bryan as he stepped in behind Kate on the dance floor. What the hell was wrong with that guy?

Kate turned and glanced at Bryan, then shook her head and held up her hands as if to ward him off. Bryan smiled and reached out to touch her bare shoulder. Seeing that man's hand against Kate's creamy skin had Gray making his way across the floor.

The jerk stepped into her when a slow song started and the tension on Kate's face made Gray's anger skyrocket. He was sure his face showed his every emotion but right now he didn't give a damn who saw him or what others thought. He was putting a stop to this now.

"Go have another drink, Bryan. This dance is mine."

Gray instantly wrapped an arm around Kate's waist and took her hand in his. From the corner of his eye, Gray saw Bryan still standing there. Spinning Kate in a circle, Gray stepped on Bryan's foot and was rewarded with a grunt.

"Still there?" Gray asked over his shoulder.

The guy finally disappeared through the crowd of dancers.

Kate's eyes were wide, but Gray would rather she be uncomfortable with him than with some idiot who didn't know what a treasure Kate was.

"He's harmless."

Gray narrowed his gaze. "And I'm not?"

She merely tipped her chin in defiance. "I could've handled it myself."

Gray offered her a smile. "You always say that."

"Because I can."

"I'm aware." He spun her around again, keeping his firm hold on her. His Kate was extra prickly today. "But we haven't danced yet and I had a few minutes to spare."

Her eyes continued to hold his. "And what were you doing those few minutes you were glaring this way?"

Damn if she wasn't adorable when she was fired up. "Some people take a smoke break. I don't smoke, so I take a glare break."

Kate stared for another moment before she finally shook her head and let out a soft laugh. "You're incorrigible. You know that, right?"

A bit of tension eased from his chest at her sweet laugh. "It's only because I care and Bryan is not the guy for you. Not even as a dance partner. Hell, he's not even your drink provider."

Kate arched a brow. "So now you're screening my guys?"

Screening them? Hell, if that was a possibility he damn well would be first in line to sign up for that job. If he hadn't been overseas during her ill-fated engagement, perhaps he could've prevented her heartache. But Gray hadn't even met the ex because he'd come and gone while Gray had been serving. So, yeah, perhaps he was looking out for her. Isn't that what friends did?

"Maybe dancing with a guy like Bryan made my list."

Here she went with that damn list again. He'd like to see exactly what was on that thing.

"Tell me more about this infamous list."

He spun her around again, slowly leading the way toward the edge of the dance floor, where there weren't as many people. He found he didn't want to share Kate right now. He wanted to keep her talking, keep her dancing. Though dancing wasn't his thing, it was an excuse to get her in his arms.

He glanced around as he led her. He recognized many people from town. The St. John brothers and their wives were all dancing. Several other couples who frequented his bar were also dancing and having a good time.

Gray actually hadn't seen the bride and groom for a while, though. Perhaps they'd already slipped out once the bouquet and the garter had been tossed. Most likely they'd been in a hurry to get to their honeymoon.

"I'm keeping my list to myself for now," she replied.

Gray stared down into her blue eyes. She hadn't brought up last night and he wasn't about to, either. They hadn't wanted things to change between them, but the tension had become palpable and he wasn't sure how to erase it.

Eventually they would have to discuss what happened. Might as well be now, while he had her undivided attention. Maybe having everyone around would help ease the tension. If they were alone again and trying to talk, Gray wasn't so sure he could prevent himself from touching her again. Touching her now was safe, smart.

"About last night—"

Kate's eyes widened a fraction. "I need to find Tara," she said, breaking from his hold. "We'll talk later."

And then she was gone, leaving him all alone with a slew of couples dancing around him. Gray fisted his hands at his sides. He hadn't expected Kate to run. He hadn't expected their night to scare her away. She'd always been comfortable with him.

But then he'd turned into the guy who had sex with his best friend on top of a bar.

Raking a hand through his hair, Gray left the dance floor and went back to what he could control. The alcohol and the servers. Right now, Kate was utterly out of his control. Perhaps they needed space. Maybe she needed a breather after what had happened.

One thing was certain, though. He'd had her only one time and he knew without a doubt he wanted more.

Kate sank onto the chaise in the seating area of the women's restroom. She slid out of her heels and resisted the urge to moan. Between all the food she ate and dancing and the lack of sleep, she was ready for bed.

It was that whole lack of sleep—or the reason behind it—that had her escaping to the restroom to hide for a bit. She'd known Gray would bring up their situation, but their friend's wedding was sure as hell not the place she wanted to hash things out.

She couldn't think when he was holding her, because now that they'd been intimate, any type of touch triggered her memories…not that the images of last night had ever faded to the background. Would they ever?

Besides, Kate had no clue what she wanted to say anyway. Did she say thank you? Did she compliment him? Or did she broach the fact that she'd had her first taste of alcohol and it wasn't that bad? What exactly did she lead in with after such an epic, mind-boggling night?

The bathroom door opened, but Kate kept her eyes in her lap, not wanting to face any guests.

"Who are we hiding from?"

So much for not facing anyone.

Kate glanced up to see Tara and Lucy holding the skirts of their gowns and coming in from the madness and noise outside. Once the door shut, her friends waited for her answer in silence.

"Tara—"

"Is it Bryan?" Lucy asked, rolling her eyes. "I swear, he and Noah are close, but I had no idea how annoying that man could be when presented with a single woman. Guess he thinks he has a chance with you."

Kate blew out a sigh. If her only problem involved a man who was a complete goober and found her attractive, she'd be golden and certainly wouldn't be hiding in the bathroom.

No, her issues came in the form of a six-foot-four-inch bar owner who could make her tingle just from the slightest brush of his fingertips.

"This isn't about Bryan. I'm just taking a breather," she told them, which was the absolute truth.

Lucy gathered the full skirt of her wedding dress and flopped next to Kate on the chaise. Tara crossed and sat in the floral armchair.

"I told you something was up," Tara stated, looking at Lucy.

"This is her wedding day." Kate glared at her friend. "You told her you thought something was up with me when she should be focusing on how quickly she and Noah can get out of here and head to their honeymoon?"

Tara's eyes widened as she shrugged. "We're friends. She can go have sex with Noah whenever. I need to know what's going on with you and Gray."

"Are you two arguing again?" Lucy asked. "I swear, you're like an old married couple, just without the sex."

Kate nearly choked on the gasp that lodged in her throat. Fortunately, she recovered before giving herself away. She was nowhere near ready to spill her secret. Her friends would be completely shocked if they learned she'd had sex with Gray. Kate was still reeling from the fact herself.

"What? No, we're not arguing." They couldn't argue when she was running away and dodging the issue. "Why would you think that?"

"Because you two were dancing, then you rushed out in the middle of the song."

Kate stared at Tara. "I didn't see you on the dance floor."

"I wasn't there. I was getting Marley another plate of fruit and dip when you scurried by," Tara explained. She pinned her with those bright eyes. "I'd assumed you were running from Bryan, but I saw Gray's face as he watched you."

Oh, no. *Damn it.* Kate didn't want to ask what emotions Tara had seen on his face, what feelings he'd been unable to mask. She honestly had no clue what he was feeling because he'd been so good at keeping that to himself since last night.

Of course, if she'd waited to hear what he had to say, maybe she'd be better in tune with what was happening in his mind.

"He stepped in and saved me from Bryan. You know how Gray is," Kate explained, smoothing down her chiffon-overlay skirt. She had to convince them there was nothing more than what was on the surface. "We just danced a few minutes until Bryan was gone. That's all."

Silence filled the room, which was good because the door opened again and an elderly lady came in. Kate didn't know her, but she'd seen her on the groom's side during the ceremony. Considering Noah wasn't from here, it would make sense that there were guests Kate didn't know.

"Would you go back out to your husband?" Kate hissed. "I'm just taking a break from those killer heels. Nothing is wrong."

Lucy took Kate's hand and squeezed. "Promise?"

"Of course." Kate nodded. "Go on."

Lucy finally got up and left. Once the other guest left as well, Kate was alone with Tara and her questioning gaze.

"What?" Kate demanded. "Can't a girl just take a break?"

"Lucy can and I can, but not you." Tara crossed her legs and leaned back in the seat. "You are always on the go, always planning the next thing, and I've never seen you relax. So what's really going on? And don't lie. I'm done with lies."

Kate swallowed a lump of guilt. Tara had been dealt too much lately, but there were just some things Kate wasn't about to share. That was not a reflection of their friendship. She'd tell her and Lucy... someday.

"Not now, okay?"

Tara's curiosity quickly turned to concern. "Promise me you'll come to us if you need anything. I know what it's like to be lost in your own thoughts and worry what to do next."

True story. Tara and Sam were going through hell all while trying to keep their daughter out of the fires.

"Same goes." Kate reached over and took her friend's hand. "Sam looked like he was doing really well."

Tara nodded. "He is. He left me a note on my windshield this morning."

How could anyone not find Sam and his handwritten notes simply heart-melting? He'd done that when they'd been married and since their split, he continued to leave her notes. Tara always mentioned them and Kate wondered what it would be like to have a man who cared that much.

The man was a hopeless romantic who'd just made some bad choices. Kate didn't blame Tara for being cautious, though. Some obstacles were just too great to overcome.

"We should get back out there." Kate came to her feet and stared down at her heels. "If I ever get married, we're all going barefoot."

Tara laughed as she stood up. "Deal."

Kate had pushed marriage thoughts out of her head long ago when her engagement ended. The whole ordeal had left her a bit jaded, but seeing Noah and Lucy come together after they'd both experienced such devastation in their lives gave Kate hope. She wanted to marry one day, to have a husband who loved her, start a family and live in the picturesque mountains of Tennessee.

One day, she vowed. But first she was going to have to figure out how to get back on that friendship ground with Gray. Every time she thought of him now, she only remembered him tearing off her underwear and climbing up on that bar to get to her.

And her body heated all over again. She had a feeling the line they'd crossed had been erased. There was nowhere for them to go that was familiar and comfortable because they were both in unknown territory.

Chapter Five

Gray slid another tray of glasses beneath the bar. For the past five days he'd gone about his business and mundane, day-to-day activities. This wasn't the first time, and wouldn't be the last, that he couldn't shake the void inside him. Something was missing, had been for quite some time, but he'd never been able to quite place it.

His father always said it was a wife and children, but Gray didn't believe that. He wasn't looking to settle down and worry about feeding a relationship. His parents had been completely in love up until his mother's death when Gray had been five. He'd seen how the loss had affected his father, seen how the man had mourned for decades. Gray didn't want to subject himself to that type of pain.

Besides, he'd never found anyone who would make him even think about marriage.

He'd been hand-delivered this bar when he'd come home from the army, just like his father before him. Gray's grandfather, Ewan Gallagher, had opened the doors when he'd retired from the army after World War II. Right after that, he'd married the love of his life and started a family. Same with Gray's father, Reece.

They'd both had a plan and been the happiest men Gray had ever known. Not that Gray wasn't happy. He knew how fortunate he was to have served his country and come home to a business with deep familial roots and heritage. Some men never came home, and some guys who did weren't even close to the men they'd been before they were deployed.

But beyond all of that, something inside him felt empty. The void that accompanied him every single day had settled in deep and he had no clue how to rid himself of it.

Gray pushed those thoughts aside and headed to the back office. He needed to get his payroll done before they opened this afternoon.

He sank into his worn leather office chair and blew out a sigh. He couldn't even lie to himself. It wasn't just the monotonous life he led that had him in a pissy mood. He hadn't seen Kate once since she'd deserted him on the dance floor.

They'd texted a few times, but only about safe topics.

Safe. That word summed up Kate. She did things by the book. Hell, the book she carried with her was like her lifeline to the world. She always had a plan, excelled at making her life organized and perfect.

Gray was anything but organized and perfect. He ran a bar. Things got messy and out of control at times. He'd obliterated her perfect little world when he'd taken their relationship to an entirely unsafe level.

Still, he was going to let her hide for only so long. "Hello?"

Gray stilled at the unfamiliar voice coming from the front of the bar. He came to his feet and rounded his desk. He always left the doors unlocked while he was here working. Stonerock was a small town where everybody knew everybody. Crime was low and people usually respected his bar's hours.

Sometimes his buddy Sam would stop in during the day to talk or just to unwind. After all that man had been through, Gray wasn't about to lock him out. Sam needed support now more than ever and if he was here, at least Gray could keep an eye on him and be part of that support team.

"Anyone here?"

Definitely not Sam. Gray had no idea who'd decided to waltz right into his bar in the middle of the morning.

He stepped from the back hall and came to stand

behind the bar. The man who stood in the middle of Gray's restaurant clearly had the wrong address. Nobody came in here wearing a three-piece suit and carrying a briefcase. Who the hell even owned a suit like that? Nobody in Stonerock, that was for damn sure.

Gray flattened his palms on the bar top. "Can I help you?"

The stranger offered a toothy smile and crossed the space to the bar…third stool from the left. Now his favorite place in the entire building.

"You the owner?"

Gray nodded. People came in looking for donations for schools, ball teams, charity events…but Gray couldn't pinpoint exactly what this guy was nosing around about.

"My name is Preston Anderson. I'm from Knoxville."

Preston Anderson sounded exactly like the type of man who'd own a suit as confining and stiff as this one. Gray eyed the man's extended hand and ultimately gave it a quick shake.

"I have enough staff," Gray replied. "But the bank might be hiring."

The guy laughed and propped his briefcase on a bar stool. "I'm here to see you. I assume you're Gray Gallagher."

"You would assume correctly."

He pulled a business card from his pocket and

placed it on the bar. Gray didn't even give it a glance, let alone touch it.

"My partner and I are looking to buy a number of properties here in Stonerock and doing some minor revamping of the town."

Gray crossed his arms over his chest. "Is that so?"

"We'd like to make it a mini-Nashville, if you will. The area is perfect for day tourists to pop over to get away from the city, but still have a city feel."

Pulling in a breath, Gray eyed the business card, then glanced back to Preston. "And you want to buy my bar."

Preston nodded. "We'll make it more than worth your while."

He took a pen from inside his jacket pocket, flipped the card over, and wrote a number. Using his fingertip, he slid the card across the bar. Again, Gray didn't pick it up, but he did eye the number and it took every ounce of his resolve to not react. There was a hell of a lot of numbers after that dollar sign.

"You really want this bar," Gray replied.

Preston nodded. "We're eager to dive into this venture. We'd like to have firm answers within a month and finalize the sales within thirty days after that. All cash. Our goal is to have all of our properties up and running before fall for when the tourists come to the mountains for getaways."

Gray had never thought of selling this place before, and now he had a month to make a decision.

His initial reaction was hell no. This was his family's legacy, what his grandfather had dreamed of.

But reality kicked in, too. That void he'd been feeling? He still didn't know what was causing it, but all of those zeroes would go a long way in helping him find what was missing…or at least pass the time until he could figure out what the hell he wanted to be when he grew up.

Gray never had a set goal in mind. He'd done what was expected and never questioned it. But more and more lately he wondered if this was really where he was supposed to be. And if it was, then why did he still feel like something was lacking?

Preston went on to explain they'd still keep the establishment a bar, but it would be modernized for the crowds they were hoping to bring in. Gray had no idea what to say, so he merely nodded and listened.

The figure on the untouched card between them spoke more than anything Preston could've said.

"So, think about it," Preston stated, picking up his briefcase. "My number is on the card if you have any questions. This isn't an opportunity that will present itself again, Mr. Gallagher."

"I imagine not," Gray muttered.

Preston let himself out the front door, leaving Gray to process everything that had happened over the past ten minutes. He reached for the card, turning it from front to back.

What the hell did he do with this proposal? True, he'd never actually wanted the bar, but it was his.

And while he may have wanted to pursue other things in his life, there were some loyalties that came with keeping up tradition. Gray would never purposely go against his family.

Family was absolutely everything to him. His father never remarried, so Gray and his dad had been a team. Then Gray's grandfather had passed only a few years ago, leaving Gray and his father once again reeling from loss.

Now that they were all each other had, this business deal wasn't going to be something easy to say yes or no to. This was definitely a decision he needed to discuss with his father. But Gray wanted to weigh his options and have some idea of what he wanted before that discussion took place.

Gray already knew where his father would stand on this from a sentimental standpoint, but his father also didn't know that Gray hadn't been happy for a while now.

Ultimately, the final decision would belong to Gray.

There was one other person he wanted to talk to. One other person who'd been his voice of reason since junior high, when she talked him out of beating the hell out of some new jock who had mouthed off one too many times.

Sliding Preston's card into the pocket of his jeans, Gray went back to working on the payroll. Kate had one more day to come to him…and then he was going to her.

* * *

Kate's color-coded binder lay open to the red section. The red section was reserved for her most important clients. Not that all of them weren't important, but some needed more attention than others.

Mrs. Clements was by far her best client. That woman wanted help with everything from organizing her daughter's bridal shower to setting up her new home office. Kate also had a standing seasonal job with the middle-aged lady when it was time to change out her closets for the weather.

Kate stared at the time on her phone. It was nearly two in the morning, but she wasn't the slightest bit tired. This plan for Mrs. Clements wasn't due for nineteen days, but Kate wanted it to be perfect before she presented it to her.

Pulling her green fine-tip marker from the matching green pouch, Kate started jotting down possible strategies. The definite plans were always in blue and those were already completed and in the folder.

Kate tapped on her phone to fire up her music playlist before she started compiling a list of possible caterers.

The knock on her door had Kate jumping in her seat. She jerked around and waited. Who would be knocking on her door in the middle of the night? Probably some crazy teenagers out pulling pranks. But the knock sounded again, more determined than just a random tap.

She contemplated ignoring the unwanted guest,

but figured murderers didn't go around knocking on doors. Plus, this was Stonerock. She knew the entire police force. She could have anyone over here in a flash if something was wrong.

Kate paused her music and carried her phone to the door in case she needed to call upon one of those said officers. Of course Noah was still on his honeymoon with Lucy, so he wasn't an option.

As she padded through the hall, Kate tipped her head slightly to glance out the sidelight. Her heart kicked up. Gray. She knew it was only a matter of time, but she certainly didn't expect him in the middle of the night.

This man...always keeping her guessing and on her toes.

Blowing out a breath, Kate set her phone on the accent table by the door. She flicked the dead bolt and turned the knob.

Without waiting for her to invite him in, Gray pulled open the screen door and stepped inside.

"Won't you come in," she muttered.

"Considering I rarely knock anyway, I figured you wouldn't mind."

She closed the door, locking it before she turned to face him. "And what on earth do you possibly need at this time of the night?"

"You weren't asleep. I saw your lights on."

No, she wasn't asleep, and he'd just come from the bar. His black T-shirt with the bar logo on his left pec stretched tightly across his broad shoulders.

She could never look at those shoulders the same way again, not after clutching them the other night as he'd given her the most intensely satisfying experience of her life.

Suddenly the foyer in her townhome seemed too small. She couldn't be this close to Gray, not with those memories replaying through her head. The memories that made her question everything and want more than she should.

Clearing her throat, Kate turned and headed to the back of the house, where she'd turned a spare bedroom into her home office.

Gray fell in step behind her. She went back to her cushy chair at her corner desk and spun around to see Gray fold his frame onto the delicate yellow sofa she'd found at a yard sale a couple of years ago.

"Why am I not surprised you're working?" he asked, nodding toward the organized piles on her desk.

"I couldn't sleep."

"There's a surefire remedy for that."

Kate stared at him for a moment before she rolled her eyes. "Did you seriously come here thinking we'd have sex again?"

Gray quirked one dark brow. He stretched his long, denim-clad legs out in front of him and crossed his ankles. He placed one tattooed arm on the armrest. Gray was clearly comfortable with this topic based on the way he looked at her, taking in her thin tank and ratty old shorts.

His gaze was anything but friendly. Well, it was friendly in the sense that he looked like he wanted to strip her out of her clothes again.

Wait. He'd never gotten her out of her clothes the first time. Perhaps that's why he was staring so intently. But he'd seen her in a bathing suit and he'd most definitely seen her lower half.

Boobs. Men always wanted boobs. It was a ridiculous thing she would never understand. Still, he continued to stare across the office as if he knew exactly what she looked like in her birthday suit.

Had he always been this intense? This potent?

Kate shivered and tucked one leg beneath her. "Why did you really stop by?"

"I missed you."

The way those words settled between them had Kate's breath catching in her throat. He said them so simply, as if the question were silly and it should be obvious why he was here.

They hadn't gone this long without seeing each other since he'd served in the army. She appreciated how he put himself out there and used complete and utter honesty.

Another reason why he was her everything. Gray never sugarcoated anything and had always been up front with her. Considering her ex had been so deceitful, having Gray in her life was refreshing and made her realize there were good men out there. This good man, however, just couldn't be for her.

"I missed you, too," she replied, because she

wanted to be just as honest right back. "I've been busy with the Savvy Scheduler, the blogs and the scheduling for upcoming giveaways, and then getting ready for the next Helping Hands meeting. With Lucy gone—"

"You're hiding from me."

She really was getting ready for the next meeting. Kate, Tara and Lucy all led a weekly support group that helped to uplift those hurting from loss. They'd all experienced it themselves on some level, so it was a labor of love.

But perhaps she was using her work and the group to hide from Gray. Still, she'd always made time for him before and he'd never pushed her away. Not once.

Fine. So maybe she wasn't being totally honest with him, but how could she be when she was trying to fumble around with her own emotions and figure it all out herself?

Kate glanced down to her lap and stared at her pale pink polish. "I don't know what to do now."

Silence settled in the room. She had no clue what he was thinking, no clue how to get them back on the comfortable ground they'd been walking on for years. How could one moment undo years of friendship? How did sex muddle so much?

When the awkward tension became unbearable, Kate turned slightly and started straightening her desk. There had never been awkwardness between them and she desperately needed to rid this moment of it. She needed her Gray back—her best friend back.

She glanced at the outline for her next week and mentally tried to prepare herself and focus. At least this was something she could control, because she sure as hell couldn't control her feelings—not now that he was in her house and staring at her as if he wanted an encore bar performance.

No. No more sex—at least not with him. She shouldn't pay attention to her body when it started getting all revved up again at just the sight of Gray. She shouldn't keep remembering how he'd felt as he'd joined their bodies. And she sure as hell shouldn't keep wondering if there was any man who could measure up to him.

"We do what we've always done, Kate."

She shivered as his soft words pierced the silence and washed over her. Leave it to him to find a simple resolution to their tension. Maybe he didn't have the juxtaposition of feelings running through him like she did. Maybe he slept just fine at night and hadn't given her or their encounter another thought.

Kate slid the green marker back into the pouch, set Mrs. Clements's folder in her desk organizer labeled Things to Do, and worked the corners of the rest of the folders until they were perfectly lined up. Now what? There was nothing else to straighten or fiddle with.

"Look at me."

Oh, that low, sultry tone. Now that they'd been intimate, she could appreciate it so much more.

Kate gritted her teeth and spun around in her chair. That piercing stare had her gripping the edge of her chair. Anticipation curled low in her belly at what he would say or do next. She'd never been on the edge of her seat with him before.

Honestly, sex changed everything. Hadn't she warned herself about that in the few moments between the kiss and the torn underwear? But her hormones had taken over and Gray had been all too convincing…and she was human.

"We're still Gray and Kate," he reminded her, pinning her with that dark gaze. "We annoy each other for fun. We watch old movies and argue over the classics. I still worry you're going to choose another loser, so I'm extra cautious and overprotective. Yes, we had sex, but we're still us."

He made things sound so simple and easy, as if sex hadn't changed a thing. But it had changed everything. She found herself looking at him differently, seeing him in a completely different light. Because for a short time he'd been not only her best friend, but also her lover.

"That's why you came?" she asked.

"You didn't think I'd let you hide forever, did you?"

Kate smiled. "I would've been at Ladies' Night this week."

That side grin flashed over his face. "You missed last week, so I wasn't sure."

Kate picked at one of the threads on the edge of her shorts. "I just needed some space."

"Had enough?"

She chewed the inside of her cheek. "Maybe."

Gray came to his feet and crossed to her. He took her hands and pulled her up against him. Kate tipped her head back to look him directly in the eyes. A punch of lust hit her faster than she'd expected. She'd hoped that need, that ache, had vanished or had been all in her mind. But no. Gray had crossed the line and had settled deep into a place inside her. And she had no clue how to categorize him.

"You're done hiding or running, or whatever the hell else you were doing." He flashed her that devilish grin. "I need you, Kate. We've been together too long to let anything come between our friendship. Can we just get back there again?"

Something akin to relief slid through her at how easily he was putting them both back on stable ground. At the same time, though, she hated that they were going back to being just friends.

How could she just ignore how she felt now that he was this close? How could she forget how he'd kissed her? How he'd looked at her, touched her?

She couldn't forget. Gray had imbedded himself so far into her soul, she truly wasn't sure she could go back. She wasn't even entirely sure she wanted to.

"We are friends," she agreed. "You have to admit this is a bit awkward."

Gray laughed. "So stop making it awkward."

He pulled her into a hug just like he'd done for years. Only this time she couldn't prevent herself from pulling in a deep breath of that masculine scent, remembering how she'd been completely enveloped by that familiar aroma and the man. His potency had been all-consuming when he'd ripped off her panties and taken her on that bar top. Would she ever get that image, that *feeling* from her mind?

"You in a hurry to get home?" she asked into his chest.

"Not really."

Kate tipped her head back and smiled. "How about a movie?"

Gray kissed her forehead. "Perfect."

Chapter Six

"Tell me about this list."

Kate stopped tapping her toes on the side of his thigh. He sat on one end of the sofa and she had relaxed on the other, stretching those legs out, propping her dainty feet against his denim-clad thigh, and driving him out of his ever-loving mind.

Gray had known facing her would be difficult. Of course they'd seen each other at the wedding, but this was the first time they'd been alone and forced to really discuss what had happened at the bar. The tension still hovered between them, but he was going to push through because as much as he wanted her physically, he refused to lose her altogether.

Other than the obvious fact she'd been dodging

him, he knew she was panicking about where they were now. He knew she'd be trying to analyze things from every which angle and she wouldn't be able to. He'd wanted her for a while, longer than he probably wanted to admit even to himself, so there was no way she could decipher what the hell truly happened when he couldn't explain it himself.

For years, he'd been able to control himself out of respect for her and their friendship. Then, over the past several months, little by little, seeing her at the bar dancing with other guys, then at the rehearsal with Bryan, it had all just become too much and he'd snapped. Every man had a breaking point and she'd definitely hit his.

"It's nothing," she finally replied.

He curled his hand around her bare toes. "Tell me about the infamous list or I'll crack your toes."

Kate's legs jerked from his lap as she laughed. "Watch the movie and leave me alone."

"We've seen this at least a hundred times," he told her as he shifted on the couch to face her. He grabbed the remote from the back of the couch and muted the TV before tossing the device between them on the cushion. "Talk to me, Kate. You can't hide it forever. I'm going to get the truth out of you, you know."

She let out a sigh and shook her head. "Fine."

When she started to get up, Gray reached out and gripped her arm. "You don't have to go get some color-coded spreadsheet that no doubt you've laminated. Just tell me. I want to hear your words, not read some damn paper."

Kate smiled as she settled onto the couch. She swung her legs back up and he instantly started rubbing her feet. Maybe if she was relaxed she'd talk, and if she was talking about this mystery list, then perhaps he would focus on that and not the fact that he wanted his best friend now more than ever.

There was still the matter of discussing the business proposition with her, but right now there were much more important things to work out. It was just another area of his life he was confused as hell about. Once he talked to Kate and his father, he'd have a clearer picture of the future…he hoped.

"Tell me why you made a list," he started, needing to reel himself in from his wayward thoughts.

Kate adjusted the throw pillow between her head and the arm of the couch. Tipping her head sideways, she stared down at him. "My thirtieth birthday just passed."

"Yes, I'm aware of that." His thumb slid up over the arch of her foot. "So, what? You think you're old now that you're thirty? I'm thirty-one. We're barely getting started."

She smiled, which is exactly the response he wanted. He loved seeing that smile, loved knowing he could get such a quick, heartfelt reaction from her.

Lacing her hands over her abdomen, Kate blew out a deep sigh. "I don't think we're old. My mom was only thirty-two when she died, which was way too young. I just… I don't know. I guess I've been thinking too much over the past year. My mom probably thought she had her whole life ahead of her with raising me. Maybe she even wanted more kids. I have no clue. All I know is I don't want to lose out on anything because I was too busy working or assumed I had more time."

Gray's hands stilled. Her words hit hard. She was absolutely right. What if he kept up his day-to-day life, wondering what else was out there, what he was missing out on? Life was fleeting and nothing was guaranteed.

Should he take that business deal? Should he accept the money and sell Gallagher's, finally moving on to fill that void? The possibilities for him would be endless and the money would allow him to fully explore his options.

But at what cost? Disappointment from his father and the unknown of what he'd do next or if he would even stay in Stonerock. The risk from either decision weighed heavily on him.

"You okay?" Kate asked, pulling him away from his thoughts.

"Fine." He switched to her other foot and circled back to her needs. He wasn't quite ready to express his own just yet. "Tell me what you've put on the list."

"You'll think I'm silly."

"We've already established I live for silly."

Kate rolled her eyes and laughed—music to his ears. "Well, I'd like to go camping."

Gray couldn't help but laugh. "Camping? What in the world brought that up?"

"I don't know. It's just something I haven't done." She stretched her legs and rotated her ankles before dropping them back to his lap. "I live in the mountains, for crying out loud, and I've never been camping."

"So you made a bucket list?"

She nodded. "I titled it My Life List."

"Of course you gave it a title. What else is on there?" he asked, resting his hands on her legs.

"I'd like to get a dog and name her Sprout. A kennel dog or a stray. I can't handle the thought of all those abandoned animals while people are paying for novelty pets. It's heartbreaking. So I'll start with one dog. Who knows how many I'll end up with."

Someone as passionate and caring as Kate would want to help the less fortunate. Just another aspect he'd always admired about her. She was always looking at how to spread her light, even when she didn't always shine it on herself.

Kate kept her eyes on his as she discussed the items from her list. "I want to go to the beach since I've never seen the ocean. I'd love to throw a *Great Gatsby*–themed party and dress up and have fun all night. I think I'd like to go on a road trip. Of course I'd have to have it mapped out, but I want to just take off in the car and visit some national landmarks.

Once I get closer to checking that one off the list, I'll make a spreadsheet."

As he listened to her, Gray realized her goals were all so obtainable and there was no reason she couldn't do those things.

"I wanted to try alcohol, so that box is already ticked off," she added.

"In bright blue marker, I'm sure."

She reached up to swat his shoulder. "No, smarty-pants. Yellow is clearly the only choice."

Gray couldn't help but laugh. Kate took her feet from his lap and crisscrossed them in front of her on the cushion.

"So what else do you have?" he asked.

"I want to do something utterly spontaneous."

Gray stared at her, waiting for her to smile or give some hint that she was kidding. But she merely stared at him, completely serious.

"Darlin', you do realize you're missing the whole point of being spontaneous if you put it on a list and schedule it."

She toyed with the frayed ends of her shorts. Gray couldn't help but watch her movements, torment-ing himself further as he stared at the white threads lying against her tanned skin. He wanted to run his hands up those shapely legs. He wanted to strip her and have her right here on this couch.

Being together in the middle of the night with nothing around to interrupt them was probably not the smartest idea, but he couldn't bring himself to leave. He was dead-tired now, but she was talking. They were getting back to a place of comfort and familiarity. And she wasn't trying to make excuses for the mistake they'd made.

Only having sex hadn't been a mistake. It had been perfect and he was hell-bent on making sure it happened again. But above all, he didn't want her to worry about the future of their relationship. He'd never let anything—including his all-consuming desire for her—jeopardize that, because he needed her just as much.

While he respected her stipulation that their one night of passion stay just that, he wasn't going to let her ignore the attraction. If the opportunity arose again, if she gave the slightest hint she wanted more, he'd be all over it…and her.

"Well, I don't know what the spontaneous moment will be," she explained. "So it's not completely ridiculous that I listed it. I just want to try to be more… I don't know. Like you. You're so laid-back and carefree. I don't even know what that would feel like. But it's a short-term goal."

He wasn't going to state the obvious of the spontaneity on the bar. She'd probably already labeled that under something else.

"If you say so," he chuckled. "Anything else on the list?"

"Well…"

She was driving him crazy. "What? You want to

jump out of a plane? See the Mayan ruins? Take an Alaskan cruise? Just spit it out."

"Jump out of a plane?" She jerked back. "First of all, I wouldn't pick something so predictable, and second of all, hell no."

Gray laughed and curled his hands over her toes. "Tell me or I start cracking."

"I want to trace my heritage."

Intrigued at her statement, he relaxed his hands and stared over at her. "Seriously?"

Kate nodded and tipped her head to the side, resting on the back of the couch. "With my parents gone, I just want to know where I came from, you know? I don't have any other family and I was just a teen when they passed. It's not something I ever thought of asking them about."

Gray had never thought of that before. His grandfather had died only two years ago, but his father was alive and well and more than willing to pass down the family stories that could trace all the way back to their roots in Ireland. Kate didn't have anything like that.

While Gray had lost his mother at a young age and always had that hole in his heart, he couldn't imagine how Kate felt, essentially alone other than having friends. But that wasn't the same as family. Nothing could ever replace parents.

She'd lived with her grandmother for a while, but ultimately she passed, too. Thankfully Kate was older when that happened.

"I want to know where I got the combination of black hair and blue eyes," she went on with a slight smile. "It's a little silly, I know, but I guess I just feel like I need those answers. Maybe I have family out there and a long-distance relative I can connect with."

Gray hated that lost tone. She'd never mentioned feeling alone before. She'd never talked like she was hurting. At least, she hadn't said as much to him. Of course, she suffered from her parents' absence. That was something she'd never get over. But he really had no idea she'd been longing to find out where she came from. Kate should have every opportunity to trace her family roots. He'd make damn sure of it.

As she went through her list, he realized that he wanted to be the one to experience those things with her. They were best friends. Yes, she had Tara and Lucy, but Lucy was newly married and Tara was still struggling with Sam and their own sordid mess.

Gray wasn't going to let Kate feel alone any longer. Hell, he'd already helped her knock trying alcohol off her list. The rest would be a joy to share with her.

"We'll do this together," he told her.

Bright blue eyes snapped up, focusing on him. "Don't be ridiculous. I wasn't hinting that I needed a partner. I wasn't going to tell anyone about this list. It's just something I'm doing for me."

"I don't plan on telling anyone," he replied. "Keep

all the secrets about it you want, but I'm not going to let you do this alone."

Kate stared at him another minute before swinging her feet to the floor. She grabbed the remote and turned the television off, then put it back on the table.

"I really should get to bed." She stretched her arms above her head, giving him a glimpse of pale skin between her tank and her shorts. "I think I'm finally tired."

Yeah, well, he wasn't. Well, he was tired in the sense that he needed sleep, but he didn't want to leave. He could sit here all night and talk with her like they had when they were younger, with fewer responsibilities. Besides, she couldn't brush him off that easily. She was running scared again. He'd offered to help and she flipped out, jumping off the couch to get away from his touch. How could she choose this over intimacy?

If they just went with the sexual pull, the undeniable attraction, it would have to be less stressful than what was brewing between them now. How could she not see that? Was she simply too afraid to face the truth?

An idea formed in his head, but he kept the piece of brilliance locked away as he came to his feet. He knew she was tired, so he'd go. But he was done letting her hide behind her fear of the unknown and what was happening here.

"You look like you're ready to drop."

Gray took in her sleepy eyes, her relaxed clothing,

and there was nothing more he wanted to do than to pick her up and carry her to bed...and stay the rest of the night. Maybe he would one day. Maybe she'd realize that the one time wasn't enough and she wanted more.

He had every intention of respecting her wishes to stay in the friend zone—but that didn't mean he wouldn't keep showing her how perfect they were together. There was nothing wrong with exploring what they'd started. Besides, he knew Kate better than she knew herself at times. She had analyzed that night from every different angle and their intimacy was never far from the front of her mind. He'd bet his bar on it.

Said bar might not be his for much longer, though. But she wasn't in the right mind-set to discuss the potential sale now, and honestly, neither was he. Tomorrow, he vowed. There was too much at stake no matter which way he decided to go. Both choices were life-altering and would change not only his entire world, but that of his father and the town.

Gallagher's had been the pride of three generations now. His grandfather had wanted to set down roots, to have something that brought people together, because he'd seen so much ugliness tearing them apart. Ewan Gallagher had started a tradition, one that the people in this tiny town had come to appreciate and rely upon.

Gray didn't want that niggle of doubt and guilt to sway his decision. He wanted to look at this from a business and personal standpoint, but it was so difficult when the two were so inherently connected.

He dropped an innocent kiss on Kate's forehead and let himself out the front door. Gray waited until he heard her click the lock back into place before he headed to his car.

He knew he needed to grab sleep, but as soon as he got up, he was putting a few plans into motion. Kate was about to check off more items on her bucket list and he was personally going to see that she accomplished exactly what she set out to do.

Morning runs sucked. They sucked even more when little sleep was a factor and really all she'd wanted was to run to the bakery and buy a donut the size of her face. And by run, she meant drive.

Kate took a hearty chug from her water bottle as she pulled her key from the tiny pouch on her running shorts. She'd ended up falling asleep on the couch after Gray left, then stumbled to her room at about six and climbed into bed. When she'd woken up for good at nine, Kate realized she'd slept later than usual, so she'd hopped out of bed and quickly headed out the door to get in her miles.

She hated running. But that was the only way she could enjoy her donuts and still fit in her clothes. Besides, the exercise was a great stress reliever…so were pastries, but whatever.

As Kate opened her front door, she heard a vehicle pulling into her drive. Kate glanced over her shoulder, her heart skipping a beat at the sight of Gray's large black truck. The thing was as menacing as the man himself. He might look like the quintessential bad boy, but he'd listened to her drone on and on about her bucket list all while rubbing her feet.

Damn it. Why did he have to be her best friend? He was the perfect catch for any woman...just not her. She couldn't—no, she *wouldn't*—risk losing him as a friend. If she'd jumped at her initial reaction after the great sex and ignored common sense altogether, she might have made a play for him. But he was the only stable man in her life. He'd filled that role for far too long for her to just throw it aside and take the risk for something more.

Even if she went for more, what would it be? Gray wasn't the type to settle down. In fact, she knew his father mentioned Gray's bachelor status quite often and Gray brushed the notion aside. He seemed just fine keeping busy with his bar. The man rarely dated and even when he did, he kept it all so private. He was definitely not someone looking for happily-ever-after.

Kate took another drink as she waited on the porch for Gray to come up her flower-lined walk.

"Didn't you just leave here?" she joked.

He glanced up, flashing that megawatt smile he didn't always hand out freely. Mercy, the man was too sexy for his own good, and now that she'd had a sample of that sexiness, she was positive no other man would ever measure up.

How did one encounter have such an epic impact? Kate had to push aside what happened. It couldn't have been that great...could it? Surely she was just conjuring up more vivid details than actually happened.

Or maybe not. Gray did in fact tear her panties off and climb up the bar to get to her.

"I feel like I did," he replied as he mounted the steps. "You're sweating."

Kate rolled her eyes. "That happens when I go for a run."

"Well, you have ten minutes to get a bag together." He hooked his thumbs through his belt loops. "And if you want to shower, you better squeeze it in that time frame."

Kate jerked back. "Excuse me? Pack a bag?"

A mischievous smile spread across his face. "We're going camping."

"What?" Shocked, she turned and let herself in her house, trying to wrap her mind around his announcement. "I can't just go camping right now. I have things to do."

Her planner lay on the table just inside the door. She fingered through the colored tabs until she landed on the red. Flipping it over, she quickly glanced at her mounting list—color-coded with her favorite fine-point markers, of course.

"You can see there's no time," she stated as Gray followed her in. She used the tip of her finger to tap on the upcoming days. "I have to finish outlining a bridal shower and start on a new client's vacation schedule. Then I have to try to come up with some way to fit in my neighbor, who swears her closets are full but won't get rid of anything. Same story with her kitchen, so at this point I'm afraid her entire house needs an overhaul. I also have eight online clients I'm working with who found me just last week through my social media sites and referrals."

"And do you plan on doing all of that today?" he asked, crossing his arms and leaning against the wall beside her.

"Well, no, but—"

"You're down to eight minutes, Kate. If you hurry, I can even swing by and get a box of donuts on our way out of town so we can have breakfast in the morning."

"That's a low blow," she stated, narrowing her eyes.

"You need a break."

She slapped her planner shut and faced him. "I can't go camping last minute. I'd need sufficient time to strategize and make a detailed list of all the things I need to take. Hell, I need to research *what* to take. I've never been, so I have no clue."

That smile assaulted her once again. Damn cocky man.

"You're in luck," he replied. "I have been multiple times so I have everything you need, minus your clothes and the donuts I'll stop and get on the road.

Look at it this way—you can check off two things on your list. Camping and spontaneity."

Kate shook her head and sighed. "I can't mark off being spontaneous when it was your idea."

And she still hadn't marked it in regards to the bar sex. That needed a whole other label of its own. How could something so life-altering be checked off so simply? No, that encounter deserved more respect than just a quick X by the words spontaneous quickie.

Gray pushed off the wall and started for the steps. "You'll want a pair of jeans for when we go hiking, plus shorts, maybe a swimsuit, comfortable shoes that can get wet. It gets cooler at night so grab a sweatshirt or something with sleeves."

Kate watched as he just headed up to her bedroom like she hadn't just laid out several reasons she couldn't go. Did the man ever take no for an answer?

Her mind flashed back to the bar as her body trembled with the onslaught of memories.

So no. No, he didn't.

And here she was, contemplating going camping? Being alone with him all night and not invoking how she felt when he'd touched her, kissed her. This was not smart. Not smart at all.

Kate headed for the steps, rushing up to her bedroom.

"You're not getting out of this," he told her before she could open her mouth.

He opened her closet and jerked a sweatshirt off

the top shelf. Two more shirts fell to the floor as a result and Kate cringed.

"You're messing up my system here, Gallagher." She crossed over and instantly started sorting the mess back into neat piles. "You cannot just start packing my bag."

He shot her a wink. "Does that mean you're cuddling up to me for warmth and skinny dipping? Hey, I'm game, but you might be more comfortable with clothes."

Kate blew out a breath and leaned back against her open closet door. "You're not going to let this go, are you?"

"Nope." He took a step closer to her, his eyes all serious now. Gone was the playful smile. "Listen, if I didn't push you into this, I'm not sure you'd actually do it. Making a list is one thing, but following through is another."

"I would do it," She felt the need to defend herself because, damn it, she would do it…at some point. "I don't know when, but I would."

He tossed the sweatshirt behind him onto her four-poster bed, then took her by her shoulders. "My truck is packed. I literally have everything we need: a large tent, food, supplies, blankets. I got Jacob to cover at the bar for me tonight. We'll be back late tomorrow evening."

Kate stared into those dark eyes and knew if anyone could help her check items off her list, it was this man. He'd clearly gone to great lengths to set this up for her and she'd be a terrible friend, not to mention flat-out rude, to turn him down.

He'd literally thought of everything and he stood before her, having rearranged his entire life for two days just to make her happy.

Kate's heart flipped in her chest. Gray always did amazing things for her, but since the sex, his actions had taken on a deeper, more intimate meaning.

"Fine," she conceded. "But step away from my neatly organized closet and let me pack. I don't trust you over there and I promise I won't be long. You swear we're stopping for donuts?"

"I promise." Gray leaned forward and wrinkled his nose. "I'll give you an extra five minutes to shower. You smell."

Laughing, Kate smacked his arm. "Get out of my room. I'll be down in twenty minutes."

Once he was gone, Kate closed her bedroom door and started stripping on her way to the shower. She dropped her clothes into the color-coded piles in her laundry sorter just inside her bathroom.

Gray Gallagher was slowly making her reconsider that whole one-night rule. For a half second she thought about packing some pretty underwear, but then snorted.

Seriously? Even if she was after an encore performance, they were camping. She'd never been, but she had a feeling lace and satin didn't pair well with bug spray and campfire smoke.

Kate stepped under the hot shower and mentally started packing. No matter how this trip went down, she had a feeling lasting memories would be made.

Chapter Seven

"I did it," Kate exclaimed, jumping up and down.

Gray glanced over to the tent she'd put together. He'd set everything out and given her instructions, and damn if she hadn't erected their tent like a pro. He knew she wouldn't give up, but she'd definitely gotten it done much quicker than he thought she would. He was proud of her.

This was by far his favorite campground, but the spot he usually chose had already been taken and he'd had to choose another. He found one closest to a hiking trail near his favorite areas in the forest. He couldn't wait to share all of these experiences with Kate.

"Looks good." Gray came to his feet and wiped

his hands on his pants. "The fire is ready if you want to roast some hot dogs for lunch."

"I don't recall the last time I had a roasted hot dog."

Gray rolled over another large log and stood it up on its end as a makeshift stool. He'd found several near the designated fire area, but set up only the two.

"We had one at the bonfire last fall," he said. "Remember the fundraiser for Drake?"

Drake St. John had been a firefighter who had encountered several issues with the then mayor. Drake had decided to run for office himself and ultimately won. Drake and his brothers were pillars in the community and Gray had happily voted for him.

"Oh, yeah." Kate picked up one of the roasting sticks and held it out for him to put the hot dog on. "So I guess that was the last time I had one."

"Then you're long overdue," he replied, getting his own roasting stick ready.

The crackling fire kept his focus on cooking his lunch....and away from the swell of her breasts peeking from the top of her fitted tank. He had no business going there. This was about Kate. He wanted this to be an easy trip, something where she could relax and just be herself, take a break from work and all those damn schedules. He was here to make sure she was taken care of, first and foremost.

Silence settled easily between them, but so much swirled through Gray's mind. Kate, their turning point, the bar, the possibilities…the unknowns came at him from every single angle.

He still hadn't spoken to his father about the proposal. There were pros and cons that Gray could easily see now, but there was no clear answer.

"I jotted down some things for us to do," Kate said after a minute. "I looked on my phone for area suggestions while you were driving and made a list—"

"I saw you. You just had to bring your planner, didn't you?"

Kate gasped and stared at him as if he'd just asked if the sky was purple. "Of course I had to bring it. How else would I know what to do? I can't keep all these places and a timeline of when to visit them straight without writing them down."

Shaking his head, Gray rotated the stick. "You can relax for a day, damn it. I've got the trip planned and details covered. We'll be fine. Chill."

"I'm relaxed," she argued. "Look at me. Cooking a hot dog over a fire, sitting on a tree stump, completely relaxed."

"Where's the planner?"

She pursed her lips and shrugged.

"It's beside you, isn't it?"

Kate blinked. "I don't know what you're talking about."

Gray pulled his charred hot dog from the fire and tested it with his fingers. Black and crispy on the outside, just the way he liked it.

"What would you do if you didn't have that colorful binder?"

"I'd be lost. This is my personal one. But I need both personal and business or I'd never be able to function."

He threw her a sideways glance. "You've got to be kidding."

Kate came to her feet and pulled her hot dog from the fire. "Why is that so strange? I have too much to remember so I just keep it all nice and neat in my planner."

"But that's just your personal one," he stated. "You still have one for work."

Gray pulled the pack of buns out and set them on the old picnic table before grabbing bottles of water from the cooler.

"This is supposed to be a nice, calm overnight trip," he reminded her. "We don't need an itinerary."

She took a seat on one of the benches and grabbed a bun. "I need a plan or I'm going to miss out on things. So, like I was saying—"

"You've got me." Gray threw a leg over the bench and took a seat. "I have plans for us so put your planner in my truck and forget about it until we start to head home."

Kate's eyes widened. "You're joking."

He stared across the table. "Do I look like I'm joking?"

"I don't like camping already," she muttered around a bite.

Gray couldn't help but smile. He was going to get her to relax if it was the last thing he did.

"After we eat there's a little place I want to show you."

"What do I need to wear?"

"You're fine the way you are."

She'd come down the stairs at her house freshly showered. Her hair had been pulled up on top of her head in some wet bun thing she sometimes wore. She'd thrown on a tank that fit her curvy body perfectly, and her shorts showed off those legs she kept toned and shapely by her constant running. Though she'd looked perfectly fine before she'd taken up that hobby. She'd started running after her jerk fiancé left. Gray never did figure out if she was using the exercise as a natural form of therapy or if she thought something was wrong with her body.

Kate was pretty damn perfect no matter her look or her shape...at least in his eyes.

They finished their lunch and cleaned up, making sure to burn what they could before putting the food back in a sealed cooler to keep the hungry animals away.

"We've got things to do that do not involve spreadsheets or strict schedules," he informed her. "I'll wait while you put your planner and cell in my truck."

Kate hesitated, but he quirked his brow and crossed his arms. Groaning, she picked up her things and put them in the cab of his truck before coming back beside him.

"Happy now?"

Gray nodded and turned to head toward the marked trail. He wasn't sure if this camping idea was the greatest or dumbest move he'd ever made. On one hand, at least he was getting her out of her scheduled shell and she was checking things off her list.

On the other, though, they would be sharing a tent. Which wouldn't be a big deal if they hadn't already slept together. He'd warned her not to make things awkward between them, so he needed to take his own advice.

Still, anticipation had settled in deep because he had no idea how the night would play out once they were alone lying mere inches from each other.

"How far are we going?" she asked from behind him.

"About a mile."

She came up beside him. "I could've skipped my run this morning."

"You could skip it every morning and be just fine," he growled.

He hadn't meant to sound grouchy, but she worried about her body when her body was perfect. Why did women obsess about such things? Confidence was more of a turn-on to him than anything. Kate had to know how amazing she looked. Damn that ex of hers for ever making her doubt it.

They walked on a bit more in silence before they came to the top of a hill. He reached for her arm to stop her. With careful movements, he shifted her to stand and turn exactly to the spot he'd been dying for her to see.

"Oh my word," she gasped. "That's gorgeous."

Gray looked down into the valley at the natural waterfall spilling over the rocks. "This is one of my favorite places."

She glanced over her shoulder. "How often do you come here?"

"Not enough. Maybe once a year."

"And you've never brought me?"

Gray shrugged. "I tend to come alone to recharge, plus I never knew you had an interest in camping."

Kate turned her attention back to the breathtaking view. "I didn't know I had an interest, either, but I'm starting to love it. There's not a worry in the world up here. How could anyone even think of their day-to-day lives when this is so…magical?"

Something turned deep inside him. He couldn't put his finger on it, but as he stood behind her, seeing her take in this sight for the first time, Gray knew he'd be bringing her back.

This one night out here with her wouldn't be enough. Just like the one night of sex wouldn't be enough. Kate was a huge part of his life. He couldn't just ignore this continual pull between them.

Gray had always loved being outside, there was a sense of freedom he didn't have when he was behind the bar or doing office work. Knowing that Kate might share this…well, he was starting to wonder just how right they were together in areas he'd never fathomed.

"Can we climb down there and get a closer look?" she asked.

"We can, but you'll want to change."

She turned back to face him. "Why?"

"There's a natural spring you can swim in."

Her face lit up and she smacked his chest. "Then what are we waiting for? Let's get to it."

She circled around him and started heading back down the narrow, wooded trail. Gray watched her go and raked a hand down his face. First camping alone and now getting her in a bathing suit. Yeah, this whole adventurous weekend was a brilliant idea… for a masochist.

Kate smoothed her wet hair back from her face as she climbed back up the shoreline toward the grassy area with a large fallen tree serving as a makeshift bench. She grabbed her towel from the tree and patted her face.

Pulling in a deep breath and starting to dry her legs, she threw a smile at Gray, who had yet to put his shirt back on.

How long was he going to stand there? They'd splashed in the water, floated on their backs, then chatted a bit while just wading. Thankfully the conversation had stayed light, mostly about the beauty of the area and its peacefulness. There was something so calming and perfect about it. Kate was convinced no problems existed here.

Gray had gotten out of the water several minutes ago but still wasn't making any moves to get dressed. And that was pretty much the only reason she'd gotten out. They needed to get back to camp so he could put some damn clothes on and stop driving her out of her mind. Those water droplets glistening all over his well-defined shoulders, pecs and abs. The dark ink curving over his shoulder. There wasn't a thing about her best friend that she didn't find attractive.

Yes. He was definitely driving her out of her mind.

Unfortunately, Kate had a feeling he wasn't even trying.

She pushed aside her lustful thoughts. Okay, she didn't push them aside so much as kept them to herself as she turned her attention toward the brooding man. Something was up with him, but it could just be the sexual tension that continued to thicken between them with each passing day.

"That was amazing," she stated, blowing out a breath and glancing toward the crisp blue sky before looking back at Gray. He said nothing, didn't even so much as crack a smile. "But I guess we can't stay here forever."

Kate tightened the knot on her towel and when she lifted her eyes back up, those dark, mesmerizing eyes were directed right at her. She couldn't quite decipher the look, but whatever it was had her clutching the knot she'd just tied.

"What's wrong?" she asked.

Gray wrapped his towel around his neck, gripping the ends in one hand. "I've had something on my mind I want to discuss with you."

Instantly, Kate stilled. The only major thing between them was the new state of their relationship that they hadn't fully fleshed out. They'd brushed it aside in an attempt to get back on safer ground.

Was he about to open the memory bank and dig deeper? Fine. She needed to just remain calm and do this. They had to hash it out at some point, and better before they fell into bed together than later, so to speak.

Gray sank down onto the large old tree stretched across the ground. Without waiting to see what he was about to say or do, she took a seat beside him.

"What's up?"

Gray rested his forearms on his knees and leaned forward, staring out at the waterfall. The way stress settled over his face, Kate worried something else was wrong. If he wanted to discuss the other night, he'd be more confident. Right now, Gray appeared to be…torn.

Kate honestly had no idea what he was going to say, but the silence certainly wasn't helping her nerves. *Was* there something else wrong? Had he actually brought her out here to tell her he was sick or dying?

"Gray, come on," she said, smacking his leg. "You know my anxiety and overactive imagination can't handle this."

"I had a visitor at the bar yesterday morning."

Okay, so he wasn't dying. That was good. So what had him so upset and speechless?

Kate shifted to block the sun from her eyes. She waited for him to go on, but at this rate it would be nightfall before he finished the story. Whoever this visitor was had Gray struggling for words. Either that or he was battling something major and trying to figure out how to tell her.

"He offered me an insane amount of money to buy the bar."

His words settled heavily between them, rendering her speechless as well. Sell the bar? Is that something he actually wanted to do? She'd never heard him mention wanting away from something that she'd always thought held so much meaning. What would his dad say? Had he even talked to his dad?

There were so many questions crammed into one space and she wanted all of the answers now.

"Are you selling?" she finally asked when it was clear he wasn't going to add more to his verbal bomb.

Gray lifted one bare shoulder and glanced over. "I have no idea. I never wanted the bar, it was just assumed I'd take it over. When I came home from the army, it was there, so I stepped into role of owner."

"What would you do without it?"

He raked a hand over his wet hair and blew out

a sigh. "I have no idea, but I've always wondered. I mean, with the amount I was offered, I could do anything."

"You haven't talked to your dad."

Gray shook his head, though she hadn't actually been asking.

"Is that why you brought me camping?" she asked. "So you could get my opinion?"

Gray reached for her hand. "No. I mean, I knew I wanted to talk to you, but the second you mentioned that list and started naming things off, I knew I was going to bring you here as soon as I could get everything lined up. It just happened to be rather quickly."

Kate couldn't help but smile as she glanced down to their joined hands. "Have you made a list of reasons to stay and reasons to go?"

His lips twitched into a grin of their own as he shook his head. "No, ma'am. I leave the list-making to you."

Her mind started rolling on all the good things about owning a family business. There was just so much, but only Gray knew what he loved most about the place.

On the downside, once you owned a business, you were married to it. Randomly he would take a day, like this, but the man was loyal and that bar was his wife, baby. Plus, he carried on the small-town tradition his grandfather had started.

Family heritage meant everything to someone like Gray. Money could only go so far. She was surprised he even considered selling the bar, which meant he must really be looking for something else in his life.

Kate's heart ached for him, for this decision. If she were in his place she wouldn't even have to think about it. She had no family and would kill to carry on this kind of legacy.

"Your silence is making me nervous."

Kate smiled and patted his leg. "You should be nervous. The pros and cons are already lining up inside my head."

Gray led her back to camp and she was somewhat grateful for the distraction. Though she didn't think anything could fully take her mind off the ripped torso covered with tats that he still hadn't covered. She'd be lying if she didn't admit her nerves had settled in at the thought of spending the night in that tent with him.

But first, she'd help him figure out what to do about this business proposition. Surely that would crush any desires...wouldn't it?

Yes, if they just continued to focus on the bar and his proposal, then any desires they shared would be pushed aside and they could reconfigure their friendship.

Kate would keep telling herself that until it became the truth.

Chapter Eight

The fire crackled, the stars were vibrant in the sky, and beside him, Kate continued to jot down notes. She'd mutter something, then mark out what she'd just written. Every now and then she'd ask him a question and scribble something else down.

Her system was driving him insane. She fidgeted, pulling her hair up into a knot, then taking it down and raking her fingers through it. Then she'd start the process all over again. Watching her was killing him, mostly because her mind was working overtime, but just seeing her in her element was too damn sexy.

Kate let out a groan. "I need my colored markers so I can see the overall picture clearer."

Gray had had enough. He reached over, jerked the planner from her lap and tossed it into the fire.

"Gray!" Kate leaped to her feet and stared down as the pages curled, turned black, and drifted up in ashes. "That was my personal planner. You can't just—"

"Too late. I just did."

Okay, maybe he should feel bad, but she needed to relax because until she did, he couldn't. She'd brought the damn thing camping when this whole night should be about taking a break from reality.

Now she sat here working on his life like he was one of her damn clients. No more.

"Not only does that have my whole life in it, I had the lists for you about the bar."

Kate spun around and propped her hands on her hips as she stared down at him. He picked up the long stick he'd had beside him and poked around at the fire, shoving the last bit of the planner further into the flames for good measure. It was better than seeing that snug little tank pulling across her chest or the creamy patch of skin between the hem of her shirt and the top of her pants.

"You're a jerk."

She stomped off into the darkness, heading toward his truck. Gray bit the inside of his cheek to keep from laughing. She most likely had a backup planner at home and he knew she kept duplicate electronic files. He felt only a little guilty. She'd be fine. Knowing Kate, she had everything logged into her memory bank anyway. Someone who was so focused on details and schedules and color coding the hell out of every minute of life would definitely know her schedule by heart.

The slam of his truck door had Gray glancing in that direction. Seconds later, Kate came stomping back with her cell in hand. She flopped back onto the fat stump she'd been using as her seat. The glow of her phone added a bit more light to their campfire area.

"You can't be serious," he grumbled.

Without looking up, she started typing like a mad woman. "Oh, when it comes to schedules, I'm dead serious. And even though you just ruined my life by burning my planner, I'm still going to help you work this out."

Gray tossed the stick back to the ground. "I'm not making a decision tonight, so relax."

"You keep telling me to relax, but if I don't worry about it and try to come to a conclusion, who will?"

Gray stood and took a step toward her. She jerked her phone behind her back and tipped her chin up in defiance.

"You're not throwing this in the fire," she said, and he thought he saw a ghost of a smile on her lips.

"No," he laughed. "But I'm not worrying and neither are you. I'm tired and it's late so I thought we could get our sleeping bags rolled out and get some rest. I want to get up early and hike to the top of the peak so you can see the sunrise."

"Sounds beautiful."

"Words can't describe it." Gray held out his hand to help her up. "So you may want to get some sleep or you'll be grouchy when I wake you."

"I'm grouchy now," she muttered, placing her hand in his. "You owe me a new planner, but I get to pick it out. I don't trust you anymore."

He helped her up, but didn't let go of her hand. "Now, where's the fun in that? You may love the one I choose."

"Please," she said, and snorted. "You have terrible taste. I've seen that painting over your sofa."

"Hey, *Dogs Playing Poker* is a classic. I paid good money for that."

"From a flea market, maybe," she muttered. Kate shook her head and blew out a sigh. "We better just go to bed and stop arguing."

Gray wasn't sure why he hadn't let her go, or why he continued to watch as the orange glow from the flames tinted her cheeks. Now her hair was down from the knot she'd been wearing. It had air-dried from the swim earlier…a swim that he took way too long to recover from. She'd only worn a simple black one-piece, but he knew exactly what she had hidden beneath that suit. She may as well have been naked. The V in the front and the low scoop in the back had been so damn arousing, he'd had to recite all fifty states in alphabetical order to get himself under control.

Gray kept hold of her hand, pulling it up to his

chest. Her eyes remained locked on his. Sounds from crickets filled the night, the crackling of the fire randomly broke into the moment.

"Gray," she whispered.

"Kate."

Her eyes closed as she pulled in a deep breath. "You're making this difficult."

"None of this has to be difficult," he countered. No reason to pretend he didn't know what she spoke of. They both had the same exact thing on their minds.

"No, it shouldn't be," she agreed, lifting her lids to look at him again. "But when I'm around you, I just remember the bar and how that felt. And then I wonder if my memory is just making the whole scenario better than it actually was."

Good. He'd been banking on her replaying that night, but he hadn't expected such an honest compliment. He sure as hell remembered, too, and not just when he was with her.

Even when he was alone or working, especially working, he recalled how stunning she'd been all spread out across the gleaming mahogany bar top. She was like a fantasy come to life.

There wasn't a doubt in his mind that she wanted him, too. He could see the way her gaze kept dropping to his mouth, the fact she hadn't let go of his hand, the way she'd avoided him for days after their intimacy. She was afraid of her feelings, of taking what she wanted.

"I don't expect anything once we go in that tent," he explained. The last thing he wanted was for her to think that was why he actually brought her here.

"I didn't think that." She licked her lips and curled her fingers more tightly around his hand. "You understand why I made the one-night rule. Right?"

She might need him to know, but that didn't mean he wanted to. All Gray cared about was how they felt, and ignoring such intense emotions was only going to complicate things further down the line. The resulting tension would eat away at their friendship and drive a wedge between them much more than taking a risk would.

"I can't lose you, Gray," she went on, staring up at him like he was everything in her life. "It would destroy me."

Kate had looked at him that way before, when her parents died and when he'd come home from the army. He didn't want to be some type of hero to anybody.

No, that wasn't right. He did want to be her hero, but not someone she thought needed to be on a pedestal. He wanted to be her equal, to prove to her that they were good together.

Fortunately, he didn't need to prove such things. She already knew just how good they were…and that's what scared the hell out of her.

"You're the only constant man in my life." She squeezed his hand. "Do you even know how important that is to me? Tara and Lucy are great, but they're not you."

Gray swallowed the lump in his throat. He didn't get emotional. Ever. But something about her raw honesty, her vulnerability got to him.

"You really think I'd let something happen to our friendship?" he asked, staring into her expressive eyes.

"Neither of us would mean for anything to happen to it," she countered. "But are you willing to take that chance?"

"I'd never risk hurting you," he stated. Gray palmed one side of her face, stroking his thumb beneath her eye. "You think I don't understand where you're coming from? You have to notice you're the only constant woman in my life basically since we met."

A smile played over her mouth. "You date."

"I do, but serious relationships aren't my thing. I'm too busy with work to feed a relationship or worry about a woman." He took a half-step closer until they were toe to toe. "I need this friendship just as much as you do, but I'm not going to ignore these feelings forever, Kate."

Her eyes widened. "You promised—"

"—that I wouldn't let you lose this friendship and that I wasn't pressuring you for anything tonight. But you can't run from your feelings forever. I won't let you deny your own feelings, either."

Unable to resist, Gray dropped a quick kiss on

her lips, not lingering nearly as long as he would've liked. After releasing her and taking a step back, he finally turned and headed to the tent.

This was going to be one long, uncomfortable night.

Kate rolled over in her sleeping bag for what seemed like the eighteenth time in as many minutes. Facing Gray now, she narrowed her gaze to adjust to the darkness and make out his silhouette.

How dare he throw down that gauntlet and then lie there and get a good night's sleep? How did the man turn his emotions off and on so easily?

She wanted to know the secret because this jumbled up mess inside her head, inside her heart, was causing some serious anxiety issues. As if she didn't have enough to handle where this man was concerned.

Kate couldn't make out his face in the dark. But she knew it by heart just as well as she knew her own. The faint lines around his eyes and between his brows gave him that distinguished look she found sexier than she should. His dark lashes always made the perfect frame for those dark as night eyes. She'd bet they were fanned out over his cheeks right now as he slept peacefully.

When he'd come home from the army, he'd been harder than when he'd left. Whatever he'd seen overseas had done something to him, something she never could put her finger on. But then he'd jumped right in and taken over the family business.

Some men came home a shell of who they'd once been. While Gray might be harder and more closed off to some, he was alive and thriving in their little town. He might not like the word *hero*, but he was hers. Honestly, he always had been.

Just another reason she couldn't keep exploring these new sexual feelings. The friendship was so, so much more important.

When Gray had implemented Ladies' Night at Gallagher's, the women around town had flocked there, all trying to catch the attention of the town's most eligible bachelor. Ladies from surrounding towns also came in to see the sexy new vet turned bartender.

Kate had always been aware of Gray's ridiculously good looks. She wasn't blind or stupid. She'd just never thought about acting on her attraction. She could be attracted to someone and still be friends... right?

Well, she'd been doing just fine at managing both until he propositioned her on the bar top. The sex couldn't have been as good as she remembered. It simply couldn't. And yet it was all of those overexaggerated flashes in her mind that had her all jumbled and aching now when she had no right to be.

"Are you going to stare at me all night?"

Kate jerked at Gray's mumbled words. He hadn't even cracked an eyelid open, so how did he know she was staring? Her heart beat faster at the abrupt break in the peaceful silence.

"I can't sleep," she answered honestly. No need to tell him her insomnia was due to him. Gray wasn't stupid.

"I can tell from all the flopping around you've been doing."

Now he did open his eyes. Even though she couldn't make out the color in the dark tent, she knew they were fixed on her.

"Sorry I kept you awake," she whispered, though why she was whispering was lost on her. Maybe because everything was so peaceful around them and she needed to hold on to that just a bit longer. Lately, so much in her life didn't seem calm. Well, maybe not so much. Mostly just Gray and their friendship, which trickled down to everything else because she couldn't stop thinking of him, of what had happened, and how to move on.

Gray shifted in his sleeping bag. When his knee bumped hers, a jolt shot through her. Being hyper-aware of him in the middle of the night with these sexual urges spiraling through her was not good. Not good at all.

But there wasn't one thing she could do to stop how she felt. Why did these feelings have to be awakened inside her? How long had she had them and not even realized it?

Yes, she'd wondered if they could ever be more than friends. She'd thought of sex with him. He was hot. She was a woman. It was the natural order of things. But she'd always pushed those thoughts aside and focused on their friendship.

That wasn't the case right now.

"Your movement didn't keep me awake," he countered.

Kate curled her fingers around the top of her sleeping bag and tried to resist the urge to reach out. So close. He was so close she would only have to lift her hand slightly to brush the side of his face. She knew from firsthand experience exactly how that bristle would feel against her skin.

Kate swallowed. She shouldn't be fantasizing about that stubbled jaw beneath her palm. She shouldn't wonder if they both could fit into one sleeping bag. And she sure as hell shouldn't be thinking how quickly they could get their clothes off.

"What's keeping you awake?" he asked.

Kate snorted. "You're joking, right?"

"Do I sound like I'm joking?"

No. He sounded sexy with that low, growly voice she'd never fully appreciated until now.

"You've got me so confused and worked up," she confessed. "Why couldn't we just keep things the way they were?"

"Because attraction doesn't follow your rules."

Kate closed her eyes and chewed on her lip. What could she say to that? He was right, but that didn't mean she wouldn't keep trying to compartmentalize her emotions. They had to stay in the friend box.

They had to. Everyone in her life had a special area inside her heart, but Gray kept stepping out of his designated spot and causing all sorts of confusion.

"You're not the only one losing sleep over this, Kate."

Oh, mercy. Those were words she wished he hadn't thrown out there to settle between them. Not now, when they were being held hostage by the circumstances surrounding them. The dark night, the enclosed tent, the sexually charged energy that seemed to be pulling them closer together.

Her heart beating a fast, steady rhythm, she reached out. When her fingers found his jawline, she slid her hand up the side of his face. That prickle of his coarse hair beneath her palm had her entire body heating up.

"What if…"

She couldn't finish. This was insane. This entire idea was absolutely insane and not smart. But she ached…for this man.

His warm, strong hand covered hers as he whispered, "What if what?"

"One more time," she murmured. "We do this just once more."

"Are you going to regret it this time?"

Kate eased her body closer. "I didn't regret it last time."

He released her hand and jerked on the zipper of his bag before sliding hers down as well. In another swift move, he was on her, taking her hands and holding them on either side of her head.

"Tell me now if you want me to stop."

Kate arched against him, pulling against his hold. "Now, Gray."

Chapter Nine

The green light couldn't be brighter. And one time?
Sure, he'd heard that before. Whatever. He'd take this
time and show her again exactly how perfect their
special bond was.

Gray eased up just enough to slide his hands beneath the long-sleeved T-shirt she had on. He hadn't
been able to appreciate her before at the bar, and it
was so damn dark he could barely see, but he was
going to get her naked and not fumble around ripping underwear like some inexperienced, out-of-
control teen.

With some careful maneuvering and assistance
from Kate, Gray had her clothes off in record time.

His hands settled on her bare hips as she reached up to frame his face.

"You're still wearing clothes."

Gray gripped her wrist, kissed her palm and put her hand on his shirt. "Then take them off."

Her hands trembled as she brought them to the hem of his tee. She jerked the material up and over his head. When she grabbed the waistband of his shorts, he sucked in a breath. Those delicate fingers on his body might be more than he could handle. To say he was hanging on by a thread would be a vast understatement.

Since she'd paraded around in that swimsuit, he'd been fighting the ache to take her hard and fast. Gray covered her hands with his and took over. Within seconds, he was just as bare as her.

Kate eased her knees apart, making room for him. Her fingertips grazed up his arms and over his shoulders. "I wish I could see you better."

Gray reached over, taking the lantern-style light he'd brought. He flicked the switch on and left it against the edge of the tent. When he turned his attention back to Kate, his breath got caught in his throat. A vise-like grip formed around his chest.

She lay beneath him, all of that dark hair spread around her, eyes bright and beautiful and solely focused on him.

"You're stunning."

He hadn't meant to say the words out loud. He'd wanted to keep this simple—or as simple as they could be, considering their circumstances. But now that they were out, he wasn't sorry. Maybe Kate needed to hear this more often. Maybe she needed to realize just how special and amazing she was.

A smile spread across her face. "I'm already naked," she joked. "You don't need to flatter me."

If she wanted to keep things light, that was fine. Having Kate here with him, like this, was more than he thought would happen.

But he didn't want more words coming between them. All he wanted was to feel this woman, to take his time with her, and show her how much she was treasured. Above all else, he never wanted her to feel like she was just a one-night stand. Even if they agreed to stay friends, he needed her to know she was worth more than quick actions and meaningless words.

Gray covered her body. Then he covered her mouth. Her delicate arms and legs wrapped all around him.

"I need to get protection," he muttered against her lips.

Her hold tightened. "I'm on birth control and I trust you."

The whispered declaration had him battling over what he should do. There was nothing more he wanted than to have no barrier between them and he trusted her, too. He'd never gone without because there wasn't a woman he trusted that much.

But he knew his Kate and he wasn't about to move

from this spot, not when she was holding on so tight and looking at him like she couldn't take another second without his touch.

Gray settled himself between her thighs, bracing his forearms on either side of her face. He smoothed her hair back, wanting to see every emotion that flashed across her face when he joined their bodies.

And he wasn't disappointed.

The second they became one, her lids fluttered down, her breath came out on a soft sigh, and she arched against him.

Kate's fingertips threaded through his hair as she urged him down, opening for another kiss. How could he ever agree to just one time with her? Hell, he already knew that twice wouldn't be enough.

She muttered something against his lips, but he couldn't make out what. Her hands traveled down to his shoulders, then his back as she tossed her head to the side. Raven hair covered a portion of her face as she cried out, her legs tightening around him.

Gray shoved her hair out of the way, basking in the play of emotions. He'd never seen a more beautiful, expressive woman than Kate. His Kate. No matter what happened, friends or more, she'd always be his.

In no time he was pumping his hips, capturing her mouth beneath his. Kate's nails bit into his back and that was all he needed to send him over the edge. Nothing had ever felt like this…well, nothing except their encounter at his bar.

Gray held on to her, nipping at her lips as he trembled. After several moments, and once his body stilled, he gathered her close and pulled the open sleeping bag over them. He didn't care about their clothes, didn't care that there was a little chill in the mountain air. He leaned over with his free hand and clicked the light off.

"That was the last time," she muttered against his chest. "I mean it."

Gray smiled into the dark. He'd never agreed to that bargain to begin with.

"These new pamphlets turned out so nice."

Kate glanced to Tara, who was waving around the stack of brand-new promotional material for their grief center. Judging by the look on her face, she'd been talking for a while, but Kate had zoned out.

"What? Oh, yes. They're pretty. Lucy did a great job with the design and the colors."

They'd just had new pamphlets done a few months ago, but with the popularity of their weekly meetings, Lucy had taken it upon herself to design the new ones, adding some testimonials from the regulars and having nicer pages printed online.

"You're distracted," Tara stated, dropping the stack to the table at the entryway of the community center. "Does this have anything to do with the camping trip?"

Kate shook her head. "No. Gray and I just went away for a day. It was pretty cool. I can't believe

I live in this gorgeous state and have never taken advantage of the mountains. I'm definitely going camping again."

The waterfall had been amazing, but the sunrise only hours after making love had been something special. She wasn't sure where Gray's thoughts were, but for her, something had changed. She needed a breather and she needed to do some serious reevaluating of where she stood on her feelings for her best friend.

What had she been thinking, telling him not to use protection? Not that she didn't believe him that he was safe, but that bold move was, well…bold. They'd taken their intimacy to another level when she knew full well they couldn't do that ever, ever again.

But when she'd been lying beneath him, cradled by his strength and seeing how he looked at her, she simply hadn't wanted him to move away for anything. She'd wanted him and only him.

Besides, they were fine. She was on the pill and neither of them had ever gone without protection before.

"What's up with the two of you lately?" Tara asked.

Before Kate could answer, she was saved by the adorable five-year-old running around the tables and singing something Kate didn't recognize.

"Marley Jo Bailey," Tara scolded. "You cannot run in here. I brought your bag in and put it back in the kitchen. You have crayons, a coloring book and your new baby doll to play with."

Marley stopped at her mother's abrupt tone, or maybe it was the use of her full name. Either way, the little cutie started skipping toward the back of the building, where the kitchen was located.

"Sorry about that," Tara said, turning her focus back to Kate.

She wasn't sorry one bit. Marley's running got Kate out of answering the question that had been weighing on her, because honestly, Kate had no idea what was going on with Gray.

"Is Sam working?"

Tara nodded. "He's always good to keep her on meeting nights, but he got a new job and he's worried about asking off."

Kate smiled. "Sounds like he's getting things back in order."

"He left me another note."

"He wants forgiveness," Kate stated. "It's obvious he loves you."

Her friend nodded and glanced back toward the kitchen area. "I know he does. That's never been the issue."

Kate couldn't imagine what her friend struggled with. Between losing her husband to addiction only to have him fight and claw his way back, and having a sweet, innocent child in the mix…there was so much to take in and Tara was handling things like a champ.

"So, back to Gray."

Kate resisted moaning. There was no way she was going to offer up everything that had happened between them. She and Gray were still friends and that's what they'd stay, because the other night was it. No more taking her clothes off for her best friend.

"He's just going through some personal things right now and needed to escape and get some advice."

There. That wasn't a total lie. She'd offered him advice, hadn't she? She'd told him to take his clothes off.

"And you gave him advice?" Tara asked, her raised brows almost mocking.

"Well, I was trying to until he tossed my planner into the fire."

Something she was still pissed about, but seemed to have forgotten about the second he'd touched her and made her toes curl all over again. Damn that man for making her want things she couldn't have—and for destroying her beloved planner.

And in answer to her question from days ago, yes. Yes, the sex was just as fabulous as she'd remembered. Maybe more so since they'd both gotten out of their clothes this time. Gray had been rather thorough and her body continued to tingle at just the mere thought of how gloriously his hands had roamed over her as if memorizing every aspect.

"The fire?" Tara gasped, throwing a hand to her chest. "Tell me he didn't burn the cherished planner."

"Very funny." Kate playfully smacked Tara's shoulder. "He said I needed to relax."

Tara laughed. No, she doubled over laughing, which had Marley running from the kitchen with some blond baby doll tucked beneath her arm.

"What's so funny?" Marley asked, her wide eyes bouncing between her mother and Kate.

"Oh, just something Kate said, honey." Tara swiped beneath her eyes and attempted to control her laughter. "So he told you to relax, which I'm sure you immediately did. And then he watched your planner turn to ash?"

Kate crossed her arms. "Pretty much."

"And he's still breathing?"

"Barely," Kate replied. "He owes me a new planner and don't think I'm not going to pick out the most expensive, thickest one I can find. It will have quotes on every page and a gold-embossed font, and I may just have him spring for the twenty-four-month one instead of the twelve."

Uninterested in the grown-ups' conversation, Marley started skipping around the room with her baby in the air.

"Oh, hitting him in his wallet." Tara feigned a shudder. "That will teach him never to mess with your schedules."

Kate dropped her arms to her sides and rolled her shoulders. "I don't know why the closest people in my life mock my work," she joked. "I mean, I make a killer living off organizing lives. I could help with yours if you'd let me."

Tara held up her hands. "I already let you into my closet. I'm still afraid to mess up those white shirts hanging next to the gray for fear you've set some alarm in there and you'll know if I get them out of order."

Kate laughed as she went to the food table on the back wall. "I'm not that bad," she called over her shoulder. "Besides, your closet was a disaster."

After Sam had left, Tara had needed something to occupy her time, and she'd had Kate and Lucy come over for a girls' night. One thing turned into another and the next thing Kate knew, she was knee-deep in a three-day project to revamp her friend's closet.

"I'm still upset you tossed my favorite sweatshirt," Tara griped, coming to lean against the wall by the table.

Kate rolled her eyes as she straightened up the plastic cups next to the lemonade and sweet tea. "That sweatshirt needed a proper burial and I just helped things along."

"It was a classic."

"No, it was from the junior high volleyball camp we went to and it was hideous."

"Still fit," Tara muttered.

Kate patted her friend's arm. "And that's why I threw it away and secretly hate you. You have never gained an ounce of fat other than when you were pregnant."

Tara quirked a brow. "High metabolism and good gene pool?"

"Still, I can hate you." Kate stepped back and glanced around. "I think we're good to go."

The meeting was due to start in fifteen minutes, which meant people should be rolling in anytime. They always had their regulars, accounting for about eight people. Randomly others would filter in. Some stayed only a few sessions. Some they never saw again.

Ironically, this uplifting support group was how Lucy and Noah met. They would've eventually met at work since he was an officer and Lucy had been a dispatcher. But, as fate would have it, Noah had slipped into the back of the meeting one day and Lucy had made a beeline for him when he tried to sneak out. Noah had lost his wife before coming to Stonerock and Lucy had lost her husband in the war a few years ago. If nothing else came from Helping Hands, at least Lucy and Noah had found true love and a second chance at happiness.

Kate wished that Tara and Sam could do the same, but things weren't looking good. Marley skipped back into the room and ran up to her mom. Tara picked her daughter up and squeezed her tight.

Something flipped in Kate's chest. She wanted a family, a husband to share her life with. But she'd been too busy with her career, a failed engagement and the launch of Helping Hands to make it happen.

An image of Gray flashed through her mind.

No. That was not the direction she needed to take her thoughts. Gray wasn't the marrying type. His father had pressured him over the past few years to settle down, but obviously that wasn't something Gray wanted.

And she needed to remember that he was her everything. She couldn't allow herself to hope for more with him. No, when she married and settled down it wouldn't be with a hunky bar owner with a naughty side and a sleeve of tattoos.

Chapter Ten

Gray finished pulling the wood chairs off the table-tops. He still needed to complete the invoice for next week's beer order and return a call to a new vendor before they opened in two hours.

Owning a bar wasn't just mixing drinks and writing paychecks. There was so much more that went into it, but he'd done it so long—hell, he'd grown up here—he pretty much did everything on autopilot.

Is that how he wanted to spend the rest of his life? Doing the same thing day in and day out? How could a thirty-one-year-old man not have a clue what he wanted to do with his life?

The tempting business proposal from the random

stranger still weighed heavily on him and kept him awake at night.

Granted, the looming deadline wasn't the only thing keeping him awake. A raven-haired vixen posing as his best friend had him questioning everything he'd ever thought to be a truth.

Gray set the last chair on the floor and turned to head toward his office. The old black-and-white picture hanging behind the bar stopped him. He'd seen that picture countless times, passed it constantly, but the image of his grandfather standing in his army uniform outside the bar on the day he bought it seemed to hit home this time.

The back door opened and slammed shut. Only a handful of people used the back door. A sliver of hope hit him as he stared at the doorway to the hall, thinking he'd see Kate step through.

But when his father rounded the corner, Gray smiled, hating how disappointment over not seeing Kate had been his first reaction.

She'd retreated again after their trip. Her pattern shouldn't surprise him, but it did. Whatever she was afraid of, he could battle it. Seriously. Did she not think all of this was freaking him out a little, as well? But there was no way in hell he was just going to ignore this pull toward her. He knew without a doubt that she was being pulled just as fiercely.

"Want a beer?" Gray asked as he circled the bar.

Reece Gallagher went to the opposite side of the

bar and took a seat on one of the stools. "You know what I like."

Gray smiled as he reached for a frosted mug and flipped the tap of his father's favorite brew. He tipped the mug enough to keep the head of the beer just right. Another thing he simply did without thinking.

He'd been meaning to call his dad, but now that he was here, there was no better time to discuss the future of Gallagher's.

Gray set the beer in front of his dad, the frothy top spilling over. He pulled a rag from below the counter and swiped up the moisture.

"Had a visitor the other day," he told his dad.

"Oh, yeah?" Reece took a hearty drink of his beer before setting the mug back on the bar. "Something tells me there's more to the story."

"He offered me more money than I'd know what to do with if I sell him this bar."

His father's dark eyes instantly met his. "Sell Gallagher's? I hope you told him where he could stick his money. Who the hell was this guy?"

Gray swallowed, resting his palms on the smooth bar top. "Businessman from Knoxville. He left me his card and told me I had a month to think about it."

His dad's silver brows drew in as he shifted on his stool and seemed as if he was about ready to come over the bar. "What's there to think about, son?"

Gray figured his father would have this reaction. The bar had been in their family for years and selling had never been an option. Hell, Gray had never thought about selling the place until he'd been presented with the option.

He had to be honest with his dad. There was no reason to gloss this over and pretend everything was fine and he wasn't contemplating the change.

"Maybe I'm not meant to run this bar."

Silence settled between them as the words hung in the air. Gray didn't back down. If his father and the military taught him one thing, it was to never back down from what you believed in.

"You're actually considering this."

Gray nodded even though his father hadn't actually asked. "Something is missing in my life," he said.

His father's response was another pull of his beer. Gray figured he should just lay it all out there. His dad might not like the direction of Gray's thoughts, but he did appreciate and expect honesty.

"I'm thankful for this, all of it. I know you and Grandpa worked hard." He pulled in a deep breath. "I'm just not sure this is what I was meant to do in life."

Reece Gallagher tapped the side of his mug. Whatever was rolling around in his mind, Gray knew his father was formulating a plan to convince him to stay.

"How much were you offered?" his dad finally asked.

Gray threw out the number which resulted in a long, slow whistle from his father.

"That's a hell of a number," he agreed. "And you think this money will ultimately buy you what you want in life? Which is what, exactly?"

Gray shrugged. "I have no clue. There's a void, though. I haven't been able to put my finger on it."

"A wife? Kids?" his dad suggested. "Settling down is a logical step."

Gray pushed off the bar. He was going to need a beer of his own if this was the path the conversation was going to head down.

"I'm not looking for a wife, let alone children."

He pulled a bottle from the cooler behind the bar. Quickly he popped the top and tossed it into the trash.

"I know that's what worked for you and Grandpa," he went on, resting his bottle on the bar. "But I'm not you or him. I'm my own person, and is it so bad that I'm not sure what I want?"

"No," his father agreed. "But I also don't want you making decisions based on money alone, and I certainly don't want you letting all of this go only to find that what you were looking for was here all along."

What the hell did that mean? Stonerock was a great town, but it wasn't necessarily where he wanted to spend his future.

"The decision is ultimately up to you," he dad went on. "You have to understand that I'm not giving you my blessing if you choose to sell. What does he want to do with the bar, anyway?"

Gray took a drink of his beer, then leaned onto his

elbows. "He and his business partner want to make Stonerock like a mini-Nashville. I guess they're looking to buy more businesses in the area and revamp them to draw more tourists."

Reece wrinkled his nose. "That's absurd. Stonerock is just fine the way it is."

Gray finished his beer and tossed his bottle. Then he grabbed his dad's empty mug and set it in the sink below the bar.

"I won't contact him without talking to you first," Gray assured his dad. "I don't want you to think that your opinion doesn't matter or that I'm only looking at dollar signs."

His dad came to his feet and tapped his fingertips on the bar. "I know money can sound good, especially that much, but family is everything, Gray. At the end of the day you only have a few friends and your family that you can count on. Money is just paper."

Why did his dad have to make him feel guilty? Why did he have to add more doubts in his head when he was so close to making a decision?

Reece headed for the back hallway.

"Wait a second," Gray called out. "What did you stop by for to begin with?"

Tossing a glance over his shoulder, his father shook his head. "It's not important."

His footsteps echoed down the hall until they disappeared behind the closing door. Gray stared out at the empty bar, knowing that in just over an hour it would be bustling. That was definitely the main perk to this place. He'd never had to worry about patrons or making money. Gallagher's was the only bar in town and it was a nice place to hang. He was proud of that accomplishment, of the tradition he carried on here.

Emotions filled his throat and squeezed his chest. No matter the decision he made, he'd always wonder if he'd made the right one. If he left, he'd look back and wonder if his father thought him a disappointment. If he stayed, he'd always be looking for something to fill the void. Could he achieve what his heart desired?

Gray wasn't going to be making any decisions tonight. Between the bar and Kate, he wasn't sure how the hell he was supposed to maintain his sanity.

"I have to go," Kate said around a yawn. "I have to meet a client early in the morning to discuss reorganizing her basement for a play-work area."

Lucy put a hand on Kate's arm. "Don't go. I haven't even gotten to the part about the hammock."

Tara busted out laughing and Kate groaned. "Seriously, Lucy. Keep the honeymoon stories to yourself. You came back just as pale as when you left so I know what you were doing."

Lucy shrugged. "But the hammock story is hilarious. Can you even imagine how difficult—"

Kate held up her hands. "I'm getting the visual."

Lucy had been back from her honeymoon only a

day, but they'd been in need of some long overdue girl time. The wedding planning and showers and anticipation had filled their schedules over the past several months.

Tara had invited them over to her house and opened a bottle of wine, and they'd proceeded to just decompress and gossip. Sweet Marley had gone to bed an hour ago, leaving the women to some much-needed adult conversation that wasn't centered around dresses, registries and invitations.

Kate didn't partake in the wine, though. The last time she drank, the *only* time she'd drunk, had changed her entire life, and she was still reeling from the results. Maybe this would just her new normal and she'd have to get used to these unfamiliar emotions that seemed to have taken up residence in her heart.

"Will you hang a bit longer if I promise to hold off on describing the hammock incident?" Lucy asked as she refilled her own wineglass.

Kate shook her head. "I've seriously got so much to do."

"Did you tell Lucy about the planner and the campfire?"

Kate shot a glare at Tara, who sat across on the opposite sofa. The smirk on her friend's face was not funny. Not funny at all.

"A fire and your planner?" Lucy gasped. "I have to hear this. I swear, tell me this and I won't bring up the hammock again."

Kate realized she wasn't going anywhere anytime soon. She sank back into her corner of the couch and replayed her camping story—minus the sex and lustful glances—to her best friends.

"Wait." Lucy held up her hands. "You went camping? That's almost as shocking as the fact Gray burned your planner."

"He forced my hand on the camping thing," she stated. "Well, he didn't force me. Camping was on my life list and he just showed up unannounced—"

"Hold up," Lucy said, incredulous. "What's this life list? Good grief. A girl gets married, has awkward sex in a hammock and misses so much that has happened. Start at the beginning."

"No hammock talk," Kate reminded her.

Lucy shrugged. "Minor slip."

Tara refilled her glass, then propped her bare feet on the couch. "Yes. The beginning of this camping adventure, please."

Kate rolled her eyes. "You already know everything."

"Still makes for a good bedtime story." Tara shrugged. "Besides, I think something is brewing between you and Gray."

"Nothing is brewing. You know we drive each other insane on a good day."

Kate was quick to Δdefend herself, but she and Gray were friends. No, really. No more sex. Just the one time...times two.

"I made a list," Kate started. "I guess you could

call it a bucket list. With turning thirty, I started getting a little anxiety about inching closer to the age my mom was when she died. I figured I better start doing some of the things I really want to try. You just never know how much time you have left."

"Camping made your list?" Lucy asked. "I'm intrigued by what else you've put on there."

Kate slipped off her sandals and pulled her feet back under her. She didn't want to get into the full details of her wishes because…well, she felt that was something she and Gray shared. As strange as that sounded, she'd originally wanted to keep it all to herself, but since he knew, Kate wanted to keep things just between them.

The secrets between her and Gray were mounting up.

"I tried to think of things I'd never done, so, yeah. Camping ranked high," Kate explained. "Once we got settled in and took a hike, I could tell something was bothering Gray. He finally opened up and dropped a bomb on me that someone wants to buy his bar."

"What?" Lucy and Tara both asked.

Kate met her friends' wide eyes and dropped jaws with a nod. "He said some guy came in and offered him an insane amount of money to purchase Gallagher's. Said something about buying properties around the town to update them and make them more city-like."

"Our town doesn't need updating," Lucy stated.

"The reason people live here is because they like the small-town atmosphere. If they wanted a city feel, they'd move there. I wonder if Drake is aware of this. Surely these guys had the decency to talk to our mayor."

Kate shrugged. "Just telling you what I know."

Tara set her wineglass on the coffee table and shifted to face Kate. "Is Gray seriously considering giving up the bar?"

"He hasn't turned the offer down."

Which honestly surprised her. He'd explained the whole thing about feeling something missing in his life, but at the same time, this was his family's legacy. A piece of history that had just been handed to him. Did he even realize how lucky he was? She'd give anything to have a piece of her parents handed down to her, some way to still hold on to them.

Which was why tracing her family genealogy had made her list.

"Wow." Lucy took another sip of her wine. "When will he decide what he's doing?"

"The guy gave him a deadline. Next week sometime." Kate stretched her legs out and felt around for her shoes. She really did need to get going. Not just because of the work thing. She didn't want to get back into the camping conversation and Tara's speculation that something was up. "He's going to talk to his dad and feel him out, though I imagine that won't go very well."

No doubt he'd let her know exactly how that talk

went. Then he'd probably call her out on dodging him since they'd returned from their trip. She hadn't been dodging him, exactly. She'd been working and she assumed he had, as well.

Besides, she just needed a break after those two days together. The man consumed her every thought lately and when they were together he was...well, even more irresistible and in her face.

What did all of this mean? How could she let her Gray go from being her best friend to lover, then try to put him back in the best friend zone? It shouldn't be that difficult to keep him locked away in that particular section of her heart. Isn't that what she did for a living? Put everything in a neat and tidy order?

So why the hell couldn't she do that with her personal life?

Kate finally said her goodbyes to her best girlfriends and agreed to meet them at Ladies' Night on Wednesday. She hadn't been for a while and was overdue—something Gray had noticed and called her out on. And, well, she could use a night of dancing and just having a good time.

That would prove to Gray that she wasn't dodging him...right?

Kate headed home, her mind working through all she needed to get done over the next couple of days. She was still in need of a good personal planner. She had looked at a few, but hadn't made a commitment yet. Whatever she chose, Gray would feel it in his wallet. That would teach him not to mess with her things anymore.

As she pulled into her drive, she noticed a sporty black car parked on the street directly in front of her house. Her eyes darted to the porch, where a man in a suit sat on one of her white rockers.

Kate barely took her eyes off him as she put the car in Park and killed the engine. Of all people to make an unexpected visit, her cheating, lying ex was the last man she ever expected to see again.

Chapter Eleven

Gripping her purse, Kate headed up her stone walk-way. "What are you doing here, Chris?"

Always clean-cut and polished, Chris Percell came to his feet and shoved his hands in his pockets.

Who wore a suit at this time of night? And in this humidity? Not that his wardrobe was a concern of hers. No, the main issues here were that he stood on her porch without an invitation and she hadn't heard a word from him in years. Granted, once he'd left, she hadn't wanted to hear a word from the cheating bastard.

Kate didn't mount the steps. He had about three seconds to state his business and then she was going in her house and locking the door. She hadn't been lying when she told her friends she was tired and still had some work to do, so this unexpected visitor was not putting her in the best of moods.

"You look good, Kate."

Chris started down the steps toward her. Now she did dodge him and go on up to her porch. When she turned, he stood on the bottom step, smiling up at her.

"It's been a long time," he stated.

"Not long enough. What do you want?"

With a shrug, he crossed his arms and shifted his stance. "I was hoping we could talk."

"Most people just text." She'd deleted him from her phone long ago, but still. Showing up unannounced was flat-out rude. Not that he had many morals or even common decency.

"I wasn't sure if you'd respond."

"I wouldn't," she told him.

He propped one foot on the next step and smoothed a hand over his perfectly parted hair. "After all these years, you're still angry?"

She didn't know whether to laugh at his stupidity or throw her purse at him and pray she hit him in the head hard enough to knock some damn sense into him.

No purse should be treated that way, so she adjusted the strap on her shoulder and held it tight.

"Angry?" she asked with a slight laugh. "I'd have to feel something to actually be angry with you."

"Kate." Chris lowered his tone as if to appeal to

her good side. She no longer had one where he was concerned. "Could I come in for a bit just to talk?"

"No. And actually, it's a bit creepy that you're on my porch waiting on me to get home."

"I haven't been here long," he assured her. "Maybe I should come back tomorrow. Can I take you for coffee?"

Kate stared down at the clean-cut man who probably still got bimonthly manicures. She couldn't help but wonder what in the hell she'd ever seen in him to begin with. Coffee with a man wearing a suit? She'd prefer champagne served up by a sexy tattooed-up bar owner.

Oh, no.

No, no, no.

Now was not the time to discover that her feelings were sliding into more than just friendship with Gray. Chris continued to stare at her, waiting for her answer, but she was having a minor mental breakdown.

"I'm busy tomorrow," she finally replied. "Good night, Chris."

Without waiting for him to respond, Kate pulled her key from her purse and quickly let herself into the house. She flicked the dead bolt back into place and smacked the porch lights off.

What on earth had flashed through her mind when Chris mentioned taking her for coffee? She loved coffee and Stonerock had the best little coffee house on the edge of town. Not that she would even entertain the thought of having coffee with that slime bag.

But Gray?

Everything in her thought process lately circled back to that man. Her planner, her bucket list, her drinks, her most satisfying sexual experiences.

Kate groaned as she made her way toward her bedroom. What she needed to do was spend more time with Tara and Lucy. So much one-on-one with Gray had obviously clouded her judgment and left her confused and mixing amazing sex with feelings that shouldn't be developing.

But Tara was busy with her own life and Lucy was still in that newlywed bliss phase. Ladies' Night would definitely be her best bet to get back to where she needed to be mentally. Letting lose, being carefree, and not worrying about anything would surely cleanse her mind of all lustful thoughts of her best friend.

Sex really did cloud the mind. And great sex... well, maybe she just needed sleep. If she weren't so exhausted, perhaps Gray wouldn't have filled her mind the second Chris started talking about taking her out.

Gray hadn't even taken her out. They weren't in any way dating. They were going on about their way like always—just adding in a few toe-curling orgasms along the way.

Kate pushed aside all thoughts of Chris showing up, Gray and his ability to make her want more than she should and the fact he may be selling his bar and leaving. She couldn't get wrapped up in lives and circumstances she had no control over. As much as she thrived on micromanaging, realistically, she had to let go.

After pulling on her favorite sleep shirt, Kate slid beneath her sheets and adjusted her pillows against the upholstered headboard. She unplugged her iPad from the nightstand and pulled up her schedule for the following day. Yes, her schedule was in both paper and e-format.

After glancing over her schedule, she went to her personal blog. So many blogs failed, but Kate prided herself on being a marketing genius. She honed in on her niche market, taking full advantage of social media platforms that drove her clients to her site, thus turning them into paying customers.

Not many people could do their dream job and work from home. Kate knew how blessed and lucky she was to have such a fabulous life.

Though seeing Lucy so happy with love and Tara with sweet Marley made Kate wonder if she was missing out.

Tara clicked on the tab to bring up her bucket list. At the bottom she added the word "family" in bold font. Ultimately that would be her main goal once she'd achieved the others. She wasn't going to rush it, she wanted to wait on the right man to come along. She was definitely ready to take that step toward a broader future.

Stifling a yawn, Kate placed her device back on her nightstand and clicked the light off. As she fluffed her pillows and rolled over, she hoped she would fall asleep right away and not dream of the sexy bar owner who had occupied her thoughts every night.

But she found herself smiling. She couldn't help herself. There was no greater man in her life, and even though things were a little unbalanced right now, she fully intended on keeping him at an arm's length. For real this time.

"Thanks, darlin', but I'm busy tonight."

Ladies' Night always brought in the flirtatious women with short skirts and plunging necklines. Being single didn't hurt business, either, but he'd never picked up a woman in his bar. That wasn't good business and certainly not a reputation he wanted hovering over his establishment.

Gray extracted himself from the clutches of the blonde at the table in the corner. That's what he got for coming out from behind his post. His staff had been busy so he'd taken the table their drinks.

Back behind the safety of the bar, Gray tapped on the computer and started filling more drink orders. Jacob ran the finger foods from the kitchen. The menu remained small and simple but enough to keep people thirsty, because the drinks were by far the moneymaker.

The DJ switched the song to one that seriously

made Gray's teeth itch. "It's Raining Men" blared through the hidden surround sound speakers. Considering the crowd and the cheers and squeals, Gray was definitely in the minority here.

One night. He could live through terrible music for one night a week. Wednesday nights brought in the most revenue. Women from all walks of life came out in droves. Some were celebrating bachelorette parties. Some were stay-at-home moms who needed a break. Sometimes a group of employees got together to decompress after work. Whatever their situation was, Gray—and his bottom line—was thrilled he'd decided to add this night when he'd taken over.

As he placed three margaritas on the bar for one of his staff to take to table eleven, he glanced at the front door when it opened.

Finally.

Gray didn't even care that his heart skipped a little at the sight of Kate. He was done ignoring the way he felt when she was near. He just…damn it, he wanted her to stop avoiding him. He needed her stability, the security she brought to their friendship.

He hadn't spoken with her since he'd talked to his dad. Just the thought of that conversation had him questioning what to do. Clearly his father would be heartbroken over losing Gallagher's, but Gray just kept thinking back to how free he would be if he was able to explore his own interests.

His eyes drifted back to Kate. She'd settled in a booth with Tara and Lucy. When her gaze landed on him, she might as well have touched him with her bare hands. Immediate heat spread through him, and the second she flashed that radiant smile, Gray nearly toppled the glass he'd been holding.

After returning her smile, he returned his focus to the orders. No woman had ever made him falter on the job before. Then again, no woman was Kate McCoy.

As he worked on filling orders, he randomly glanced her way. He knew exactly which drinks were going to that table. Those three were so predictable. Tara always wanted a cosmo, Lucy stuck with a light beer and Kate went with soda.

It wasn't long before another song blared through the speakers that had Gray cringing, but the dance floor instantly filled with women. Kate and her friends were right in the midst of the action.

That little dress she wore had his gut tightening. The loose hem slid all over her thighs as she wiggled that sweet body on the dance floor. She'd piled her hair up on top of her head, but the longer she danced, the more stray strands fell around her face, her neck.

Get a grip.

"Hey, baby. You ever take time for a dance?"

Gray flashed a smile to the redhead leaning over the bar at just the right angle to give him a complete visual of her cleavage and bra of choice.

"Who would make all these drinks if I went dancing?" he yelled over the music.

She reached across the bar and ran her fingertip down his chest. "I think if you got on that dance floor, we'd all forget about our drinks. At least for a little while."

Someone slammed a glass next to him, jerking Gray's attention from the flirtatious patron.

He turned just in time to see Kate walking away, her empty glass on the bar.

"Looks like you made someone's drink wrong," the redhead stated, lowering her lids. "You can make me anything you want."

Gray stepped back, causing her hand to fall from his chest. "Where are you and your friends sitting?" he asked. "I'll send over a pitcher of margaritas."

Her smile widened as she gestured to their table. Apparently the idea of free booze was more appealing than him...which was perfectly fine. Right now, he was more intrigued with the way Kate had acted. She'd slammed that glass pretty close to his arm on purpose and then walked away without a word.

Jealous?

Gray couldn't help but smile as he got the pitcher ready. If Kate was jealous, then maybe she was ready to see where this new level of friendship would take them. Perhaps she'd missed him in the days they'd been apart and she'd thought more about their time in the mountains.

Maybe she'd finally realized how good they were together and that it was silly to put restrictions on their intimacy. He spotted her back out on the dance floor talking to Lucy. Lucy nodded in response to whatever she said and Kate walked away.

Gray picked up empty glasses and wiped off the bar where a few ladies had just sat, all the while keeping his gaze on Kate. She went back to the booth and grabbed her purse.

Well, hell. She was pissed and leaving? All because some woman flirted with him?

If she was that upset, then she was definitely jealous. Gray had every intention of playing right into that little nugget of information.

Gray lost track of Kate, but he never saw the front door open, which meant she had to be inside somewhere. He glanced at his watch and realized they still had another two business hours to go. He couldn't get to Kate for a while, but she better be ready for him, because he wasn't backing down from this fight. He was damn well going to call her out on her jealousy and forbid her to make any excuses for why they shouldn't be together.

Gray couldn't wait to get her alone again.

Chapter Twelve

This was the most ridiculous thing she'd ever done in her entire life. But hey, at least she could mark spontaneity off her life list.

Kate stared at the clock on Gray's nightstand. The bar had closed thirty minutes ago. She knew he had cleanup down to a science and he should be wrapping things up any minute.

She thought coming up here to cool off would help. Seeing that trampy redhead raking her false nail down Gray's chest had set something off inside Kate she didn't want to label…because it smacked her right in the face with jealousy.

Why was she jealous? Kate knew full well that women found Gray sexy and did nearly anything to get his attention. But things were different now. Yes, they were just friends, but everything had changed.

What would he say when he came up here and found her in his bed? Would he tell her they'd agreed to call it quits after the camping? Would he climb in bed and give her another night to remember?

Kate came to her feet and grabbed the dress she'd flung at the bottom of the bed. This was a mistake. She looked like an utter fool. No, a desperate fool, and she needed to get the hell out of here before Gray came in.

The front door to his apartment clicked shut, followed by the dead bolt. Too late to run.

She clutched the dress to her chest, feeling even more ridiculous now. Why had she put that damn "be more spontaneous" idea on her list? And why had she let that busty tramp bring out the green-eyed monster?

Heavy footsteps sounded down the hall seconds before Gray filled the doorway. His dark eyes widened as they raked over her. There was no way she could move. Just that simple, visual lick he gave her had her rooted in place.

His eyes snapped back up to hers. "Put the dress down."

Kate dropped it at her feet before thinking twice. That low command gave her little choice but to obey. Warmth spread through her. There was no denying exactly why she'd come up here, just as there was no denying that heated look in his eyes.

"You came up here a while ago." He leaned one broad shoulder against the door frame and continued to rake his eyes across her body. "What have you been doing?"

"Second-guessing myself," she murmured.

Gray's lips twitched. "Is that so? I don't recall sneaking into a man's bedroom on your life list."

"I was trying to check off spontaneity."

"Is that so?"

Kate crossed her arms over her chest. "I'm feeling a little silly standing here like this. Are you just going to stay over there and stare at me?"

"Maybe I'm looking at you because you deserve to be valued."

Oh, no. He couldn't say things like that to her. Statements so bold only pushed them deeper into this …whatever the technical term was. *Friends* seemed too tame of a label considering she stood in his bedroom wearing only her underwear.

"Chris showed up at my house."

Why did she blurt that out? She prided herself on planning everything, even her words. But somehow hearing him mention her being valued made her think of the jerk who thought the opposite.

Gray stood straight up and took a step toward her. "What the hell did he want?"

Kate laughed. "To talk. He invited me to coffee."

The muscle in his jaw clenched. "Did you go?" he all but growled.

"No. I demanded he leave and I haven't heard from him since."

Gray's eyes narrowed. "He's trying to get you back."

"After all this time and after what he did? He's a fool."

"Tell me if he comes back."

Kate stared up into those dark eyes. "You're jealous."

Gray slid his palms up her bare arms, over her shoulders, and hooked his thumbs in her bra straps. "Like you were jealous downstairs?"

Tipping her chin up, she met his mocking stare. "I was not jealous."

Gray's fingertips left the straps and slid over the swell of her breasts. Tingles raced through her body.

"You cracked the glass you slammed down." One finger slid between her breasts and back up. "Seemed like you were upset about something."

"Consider the glass payment for the panties you ripped off me."

If possible, his eyes darkened at the mention of her underwear. In one swift move, he flicked the front closure of her bra and had it off. When he gripped the edge of her panties and met her eyes, she smiled.

"You going for two?" she asked, quirking a brow.

He gave a yank, and the sound of ripping material answered her question. Suddenly she stood before him completely naked and in the bright light of his bedroom while he was completely clothed.

"This is hardly fair," she informed him.

"You snuck up to my apartment and came to my bed," he reminded her. "You're playing by my rules now, Kate."

How did the man continually get sexier? Seriously. Looks were one thing, but the way he treated her, spoke to her…how would she feel when this came to an end?

"I wasn't going to do this again," she muttered, mostly to herself.

"And I wasn't going to let you run, either." He banded an arm around her waist and jerked her body against his. "Why is there a time limit on what we're doing? We both like it. Neither one of us is dating anyone. It makes sense."

Kate closed her eyes. "Because we could lose ourselves and forget who we really are."

He leaned down and nipped her lips. "Maybe we're only just discovering who we really are."

Those words barely registered before he lifted her off her feet and carried her to his bed. He eased her down onto the plain gray sheets that were still rumpled from when he'd gotten out of them. She'd never been in his bedroom. They'd been friends forever, but crossing this threshold was taking things to a whole new territory.

Gray eased back, leaving her lying spread out. She watched as he reached behind his neck and jerked the black tee up and over his head. After he tossed it into the corner, he started unfastening his jeans, all while keeping those heavy-lidded eyes on her.

"You look good here, Kate."

She closed her eyes. Maybe if she didn't look at him when he said such meaningful words, they wouldn't penetrate her soul. But he kept saying little things. No, not little, not in the terms of the impact they had.

Instead of responding, because she truly had no words, she lifted her knees to make room for him. Once he'd gotten protection from his nightstand, she reached out, taking him in her arms. His weight pressed her further into the bed. She wasn't sure how she looked here, but she knew she liked it. Being wrapped up in Gray and knowing they shared something no one else knew about…there was a thrill to what they were doing.

A thrill she wasn't sure she ever wanted to see end.

But was he on the same page? If she threw out that she was having stronger feelings, what would he say? Would he tell her they were done with sex? Would he tell her they could be friends and have sex only as long as they were both single? Because suddenly, she wondered if there could be more.

"Hey."

Kate focused on the man who flanked her head with his forearms and smoothed her hair away from her face.

"Stay with me," he murmured.

Curling her fingers around his bare shoulders, Kate smiled. "I wouldn't be anywhere else."

Gray joined their bodies and Kate locked her ankles behind his back. She wanted to stay just like this, to forget the outside world, to ignore any warning that went off in her head about what could go wrong. Because right now, everything in her world was absolutely perfect.

Gray's lips slid over her skin, along her jawline, down her neck, along her chest. Kate arched into him, needing more and silently begging him to give it to her. Gray murmured something into her ear and she couldn't make it out. He'd done that before and she wondered what he was saying, but that was something she'd ask later. She'd rather enjoy the euphoria and sweet bliss of being in his arms…in his bed.

In a move that shocked her, Gray held on to her and flipped them until he was on his back and she straddled him. The way he looked up at her…

A girl could get used to a man looking at her like she was the only good thing in his world.

Gray gripped her hips and Kate's body instantly responded to his strength. His fingers bit into her as she flattened her palms on his chest and let the moment completely consume her.

Before Kate's body ceased trembling, Gray's stilled beneath her. His lips thinned. His head tipped back. His eyes shut. But his grip on her never lightened. She remained where she was, watching the play of emotions across his face.

Slowly he relaxed beneath her. As he slid his hands up over the dip in her waist and urged her down, Kate smiled. She fell against his chest and closed her eyes.

"What now?" she asked, unable to stop herself.

His chest vibrated with the soft rumble of laughter. "We don't need to plan the next move. Relax."

When she started to set up, he flattened his hand on her back. "You can stay just like this a few more minutes."

She could, but she had questions. So many questions and only he could answer them. Well, they could figure them out together, but what was going to happen when she told him she might want more? He'd never even acted like he wanted a relationship. They had sex. They had never even been on a real date.

Kate couldn't take it anymore. She sat up and shifted off him. With her back to Gray, she sat on the edge of the bed and leaned down to pick up her discarded dress.

"We really need to talk."

Silence filled the air, as she'd expected it would once she uttered those five words that would put any man's hackles up.

Kate threw a glance over her shoulder. Gray lay there naked as you please, with his arms folded behind his head. His eyes held hers, but he still said nothing even when she raised a brow, silently begging him to speak.

"Why are you making this difficult?" she asked.

She came to her feet and threw her dress on, sans all undergarments. When she spun around toward the bed and crossed her arms over her chest, Gray merely smiled. Still naked, still fully in charge of this situation, because he just watched her. The man could be utterly infuriating.

"What are we doing?" she muttered, shaking her head. "Seriously? Are we going to keep doing this? Is there more?"

Her heart beat so fast, she wondered if he could see the pulse in her neck. Again without a word, Gray came to his feet and strutted from the room.

She threw her arms out. "Well, that went well," she whispered to the empty room.

Moments later, he came back in, still not the least bit concerned with his state of undress. He carried two wine stems between his fingers and in the other hand he had a champagne bottle.

"This is another bottle of what you had the other night." He set everything on the nightstand and poured her a glass. "You need another drink if we're going to get into this discussion."

"Drinking isn't the answer," she retorted.

He picked up the glass and handed it to her. "I never said it was. But I brought this bottle up earlier and got sidetracked when I found you naked in my room."

She took the glass but didn't take a sip yet. "Why

did you bring it to begin with? I didn't take you for a champagne drinker."

"I'm not, but I knew you were up here so I brought it for you."

Kate jerked. "How did you know I came up here? I was discreet."

Gray laughed as he filled his own glass and then downed it in one gulp. He set the glass back on the nightstand and turned toward her.

"I'm a pretty smart guy, Kate." He pointed toward her glass. "You're going to want to start on that."

She took a small drink, relishing the bubbles that burst in her mouth. Champagne really wasn't bad at all.

"You were jealous," he started, holding up his hand when she opened her mouth to argue. "You were, so be quiet for a minute."

Kate took another drink and sank onto the edge of the bed. "Could you at least put something on? It's hard to concentrate with all that hanging out."

Gray laughed and turned toward his dresser, where a stack of clean laundry lay neatly folded. He grabbed a pair of black boxer briefs and tugged them on.

"Better?"

Actually, no. The briefs hugged his narrow hips, drawing her attention to that perfect V of muscles leading south. Mercy, how had she missed all of his flawless features in the past?

She took another drink.

"So you were jealous," he went on.

"Move to something else," she growled.

Gray laughed, propping his hands on those hips she tried so hard to stop staring at. "Fine. Then I saw you grab your purse and disappear, only the front door didn't open and I couldn't get a clear view of the back hall. Nobody goes that way, but I had a feeling my Kate had done just that."

She narrowed her eyes. "Jacob told you."

"He didn't have to say anything."

Kate polished off her champagne and set her empty glass next to his. When she glanced back up at him, she shivered at the look in his eyes.

"You didn't like that woman flirting with me. That was a good piece of information to have."

Kate hated that she'd let her emotions get the better of her. "Fine. I was jealous."

Gray knelt down in front of her and clasped her hands in his. "I didn't think you'd admit it."

"Why hide it? We may just be having sex, but that doesn't mean I want to see some woman pawing you."

Kate stared down at their joined hands and willed herself to be strong and just say what she wanted to say. But before she could tell him her thoughts, he placed one hand beneath her chin and tipped her face to meet his.

Gray leaned forward and nipped at her lips before murmuring, "Marry me."

Chapter Thirteen

Why wasn't she saying anything?

Gray waited.

"Kate?"

She blinked. "Marry you? But we've never discussed anything like that."

When she came to her feet, her abrupt movement had him standing as well. Then she began to pace his room. She couldn't go far in the small space, but since he had only a bed and dresser, she didn't have much to maneuver around.

"Marry you," she repeated beneath her breath as she turned on her heel to walk in the other direction.

"Why not?" he asked. "We get along, we're good

together in bed, and we just understand each other. That's more than most married couples have."

She stopped and stared at him as if he had grown another nose on the side of his head. "Why on earth do you want to marry me?"

"I talked to Dad about selling the bar." Now it was his turn to pace because the thought of everything closing in on him made him twitchy. "He's most definitely not on board and he seems to think I just need to settle down. Perhaps this way, I could sell it and you and I could use that money to start over somewhere. Or hell, build a house here. Whatever. We'd have freedom and that's all that matters."

He'd come to stand directly in front of her, but she continued to stare. No, glare would best describe what she was doing now. There was something he couldn't quite pinpoint in her eyes. Gone was the desire he'd seen moments ago.

"So, what, I'm just a means to pacify your dad so you can collect a check?" she asked. With a shake of her head, she let out a humorless laugh. "I was already going to marry one jerk who obviously didn't get me. It's quite clear you never understood me either if you think I'll marry you."

Anger simmered within him, but he didn't want to lash out.

"What the hell is wrong with marrying me?" he asked.

"I want to know your first thought when I asked why you wanted to marry me. Don't think about what I want to hear. Just tell me the first thing that comes into your head."

This was a trap. Somewhere in that statement she'd set a trap for him and he was about to fall headfirst into it.

"I think it makes sense," he answered honestly. "What's there to think about?"

She stared at him a bit longer and that's when he saw it. Hurt. That emotion he couldn't pin down before had been pain and it stared back at him plain as day. He'd seen that look before from patrons who wanted to drink their worries away. He'd seen it too often. But he was completely baffled by why the hell she stared at him with such anguish.

"What did I say?"

She chewed on her bottom lip for a moment before skirting around him and picking up her underwear and bra. He watched as she dressed fully and then sat on the edge of his bed to pull her sandals on.

"Where are you going?"

Without looking up, she adjusted her shoe and came to her feet. "Home. I've had enough of…whatever this is. We never should've slept together."

He crossed the room and took her shoulders, forcing her to face him. "What the hell are you talking about? Is this because I asked you to marry me?"

Her eyes swam with unshed tears and he wished like hell he knew why she was this upset.

"Do you love me, Gray?"

"What?" Her question stunned him. "Of course

I love you. I've loved you since the seventh grade. What kind of a question is that?"

She blinked, causing a tear to spill down her cheek. He swiped the pad of his thumb over her creamy skin. His heart ached at seeing her hurt, but hell if he knew how to fix this.

"It's a legitimate question, considering you proposed," she said, her voice soft, sad. "This isn't working for me anymore."

Kate shrugged from his arms and stepped back. She tilted her chin and squared her shoulders as if going into warrior mode before his eyes.

"You want freedom?" she asked. "Then go. Take that fat check, sell the bar and just go."

"What the hell are you so angry about?" he asked...well, more like yelled, because damn it, he could not figure her out.

"I never thought you'd use me or consider me plan B for your life." She swatted at another tear that streaked down her cheek. "You're only asking me to marry you to pacify your father. That man would do anything for you and he's all you have left. Do you know how lucky you are? Do you understand that if I had a parent in my life, I'd do anything to make them proud of me?"

Now he was pissed. Gray fisted his hands at his sides and towered over her as he took a step forward. "You think my father isn't proud of me? Of what I've done here? You know I'm sorry about your parents, but damn it, Kate, you can't always throw that in my face."

She recoiled as if he'd hit her. Gray muttered a string of curses beneath his breath as he raked a hand through his hair.

"That's not what I meant," he said.

She held up her hands. "You said exactly what you meant. We don't see eye to eye on things anymore. Just another reason why I need to go and this…all of it has to stop."

His heart clenched. "What do you mean, 'all of it'?"

"I knew we couldn't keep our friendship and sex separate," she cried. Tears streamed down her cheeks and she didn't even bother swiping them away. "Then you throw out an engagement like it's a simple fix to your problems. Did you ever think that maybe I'd want to marry someone who actually loves me? That I don't just want to settle?"

"I said I loved you," he practically shouted. "What more do you want?"

The brief smile that flashed amid the tears nearly gutted him. Pain radiated from her and if he knew what he'd done to crush her, he'd fix it.

"You don't mean it," she whispered. "Not in the way I need you to."

A rumble of thunder and a quick flash of lightning interrupted the tense moment. Within seconds, rain pelted the windows. Kate stared at him another second before she turned away and headed toward the door. Gray had a sinking feeling that if she walked out that door, she might never come back...not even as his friend.

"Don't go, Kate. Not like this."

She stilled, but didn't face him.

"We can work this out."

"I think we've said enough," she replied.

He took a step toward her, but didn't reach for her like he desperately wanted to. "At least let me drive you home. You're upset and it's starting to storm."

Those bright blue eyes shining with tears peered over her shoulder. "I'd rather take my chances with the storm outside than the one surrounding us."

And then she was gone.

Gray stared at the spot where she'd just stood, then he glanced to the empty glasses, the rumpled sheets.

What the hell had just happened here?

Well, there was the proposal that had taken them both by surprise. But in his defense, the moment the words were out of his mouth, he hadn't regretted them.

He did love her. They'd been friends forever, so what kind of question was that? And what did she mean by saying he didn't love her the way she needed him to? He'd always been there for her, hadn't he?

Gray turned from the bedroom. He couldn't stay in there, not when the sheets smelled like her, not when just the sight of that bed had him recalling how perfect she'd looked lying there.

He stalked down the hall and into the living room. The storm grew closer as the thunder and lightning hit simultaneously. The electricity flickered once, twice, then went out.

Perfect. Pitch black to match his mood.

Gray went to the window and looked down into the parking lot beside the bar. Kate's car still sat there.

Without thinking, he fumbled his way through the dark to throw on a pair of jeans, not bothering with shoes. He raced down the back steps and out the rear entrance.

Instantly he was soaked, but he didn't care. If Kate was still here, she was sitting in her car, upset. He knew that as well as he knew his name.

He tapped on the driver's window. Kate started the car and slid the window down a sliver.

"Get out of the storm," she yelled.

"I will when I know you're all right."

The damn street lights were out so he couldn't see her face, but he saw enough shimmer in her eyes to know she wasn't fine, not at all.

"You're soaked. Go inside, Gray. We're done."

He jerked open her door, propping one arm up on the car, and leaned down to get right in her face. "We're not done, Kate. You can't brush me aside."

The lights from her dash lit up her face. She stared at him for a moment before shaking her head.

"I'm going home. I need some space."

He knew what that was code for. She wanted

to push him away and try to figure everything out herself. Hell no. Yes, he'd upset her, but he wasn't backing down. This was bigger than selling the bar, pleasing his father or some lame marriage proposal.

Kate had legitimately been hurt by their conversation. She'd opened herself and came to his room. He could only imagine the courage that had taken.

"You can have your space," he told her, swiping the rain from his eyes. "But know that you can't keep me away. I'm not going anywhere, Kate."

He didn't give her a chance to reply. Gray gripped the back of her head and covered her mouth with his. Quick, fierce, impossible to forget, that's the kiss he delivered before he stepped back and closed her car door.

The window slid up as she put the car in Drive and pulled out of the lot. He stood in the midst of the storm, watching her taillights disappear into the dark night.

The thunder continued to rumble and a bolt of lightning streaked across the sky. Gray rubbed his chest as he headed back inside. He'd always ached for her when she'd gotten upset. But this was different.

Somehow with that surprise proposal, he'd severed something they shared. He'd tainted their friendship and put a dark cloud over their lives. All he'd wanted to do was make his father happy and somehow that had blown up in his face.

Gray knew sleep wasn't coming anytime soon,

so he started plotting. If the damn electricity would come back on, he could put his plan into motion and maybe salvage some semblance of this friendship.

Chapter Fourteen

Kate clicked Send on her blog and sat back to admire the new layout she'd implemented on her site. Thanks to sleepless nights, she'd had plenty of time to work on cleaning up her pages a bit. She now had everything organized and easier to maneuver.

But she was in no mood to celebrate. For the past two mornings she'd been sick as a dog. She'd also missed her period and there was a home pregnancy test in her bathroom that mocked her every time she went in. There was no need to take it. She knew.

The birth control she'd switched from pill to patch had come during their camping trip, there was no questioning how this happened.

She hadn't heard from Gray in two weeks. The

deadline had passed for him to make a decision on the bar, but he hadn't told her anything. He hadn't texted, hadn't called. He'd warned her he'd give her space and he'd kept his word.

Damn it, why did she have to miss him so much? What was he going to say when she told him about the baby? Most likely he'd take that Neanderthal attitude and try to convince her to marry him.

Kate glanced at the clock. She really needed to get some lunch. The crackers and ginger ale this morning had worn off. Well, they hadn't stayed down, so they'd worn off immediately.

She scrolled through her newly uploaded blog discussing why organization made for a better attitude. People in general were calmer if the world around them was in order so they didn't feel as if they were living in chaos. She'd even added a new buy button to the site, along with a note stating that all first-time clients would receive a 10 percent discount.

Her newsletter was set to go out this evening, so the timing of this post was perfect. Of course, she'd planned it that way.

Kate pushed her chair back and came to her feet. A slight wave of dizziness overcame her. Gripping the edge of her desk, she closed her eyes and waited for it to pass.

What would Lucy and Tara say? They didn't even know she and Gray had been intimate. They would be hurt that she hadn't confided in them, but she just hadn't been ready and then she thought things were going to go back to normal and now…well, this was her new normal.

Kate's cell buzzed and vibrated on her desk top. She sank back into her chair and stared at the screen, not recognizing the number. New clients contacted her all the time, so ignoring the call wasn't an option.

"Hello?"

"Ms. McCoy?"

She didn't recognize the male voice on the other end. "Yes."

"My name is Steven Sanders. I'm with a group out of Nashville called Lost and Found Family."

Intrigued, Kate eased back in her seat and kept her eyes shut. The room had stopped spinning, but she wasn't taking any chances right now.

"What can I do for you, Mr. Sanders?"

"Actually, it's what I can do for you," he countered. "I was given your contact information by Gray Gallagher. He wanted me to talk with you about tracing your family and finding your heritage. Is this a good time to talk?"

So many things swirled around in her mind. Gray had called someone to help her find her family? But he hadn't talked to her or even texted. Why hadn't he told her about this? Why was he being so nice when she'd turned him down and left in the midst of a storm?

"Sure," she replied. "Um…sorry. This is all just a bit of a surprise."

The man chuckled on the other end of the line.

"Gray was adamant I call you as soon as I could, but I was trying to get another case wrapped up before contacting you. He made me vow to give your case special attention."

Something warmed inside her, something that brought tears to her eyes. She leaned forward, resting her elbows on her desk.

"Well, I appreciate that," she replied. "But I understand I'm probably not your only client. What information do you need from me?"

Steven went on to explain the information Gray had already delivered to him. He asked her about her mother's maiden name, her skin color, eye color, hair color. He went through her father's description. Then he asked for birthdays, where they were born and any grandparents' names she might know.

"This gives me a bit to go on to get started," Steven said after about a half hour of gathering information. "Should I call or email you when I have more questions?"

"I'm fine with either," she replied. "I can't thank you enough. I never knew really who to call to get started on this. You can bill me through email and I'll—"

"Oh, no, ma'am. Mr. Gallagher already took care of the bill, and any further charges will be sent to him."

Kate wasn't going to get into an argument with this guy. He had no clue about the whirlwind of emotions that continued to swirl around her and Gray. The poor guy was just doing his job.

"Thanks so much for taking on this case," she replied. "I look forward to hearing from you."

"I'll be in touch."

She disconnected the call and stood back up, thankfully no longer dizzy. As she made her way toward the kitchen, she went over in her mind what she wanted to say to Gray. He'd already helped her by tracking down someone who could research her ancestry. He didn't need to pay for it, too. And he'd done all of this after they'd stopped speaking.

The idea that he'd started working on a portion of her life list had tears burning her eyes. No matter what had transpired between them, he was still determined to be there for her.

Kate made a quick peanut butter sandwich and grabbed a bottle of water and a banana before heading back to her office. There was no dodging Gray anymore. She needed to thank him for hiring the genealogy investigator, plus tell him about the baby.

If she thought their dynamics had been changed before with just sex, this would certainly alter everything they'd ever known. She had to be positive before going to him and she had to know exactly what to say.

Kate would definitely take the test to be sure, but he deserved to know. This was definitely something they needed to work on together.

Looked like she wasn't going to be putting him in

that friend category anymore. She wasn't ready to put him in the husband category, either. He'd honestly hurt her when he'd said why he wanted to marry her.

How could he be so blind? How could he not see that she wanted someone who genuinely loved her? Like *in love* with her?

She'd been on the verge of telling him she was falling for him when he blurted out the proposal, destroying any hope she might have had that their bond could go deeper than friendship. And now she was carrying his child. If this wasn't the most warped situation ever, she didn't know what was.

Ladies' Night was tonight and in their group texts, Lucy and Tara had already been vocal about wanting to go. Kate figured now would be as good a time as any to go out, try to have fun and not freak out about her entire life getting turned upside down.

Because as scared, nervous and anxious as she was about this child—along with a gamut of other emotions—the truth of the matter was…she was happy. She had no family, but she was creating her very own. No, this was definitely not planned and, surprisingly, she was okay.

This wasn't a schedule or a job. This was a child. Her child.

Would Gray still want to take the money from the sale of the bar? She couldn't stand the thought of him leaving, but he needed to be aware of just how much their lives were about to change.

Tonight. She'd go tonight and thank him for the

genealogy specialist. Then, once the bar closed, she'd take him upstairs and tell him about the baby.

First, though, she had a test to take.

As Wednesday nights went, the bar was crazier than usual. He'd begged one of his waitresses to come in on her night off. He never begged. He'd even offered her an extra paid day off if she just came in for a few hours to help bartend. Jacob was in the kitchen filling in for the cook, who'd come down with some cold or whatever.

It was just a crazy, messed up day.

And Kate had strolled in with her friends and hadn't come up to the bar once to speak to him. In the two weeks he'd given her space, he'd damn near lost his mind.

More orders flooded the system and Gray didn't slow down or stop. If Kate was here, then she was here to talk. She'd missed Ladies' Night last week and, like a fool, he'd watched the door. But he'd been so busy over the past fourteen days trying to get this place ready to sell that he'd let himself get wrapped up in the business.

He still hadn't made up his mind, but he had texted the guy and bought more time. Gray was inching closer to realizing he might never get a chance like this again. If he ever wanted to get out and see what he'd been missing in his life, now was the time.

What seemed like an eternity later, the crowd started winding down. Gray had caught glimpses of Kate, Lucy and Tara dancing, but now he only saw Kate in the corner booth alone and looking at something on her phone.

He left the bar to his employee and promised to be away only two minutes. Now that things weren't so insane, he wanted to talk to Kate.

As he crossed the bar, weaving through the tables and the stragglers who were still hanging out, Kate looked up and caught his gaze. Her eyes widened and with her tense shoulders and tight smile, Gray knew something was up.

Without asking, he slid into the booth across from her. "Didn't expect you to show up tonight."

She laid her phone in front of her and shrugged. "I needed to get out of the house. Plus, I needed to thank you for having Steven Sanders call me."

Gray eased back in the seat. "So he's on it. Good. I was giving him two more days to contact you before I called him again."

"He has other clients, you know."

Gray didn't care. What he cared about was helping Kate with her list and finding some sort of family for her to call her own.

"I hope he can find what you need," Gray replied.

Silence settled between them as she glanced down at her hands. She'd laced her fingers together and the way her knuckles were turning white made him wonder what was really on her mind.

"You're upset that I contacted him?" he guessed.

"No, no. I'm surprised and thankful," she corrected him.

"What's wrong?" he asked, leaning forward. "Lucy and Tara took off a while ago but you're still here."

Her eyes darted to the dancing women on the dance floor.

"Kate."

She turned her focus to him, but that didn't last long. Her gaze dropped once again to her clasped hands. "We need to talk. Can I wait until you're closed?"

Gray glanced to his watch. "We've got another hour. Do you want to go upstairs? You look like you could fall over."

And she did. She'd gone sans makeup, which wasn't unusual, but he could see the dark circles under her eyes, and she was a bit paler than normal.

"You feeling all right?" he asked.

She attempted a smile, but it was lame and forced. "Fine. I think I will go upstairs if you don't care. I can't leave without talking to you alone."

When she slid out of the booth, Gray came to his feet as well. She reached for the table with one hand and her head with the other as she teetered.

"Kate." He grasped her arms, holding tight. "I didn't make a drink for you. What have you had?"

She waved a hand away as she straightened. "I'm just tired and stood up too fast. I've only had water."

"Do you need something to eat?"

Shaking her head, she tried for a smile once again. "Really, I'm okay. I'll meet you upstairs when you're done."

He watched her head behind the bar and into the back hallway. Never in all his years as owner had he wanted to close up early and tell everyone to get the hell out.

Something was wrong with Kate. After all the running she'd done, something had pulled her back to him and he knew it wasn't the fact he'd called a genealogy specialist.

The next hour seemed to drag as he busted his butt to get the place ready to shut down for the night. He could sweep the floors and do a thorough wipe down in the morning. Once all the alcohol was taken care of, the kitchen was shut down properly and the employees were gone, Gray locked up and headed upstairs.

When he opened the door and stepped into the living room, he froze. There on his sofa was Kate all curled up in one corner. She'd removed her shoes and her little bare feet were tucked at her side.

She didn't look too comfortable at the angle her head had fallen against the back of the couch. Had she not been sleeping at home? Had she thought about his proposal and was here to…what? Take him up on it?

Gray turned the knob and slowly shut the door, careful not to click it into place. He crossed the room and took a seat directly in front of her on the old metal trunk he used as a coffee table. He watched her for a minute, torn between waking her and letting her get the sleep she seemed to desperately need.

After several minutes of feeling like a creeper, Gray reached out and tapped her leg. She didn't move. He flattened his hand around her thigh and gave a gentle squeeze.

"Kate," he said in a soft tone.

She started to stir. Her lids fluttered, then lifted. She blinked a few times as if focusing. Then she shot up on the sofa.

"Oh my gosh." Her hands immediately went to her hair, pushing wayward strands back from her face. "I didn't mean to fall asleep."

He held out his hands. "Relax. It's no big deal."

She swung her legs around and placed them on the area rug. The side of her knee brushed his as she propped her elbows on her thighs and rubbed her face.

"What's wrong, Kate?" He couldn't stand it any longer. "I gave you the space you asked for, but you show up here looking like a small gust of wind could blow you over. Are you sick? Don't lie to me."

Damn it, fear gripped him and he didn't like this feeling. Not one bit.

"I'm not sick." She dropped her hands in her lap and met his gaze dead-on. "I'm pregnant."

Chapter Fifteen

Kate stared at him, worried when the silence stretched longer than was comfortable.

She hadn't meant to just blurt that out, but honestly, was there a lead-in to such a bomb? Gray sat so close, their knees bumped. And for the second time in their years of friendship, she couldn't make out the expression on his face.

His eyes never wavered from her, but he reached out and gripped her hands in his. "Pregnant? Are you sure?"

Before she could answer, he shook his head. "That was stupid. You wouldn't tell me unless you were sure."

"I've suspected for a few days, but just took the test today."

Now his eyes did drop to her stomach. "I don't even know what to say. Are you... I mean, you feel okay?"

"I'm nauseous, tired, look like hell. Other than that, I'm fine."

Gray shifted his focus from her flat abdomen to her eyes. "You've never looked like hell in your life."

"You didn't see me hugging the commode this morning," she muttered.

His thumb raked over the back of her hand. "Did you come here to tell me you'd marry me?"

She'd been so afraid he'd say that. That he would just assume a baby would be a reason to marry. If the marriage wasn't going to be forever, how was joining lives the right thing to do?

"I'm not marrying you, Gray."

His dark brows drew in as he continued to stare at her. "Why not? This is all the more reason to get married. We're going to be parents. I can sell the bar, get the money, and we can go wherever you want. Hell, we'll travel and then decide where to settle down. Name it."

Kate shook her head and removed her hands from his. She leaned back on the couch and curled her feet back up beside her where they'd been.

"That's not the answer," she countered. "I don't want to keep doing this with you. We have time to figure out what the best plan will be for our baby."

"So if I sell the bar and leave, you'll what? Stay here? I want to be part of our child's life."

She knew he would. She expected him to be. Gray would be a wonderful father. He'd be a fabulous husband, just not in the way he was proposing. Literally.

"I'd never keep you away from the baby," she told him. "I'm hurt you would even suggest such a thing. If you leave, that's on you. I'll be right here in Stonerock."

He stared at her another minute and then finally pushed to his feet. "Stay here tonight," he said, looking down at her. "Just stay here so we can figure this out."

Kate smiled, but shook her head. "Sex isn't going to solve anything."

"Maybe I just want you here," he retorted. "Maybe I've missed you and now, knowing that you're carrying my child, I want to take care of you."

The tenderness in his voice warmed her. She knew he'd want to take over and make sure everything was perfect for her. He'd want to make her as comfortable as possible.

Unfortunately, through all of that, he just couldn't love her the way she wanted to be loved. The way she loved him.

Tears pricked her eyes. She dropped her head and brought her hands up to shield her face. Damn hormones.

"Kate." The cushion on the sofa sank next to her. One strong arm wrapped around her and she felt herself being pulled against his side. "Don't cry. Please. I'll figure something out."

Couldn't he see? This had nothing to do with the bar and if he kept it or sold it. If he loved her, truly loved her like a man loved a woman, she'd go anywhere with him. But she couldn't just uproot her life for a man who was settling and only trying to do the right thing.

"Stay," he whispered into her ear as he stroked her hair. "Sleeping. Nothing more."

She tipped her head back to peer up at him.

"Please."

She knew he only wanted to keep an eye on her, plus it was late and she was exhausted. Kate nodded. "I'll stay."

Gray left Kate sleeping and eased out of the bed. He glanced back down to where she lay wearing one of his shirts, her raven hair in a tangled mess around her, dark circles beneath her eyes. She'd been so exhausted when she'd come to the bar last night.

And she'd dropped the biggest bomb of his life.

A baby. He was having a baby with his best friend and she refused to marry him.

Gray had to convince her to. Before she'd changed his entire life with one sentence, he'd nearly talked himself into selling Gallagher's. Now that he knew he was going to be a father, well, he was sure he wanted to sell. He could use that money and make a nice life for his family...just as soon as he convinced

Kate to marry him. Didn't she see that this was the most logical step?

He hadn't planned on getting married, but with his dad always hinting that he should, with the new chapter of selling the bar, and with Kate pregnant... hell, he had to move forward with his plan and make her see this was the best option for their future.

Quietly he eased the door shut and went to the kitchen to make breakfast. He had no clue what was on her agenda today, but hopefully after a good night's sleep, they could talk and try to work things out. Well, he'd try to get her to see reason.

Gray checked his fridge and realized he hadn't been to the store in... Honestly, he couldn't remember the last time he went to the store.

He headed down to the bar and raided that kitchen, then ran back upstairs. Now he could actually start cooking something. Kate still slept, so he tried to be quiet. His apartment wasn't that big, but it worked for him.

That is, this space had always worked until now. He couldn't exactly expect Kate to raise a baby here. She valued family and the importance of home. Kate and the baby deserved a house with a yard, somewhere they could put a swing set. Something the total opposite of a bachelor pad above a bar.

Gray fried some potatoes he'd snagged from downstairs and pulled out the ham steaks from his freezer. Kate was more of a pancake girl, but she'd have to adapt today. He would see to it that she was cared for, whether she liked it or not.

He'd just dished up the plates when he heard running down the hall and then the bathroom door slamming shut.

Muttering a curse, he left the breakfast and went to the closed door. Yeah, she was definitely sick. He rubbed his hands down his face and stared up at the ceiling. How the hell could he make her feel better? He couldn't exactly fix this or take it from her.

He stood on the other side of the door and waited until the toilet flushed. He heard water running and, moments later, she opened the door. Gray hated how pale she was, how her hand shook as she shoved her hair away from her face.

"Sorry about that," she murmured, leaning against the door frame. "It hits quick."

He reached out and framed her face in his hands. "Never apologize to me. I made breakfast, but I'm thinking maybe you're not in the mood."

Her eyes shut as she wrinkled her nose. "Do you just have some juice?"

"Downstairs I do. I'll be right back."

In record time he had the juice and was racing back upstairs. As soon as he stepped into the apartment, he heard Kate talking.

"No, Chris. This isn't a good time."

Gray set the bottle on the small dining table and headed down the hall toward her voice. Chris, the bastard ex.

"I never agreed to meet up with you, so if you thought I did, then you're mistaken."

When Gray hit the doorway of his bedroom, he saw Kate sitting on the edge of his bed, her back to him. She had her head down and was rubbing it.

Anger bubbled within him. Who the hell was this guy who suddenly came back into her life? Why did he think she would want anything at all to do with him after the way he'd treated her?

"I don't care how long you're in town," she replied. "I'm busy."

She tapped the screen and tossed her cell on the bed.

"Has he been bothering you?" Gray asked, stepping into the room.

Kate turned to glance over her shoulder. "Just a few calls and texts. He only showed up at my house the one time."

If this jerk planned on staying in town, Gray intended to track him down. It was time for Chris to find out for good that he'd lost his chance at anything with Kate.

"I have your juice in the kitchen," he told her. "How are you feeling?"

She let out a slight laugh. "Confused. Scared. Powerless."

It probably wasn't the best time to tell her he felt the same way. Kate needed him to be strong, needed him to be there like he always had been. Even more so now.

Gray crossed the room and came to stand in front of her. "Don't answer me now, but think about marriage, Kate. There are so many reasons this is a good idea."

She stood, easing around him. "Not now, Gray. Just...not now."

"I'm just asking you to think about it."

He followed her down the hall to the kitchen. Grabbing a glass from the cabinet, he set it on the counter and poured her juice.

"I'm not asking for an answer today," he told her as she drank. "But you can't dismiss the idea completely."

She licked her lips and leveled her gaze. "Are you selling the bar?"

Gray swallowed, knowing he was going to have to say it out loud at some point. "Yes."

Kate pulled in a slow breath and nodded. Then she finished the last of the juice and handed him back the glass.

"Then go do what you need to do," she told him. "You wanted to figure out what your life was missing, and I sure as hell don't want to be the reason you stay. I won't be someone's burden and I won't let this baby feel that way, either."

Gray slammed the glass on the counter and took her by her shoulders. "You're not listening to me, damn it. You're not a burden, Kate. This baby isn't a burden. But selling the bar makes more sense now than ever. What? You want to live up here and raise a child?"

"We're not getting married or living together, so it's a moot point," she threw back at him. "I don't like this, Gray. We're always arguing and I just want my friend back."

Her voice cracked on that last word and he hauled her against his chest. He wanted his friend back, too, but they'd obliterated the friendship line and now they were adding a baby to the mix.

"We can't go back," he told her. "But I won't let you go through this alone. I'm here."

She eased back, piercing him with those blue eyes full of questions, but she asked only one.

"For how long?"

Chapter Sixteen

Well, there was no more dodging the inevitable.

Kate had asked the girls over since she knew Sam had Marley. This was definitely not a conversation for little ears.

She'd ordered pizza, made cookies, had wine and water on hand—everything was all set for the big reveal. Just then, her front door opened and Tara and Lucy came in, chattering.

Kate heard Lucy saying something about her stepdaughter, but couldn't make out exactly what it was. When she'd married Noah, she'd gotten an instant family and was filling the role of mom beautifully. Tara excelled at motherhood, despite the roller coaster she'd had to endure these past several months with Sam and his addiction.

Looked like Kate couldn't have asked for two better women to call on for support. She only hoped they weren't too angry with her for keeping the situation with Gray a secret.

Kate stepped from the kitchen into the living room. "Hey, guys."

"I smell pizza," Tara stated. "Please, tell me you got extra bacon on at least part of it."

Kate rolled her eyes. "Have I ever let you down? I even bought your favorite wine, though wine and pizza always sounded like a bad combo to me."

Lucy set her purse on the accent chair and dropped her keys inside. "Wine goes with everything and so does pizza, so it only makes sense to pair them together."

Kate attempted a smile, but her nerves were spiraling out of control. She could do this. There was nothing to be afraid of and her friends would be there for her. Isn't that what they did? They banded together during the best and worst of times.

"Oh, no." Tara took a slow step forward. "I thought we were just having a random girls' night. What's wrong, Kate?"

"You guys might want to sit down with a glass of wine first."

Lucy crossed her arms over her chest and shook her head. "Not until you tell us what's wrong."

"Nothing is wrong, exactly," she replied. "Gray and I—"

"Finally." Tara threw her hands in the air. "I knew something was going on with the two of you. What is it, though? You seem, I don't know…nervous."

"Are you and Gray together?" Lucy whispered as if this was some sacred secret.

"You could say that."

Kate looked from one friend to the other. They'd barely made it inside the front door, and from the determined look on their faces, they weren't moving any further until she confessed.

"I'm pregnant."

Tara's eyes widened. Lucy's mouth dropped. Neither said a word, but their shock spoke volumes.

"We were just fooling around," Kate went on. "I mean, there was the night of the rehearsal dinner, then camping—"

"I called this," Tara repeated. "Well, not the baby. Damn, Kate. You're having a baby?"

Kate couldn't help the smile and shrug. "Of all people, the CEO of Savvy Scheduler did not plan this."

Lucy stepped forward and extended her arms. Kate shook her head and held her hands out, silently telling her friend no.

"I can't do comfort right now," she explained. "I'm barely hanging on here and I just need to come to grips with this—"

Lucy wrapped her arms around Kate and that was

all it took for Kate to finally crumble. Tears fell, fear took hold, and soon Tara's arms were banding around them as well.

"It's going to be okay," Tara stated. "A baby is a wonderful blessing."

"What did Gray say?" Lucy asked, easing back slightly.

Kate sniffed and attempted to gather herself together. "He proposed," she whispered.

"That's great," Tara exclaimed. "I always thought you two would end up together."

Swiping her face with the back of her hand, Kate pulled in a shaky breath. "I turned him down."

Tara gripped her shoulder. "What?"

"I'm not settling," Kate explained. "I want to marry someone who loves me, who isn't marrying me because of some family pressure or a pregnancy."

Kate stepped back to get some space. She didn't want to cry about this, didn't want pity. She wanted to figure out what her next step should be and she needed to be logical about it.

Maneuvering around her friends, who continued to stare at her as if she'd break again, Kate went to the sofa and sank into the corner.

"He proposed before I told him about the baby," she explained. "He's got that offer to sell the bar and his father has been on him for years to settle down. Gray wants to move ahead with the deal and figured if we got married, maybe his dad wouldn't be so upset about losing Gallagher's. Then when I told him about the baby, well, he thinks it's only logical."

Tara sat on the edge of the accent chair across from the sofa. "What's logical is that you should tell him how you really feel so the two of you can move on."

"You do love him, right?" Lucy asked as she sat in the chair right next to Tara's hip. "I don't mean like you love us as your friends. I mean, you love Gray. I know you do or you never would've slept with him."

Kate couldn't deny it—she didn't want to. She was tired of the sneaking, the secrets, the emotions.

"I do," she whispered. "But it's irrelevant because he doesn't see me like that."

"Men are blind." Lucy reached over to pat Kate's knee. "Sometimes you have to bang them over the head in order for them to see the truth. You need to be honest with Gray. He should know how you feel."

Kate had put her love out there before. She'd had a ring on her finger and a dress in her closet, but that love—or what she'd thought was love—had been thrown back in her face.

She loved Gray more than she ever did Chris. Gray was…well, he was everything. How would she handle it if he rejected her? At least if she kept her feelings locked inside her heart, they could remain friends, raise the baby and not muddle up their relationship with one-sided love.

"How are you feeling, other than Gray?" Tara asked. "Physically, I mean. Have you been sick?"

"Gray made me potatoes and ham for breakfast and the smell woke me when my stomach started rolling. Sick doesn't begin to describe my mornings."

Lucy's eyes widened. "He made you breakfast? That's so sweet."

Kate laughed. "He's always taken care of me. That's not the problem."

"The key to any good relationship is communication," Tara stated, and the wistfulness in her tone had Kate turning her focus on her. "Trust me. You need to tell him how you feel."

Kate tucked her hair behind her ears and wondered what would be best. Baring her heart to Gray as to her true feelings or just waiting to see what happened? For all she knew, he would sell the bar, go on some grand adventure to find himself and then discover that he never wanted to return. Then what?

"I honestly don't know what to do," she muttered. "I don't want him to feel sorry for me or think I fell in love with him because of the pregnancy. I've loved him… I don't even know how long. Maybe forever, but I didn't realize it until recently."

Lucy grabbed Kate's hand. "Well, right now let's focus on you and this baby. I'm confident Gray will come around."

Kate wished she had Lucy's confidence and Tara's courage. But this was her life and this pregnancy was the biggest thing that had ever happened to her. And she didn't want to put her heart on the line again because she'd been right from the very beginning. She could lose Gray's friendship if all of this went wrong. Losing the one constant man in her life wasn't an option. Especially now that the same man would be needed as a constant for their baby.

Gray set the glass of sweet tea on the counter in front of Sam. The bar didn't open for another hour and Sam had stopped by after a long week at his new job. Gray admired the man for putting his family first, for selling his own company and humbling himself to get counseling before going to work for another construction company.

He'd helped himself but may never get his wife back. The harsh reality was a bitch to bear, Gray was sure. Sam was a great guy who'd made poor decisions.

"Are you really selling the bar?" Sam asked, gripping the frosted glass.

Gray flattened his palms on the rolled edge of the bar. "I am. I haven't contacted the guy from Knoxville yet, but I plan on calling Monday morning."

"What does your dad say about it?"

Gray didn't like to think of the disappointment he'd seen in his father's eyes. He knew his dad wanted to keep the bar in the family, but would ultimately support Gray no matter what.

The problem was, Gray wasn't a hundred percent sure what he wanted. He did know that the money from the sale would put him in a perfect spot to provide for Kate and the baby.

He hadn't mentioned the baby to his dad because that would've brought up a whole other set of issues...like the fact that she wouldn't marry him.

But he knew where her doubts were coming from. Kate had been left so shaken when her parents had passed. Then her fiancé had revealed his true colors and broken her heart. Gray never wanted her to question where her foundation was again. He knew she was scared with this pregnancy—hell, he was, too. But there was nothing he wouldn't do for her even if she refused to marry him.

"Dad isn't happy," Gray finally replied. "But he respects my decision. He'd like to see me settled down with a wife and a bunch of little Gallaghers running around and gearing up to pass this place to them."

Sam took a hearty drink of his tea and set the glass back down. "That's not what you want, I take it."

Gray gave a slight shrug, feeling something tug on his heart. "I don't know what I want, but has been on my mind."

Especially now.

"It's not for everyone, that's for sure." Sam slid his thumb over the condensation of his mug. "Tara is everything and when you find a love like that, it's worth fighting for. I really messed up, Gray. Don't learn from my mistakes."

Gray gritted his teeth and tried to sort through the thoughts scrolling through his head.

The most dominant thought was love. Love worth fighting for. He loved Kate. Hadn't he told her as much? They'd loved each other for years, so why was she so adamant about not marrying him? Wasn't any level of love a good basis for a marriage?

But she'd told him she wouldn't settle, that she wanted to be with a man who loved her the way a husband should love his wife.

He didn't even know what that meant. He thought she'd be happy with him, that they could be happy together. Obviously she had other expectations about her future.

"How are things with Tara?" Gray asked.

Sam shrugged. "Still the same. We get along for Marley and we're always civil, but it seems so shallow, you know? We just go through the days, same cycle, same fake smiles, like we're both not hurting."

Gray hated seeing his friends so torn. Yes, Sam had made mistakes, but he was human and he'd fought like hell to get clean and make up for the pain he'd caused.

Is this how Gray and Kate would be? Would they be moving through the days just living civilly and trying not to break? Would they bounce their child back and forth and pretend everything was okay?

And what would happen if Kate wanted to go on a date or brought a man home?

Jealousy spiraled through him at the mere thought of another man in Kate's life. Another man in their child's life.

Gray went about getting the bar ready to open. He chatted with his employees when they came in the back door and he welcomed the first customers who started to filter in. Sam remained on his stool, sipping his tea, then finally beer. Gray made sure to always keep an eye on his friend when he came in, and Sam usually limited his drinking to one or two beers. He seemed to be on the road to getting his life back under control.

Too bad Gray couldn't say the same.

Chapter Seventeen

"This was a mistake," Kate growled as Lucy practically dragged her inside the front door of Gallagher's. "A pregnant woman shouldn't be hanging out at the bar."

Lucy held onto her arm. "This is exactly where that pregnant lady should be when the man she loves is the owner. Besides, Tara is home with Marley tonight and Noah took Piper on a father-daughter date to the movies. I wanted to get out, so you're stuck with me."

Kate shouldn't be here. Then again, she shouldn't have put on her favorite dress and curled her hair, either. She didn't do those things for Gray. Absolutely not. She did them for herself because...

Fine. She did them for Gray because no matter how much she wished it, she couldn't just move on and forget her feelings for him. Pregnancy aside, Kate wanted Gray just as much as ever. Even if she hadn't been carrying his child, she would be completely in love with him.

For years she'd wanted a family of her own. She'd dreamed of it, in fact. Then she'd started her little business and focused on that after her world was rocked when Chris left. Now she was being given a second chance at a family, but Gray wasn't on board...not in the way she needed him to be.

Inside Gallagher's, an upbeat country song was blasting as several couples danced. The tables were full, except for one table right smack-dab in the middle of the floor. Fabulous. Why couldn't their usual corner booth be open? That real estate should always be on reserve for her.

Kate dropped to the hard wooden seat and hung her purse on the back. This was not ideal, not at all. Here she was, front and center of the bar, almost as if fate was mocking her.

A slow, twangy song filled the space and even more couples flooded to the dance floor.

"Fancy seeing you here."

Kate turned around, barely registering the cheesy line and her ex before he whisked her out of her seat and spun her toward the dance floor.

In a blur, she saw Lucy's shocked face.

"Chris, what in the world," she said, trying to

wriggle free of his grip on her hand. "I don't want to dance."

Banding an arm around her waist, he took her free hand in his and maneuvered them right into the midst of the dancers.

"Just one dance," he said, smiling down at her as if he had every right to hold her. "Surely you can give me three minutes to talk and then I'll leave you alone."

Kate didn't want to give him three seconds, let alone three minutes. She didn't get a chance to say anything because Chris was jerked from her and then Gray stood towering over him.

"You're Chris?" Gray asked, his body taut with tension.

Kate stepped forward and put her hand on his back. "Don't, Gray."

Ignoring her, he took a half step forward, causing Chris to shove at Gray. "I'm talking to Kate, if you don't mind."

"I actually do mind," Gray growled over the music. A crowd had formed around them.

"It's fine," Kate insisted. She didn't want an altercation.

"You heard the lady," Chris said with a smirk. "It's fine. Now go back to making drinks."

Kate didn't have time to react as Gray's fist drew back and landed right in the middle of Chris's face. Her ex stumbled back, landing on a table and upending another one.

Gray shook his hand out and Kate stepped around to stand in front of him, worried he'd go at Chris again. The last thing Gray needed was to get in a fight in his own bar. That wouldn't be good for business.

"Stop it," she demanded.

The look on his face was pure fury. Finally, he took his gaze from Chris and landed it on her. "Keep your boyfriend out of my bar."

Kate drew her brows in and dropped her hand. "What is wrong with you?"

"What the hell?"

Kate turned around to see some guy helping Chris up. The stranger turned his attention to Gray. "This is how you run a business?"

Gray moved around Kate and walked past Chris, the stranger and the crowd. Kate stared at his retreating back and was startled when a hand fell on her shoulder. She spun around to find Lucy.

"That was...territorial."

Kate shook her head. "What just happened?"

"I'd say your guy got jealous, but who was the other man who stepped in?"

Gray stalked back over to Chris and the other man. Kate watched, waiting and hoping there wasn't going to be another altercation.

"The bar isn't for sale." Gray stood directly in front of the two guys. Chris held his jaw, working it back and forth. "You two can get the hell out of here and don't come back."

Gray and Chris sparring wasn't something she thought she'd ever see. But no doubt about it, Chris wasn't going to win this fight no matter what he threatened.

"I'll sue you," Chris spouted. "My partner and I were going to give you a lot of money for this place."

"Sue me," Gray said, crossing his arms over his massive chest as if he didn't have a care in the world. "But leave."

He turned back around and went back to the bar. Kate watched as he started making drinks like his whole life hadn't just changed. Chris was a bastard, no doubt about it.

He'd wanted to sell the bar. He'd been pretty set on doing just that. What had changed his mind? He hadn't said a word to her. Between Gray's silence and Chris's betrayal, Kate wasn't sure how to feel, but pissed was a great starting point.

Then dread filled her. Had he done this because of the baby? Was he giving up what he truly wanted to make her happy? Because he'd done that with his father, when he'd taken over the bar after his tour of duty just to appease him. And here he was putting his own needs aside again. Kate intended to find out why.

Chris and his business partner turned and left, leaving many talking about what had just happened. Obviously the other guy was the one who'd made Gray the exorbitant offer.

"I can't believe he just hit him," Kate muttered.

Lucy laughed. "I recall him hitting another guy who got in your face several months ago."

Kate ran a hand through her hair as she met Gray's dark eyes across the bar. "At least he's consistent."

"Heard you made a little scene at the bar last night."

Gray rubbed his eyes and attempted to form a coherent sentence. His father had called way too early, knowing full well that Gray would still be asleep. The man had run the same bar for thirty years. He knew the routine.

"Nothing I couldn't handle."

Gray eased up in bed and leaned against the headboard because he knew his father didn't randomly call just to chat.

"Also heard you turned down the offer to sell."

Gray blew out a breath. Yeah. He had. That hadn't been an easy decision, but definitely the right one. The second he'd seen Kate in another man's arms, Gray had lost it. Then, on his way over, he'd heard Kate call the guy Chris and Gray nearly exploded. Okay, he did explode, but that guy deserved the punch—and more—for what he'd done years ago.

Kate was his family. Kate and their child was his family. The future had seemed so clear in that moment. All the times he'd waited for a sign, waited for some divine intervention to tell him what to do. But Kate and their family was everything. And he'd found that he wanted to continue that tradition with his child, boy or girl.

"I'm keeping the bar," Gray confirmed.

"Who changed your mind?" his dad asked.

Gray instantly pictured Kate. He couldn't help but smile though he was dead tired. He'd screwed up things with her. He'd legit botched up their relationship from the friendship to the intimacy. But he had a plan.

"I just realized nothing is missing from my life," Gray replied. "I'm staying here and Gallagher's will remain in the family."

"That was a lot of money to turn down, son."

Funny, but that didn't bother him anymore. "It was," he agreed. "Family means more."

Family meant *everything*.

He needed to tell his dad about the pregnancy, but he wanted to talk to Kate first. He had quite a bit to talk to her about, actually.

"I'm proud of you," his dad finally said. "Your grandfather would be, too, knowing you decided to stay in Stonerock, keep the tradition alive."

A lump formed in Gray's throat. "I wouldn't be anywhere else."

"Well, I guess I'll let you get back to sleep," his dad chuckled. "But Gray. Let's lay off the hitting. I know you have a thing for Kate, but control yourself."

His dad hung up before Gray could say anything about Kate or his self-control. He tossed his phone onto the rumpled sheet next to his hip. Raking his hands over his face, Gray attempted to sort his thoughts, his plans. Today he was taking back his life. Taking what he'd always wanted, but never knew he was missing.

And Kate wasn't going to get away again.

Chapter Eighteen

She hadn't seen Gray since the night before last. He'd punched Chris, turned down an enormous business deal and gone back to brooding.

Out of the blue, he'd texted this morning to tell her she'd left something at his apartment. There was no way she'd left anything there because she was meticulous about her stuff and knew where everything was.

Clearly he wanted her there for another reason. Kate found herself sipping her ginger ale and clutching a cracker as she mounted the outside back steps to the bar apartment.

Shoving the rest of the cracker in her mouth, she gripped the knob and eased the door open.

"Gray?" she called out as she stepped inside.

She'd never knocked before, so she didn't now, plus he knew she was coming.

Kate stepped into the living area and stopped short. The picture over the sofa was no longer the tacky *Dogs Playing Poker*. Tears pricked her eyes as she stepped closer to the image, one she'd seen so many times, but never like this.

A young Kate stared back at her. On either side of her in the portrait were her parents. All three smiling, not knowing what the future held. Kate had this exact picture in her bedroom.

"You like it?"

Kate was startled as Gray's easy question pulled her from the moment. Without turning, she nodded. Emotions formed heavy in her throat as her eyes burned with unshed tears.

"I remember that day so vividly," she told him, taking in every feature of her parents' faces. "We'd just gone for a picnic at one of the state parks. Then Dad took us on a small hike. My mom tripped on a rock and tore a hole in her tennis shoe. We laughed because she was always so clumsy."

She could still hear her mother's laugh—so sweet, almost wistful. "Not a day goes by that I don't miss them."

"They'd be proud of you."

Kate smiled as she turned to face Gray. "I hope so. I wonder what they'd think of me becoming a mother. Not having mine right now is…"

She blew out a breath and tried to gather her thoughts.

"I'm sure it's difficult," he told her as he remained in the doorway to the bedroom. "My mother passed when I was little, so I don't remember her. You're going to be a great mother and you've got those fond memories that will help."

She met his gaze, biting her bottom lip to cease the quivering.

"And you've got me," he added.

Kate blinked away the moisture and turned back to look at the picture. "Why is this hanging here?" she asked.

"This is your birthday present. It didn't come in on time, but I want you to have it."

This is what he'd done for her. For years he'd given her chocolate-covered strawberries, and this year had been no different. But he'd gone a step further and done something so thoughtful, so unique. Damn it, why did love have to be a one-way street with him?

"How did you get a copy?" she asked.

"Social media. I pulled it from one of your accounts and had it blown up on the canvas."

Crossing her arms, Kate turned her attention back to Gray. "If it's my birthday present, why is it hanging here?"

"Because you didn't like the other painting."

Confused, Kate shook her head. "I don't understand."

Gray pushed off the doorway and closed the distance between them. He stood directly in front of her, within touching distance, but didn't reach for her. As she studied the fine lines around his eyes, she realized he was tired. Had he not slept lately? Was he regretting his decision not to sell the bar?

"You and this baby are my priority now," he stated simply. "Not the bar, not moving and taking that money. Nothing else matters but my family."

What? Did he mean…

"I don't care where we take the picture I got you," he went on. "If you want to live here, we leave it here. You want to stay in your house, we hang it there. Our child will know your parents and I want to create a family with you."

"Gray," she whispered.

She dropped her face to her hands as another wave of emotions overcame her. He was only saying this to appease his dad, to make his father see that Gray was ready to settle down.

Kate swiped her face and met Gray's eyes. "We've been over this."

Now he did reach for her. Those large, strong hands framed her face. "No, we haven't, because we're about to have a whole new conversation. I need your undivided attention when I tell you I'm in love with you."

Kate's heart clenched. She stared up at him, gripped his wrists, and murmured, "You—you're in love with me? As in…"

"As in I want to make you my wife, not because of the baby and not because I'm staying here and keeping the bar." A ghost of a smile formed on his lips. "All these years I thought there was a void, but there wasn't. You were here all along and the only thing missing was having you even deeper in my life. That was the void. I need you, Kate. I know you'd be fine without me and we could share joint custody of our baby, but I want this life with you. I want this child and more with you."

Tears spilled and there was no way she could even think of holding them back. "You're serious?"

Gray laughed, then nipped at her lips. "You think I'd get rid of my dog picture for just anybody? I love you, Kate. I love this baby."

"But you were so angry the other night and I thought…"

"I wasn't angry with you," he assured her. "I was angry with that jerk who held you in his arms. I was angry with myself for being a dick to you, for not realizing sooner exactly how much you mean to me."

Gripping his wrists tighter, she so hoped he meant that. Every part of her wanted him to love her, to love this baby and to want to be a united family.

"Are you sure this isn't because of the baby?" she repeated.

"It's because of us," he stated, swiping the moisture from her cheeks. "If you weren't pregnant, I'd still be in love with you. I'd still want to spend my life with you."

"Spend your life with me?"

Gray let out a soft chuckle as he stepped back and dropped his hands. "You keep answering me with questions."

Kate watched as he went to the bedroom and came out a moment later holding something behind his back.

"I got something else for you."

Honestly, she wasn't sure how much more she could take. Between the photo and the declaration of love, she had more than she'd ever wanted.

Gray pulled out a thick book from behind his back. No. It wasn't a book at all.

Kate busted out laughing. "A planner?"

Gray got down on one knee and her breath caught in her throat. "Not just any planner, babe. Our life starts now. Marry me."

The front of the planner had a big gold heart on a white background. Gray opened the cover to reveal an attached satin ribbon to use for marking pages.

"Gray," she gasped.

Tied to the satin ribbon was a ring.

"I was just going to propose with the planner because I realize that's more important than jewelry to you," he joked. "But I hope you'll take this ring. It was my mother's. My dad saved it for me to give to the woman I love. There's nobody else I would ever give this ring to."

Kate's nausea chose that moment to make an appearance. She swayed on her feet, and Gray instantly came to his and wrapped an arm around her waist.

"I hope that's the baby and not my proposal," he said, guiding her to the couch.

"Definitely the baby," she told him.

He set the planner down on the old, antique trunk. "What can I get you?"

Kate closed her eyes, willing the dizziness to pass. "The ring on my finger, for starters."

She risked looking over at him and found him smiling, his eyes misting. "Are you going to cry?" she asked.

"Me? No. I don't cry." He sniffed as he untied the ring and held it up to her. "My dad said my mom loved pearls, but if you want a diamond or, hell... I don't know. I'll get anything, Kate. I just want you."

She held out her left hand. "And I want you and this ring that means so much to you."

Gray slid the ring onto her finger and let out a breath. "I so hoped this would fit."

Kate extended her arm and admired the ring. "It's perfect."

He pulled her into his arms. "We're perfect. I'm sorry I didn't see this before. When you said you needed me to love you like you deserve, I didn't get it."

Kate slid her arm around his abdomen and toed off her sandals. She propped her feet on the trunk and nestled deeper into his side.

"I've always loved you," he went on. "I even loved

you like a husband should love a wife, but it took a reality check for me to fully realize it."

"Was it Chris coming back to town?"

"Part of it," he replied, trailing his fingertips up and down her arm. "When you weren't here, I felt empty. Once we slept together that first time, everything changed. I wanted you more and more, not just for the sex, but because I felt alone without you."

Kate smiled and eased up. "Then you took me camping to seduce me."

A naughty grin spread across his face. "I took you camping to mark an item off your bucket list. The seducing was just a handy by-product."

His face sobered as he studied her. "I meant what I said before about helping you fulfill your list. Have you heard any more from the genealogy expert?"

"Not yet, but he's starting his research and that's a step in the right direction."

Gray kissed the tip of her nose. "What do you say we go pick out that dog you wanted? Sprout, right?"

Her eyes widened. "Right now?"

With a shrug, Gray sat up. "Why not? The local shelter is open."

Of course he'd want a shelter dog. As if the man couldn't be more perfect. She reached out and fisted his unruly hair in her hands, pulling his mouth down to hers.

"You're so perfect," she muttered against his lips. "Let's go get our Sprout."

"Want to get married, too?"

Kate stilled. "Today?"

"You still looking for something spontaneous for your list?"

The planner inside her started to have anxiety, but the woman who stared at this man wanted him to be hers in every single way.

"Don't worry about the perfect venue or the gown or flowers," he told her. "Marry me, Kate. Now. Today."

She let out a laugh, completely shocked at her response. "Let's do it."

Gray lifted her up into his arms and held her tight. There was no one else on earth who could make her want to ignore her plans and throw caution to the wind. But Gray made her want to live in the moment.

"Maybe I should write this in my planner," she told him.

He set her down on her feet and smiled as he reached down to flip the pages of the planner. "I already did. I had a feeling you'd say yes."

Kate glanced at the open pages. Her heart leaped in her chest at Gray's writing on today's date: Making Kate My Wife.

She smacked a kiss on his cheek. "I'm going to turn you into a personal planner after all."

"As long as you're mine, I'll make a thousand lists with you."

Epilogue

Sam stood outside his front door. Well, not *his* front door, since he and Tara had separated. Everyone thought their divorce was final and he'd never said otherwise. Tara had wanted the divorce, and he deserved all of her anger, but he'd never signed the papers. Sam Bailey never gave up and he sure as hell didn't intend to now—even when his entire world was slipping from his grasp.

He tapped his knuckles on the door—a door he'd installed when they'd bought the house only three years ago, a door he'd walked through thousands of times without thinking twice. Those days were gone. He'd severed his right to just walk in. At this point, he just hoped Tara talked to him.

The dead bolt flicked and Tara eased the door open, pulling her robe tighter around her chest.

"Sam, what are you doing here?"

She always looked gorgeous. Whether she wore her ratty old bathrobe or she had on a formfitting dress. His Tara was a complete knockout. Only she wasn't his anymore.

"Marley called me."

"What?"

"She said you'd been crying." He studied her face but didn't notice any traces of tears. "Everything okay?"

"I wasn't crying," she stated, but her swollen, red eyes gave her away. "Nothing for you to worry about. What else did she tell you?"

Sam swallowed. This wasn't the first time Marley had called him, trying to find a reason to get him to come over. He knew his little girl wanted her parents to live together again, but it just wasn't possible right now.

Even so, he and Tara had made it clear they would put Marley first at all times. They didn't want her to suffer any more than necessary. Keeping her happy, feeling secure, was top of their priority list.

"I'm fine." Tara licked her lips and raked a hand through her hair, then opened the door wider. "Do you want to come in and see her? She's getting ready for bed. Or I thought she was. I'm sorry. I had no idea she called you."

Again.

The word hovered between them because this wasn't the first time, and likely not the last. But Sam would come every single time if there was the slightest chance something was wrong with Tara.

"I shouldn't come in." Though he desperately wanted to. He wanted to walk in that door and tuck his daughter into bed and then go to his own room with his wife. "I don't want her to think she can keep doing this when there's nothing wrong."

But there was so much that was wrong. So much pain, so much heartache. All of it caused by his selfish desires, his addiction. An addiction he'd put ahead of his own family.

Tara glanced over her shoulder, then eased out the front door and closed it at her back. Sam adjusted his stance to make room for her. The glow of the porch lights illuminated her green eyes. It was those wide, expressive eyes that had initially drawn him to her.

"I know you're trying to move forward, to seek forgiveness or even more from me." She looked down to her clasped hands and shook her head. "But you can't keep leaving notes, Sam."

That's how he'd originally started to get her attention when he was serious about dating her. Stonerock was a small town, so they'd known each other for years, but something had shifted. He'd leave random notes asking her out and then, once they were together all the time, he'd leave little love notes. He'd done that for years, wanting her to know how special she was.

He'd messed up. There was no denying the facts. All he could do now was try to prove to her, to Marley that he was the man they needed him to be. No matter how long it took.

"I'm a patient man," he told her, fisting his hands at his sides because he wanted to reach out and touch her. He wanted to brush her hair back from her face and feel the silkiness of her skin once more. "I know I hurt you. I know I hurt Marley. But you know me, babe. I'm going to make this right."

"It's over," she whispered. "I don't want to keep dragging this out. What happened is in the past and we both need to move forward. It's not healthy, Sam."

"No, it's not," he agreed. "I'm starting over, Tara. I'm trying one day at a time."

"Maybe you should just sign the papers," she whispered through her emotion as she went back inside.

The door closed. The click of the lock seemed to echo in the dark of the night. But Sam couldn't give up. His family needed him.

He had every intention of proving to Tara that he could be a better man.

*****

MILLS & BOON

Coming next month

RESCUING THE ROYAL RUNAWAY BRIDE
Ally Blake

"Look," Will said, stopping to clear his throat. "I'm heading towards court so I can give you a lift if you're heading in that direction. Or drop you…wherever it is you are going." On foot. Through muddy countryside. In what had probably been some pretty fancy shoes, considering the party dress that went with them. From what he had seen there was nothing for miles bar the village behind him, and the palace some distance ahead. "Were you heading to the wedding, then?"

It was a simple enough question, but the girl looked as if she'd been slapped. Laughter gone, colour gone, dark tears suddenly wobbled precariously in the corners of her eyes.

She recovered quickly, dashing a finger under each eye, sniffing and taking a careful step back. "No. No, thanks. I'm… I'll be fine. You go ahead. Thank you, though."

With that she lifted her dress, turned her back on him and picked her way across the road, slipping a little, tripping on her skirt more.

If the woman wanted to make her own way, dressed and shod as she was, then who was he to argue? He almost convinced himself too. Then he caught the moment she glanced towards the palace, hidden some-where on the other side of the trees, and decidedly changed tack so that she was heading in the absolute opposite direction.

And, like the snick of a well-oiled combination lock, everything suddenly clicked into place.

The dress with its layers of pink lace, voluminous skirt and hints of rose-gold thread throughout.

The pink train—was that what they called it?—was trailing in the mud behind her.

Will's gaze dropped to her left hand clenched around a handful of skirt. A humungous pink rock the size of a thumbnail in a thin rose-gold band glinted thereupon.

He'd ribbed Hugo enough through school when the guy had been forced to wear the sash of his country at formal events: pink and rose-gold—the colours of the Vallemontian banner.

Only one woman in the country would be wearing a gown in those colours today.

If Will wasn't mistaken, he'd nearly run down one Mercedes Gray Leonine.

Who—instead of spending her last moments as a single woman laughing with her bridesmaids and hugging her family before heading off to marry the estimable Prince Alessandro Hugo Giordano and become a princess of Vallemont—was making a desperate, muddy, shoeless run for the hills.

Perfect.

Continue reading
RESCUING THE ROYAL RUNAWAY BRIDE
Ally Blake

Available next month
www.millsandboon.co.uk

LET'S TALK
Romance

For exclusive extracts, competitions
and special offers, find us online:

f facebook.com/millsandboon

⊙ @millsandboonuk

t @millsandboon

Or get in touch on 0844 844 1351*

For all the latest titles coming soon, visit
millsandboon.co.uk/nextmonth